THE UNSEEN

(THE UNSEEN SERIES, #1)

PIPER SHELDON

QUERQUE PRESS

This book is a work of fiction created from the dregs of this author's brain juice. Any resemblance to real humans of this planet earth and current timeline is highly coincidental and totally unlikely.

No part of this book may be reproduced in any form or by any electronic or mechanical means, including information storage and retrieval systems, without written permission from the author, except for the use of brief quotations in a book review.

To J.R., always

1

Maggie

I LOVE TURNING INVISIBLE. IT'S A DEFINITE PERK AS AN investigative journalist. I mean, it's part of the reason I am an investigative journalist; it's a chicken-egg thing.

Being naked to get invisible? That part? Don't love that so much.

Right now, for example, I'm freezing my lady bits off in the closet of a swanky hotel suite waiting for a break in the story that's been driving me for the last four years. Four. Years. Of creeping around LA in only what-God-gave-me to bring down one man. *The* reason I've transformed from caterpillar Maggie May to the butterfly of revenge Miss Mayday, whistle-blower on the biggest scumbags in Hollywood.

As if on cue, Marty Zebulund strides into the suite. He lowers himself onto a blue velvet couch and runs his hand over the back like he owns it. The room is upscale and modern with a large arrangement of costly-looking flowers, about the size of a Fiat, sitting on the table in the foyer. Flowers that will be thrown in the trash at the first sign of aging. If that isn't a metaphor for this town, then I don't know what is. I'm trying not to shiver in the coat closet watching through the crack in the partially opened door. I lose my battle when the sight of him through the flowers makes me shudder.

Naked, cold, and disgusted. That could be the name of my memoir.

As much as it sucks to see Zebulund, it's why I'm here, not for the actor, though it is his press junket. James Roe doesn't interest me. Not his small-town wholesomeness or those expressive eyebrows that seem to say, "Watch out ladies, I'm sensitive." Sure, he has old-school Hollywood good looks, and yes, he does seem to have a presence that naturally lights up every room he enters with just enough mischievous glint in his eyes to hint at good times, but pfft, whatever. That don't impress me much.

I care why Zebulund is here wanting to talk to him at all.

The assistant that just brought Zebulund into the living room area stands with hands clasped. "Mr. Roe will be right out," she says with a quick, polite smile. She's tall, thin, and blond. She could be my twin. We come a dime a dozen in this town where the standard of beauty starts a lot higher. Her pencil skirt and white silk blouse are professional and flattering. I have clothes envy.

"Thankfully, I have your lovely company until then." The moment he starts speaking the hair on my neck prickles. That voice, deep and jovial with an undercurrent of bile.

My stomach reacts like missing the bottom step of a staircase. I'm naked. He's right there. I wrap my arms tight around myself as a horrible, familiar feeling of helplessness sets in. My nails dig into my palms. Think of the other girls. Think of the girls he hasn't... corrupted yet. Find the focus. I swallow down a lump.

The assistant is quiet as she mumbles a response. I can't quite hear so I glide out from my hiding spot, slipping *Under* as

I go. Going Under is what I call disappearing. It drains me so best to do it in small bursts.

"Can I get you anything while you wait?" the assistant asks as she stands in front of Zebulund, hands clasped. Zebulund's thick arm and expensive watch draw my attention as I avoid looking directly at him. She studies the wall in the way all women have perfected while having their bodies analyzed by lascivious men.

"Fantastic legs," he says as though she should feel complimented.

She clears her throat. "I better get back to work."

"Oh, come on, smile. It was a compliment." His voice is casual and yet pressing. "Sit down. I'm sure this has been a long day." His finger taps the back of the couch. There's no semblance of a question in his tone.

I know this. I've heard it. Those exact words, in fact. He must have a little black book of go-to harassment phrases he finds charming. I step around the vase of flowers wanting to protect her—to do something. My knees tingle as I look fully at him for the first time in years. He's aged some. He's always been an imposing man and time has not diminished that. His features refined are framed by silver hair over his ears, proving there's no justice. There was a time I found him attractive and this knowledge makes it difficult to look at his face, except in discreet glances that cost me.

"I need to get coffee for Mr. Roe. I'd be happy to get you something," she says still standing.

The only sign of irritation is the quickening of his tapping fingers along the back of the couch. People do not deny Zebulund. "I thought Mr. Roe would be interested in this meeting, but maybe he's too busy."

The assistant keeps a cool demeanor but inside there's bound to be an explosion of mixed emotions. Stay and play nice with the man that could help her boss's career or protect herself?

He's a class-A manipulator. Anger and panic war within me and to my disgust I freeze. Incapacitated. Just like the first time I was in a hotel room with him.

"You don't want me to get bored, do you?" A smooth grin transforms his strong features as he waves to the seat next to him on the couch.

She hesitates, glancing where he indicated.

It breaks through my fear and I step forward, imagining my bony knee slamming right into his junk. Exposé be damned. I will not watch her be forced into the same position I was. This will not happen again.

A voice cuts through the air. "Rachel, where's that coffee I asked for?"

Rachel and I both back up a step. She smoothes her skirt. "Yes, Mr. Roe." She angles toward the door. "I'm going to get it right now."

The relief is instant in me and in the released tension of her shoulders.

James Roe walks into the room from a bedroom so his back is to me. The fibers of his gray tee are stretched to their maximum capacity around his torso. It clings tightly to his expansive and highly defined shoulders then tapers down to his trim waist. Hollywood is an equal opportunist when it comes to crippling body image standards.

"Hey now, there's no rush." Zebulund's beefy paw runs up and down his own thigh. "I was just getting to know... Rachel is it?"

"I asked for it ten minutes ago." The hand at Roe's side clenches into a fist before releasing, almost unnoticeable. "If she did her job, I'd be drinking it already."

Rachel turns to catch her boss's eye and her face falls. "Yes, sir. I'll be right back."

"Get that coffee that I like," Roe snaps.

I frown at his tone.

"The one across town?" Rachel clarifies.

"Is that a problem?"

"No, sir. I'll be back as soon as I can." Rachel's gaze flicks from man to man. In LA traffic that could take an hour. "Your next appointment is in twenty if I'm not back in time."

Zebulund, who has been watching this with good humor, frowns.

"They'll have to wait until Mr. Zebulund and I are done," Roe says.

"Yes, sir." And with that, Rachel turns to leave. I step back right before she brushes past me. She halts momentarily and looks in my direction. My pulse jumps. Her eyes focus behind me and around me but never settle on me.

This happens sometimes. I mean, I'm still here. People sense other people even if they don't see them. All of my body-washes and lotions are fragrance-free but everyone has their scent. We all have a presence no matter how we try to stay hidden.

Rachel's eyes set with a glare of determination. She's gone again without another look back.

Since I'm already in my invisible uniform so to speak, I skulk toward the open door. Roe chooses the chair across from Zebulund, still pointed away from me, so I can't see his face. Not that I want to see his face. He settles back with one leg crossed casually over the other knee. His guest's eyes remain locked on Rachel's retreat.

"What can I do for you, Mr. Zebulund?" Roe asks.

"Please, call me Marty." He returns his focus to Roe. "I came here alone for a reason. To speak man to man."

Roe asks, flicking a piece of fuzz off his pants, "About what?"

"I think you and I are destined to be friends." He slips into a more professional tone. "Your star's rising. I have a lot to offer."

Zebulund was the most powerful man in this town. Everybody knew it. That's why after all this time I've made almost no progress getting the information I need on him.

I step closer.

Prior research revealed that these two had never worked together on any projects. How could Roe have made it this far without Zebulund on his team? When O.G. sent me here today I didn't know James Roe would be a part of this. Was this conversation that I was supposed to hear? O.G., you sneaky, sneaky wabbit.

"Here I am." Roe's arms relax to the side, palms up. "No mystery. Just a kid from Nebraska."

"You're awfully quiet about your past. Makes for good gossip."

Roe shakes his head and chuckles good-naturedly and I catch his profile. Dammit, he's handsome.

Okay, so I definitely see his draw. He does have something.

"No mystery. My parents have a good marriage. I've got an older sister and a younger brother. Happy childhood. No drama. Doesn't make for interesting TV."

"Ah, so that's your angle. The less known the bigger the intrigue."

"Sure." Roe chuckles again but there's a strain to it.

There's always an angle. Some image. Some face that's presented to the world. Nobody in this industry is real. Everybody is as fake as their teeth and tans. I glare at Zebulund, hoping for laser vision. My entire life course derailed because of him and he wouldn't know me if he tripped on me.

A small part of me is begrudgingly impressed by Roe's reaction. I've seen enough actors over the years act like total nutcases to get in Zebulund's inner circle. It's not attractive to see a full-grown man all but grovel to be invited to a poker game. Yet, Roe remains stoic and hard to read.

"I like your talent and I think you'd make a great lead in the Space Wars movies." Zebulund's fingers resume their tapping.

A new tension in Roe's shoulders is the only thing to give him away. Those movies are the most anticipated films to come to Hollywood in ages. If he gets the lead, it would change the trajectory of an already stellar career.

"Why me?" Roe asks.

"If we team up, it'll take Hollywood by storm."

"What do you get out of it?"

"I'll be the man that made James Roe a living legend. Think Bogart, Nicholson, Brando. More than a short-term, it-man. A serious career actor. Lasting power."

"So long as they're your films? Slingers Production Company only? Is that it?"

The other man nods smoothly. "We make enough movies and you could have your pick. From indie to blockbuster, whatever you want. You come work for me and I make you wealthy beyond your wildest dreams. I get you in places you don't even know exist. Nobody can touch you."

"And you want to do this out of the goodness of your heart?"

Zebulund stops tapping and forces Roe to hold his stare. "I would get exclusivity. You do my movies, my press junkets, etc."

He makes it sound like that's the real treat. And truthfully his production company, Slingers, is the biggest and most successful Hollywood franchise. I don't understand Roe's hesitation, unless this is some power play. Maybe he's pirouetting on the inside.

"I'm interested but I'd like to hear more of the details." Roe turns his head like he's going to look in my direction.

Something about that movement causes me to shrink back toward the safety of the closet. I stay Under, even though I'm starting to feel like a dried-out husk.

"Good. Good to hear." Zebulund stands. Okay, so conversation over. "Think on it. We're both busy men. The price we pay, am I right?"

Roe stands too, with his hands stuffed deep in his pockets. "Too true."

"I'm having a bit of a party on my yacht this weekend. Nothing crazy. A celebration of life. We can talk more details then. There'll be food, booze, and..." he shrugs and thumbs his nose, "Anything else you might need to party."

"Ah."

This is good. This is really good. Roe's being invited to an exclusive Zebulund Yacht party? These things are legendary. I steady myself. This doesn't change anything, Roe was invited, not me. And yet, I've got a good feeling about this.

"Not a lot of people have this number. Keep it to yourself." Zebulund slides a card to Roe, who tucks it into the breast pocket of his tee.

How close would I need to get to try to slide that out? I've had worse jobs over the years than trying to feel up James Roe.

"Will do," Roe says.

"I expect to see you this weekend." Zebulund speaks as though it's already written.

Roe responds with a tight smile.

"Feel free to bring that assistant of yours."

They walk toward the exit and I keep myself tucked behind the open door to the living room. I'm getting tired. I never know how long this power will last and the worst thing would be to collapse in a heap in front of these two. I squeeze my eyes shut. I came here with one goal and I can't afford to be distracted... and yet if I can get to Roe, I can get to Zebulund. I need him to move. I need to go follow my Moby-is-a-huge-Dick while I've got a chance. This could be golden.

Zebulund leaves the suite. Roe's holding the door open to watch him walk to the elevator. The door is wide open. I just need to sprint after him. And yet my feet aren't moving. I'm frozen with indecision. It's not like me. I need to make the right choice, but my gut instinct is the Scarecrow pointing both directions.

Zebulund is almost to the elevator. A cell phone rings and it adds to the stimulus overload as I try to make the smart choice. I look once more to the elevator and back to Roe as he answers the call.

I make my decision.

2

Roe

I DROP TO THE EDGE OF THE BED AS MOM TAKES A DEEP BREATH on the other end of the line. Whatever she's about to say will be the cherry on top of this shit sundae weekend.

The smile I put on before I answered her call slides off my face and tension cramps the muscles of my neck. After Zebulund leaves, I'm left with a sticky feeling I can't shake. I had hoped hearing Mom would be a welcome respite from the superficial day but the second I hear her voice I know I'm wrong. Turns out I can hear if she's not smiling through the phone too.

"What's wrong?" I ask.

"Everybody's okay. Don't worry," she repeats.

"The more you say that the less it works, Ma." The feeling of being watched is so tangible I get up and shut the door. Maybe this place is bugged. Nothing surprises me at this point. Being a celebrity means you lose your right to privacy. I can't have an opinion or a personal life. Hell, I can't even take a ten-minute break.

Man, I sound ungrateful sometimes. At least I keep it to myself.

"It's about, uh, Uncle Jack." Her voice is thin.

I don't have an Uncle Jack. That's code for the company I'm funding. The company that's keeping the majority of my hometown employed, including both my parents.

"Is he okay?"

"I don't think so. There's some internal bleeding."

"I'll be there tonight." I reach for my laptop to buy a flight.

"You can't leave right now, sweetie. Your movie premieres soon. Paul's on his way there. He'll be there tonight. Can you meet him at nine?"

"Yeah, of course." My schedule is booked solid but the worry in my mom's voice is enough to motivate me to cancel all plans. "Where?"

"What hotel are you at?" Paper shuffles and I picture her in the kitchen digging through the junk drawer, frowning as she tries one dried-out pen after another before putting them all back. It's almost enough to make me smile.

"No. Not here." I glance around the room, feeling increasingly paranoid. "How about the place I took you and Dad the first time you ever came for a visit. You remember?"

"Sure, the—"

"Send him there. And don't tell anybody else."

"Are you okay, honey?"

"I'm fine, Mom."

At that moment, there's a tentative knock on the door which causes me to jump about a foot in the damn air. I run a hand over my face at my reaction to my ridiculous behavior. What I'd do for sleep.

"You don't sound fine"—slight pause—"are you eating enough?" she asks like she has to walk on eggshells with me.

"Yes, Mom."

"Make sure you're not burning the candle at both ends."

I feel the kind of guilt that only mothers can cause. "Yeah. Look, I gotta go. Tell Paul I'll see him tonight. Love you."

"Love you too."

We disconnect and I stare at the picture of her and my dad that I use as their caller ID photo. It was one of the few times they'd come out here to visit. I don't like this world mixing with my real life. My homesickness is so acute sometimes it's worse than the stomach pains.

The knock comes again. I drop the phone on the bed and go to the door. "Coming."

Rachel is back already and holds up a cup of coffee.

I squint skeptically.

"Traffic wasn't that bad?" She grins as she shrugs.

"Right." I take a long sip even though it burns my tongue and tastes like cheap hotel coffee.

"That and I got you a cup from downstairs and watched until he left." She brushes past me and examines the room.

"Yeah. Sorry about that. You know... with guys like that..." I feel like an ass for treating her the way I did. Why can't I finish the sentence? Luckily I don't have to.

"Trust me, I get it. Gotta play the tough guy. But if you snap at me again, I may kick your ass."

"And that's why I keep you around."

Zebulund's reputation for big parties and extravagant gifts is matched only by the rumors of his immorality. I've never met the guy before today and wasn't impressed. He carries himself like being allowed to breathe the same air as him is a gift.

"So?" she asks with eyes wide in excitement. "How'd it go? What'd he say?"

We move to the living room where I spent most of the day being interviewed. I'm too restless to sit down but she does.

"You were right. He wants me to do the Space Wars movies."

"Yay!" She claps rapidly.

I scratch at my chin, rough with a five o'clock shadow.

"Why the face? This is huge."

"I don't know." I shake my head. "It feels off. A big decision."

"Good news, you don't have to marry him. You don't even have to decide right now."

I nod and pick up a stress ball from the free swag table. I lob it into the air and catch it a few times. In my peripheral vision Rachel is dying to say something.

I wave her on. "Out with it."

"This could be the thing that makes you a household name."

Why me? Almost slips out of my mouth but it seems a little self-indulgent so I toss the ball a few more times.

"I guess."

"You've told me countless times you hate being called the 'it guy' because it implies you aren't going to be 'it' forever. Well, this is how you make *it* last."

My stomach rumbles loudly, and it's the reminder I need. Once you've come close to starving, you'll do anything not to go back to that place. I'll do what it takes to stay in this game. Feed myself and my family. Even if it starves my soul.

"You've heard the rumors about him, his reputation. I don't know if I want to be associated with that."

"Yeah, I've heard." She chews her lips as she mulls.

"You didn't get a vibe?"

"I do from a lot of men in this town."

It shouldn't be that way. I regret not calling Zebulund out on the spot.

"He invited me to a party this weekend." I casually change the subject.

"Oh?"

"On his yacht," I say with affected arrogance.

"Roe!" she yells with indignation.

"Rachel!" I mimic her tone.

"You have to go." She glares.

"I'll think about it."

Zebulund's party is the last thing on my mind. My mother's worried tone flashes through my mind and I replay her words, "internal bleeding." I need clear tonight's schedule to talk to Paul. I'm booked solid until the press tour is over and I start shooting the next film. Then the whole damn cycle starts over again.

"When is it? I'll move things around."

The ball slips out of my hand and rolls toward the closet in the foyer. "Stop giving me that face," I call out as I half stoop to chase after it.

She starts to speak but whatever she says blurs into the background as my brain fights to take in the scene in front of me.

A naked woman stands in front of me. I'm talking right in front of my face. Were her arms not crossed casually in front of her, I would know her waxing preferences. She has a bored expression. My shock must show because finally, she reacts. She frowns and looks behind her like I'm the one out of place in this scenario. Her mouth falls opens.

Peers have shared stories of crazy fans sneaking their way into rooms, of men and women draped naked across beds when they get home. But never, not once, have I experienced anything at this level.

I'm on a delay but then reality hits me. Crazy naked lady in my closet!

I scream something I'm not proud of and shoot upright. I scramble back, slamming into the table so hard the large arrangement of flowers wobbles precariously. I have to use my whole upper body to steady it.

"What's wrong?" Rachel is at my side in an instant.

I point to the closet with a shaking hand. We turn in unison to examine the empty area.

"Someone's in here." As I speak I'm whipping all around to find the missing woman.

"What? Where?" Rachel, to my surprise, immediately picks up her phone, ready to act with whatever power she can wield.

"You didn't see another person?" I ask.

Rachel scans the room as she calls down to the front desk. "Send security." She pushes open doors and checks the room as she explains the situation.

My tiny assistant checks closets and calls for help as I stand pointless near the exit, half-cowering behind the safety of the doorway. It's not my finest moment. Barely five minutes later a hulking guard sweeps the room and assures us that nobody is there. He leaves, insisting he'll check the cameras. I slump into the couch.

"It's been a long fucking day."

Week.

Month.

Year.

I press the heels of my palms into my eyes until tiny white spots swirl around. I saw something. Didn't I? Fuck. I can't remember the last time I slept more than an hour or two at a time. My stomach grumbles again to remind me of my other problems.

"What did she look like?" Rachel asks and, God, I could hug her for humoring the crazy man.

"Sort of like you. I mean, I think. Tall. Blond."

"Well, that could be it then. Maybe my reflection in the TV or window or something? There are a lot of shiny surfaces." She seems very sure.

But I'm sure too. There was a woman standing just inches in front of me and there was no trick of light. My cheeks heat. I'm a tool. I can't tell Rachel that the woman I saw was naked. What if she thinks I'm making some crazy-ass pass at her? Not that she seems to need my protection. If anything, it's clear that I need her as my bodyguard.

"Actually," I say, "I think you're right."

Rachel sits back and lets out a breath through puffed cheeks. "Yeah?" She watches me too closely. "I can tell you saw someone. But I was standing right there too. I didn't see anybody coming or going."

"Maybe she snuck out."

"Maybe. Regardless, I'm canceling the rest of your interviews. In fact, I'm canceling the rest of your day. You need a break."

I want to argue. These days I work until I pass out from exhaustion. Complaining is weakness. There was a time my family fought for every penny. I won't ever belly-ache about this life but I need to meet with Paul. Silver lining of losing one's mind is the readily available excuses for missing obligations.

"I do need a break." I need to clean up my act before I'm committed and not to another movie. And while any publicity is good publicity, I haven't reached that point in my career. "Yeah. Now that you say it. I bet that was it."

"Okay." Rachel purses her mouth to the side. "I'm going to go deal with the rest of the reporters."

"Thanks." I feel a ping of remorse for the people who waited all day.

"You got it." She stands up. "You rest up for the yacht party."

"I said I'll think about it." I follow suit and leave the room.

I don't want to be here any longer than I have to be. Downstairs, I sneak out a back entrance and glance at my watch. I could walk a bit before it's time to go meet Paul. I stride away from naked fans and crazy yacht parties. But when I blink, the face that stared out at me from the closet is right there. It's implanted in my brain now. We better never cross paths again.

3

Maggie

No.

There's no way.

I race down the hall. Naked. Heart racing. Mouth dry and head pounding. The hallway narrows and expands like I'm on the set of *Vertigo*. I run my hand along the moulding to keep myself from falling.

Stay calm. Assess the situation. Make a plan. Leave the hotel as soon as possible. Get dressed. Maybe not in that order. Definitely not in that order.

It is entirely possible my worst fear just happened. I have to accept that. Roe saw me because I let myself get too tired and for some reason, my power slipped. I ignored the little voice that told me it hadn't slipped, and Roe's assistant didn't see me as I sprinted out of the room while he steadied the flower vase.

My clothes and bag wait for me undisturbed in the janitor's closet where I left them. So are the three bottles of water. Dressed and feeling a little more in control, I drink the water, one bottle after another, my pulse calming with each gulp. I return to the waiting area where the rest of the reporters pack up with faces of disappointment.

A few wisps of conversation meet my ear. "Waited six hours for nothing." "I'm still billing for this." "Roe's a diva after all." "Some crazy fan."

It's that last one that has me stopping to examine a massive potted plant so I can discreetly listen.

"Are you serious?" one whispering voice asks another.

"That's what I heard. The security guard was telling his staff to be on the lookout."

With that I scurry out the rotating doors of the hotel and into the heavy foot traffic of dusk in Hollywood.

My phone vibrates in my bag. Right on cue.

O.G.'s message reads, "You have ten minutes to get here."

"Pushy, pushy," I respond as the map loads the address in the background.

"Gonna tell me what happened back there?"

When O.G. popped into my life a couple years ago, providing scant bits of information via texts, I quickly learned his value. Whether or not he knows all of my particular talents, I'm not sure. We don't really talk about it. We don't really talk at all actually. He provides info; I reply with snark. It's our shtick.

My thumbs blur as I type a response. "Nothing. All is well."

"Right. Hurry."

I send a "strong arm" emoji. A second later he buzzes me again. "Go left. Sidewalk blocked."

Just in time I see the construction signs.

"Creeper," I shoot off as I keep moving.

Whatever it is that gives O.G. his prophetic insight has never extended to Zebulund.

I stop short, in front of my destination, frowning at my phone to verify. I had assumed I'd be going to a ritzy restaurant with no reservation list, invite-only style. But it's a derelict theater straight from the golden years of Hollywood, complete with a giant fluorescent marquee that buzzes loudly. A mash-up of letters, some upside-down and some repurposed numbers, illuminate a Bogart/Bacall double feature. In the ticket booth hangs a handwritten sign declaring "Closed for private screening" with today's date. The total lack of traffic and red carpet means this is not the sort of event that draws the press.

Inside I'm greeted by the ever-present smell of popcorn and the clang of an ancient air-conditioning unit. There's a solitary concession stand where two teenage girls stand, arms crossed in mirrored images of blasé. The one on the left has a punk shaved head and piercings incongruous with her cherubic face. The other rocks razor-sharp bangs and copious amounts of eyeliner. Only their stiff, overlarge theater uniforms belie the anarchist vibe. I mean, they must care a little to have this job.

Their gazes scan me as I approach, before focusing back on their discussion in a slightly quieter tone.

"The whole theater and a big-ass tip." Bangs pauses in her conversation with Piercings long enough to spout out, "Sorry. Closed."

"Ugh, I know." My investigative journalist instincts urge me to play it cool. "I'm late. I need a water before we go in." This much is true. I don't have to fake the exhaustion and shaking hands either. I dig distractedly through my bag. "Roe should already be here." I wait a moment before looking up with a sheepish expression in time to catch them sharing a look. As anti-establishment as they think they are, Roe is a huge star. "Dammit. You didn't hear that from me." I scan them in turn and then add. "You guys look cool though." Like their confidence in my secret is a gift.

Bangs insists, "We can't let anyone in—"

"Yeah, except Paul, I know." I fake more frustration in my search for an item that doesn't even exist. Under my breath, I start my rant. "Figures he wouldn't remember me. I just keep his world running." Louder, I say, "I'm his PA, Rachel. I guess I'm not included. I'm just a woman. How important can I be?"

Bangs frowns. They share a look.

Piercings says, "Sorry, it's just that we can't."

Their gazes drop to my quivering chin.

"No, I get it. You guys have to do your job. I'm sorry for unloading. It's just we had this press junket all day. I'm so tired. And then he demands I come down here and for what? He can't even bother to remember me." I quickly dash away a tear that doesn't exist. "It's just these people. Sometimes they act like they can't even see me, you know?"

"Totally."

I sigh. "Can you just run this in?" I hold up the water. "If I don't get him water, he'll freak." I tighten my tone as I speak.

They glance at each other again.

"It's cool. Just go ahead. He's in the john anyway."

Perfect! "Thanks. You're a real lifesaver."

Bangs waves away my credit card.

"Thanks again." I'm almost through the theater door when I call out, "And don't tell anybody he's here. The paparazzi would ruin his night."

It takes a lot of effort not to grin as I walk into the dark room. The theater is blessedly empty. I scurry to the darkest corner to disrobe. Again. The theater looks like every old theater, smaller than the new ones, with several dozen old wooden seats, covered in balding velvet, half of which don't automatically fold up anymore. Heavy red fabric drapes the walls and a dusty curtain borders a giant white screen.

By the time I chug one of the waters, I'm convinced that what happened in the coat closet was a fluke. It was exhaustion and definitely not a slip in my skills. Nothing more. I can do this. I'm still in the game. I toss the other water in my purse and hide it under a seat. I go Under and not a second too soon. Light spills in from outside as a man walks through the door.

Instinctively, my arms cross over my body despite my pep talk only seconds ago.

It isn't Roe. It's another guy around his age though. Maybe a little older than him, early thirties. Under a faded blue ball cap he has very thin blond hair that flops over his ears. He looks all around the theater, his eyes traveling right over me without stopping. I let out a quiet breath of relief. Totally a fluke.

I never know if this gift will leave as suddenly as it appeared. It's my experience that if it feels too good to be true, somehow I'll end up getting screwed over.

The man, presumably Paul, tugs off his ball cap and messes with his hair. He chooses a seat toward the front center. I crawl along the aisle opposite the entrance and try not to think about what my hands are touching. In a seat a few rows back, I fold myself into a little ball. Light spills in again and I drop myself low. Roe's gaze searches the theater and snags on the other man. I'm out of his line of sight and his eyes never stop on me.

Phew.

"Paul." He holds out his arms as he approaches, and the other man stands to meet him.

They embrace with large, genuine smiles. They don't look like brothers, maybe family friends.

"Hey, man, thanks for meeting me." Paul thumbs around the empty room. "I take it that it's not a coincidence we're alone."

"I wanted you to be able to speak freely." Roe pets his eyebrow repeatedly, like he's trying to pet it into submission.

The curtains pull back to widen the screen as the lights go down. Familiar music signifies the start of the movie. White letters on a gray clouded sky illuminate the faces of the two men in front of me. The sound of the movie is loud enough to drown them out. I make my way back to the aisle and come down another row to hear better.

"It's not good. Your mom and I were going over the finances and there're big discrepancies."

Roe holds up a finger and looks around. For a moment, it almost feels as if his gaze stops on me but it moves on quickly. My heart pounds but he doesn't scream or have any sort of reaction, so I've got that going for me. I curl myself up in a ball again, sitting on one leg so none of my personal bits touch anything. I'm gonna be honest it's weird to sit with all your lady parts out there, regardless if they can be seen or not. I've found many ways to protect myself over the years. I'm weirdly proud of my ability to get naked in public.

"Did you hear something?"

"No," his companion says, but glances around. His gaze moves all over and passes me again. "Why?"

Roe shakes his head. "Go ahead."

"We can't figure out where it's going. At first, it was a charge here or there that didn't seem right. Enough that I stopped to look into it. A charge to a few companies that seemed innocuous enough. Actually, your mom saw them first. I assumed it was just some contract work or something."

"What companies?"

"I'll send you the list. I can't think of any of the names right now. They're located here in LA, though."

"That doesn't sound right. I contract all work out to the companies in the nearby towns. And there's a reason for that."

"That's what caught your mom's attention." Paul's ball cap is in his hands again, getting twisted into a tube shape.

I lean forward with interest. What was this? A little business on the side? Is he scamming people out of money? As if he needs more. That doesn't seem right either.

"We did some digging. It's only a few thousand here and there but enough to raise some red flags. It's shady."

Roe's face gives nothing away. Even his normally telltale eyebrows sit neutrally on his forehead. "I'll look into it and get back to you." Roe is lost in thought when he glances at his friend and then does a double take. "What's wrong, you seem upset still?"

Paul frowns like something more weighs on his mind. "The thing is. I researched these LA companies. Each one had a basic website, not much to them and they all seem legit, but umm, shortly after that my computer and several others on the intranet got a nasty virus. We still haven't been able to fix them. We've resorted to using old machines just to keep things moving."

"I'll ship new computers out right away. Just tell me how many you need."

"It feels weird. The timing."

"I agree. You think somebody didn't like you snooping?"

"Does that make me sound paranoid?"

"I really don't know anymore. Sometimes I think..." He stops himself short. "I dunno. Never mind. Email me every-thing you know. To the secure account. Otherwise, don't contact me at all."

Roe uses the five o'clock shadow on his chin to scratch the palm of his hand.

"I know we'll work this out." Paul clears his throat. "The things you're doing for our town. It's life changing—I wish you could see it there." The other man's voice is tight with emotion.

Roe waves him away. "You don't have to... I know. I mean. This is..." He runs his hand over his neck.

Both men look so uncomfortable with this exchange it's almost laughable. They quickly change the subject and slip into talk about work and family. I need to come Up because I'm getting dizzy and so I hide in the darkness of the corner until it looks like they're wrapping up. Paul stands up and replaces his ball cap. They hug again.

"It's good seeing you. Hey. Don't sit on this okay? I've heard some really stupid ideas about how to handle this. Ideas that could get out of control."

"What do you mean?" Roe's eyebrows scrunch together in a concerned look.

"Nobody likes the idea that someone is pulling shit over on us. They're grabbing pitchforks."

"Don't let them do anything. I'll fix it."

"I'll try." Paul scrutinized him. "Hey. Your mom told me to tell you to eat more."

They both laugh.

"Noted."

"Hollywood getting to your head?" Paul's eyes move up and down Roe.

"It's for my next role. I'm a marathon runner."

"Don't be a stranger. Darla is having number two this fall," Paul says as he heads for the exit. "And you still haven't met number one."

"Ah, man. I didn't know. Congrats to you both. I'll get out there soon I promise." His face is sheepish with genuine regret.

Paul squeezes his bill again before putting his cap back on and waving one last time. Roe stacks his hands on his head and stretches his back. The movie plays on in the background as Roe watches his friend.

Okay, so maybe I've made some snap decisions about this guy but now I'm even more intrigued. Maybe I could use this to get on Marty Zebulund's yacht. I don't know what the deal with this other drama is, but I'll find out it if helps my cause.

Finally, Roe drops his hands from his head and makes his way to the exit. He leaves, and I let out a huge breath. I come back Up and stretch out my limbs. Doing yoga in the nude never gets old. Very invigorating. Normally, I get dressed as fast as I can, but I've been Under for a while and my vision is still fuzzy. I stretch, arching my back until it cracks and turn side to side to pop it more. I do a few more stretches and grab my stuff.

The need to use the hand sanitizing wipes war with my desire to drink the water.

I finish cleaning up and head back down the aisle when the door opens. I drop into a seat, sliding my purse underneath, and go back Under.

It's Roe. Back with coat unzipped and a water bottle that makes me smack my mouth in envy. I'm beyond ready to go. My ass is sore from these old seats and the vents are massive and blow icy air in this ancient place. More urgent though, is the uncertainty of how much longer I can stay Under. It's already been such a long day.

My heart hammers as he turns up the row I sit in—not the one he had been in. I sit ramrod straight and utterly still. I hold my legs closer to my body, as though making myself as small as possible might help. He approaches without looking at me. No need to panic. He's probably enjoying some alone time.

I sit back as he makes his way to the seat two down from mine. My pulse rockets and I slowly move my arms to cover my chest, but the movement causes no reaction. His focus is the film. I would let out a sigh of relief but he's close enough to hear it. I'm terrified to even move for fear of jostling the molecules of air around him.

His arms cross over his chest and he settles in to watch the film. The action pushes something up from the breast pocket of his shirt. That's when I remember Zebulund's business card. The edge of the thick card stock makes a stark line and the top black edge peaks out. Grabbing that card would be risky and stupidly reckless.

Obviously, I'm going to try to get it.

He chugs some of his water and I watch his throat work. He re-caps the water and stretches his arms out. His wingspan is so large his fingertips almost graze me. I have to get that card. I can't risk getting that close to him... touching him. But if I gently wiggle it out... No, that's crazy. He'd feel it.

I'm moving toward him. Damn me.

No big deal. I'll slide the card out and book it. He probably won't even notice.

Humphrey is on screen talking to Bacall. People were more interesting-looking back then. Roe would have fit right in with Clark Gable and Cary Grant. He has a strong nose and knowing eyes set off by those damn eyebrows. His eyebrows are so distracting at first it takes a minute to see how startlingly handsome he is. His jaw is square with a little divot like a cartoon bodybuilder. His tan looks natural like he just spent the day tilling the earth. He's got a gentle, borderline weepy look to him that softens his intimidatingly strong form. And I think, if he were inclined to smile, a little dimple might make an appearance.

I sigh.

Part of being invisible all the time is the total loss of social graces. Sometimes even when I'm not Under I feel myself staring too long at people. I'm doing that now. I snap back to reality.

I swallow with difficulty and lift my hand slowly toward him.

Easy does it.

Even with his face totally relaxed he seems deep in thought. I'm still too far away. The chair between us is stuck down so I very quietly and slowly make my way over to kneel on it.

His gaze never wavers from the screen. I jump when he chuckles at one of Bacall's sassy comebacks. I lean even closer. The man smells like snuggling in bed on a Sunday afternoon. Is that a bottled scent?

The room rocks a little as I focus on my task.

And yet... I lean closer to him.

I've never touched anyone before while Under. Though I've run into plenty of things and am able to touch stuff, I've never touched a person or been touched. I can't remember the last time I was touched by another person, period. Even hand holding or linking arms, anything but cold isolation. Suddenly, I miss the intimacy so acutely it's a pain in my chest. My finger hovers inches above the card. I can pluck the corner with my thumb and forefinger if I get this just right.

Roe swallows. I retreat a little. He reaches for the water but decides against it. His Adam's apple moves up and down. I hadn't noticed his breathing because mine has increased unwittingly. But now I see. He breathes too quickly. On screen Bacall and Bogart embrace. Maybe that's why his pulse beats wildly yet gently at his neck, just barely noticeable under his beard scruff coming in. The card teases me as he shifts. I refocus.

My hand moves closer.

A second later his hand snatches mine out of the air like catching a fly ball.

"So, I've narrowed it down to two options." His focus remains forward but he doesn't let go of me as he speaks. "Either I'm talking to a ghost or I've completely lost my mind." He leans back a little so he can look me right in my eyes. "And I'm not sure which is worse."

4

Roe

THE WAY I SEE IT, IF I'M GOING INSANE OR BEING HAUNTED, AT
least I'll enjoy myself. My apparition is fucking gorgeous. Or
my imagination does good work. I suspected as much in the
hotel but up close and personal she's a knockout.

At first glance, she might be mistaken for the typical California Blonde, but the longer I study her shocked expression,
the harder it is to tear my gaze away. That round and innocent-
looking face has already burned its way into my memory. Her
eyes slant up, like that Icelandic supermodel, giving an air of
bashfulness even now as they widen in surprise. Her skin is
warm and smooth, and her pulse beats wildly against my
fingertips.

She rips her hand away and holds it to her body in horror.
She hasn't responded to me. What, am I not supposed to talk to
her? Is this some sort of trap? Had Paul not looked right
through her I'd think this is some prank.

Her mouth opens and closes, her light eyebrows high in

surprise. A sound, garbled and far away, leaves her mouth—like drifting to sleep and hearing someone call your name.

"I can't hear you if you're trying to say something," I say. "I didn't know ghosts could talk. Are you dead?"

She frowns with an intense glare. Her lips move and I get the distinct impression I'm being chided. I'm torn between wanting to offer her a coat... and not. Fingers snap silently in front of my face, drawing my attention back up as an arm covers her, a little too late if you ask me. She's clearly ranting about something but I still can't hear her.

"Yeah, still can't hear you," I say, pointing to my ear. Maybe she's the ghost of some old-timey actress, killed too young. She has the vibe. Her beauty is striking with flawless, glowing skin. But her hair is long and styled in a trendy way. Not retro at all. Even though her face is crystal clear, her body shimmers slightly as though she's behind fogged glass. Her legs are pulled up and crossed, otherwise, I'd be getting a full show.

"I wonder..." My hand rests on her knee. It's warm and smooth as I run it higher up her thigh.

Her hand shoots out to smack my cheek. Very real, the sharp sting assures me.

"Sorry." I take my hand back.

The haziness around her disappears and she snaps into focus.

"What the hell do you think you're doing?" the woman yells.

"You can talk?" I flinch back.

"What do you think?" She pulls herself in tighter. "Stop looking at me like that. Stop touching me. I have to think." Her knees tuck tighter against her chest, her elbows keeping her closed up tight as she rubs her temples. "This makes no sense. The other guy didn't see me." I don't think she's talking to me.

"If you don't want people to look at your goods, then maybe you shouldn't be butt-ass naked in a public theater."

"No. It's not like that. I can't believe this—wait, did you just say 'butt-ass naked'?"

"Aren't you?"

"No. You dolt, it's 'buck-ass naked.'" She shakes her head and suddenly I like it a lot better when I can't hear her. "That isn't the point. The point is you shouldn't be able to see me." Goose bumps break out over her skin as she shudders.

"You're alive?" I ask.

"Yes. I'm alive. You get a gold star."

"Hey, I'm not sure why you're mad at me for you being buck-ass naked," I enunciate clearly, "but there's no way this is my fault." I did run my hand up her thigh. I throw my arms up in the air and point with one finger where I grazed the soft skin. "You can't blame me for that. I wasn't sure you were corporeal."

She stills then studies me with a frown. Despite the chill, her cheeks turn pink. "Yeah, well, I give you a point for knowing 'corporeal.' But you can't just go touching whomever you please."

"I know that." My ears burn.

"And can you do something about those eyebrows?" She glowers more fiercely.

"What's wrong with my eyebrows?" I slowly lower them when I register their location on my forehead. "People love my eyebrows."

"I'm sure they do. Too low," she adds.

"Hey now—"

"Turn around."

"What?"

She rolls her eyes, causing her long lashes to fan out. "Turn around you philistine, so I can go grab my clothes."

I swear under my breath but do as she asks.

"Stop looking." She peers up from her bent over position and I pretend to study the ceiling.

"Now she has modesty," I mutter.

"Okay." She's in a sundress and sandals. She rubs her hands briskly over her arms.

I pull off my coat and hand it to her. She looks at it like I used it to wipe my ass.

"You wear it. It keeps you warm."

"Thanks." She slides it over her shoulders and shivers into it, slowly, like she's expecting it to bite. She reaches into her bag and pulls out an empty bottle, shaking it with a frown. "You don't have any water, do you?" Her lips are cracked and dry. I didn't notice that at first. Her pallor is alarming. I bend down to grab the bottle I brought in earlier. She snatches it from my hand and chugs it like it's the nectar of life.

"Uhh. That's good." The long column of her throat moves as she swallows. "I've never been Under that long." She wipes her mouth with the back of her hand engulfed in my coat.

"Under?"

She relaxes, leaning her head back on the seat. She looks bushwhacked. "It's what I call it when I... do that. It feels like I'm underwater or something and when I come up, it's like I can breathe again."

"When you do what exactly?" I'm lost in this conversation but she already thinks I'm an idiot. I'll have to Google 'philistine' later to prove I'm not.

"Hey, how come you can see me?"

I blink. "Because I have the gift of vision."

"No." Her little nostrils flare. "You can see me when nobody else can. I thought it was a fluke earlier."

"I knew that was you." I point and snap my fingers at her face.

"Wow, great work, Sherlock. You managed to deduce that the naked girl here was the same as the naked one from earlier as we look exactly the same."

"Has anybody ever told you how delightful you are?"

The look on her face tells me that yes, they have. What she

says finally sinks in. I know, I know, but naked woman equals blood not in brain.

"Wait, wait, are you saying you actually turn invisible and I'm the only person who sees you?"

The look on her face says exactly that. "Hi, welcome to our conversation." She stands. "Listen, I have to go." Her hand shoots out to steady herself on the back of the chair.

She can't leave. I need to know how much she heard.

I grab her wrist as she moves away. "Wait."

"Don't touch me." She flinches back.

"Sorry. Shit." My arms are back in the air. "*Sorry*, but you can't just go."

"No? Okay." She walks into the aisle.

"Who are you? Why are you stalking me?" I'm up and following her, not touching her. It's my turn to be mad. "Are you trying to get a pic of me for some tabloid or something?"

This stops her. "Please. If that's what I wanted you'd be all over the Internet by now."

"Then who are you? Have you been following me all day? How did you find me here?"

We're standing in the aisle as the changing scenes on screen lengthen and shorten the shadows around us.

"I need to go." Her arms spread out for purchase where there is none.

"Wait. Will you just sit down and talk to me? This is ridiculous." I want to force her into a seat but hesitate.

Turns out I don't need to.

She looks right at me and says, "For the record, I don't normally do this."

Then her knees give out and I catch her a second before she hits the ground.

5

Maggie

IMAGINE THE WORST HANGOVER YOU'VE EVER HAD. NOW TAKE that and multiply it by all the times you stubbed your toe on furniture. Okay, that's close to how I feel right now.

I groan with the knowledge that whatever happens next is going to suck. I can't lie in these nice smelling sheets forever. I force my eyes open and wait for everything to come into focus. The bed tilts and I feel like I'm rolling off the edge, though I'm not moving. A smart person would be wary of the water that sits on a bedside table that is not theirs, in a room they don't recognize. Alas, I chug it down and at least that's where the comparison to a hangover ends because instantly my body feels better. I grab the second bottle and chug that too because if it's poisoned at least I'll die quenched.

I lie back down and study the ceiling. Okay. Now I have the mental capacity to freak out about having no idea where I am. I groan again and recall the last thing to happen. Roe's eyebrows transitioned from frustration to worry as my world faded to black.

James Roe, who can see me when I'm Under. I groan.

I'm in a tiny but neat guest room painted cornflower blue. Not much space for anything but a full-size bed, with the aforementioned fresh smelling sheets and side table, and an antique dresser with cut flowers on it. I always hope that I'll be the type of person that goes to the farmer's market for flowers and organic produce. For now, I have no time for flower arranging between plots for revenge.

For someone who has no clue where she is, I'm awfully content. Content's not the right word. Neutral? Maybe it's the sleep or simple domestic prettiness of this room, but I'm oddly calm about everything. It's interesting considering the one thing I have going for me to stop Zebulund has been completely ruined by an actor who's seen all my nooks and crannies. I'm in some state of shock. Four years and not a single person has seen me. I can't think about what this means because if it means the end of me trying to bring down Zebulund then I'll be drifting purposeless in life. And more people will get hurt.

No. I'll figure out this Roe business and get back to work. After coffee.

The slanted morning sun shines through the room. I've slept for hours. I sit up too fast, clutching for my phone. I'm dressed in an oversized T-shirt that smells like fresh laundry and is most certainly not mine. Two soft voices talk outside the room. Only a small amount of wooziness remains as I make my way toward the door and crack it open. Down a small hallway, Roe sits at a kitchen island, talking to someone out of sight. I could try and find a way to get out of here without being seen or I could just be a grown-up and get this confrontation with Roe over. Ugh. Being an adult is stupid.

The smell of coffee greets me and the decision is made. I all but float on tiptoes following the scent. As I round the corner,

Rachel, Roe's assistant from yesterday, comes into view. I wave self-consciously at her.

"Good morning," she says sweetly.

I like her, I do. I appreciate her gusto with Roe, but right now I need coffee and she's blocking the pot.

"Hi," I say, letting my hair fall in front of my face to block my view of Roe. We don't exchange introductions. I'm not about to volunteer who I am and I'm sure my whole vibe screams, "I will cut you!"

She moves away from the pot as she sees me approach. People might think we're sisters, but I'm the evil one. Where she smiles easily, I glower.

"Hey, how're you feeling?" Roe, who stopped talking at her greeting, stands up and pulls out the chair for me at the bar.

I look at him. I look at the chair. I look back to him. Is it some sort of trap? I turn away toward the counter, reaching out with grabby fingers.

"Coffee."

"Charming as ever," he grumbles at my back.

"Just brewed a pot." Rachel is washing out a mug. "Help yourself."

"Thanks."

The cream and sugar are out in special dishes below coffee mugs hanging from hooks above the machine. I decide then and there I'll never have my life as together as this woman. Roe's gaze is tangible on my exposed legs as I reach for a cup. When I sneak a glance, he looks away quickly. I shuffle around and get myself a drink all the while feeling the weight of the silence behind me. I bet they're exchanging little looks and gestures conveying, "You speak." "No you. You brought her here." I wonder if he told her about any of it. Probably not. Who's going to believe him? And I'm not about to back him up out of the goodness of my heart.

My approach for dealing with Roe thus far has been to

pretend he doesn't exist. After I take two hearty gulps, I look to her and ask. "Your place?" Though it obviously is.

She nods.

"Thanks for letting me crash here." I sort of lift my voice at the end. This whole situation is weird, weirder than normal, but I keep my face neutral.

"Not a problem. Roe brought you." She glances to him and back. "Are you sure you're okay? You seemed out of it last night."

I nod and inhale the coffee I cling to. I don't actually remember about last night, post-faint.

There's a giant rock on her ring finger and small signs of male life around the place: a few sets of large shoes near the door, an LA Kings coffee mug, and an unmistakable masculine smell of aftershave. Could the tension I'm picking up be from the fact they're a couple on the down-low? Everybody in Hollywood is dying to know who he's hooking up with.

And yet, they're formal with each other. He stands stiffly on the other side of the island, disheveled and exhausted looking. And he's still dressed in last night's clothes. If he's living here, or even staying here, he'd have likely changed.

"Is your fiancé still asleep?" I venture.

With a shake of her head she says, "He's at his morning practice. I'm about to go meet him."

"Practice? It's early."

"He's a hockey player. They have a game tonight."

Roe watches this exchange with eyes that widen with every fact but he smoothly tries to cover it up.

"Very cool," I say.

After drying her hands, Rachel collects her bag and slides her keys to Roe. "Stay as long as you like, just lock the deadbolt when you leave."

"Will do. And thank you again..." He sort of trails off, but with his back to me, I can only assume he's gesturing to me with his eyeballs.

"Seconded," I add.

Before he can turn around, I busy myself with another mugful of coffee.

"Maggie May?"

Ah, nuts. It's not like he wouldn't have figured it out eventually.

"That's me."

"I wasn't prying but after you collapsed I had to find some ID. You're a reporter."

"Guilty again."

I recognize that it's childish to be angry at Roe for being able to see me. I recognize it, but it doesn't change the fact. He crosses his arms as a look of quiet disbelief fills his face.

"Have I offended you in some way? Because the way I see it, you're a reporter who's naked stalking me."

"I'm not stalking."

"You are."

"I'm researching."

"And the nudity?"

I set the mug down. "If I wear clothes, it defeats the being invisible thing."

"Aha! So you admit it. You can disappear." He pauses to run a hand over his face. "Your clothes don't vanish with you?"

"I'm having déjà vu. Didn't we already do this? But for the record, no they don't."

"Noted. And sorry if I'm having just a little trouble wrapping my mind around all this. If I hadn't seen it with my own eyes…" He trails off again.

"Why didn't you take me home? If you went snooping for my ID."

"I barely had time to get you dressed, you're welcome by the way, and find your badge before the paps showed up. I had to think fast. Rachel's was the only place I could think to go. Funny that they knew I was at the theater at all." His voice is heavy with insinuation.

"Weird." I can't help a little smile, hoping the concession stand girls made some money off the information.

"I said you fell asleep and I didn't want to wake you. Now there're stories online, with witnesses, that I overworked my personal assistant to the point of unconsciousness."

"Bummer."

Roe gets up and throws his arms out. "Have I done something to piss you off? This is my career you're toying around with, okay? One wrong tweet and I could be cast out with yesterday's fad diet."

I match his stance. I'm pissed too. But to be fair, I can't fully identify why yet. Coffee. Brains. Delay.

"Yeah, you have actually." And then I realize I have no follow up. No answer that I want to give. I haven't had time to process everything. I start talking without thinking. "Four years and not one person has ever seen me when I'm Under." I feel the frustration building again as I make the connections. "And now, right when I'm getting finally close to something, this happens. You've ruined everything."

"I haven't done anything."

"Seeing me is enough."

We pause in our fighting. I break eye contact first. Okay, I may be acting like a jerk. I'm not great when things don't go according to plan. There's the understatement of the year.

"Close to what?" He scratches the back of his neck.

"Huh?"

"You said you were close to something. What are you close to?"

"Nothing." I make a pouty face at my misstep. I'm really not a morning person.

"Your next story? You're so curious to crack the mystery of

James Roe?" He crosses his arms. "I'm a person, you know? I took care of you when you passed out and you treat me like I'm the aggressor here."

"I know. Okay. Thank you for that, by the way. I'm sorry for the saltiness." I groan and stare up at the ceiling. Things are so far off the plan I couldn't even see the plan. "What? You think I'm going to out you? It's not like I can tell anyone. What would I even say?"

I shake my head. Honestly, I'm not even worried about that. I can't say anything without giving too much away. "This isn't even about you," I half-mumble.

"You're gonna have to give me something here." He throws up his arms. Then he takes a deep breath. After a minute of serious eyebrow exercises, he says, "You weren't following me at all were you?" His voice is softer.

I shake my head. "At least not at first."

He's putting the pieces together. I stay quiet.

Now that I'm no longer set to defensive-mode, and I'm able to brain properly, I'm able to take in the vision of him. His jeans hang low on his slim waist, flashing a strip of black elastic, before that same black T-shirt stops. The cotton looks soft enough to rub my face all over. My focus returns to him as he speaks.

"If I guess correctly will you tell me?" He rubs his right eyebrow like he's pushing back a headache.

My knee-jerk reaction is to tell him, hell no, and to go screw himself, but I'm flailing. I need to regroup. I'm having... thoughts. The start of an idea gains traction in my mind, but I'm going to need to trust Roe at least a little until I see where this goes. I work alone. Even O.G. is an invisible partner, pun intended, but Roe does have connections. Can I trust a man who knows so much about me? Maybe he wouldn't have the power to ruin me necessarily but he already knows more about me than any other person in the world. That alone is terrifying.

He bends closer and says, "It's Zebulund, isn't it?"

Sonuva biscuit.

———

Roe

CARRYING MAGGIE MAY OUT OF THAT THEATER LAST NIGHT filled me with primal protectiveness. I sheltered her from the camera flashes and the shouted questions. I hid her face in my chest, hoping to give her some privacy that's never afforded to me. The girls behind the counter said she was Rachel. I didn't correct the press and then I had to awkwardly explain the whole situation to a half-asleep Rachel in the middle of the night. I spent most of the rest of last night replaying everything that happened and not sleeping on Rachel's couch.

It's true, I feel a deep-seated need to watch over Maggie.

But, good God, she's annoying. And mean. She's like a city squirrel: all cute and fuzzy-seeming but will fuck you up if you touch her nuts. Why is she mad at me for seeing her when nobody else can? It's not like I chose that. But as we speak it becomes clear that it was never about me. It's about her getting to someone else and me getting in the way. The flicker in her eyes when I mention Zebulund's name confirms it.

"I'm right, aren't I?" My chin lifts.

I think she's about to challenge me to fisticuffs but something else happens. Her eyes narrow and I can almost see a choice being made in them. "Yes."

Well, I'll be. "You're trying to do a story on him?"

She sucks in her lips and chews on them. I wait her out. I can wait all day, lady.

Again she says, "Yes."

"You thought by following me, you could get to him?"

"I still think that."

I frown and spill the other worry that has bothered me all night long. "How much did you hear last night? At the theater? And before, at the hotel? Were you there listening to the call with my mom?"

"I didn't mean to eavesdrop on all that stuff." She seems genuinely abashed but then adds, "Well, I mean, of course, I did but only because I thought it would relate to Zebulund. The stuff back in Wyoming I don't care about."

"Nebraska."

"Whatever."

"Not whatever. They're two totally different states."

She holds her arms wide apart. Her right hand wiggles. "New York." She wiggles her left. "LA." Then claps them together. "Everything else is cornfields and mountains as far as I'm concerned."

I laugh with incredulity. "You really are a delight. Your friends must love you."

Her little rosebud mouth purses. "Oh yeah, you're the expert on friends when the only person you could take me to was your PA, and you didn't even know she was engaged."

"I knew she was engaged." We're inches apart, facing off.

"What's her fiancé's name?"

Fuck. "This isn't about Rachel. This is about you stalking me. I can have you arrested."

"You have no proof." She pokes my chest, looks at her finger, and drops her balled fist to her side.

I probably don't have any proof. "I have no connection to Marty Zebulund. I don't even know him."

"Not yet." Her eyes light up in a particularly unnerving way. "But you did get a very special invite, if I recall."

"I'm not going to that."

"Rachel agrees that you should."

I replay what I can from that time and wonder what else

she heard. I think again of Paul and my family back home and the anger starts to return.

"What. Did. You. Hear?"

"Just from right before Zebulund got there. And calm your brows. I'm going somewhere with this. I have an idea."

"Lucky me."

"Yeah, you are lucky."

I grind my molars. I'm so sick of being told I'm lucky and that's the only reason I'm here. I won the genetic lottery, right?

"Okay, you're pouting again." She rolls her eyes. "I didn't mean to upset your delicate sensibilities. I just meant you're lucky to have me."

I lower myself back onto the stool while she gets a glass of water. I'll hear this out because, honestly, I'm too shocked by the cojones on this chick to do anything else. I don't often play the celebrity card, but even if I wanted to, this woman couldn't care less. Not about listening to my personal calls, not about following me, none of it seems to bother her conscience. She's so focused that the things most normal humans worry about, like common decency, falls to the wayside. Is that what happens when nobody can see you?

"Here's what we know. I need to get close to Zebulund. You can get on his yacht. You could help me." She leans against the tile counter and ticks off points on her fingers.

"Why would I help you? You aren't exactly charming me out of my pants over here." I step so the counter is between us.

"I'm so glad you asked." A genuine smile grows and it's transformative. "Because you need me, Mr. Roe. You need me as much as I need you."

We're leaning over the counter, face-to-face. Her eyes glint with mischief. I swallow.

"How's that?"

"I can help you find out what's happening back home in Pennsyltucky and in exchange you get me closer to Zebulund."

"That simple, huh?"

"I think so." A smile hangs on her lips until she licks it off. Her gaze roams over my face and grows concerned the longer I take to respond.

Getting involved with this woman is a bad idea. Every man-instinct yells for me to get away from her. But other instincts suggest investigating how soft her lips are.

I could hire someone or I could do the research myself. I could look into things, but it's a lot harder for one of the most trending actors to go poking around without being noticed. A person who can't be seen, well, they could get places.

"I'm going to regret this." I scrub my hands through my hair.

"Hell, yeah!" She smacks the counter and straightens. "That's what I like to hear." Her fingers tap a rhythm on her chin, wheels churning, smoke all but pouring out of her ears.

"Are you going to tell me what it is you're looking for?" I ask, hoping that while she's distracted formulating a plan I can get to the root of this.

The world is full of reporters trying to shed light on Zebulund. Hell, a few have even come close with stories of abuse and crossed lines, but the accusations fall off him like fresh snow on a windowpane. Of course, none of those reporters could disappear. There's something she's holding back.

Eventually, my question sinks in and she frowns. "What do you mean?"

"You're not telling me the whole story. I want to know what your end game is."

"You help me at the party this weekend and I'll consider trusting you."

"Well, with how open and friendly you've been, I'm dying to put my neck on the line for you."

I lean forward on the counter between us again and catch her checking out my arms. I flex. She frowns and looks away.

"Come on. I'll take you home," I say.

I push off the counter as she comes around it. We both notice her hands on my chest at the same time. She snaps them back and tucks them under her arms.

"I'm sorry. Please. Pretty please." She rounds her eyes and blinks up at me. "I need to work out the logistics of creeping around naked. Admittedly, having a partner to help with clothing and distractions may be useful."

I stiffen and give nothing away. Truth be told I'm on board with this plan, but I have to make her work for it a little bit.

"You expect me to trust you when you didn't even trust me with your name. Seems fair."

"Sorry. I'm used to working alone. But look, this could really work." The wheels are really spinning, and she begins to pace.

I let her simmer for a few minutes.

"Zebulund said I could bring someone," I say. "Go as my date."

Her face falls, and the color drains away.

"I meant as a cover." I lift an arm toward her but lower it when she can't hide the flinch. "Why do you look like the idea makes you want to puke?"

"It's not that. I just... umm... he might recognize me." Her hands shake as she untucks her hair from behind her ear to hide behind it.

"Okay. Okay." I relent a little in my teasing. I don't want her to clam up again. "We'll think of something else."

"I'll get there. I just need you to help me get close to him," she says.

"I'll do my best. Then you'll help me figure out my stuff."

"I'm going to need more information about all that."

"And I'll tell you." I tower over her. "Once you prove you're good."

"Please." She rolls her eyes. "I'm damn good at what I do."

"Prove it."

"I will."

We're facing off again. Drifting back to each other like toys floating in a pool.

"There has to be a reason," I say without thinking. I'm distracted by the way her gaze keeps dropping to my mouth.

"Hmm?"

"There has to be a reason I can see you when you're Under and nobody else can."

Her eyes slant with focus. "It is... concerning."

"We could help each other out."

I've pushed too far. I can almost see her eyes shutter closed. She steps back.

"This is the deal. Help one another but then that's it. I don't need anybody to help me. I'm the one with the skills."

"Fine." I scrub a hand over my face.

"Good."

"Great."

She swallows the rest of her coffee in one gulp and makes a "yuck" face. "Now hurry up and take me home, Pennsyltucky. I've got someone waiting for me."

6

Maggie

"Mrs. Jenkins," I yell propping open her back door with my foot. "I brought some groceries."

It's Friday morning and I'm set to meet Roe to finalize a plan before he leaves tonight. I go about putting away her eggs and milk while the distinct scuffling of her walker makes its way down the hall.

The fact is there's no way I could realistically afford to live where I do, but I got lucky with Mrs. Jenkins. I tell her time and time again I'm robbing her but she won't have it. Mrs. J's multiple sclerosis takes a toll, and she needs help with the day-to-day stuff. So in exchange for helping her with whatever she needs, I live in the adobe bungalow in her backyard for a fraction of what it's worth.

She comes from old Hollywood. Her mother was a moderately successful actress I'd never heard of. Her father was supposedly some huge Hollywood screenwriter. She's never told me who, only that that's where all her money comes from.

Mrs. Jenkins never had the acting bug and to be honest I don't think she ever worked a day in her life. She was a socialite in the days before celebrity heiresses were treated like royalty.

Her dog Pepper scampers from behind her to lick my ankles. Pepper's a mix that can't be described in terms of traditional breeds; he's more like a mad scientist's lab experiment gone terribly wrong. A Chihuahua's bugged out eyes, a Pomeranian's short body, and the long hair of I-don't-even-know-what. Top it all off with a tongue forever spilling over the side of tiny jagged teeth and you have the abomination that is Pepper.

"These are lovely," Mrs. J. says as she removes the brown paper from a small bouquet I got at a discount that morning. She leans on her elbows, a sure sign she's having a flare up. "I think I have a vase above the sink." She points a shaking finger.

Today Mrs. J. is dressed to the nines in a fabulous vintage Chanel cream suit. She probably bought it in 1975 to have lunch with someone fabulous. Her hair is tucked under a turban with a giant jewel and a turquoise feather. If I had to guess her age, I'd say somewhere between seventy and three hundred. But I'd never ask and a lady would never tell, as Mrs. J. would say.

"I got it. I'm out of town this weekend. Is there anything I can do for you before I go?"

"A fantastic trip away? Perhaps a romantic rendezvous with a foreign dignitary?" She winces as she shifts her weight.

"Close, but not quite," I tease. "Is it bad today?" I slide her a glass of room-temperature water and two pills. Normally, she's pretty self-sufficient but she has her bad days.

"Not too bad. A storm's blowing in."

"Okay. I'll make sure all the windows upstairs are closed before I go. The guys will stop by to check in."

"Those two are gossips."

I laugh out loud. Danny and Russell live next door and

work for the local morning show. Russell's the sports reporter and Danny books the guests.

"Pot meet kettle," I say.

"I never gossip."

"Right."

"Everything I say is fact and needs to be shared."

"Okay, okay."

"Are you going to tell me where you're going?" Mrs. J. asks

"Maybe. If you're lucky."

"Just lie." She adjusts the flowers in the vase. "Tell me it's a ski trip to Taos."

"In October?"

"Fine. Then a spa getaway." She closes her eyes and tilts her head back like she's imagining it. "There's a fabulous spa just north of Santa Fe..."

I've seen so many old photos of Mrs. J. that they seem to transpose themselves over her face now. No longer do I see the laugh lines and sagging skin, only the classic beauty from black-and-white photos. She was and still is a knockout.

This morning O.G. messaged that I'll be a caterer for the Marty Zebulund cruise. Trapped on a boat with him for almost three days. The text made my stomach queasy and I've been doing my best not to dwell on it. It's a big step in the right direction. That's what I have to remember when my nerves try to shake me. Not exactly glamorous. Mrs. J. doesn't need to know the hairy-knuckled details.

"Actually, it's a yacht party. With celebrities." I throw her a bone.

Her eyes go wide, and I warm up inside.

"Did I ever tell you about the time I went out with a certain Hollywood actor and his wife on their boat?" she asks. "Well, I won't go into the details, but let's just say I don't remember most of it. At some point, I couldn't tell where they ended and I began. I'm thankful we all made it back in one piece." She taps the counter with long jewel covered fingers. "People weren't as safety conscious and concerned about rules back then. Things were more fun. Innocent but more dangerous."

I've heard this spiel a thousand times, so I'm only half listening as I fold up the rest of the reusable bags and tuck them away.

"Gonna tell me who this couple is?"

"You know I can't." She shoots me a coquettish look over her padded shoulder.

"I don't think I'll get that wild, but I do have to dress fancy and rub elbows with all the hottest men in town."

She shuffles toward me and grabs my chin, tugging my face down to hers.

"With those legs and this gorgeous face, you'd better live a little. Before it's too late."

"You know it." I wink.

She plants a wet kiss on my cheek. The floral perfume that infuses the air around her makes my eyes water.

"That's my girl."

I wish I had more fun stories for her, but it's hard to have a social life when your sole purpose is to bring down one evil man.

———

Roe

I CAST A GLANCE AT MY PHONE AND ORDER ANOTHER ESPRESSO. Thirty minutes until I need to hit a press photo shoot with the rest of the *Dartango* cast. It's the most I can spare, especially since Rachel cleared my schedule for Zebulund's party this weekend. This is what we wanted and planned, but I still dread it like my annual checkup.

It's a hot California day at the bistro where I'm waiting for

Invisible Girl, but the light breeze and shade make it comfortable. I don't think I can call her that. I'm sure it's copyrighted, and some lawyer will pop out of the bushes to sue me if I say it out loud. I'll just call her Maggie. It's a sweet name. Fitting. Not of her ice queen personality but of her farm-fresh face. A face I find myself thinking about more often.

When she sits across from me I jump because it's like I willed her into existence. Even with the reek of old lady perfume, she rocks the hell out of a crop top and jeans.

"Hey." She grabs my just-delivered drink and takes a sip. "Ouch, that's hot." She glares at the cup as though it's at fault. "Can I see your menu?" She grabs it before I respond. "I'm starving. I'm assuming you're buying lunch, Mr. Moneybags? Oh, that looks yummy."

"Hello." I blink, disorientated by the different version of the zombie I met this morning. "It's okay you're late. It's not like my time is extremely valuable."

"Man." She peruses the menu. "I'm so hungry I could eat everything on here. I think I'll get this veggie panini and fruit. What are you getting?"

"I ate." I slide the coffee back my way. There's only a small bit of foam left in the glass.

"Oops sorry."

After she orders enough food to feed a whole family she says, "Okay. Here's the deal. I got a way onto the yacht. We need to hammer out a few details."

"Agreed." I lean forward and lower my voice. "I was thinking—"

"Did it hurt?" she cuts in a snide tone.

"Har har. I have ten minutes."

"You were using your three brain cells, go on."

"You're the only person who treats me like an idiot," I snap. She appears slightly abashed, so I go on before she can say more. "This whole arrangement is only going to work if we're on the same page. I get that you have this whole jaded image, but we need to work together."

"Sorry. My people skills are lacking." She chews her lip and looks away.

"I'll tell you more about the business back home, if you give me the details of your talents. I don't need you having a brain aneurysm or something while we're in the middle of the Pacific Ocean. I assume you can't be invisible all the time or you would be. God, this is the weirdest conversation. I can't believe we're discussing how you turn invisible."

"Not invisible enough, apparently." She chews on a chunk of ice from my glass of water.

"You're going to have to have a little faith in someone else. I'm not exactly keen to tell you about my issues either."

"Fine." She glances around and leans in. "But you go first."

"Okay." Now that I have her, I'm not sure where to begin. "What do you want to know exactly?"

"What's the deal with this business you own, or whatever? Why all the extreme measures to meet in secret?" she asks.

The server drops off food and Maggie digs in two-fisted while I talk.

"I'm from a small town in Nebraska. It's where my parents live and my brother and sister. Everybody I grew up with. There's a factory that I help keep open. In turn, everybody has a job and the economy thrives. I can't be linked to it in any way."

"Why? What does this factory make? Drugs? Bombs?"

"Jesus. No. What's wrong with you? We make toys for kids."

She swallows a french fry whole like a duck. No chewing, just swallowing.

"So why all the secrets?"

"It's a small town, lots of pride. They like my family and all, but they wouldn't want any handouts. Not from me."

"But you're keeping them in their houses. You're a saint. You're making toys for kids? You're literally Santa."

"No." I clear my head with a shake. She doesn't need to understand any more than that. "You need to figure out who owns these companies that I'm supposedly paying. Something's off. I can't go looking into it. Like you said, my face won't go unnoticed."

"Gotcha." She sits back and finishes off my water.

When she doesn't say more, I raise my eyebrows and gesture for her to go on.

"Calm your eyebrows. What do you want to know?"

"Oh gee, I don't know." I lean in and whisper with gusto, "When did you start—uh."

"Turning invisible?"

My wince is subtle, but she purses her lips at it.

"Don't worry, it's not contagious. I don't think." She studies the street. It's crowded with tourists and shoppers and everybody in between. "Four years ago. Though I think maybe I could always do it. I don't know. There's really no way of knowing."

"Okay. How does it work?"

"Not sure."

"Can anybody else do it?"

"I dunno."

"What do you know?" I grip my fork, to keep it from flying at her head.

She sighs and tucks her knees under her chin and sits in a little ball on the metal bistro chair. She has only stopped eating because the plates are licked clean.

"I know that I can go for about fifteen minutes at a time. Any more than that and I start to get... weird. The longest I was ever Under was that day at the theater, and you saw how that worked out."

"Damn."

"Yeah. I think it's dehydrating me or something. I get all the bad side effects of drinking: dehydration, vertigo, but none of the perks."

"Like what? Lowered inhibitions? Lack of volume control?"

She laughs high and sweet, and I feel like I've won an Oscar.

"Good point. I guess, I mean, it's not fun. That's really all I know. I didn't even know I couldn't be heard until yesterday. I'm never around anybody to practice."

I'm about to suggest that we work together to find out more but I can tell I've already pushed her way past her comfort zone.

"I could kind of hear you but not clearly," I say. "And that might be because I can see you."

"Good point." She studies a passing plane. "I have no idea why you can see me or if anybody else can. I will say, I've been doing this almost every day for four years, around hundreds of people, and not once did anybody ever see me."

"Makes you think..."

"What?" she snaps.

"I don't know? That maybe there's a reason we met."

"I wouldn't overthink it, toots. Statistically, I was bound to meet someone who could see me."

"It's crazy you have to get naked."

"I haven't figured out where the emperor shops yet." She crosses her arms over herself like a shield.

"Logistically, it must be hard to get in and out of places."

"Yeah, actually it's a pain in the ass. Especially because I need to show my press badge sometimes. I dress light and hope somebody leaves a door open."

What are the possibilities of knowing somebody invisible? Of working together? I twirl the fork on the table.

"Are your eyebrows insured?"

It's such a non sequitur that I laugh. "What?"

"It's like they have a life of their own." She's smiling but trying not to, I can tell. "They could have their own career."

"You're making them self-conscious." I cover them.

"Seriously, what if they get a call-back and you don't?"

I shake with contained laughter.

"I keep waiting for them to scoot off your face like little caterpillars. You'd be ruined."

A blush fires my cheeks and I can't believe it. I cast my gaze to random places, the light traffic, the clear blue sky, the planters along the front of the bistro filled with bright orange marigolds. Anywhere but her.

"Anyway." I stop laughing and focus. "We need to make a plan for what exactly you want to do."

"You're right."

"Are you going to have to work? Do you know how to cater?"

She shrugs, causing blond locks to fall and expose her smooth shoulder. A delectable, perfectly curved shoulder.

"I mean, how hard could it be."

"Have you ever even served food?" I glare at her.

"No. But I'll figure it out."

"Famous last words. How did you get this gig?"

She sucks in her lips.

"Okay, you don't have to reveal your sources."

"In case you're right," she admits like it costs her. "I do have a backup plan to get a terrible case of seasickness."

"You can act? Wonders never cease." Annoyance has me crossing my arms. So many people think acting is the easiest thing in the world. "You're planning on figuring that out too."

"No." She waits a beat. "I wanted to be an actress in another life."

The ice facade is back, forestalling any questions.

"I was good too. Not as good as the top half of your face, mind you," she adds, "but I did all right."

"So funny." I ball up my cloth napkin and throw it at her.

She laughs again with total abandon and I feel it at the back of my knees. I can see why she never does it. If she laughed like this all the time she'd never get anything done for the hordes of people crowding her.

7

Maggie

MY HANDS SHAKE AS I PULL MY PHONE OUT OF MY BRA AND address a text to O.G.

"You told me I would be a caterer!!!!"

Yes, I used that many exclamation points. I also throw in a few red-faced angry emojis. I have a point to make.

Getting close to Zebulund means being unnoticed. But this. This is the opposite of anonymity.

"Last minute change. Best I could do."

I send him a single middle finger emoji.

He responds with a winky face.

"I will find you. And I will hurt you."

I growl at the response that pops right up. "Good luck with that."

For some reason, I believe that if I made it my life's mission to discover who O.G. is, I never would. I'd be ninety-five on my death bed cursing his pseudonym.

"I need new friends," I say out loud to my reflection.

The 1940s style black satin cocktail dress barely covers my

ass. The sweetheart neckline is cut low on my modest cleavage but the built-in corset takes it up a smoldery notch. Itchy stockings cover my legs, complete with garters and garter belt.

I feel almost sexy until I remember that Zebulund is on this boat, only yards away. It's like a switch is flipped and I want to cover up with a sweater. Or, you know, turn invisible. My hand shakes as I correct a curl that keeps falling loose.

Just my body, not my being. Just my body, not my being.

I bend over slightly with my bottom facing the mirror. Everything is very visible if I bend even a little. The reflection of my ruffled-bloomered tushy wiggles in the mirror. "This is ridiculous."

"Did you say something?" Roe barges in and closes the door behind him.

I snap upright. The small changing room under the deck of the yacht for staff suddenly feels too small for two people. I press the front of the ridiculous costume flat over my stomach. His gaze slides over my legs and chest and face before returning to linger a little too long on my legs.

"Wow." He wipes his hand over his mouth. "I thought the point was to be low-key."

"Apparently, I'm a cigarette girl." I pat my retro updo and place a hand on my cocked hip. My other palm tips up toward the roof, like a sassy teapot. "It's the best my source could do last minute."

"It's umm, conspicuous." He steps forward and leans in, examining my face. "Are you wearing makeup?"

The eyeliner is cat-eye style and the fake lashes match the theme. I can't risk getting fired before we leave port. When I commit I go all in, even if I'm not happy about it.

"I know. It's ridiculous. It's too much."

He studies me closely. I shift and nervously play with the satin skirt's hem. I never wear makeup. In fact, I never do anything that might draw attention to myself.

"You look great." He runs a finger along the hem I've been fooling with. It accidentally grazes my thigh. "I'm concerned about you going unnoticed, though. I thought that was why you didn't want to come as my date."

"I did think about that."

I thought about not even coming on this stupid trip. Because I'm worried about how I might react to being next to Zebulund. Will I punch him or start crying? Will I lose my cool and scream at him? But this whole trip is all my brilliant plan. I need to toughen up if I'm going to bring down a titan like Marty Zebulund.

"My plan is to avoid Zebulund all costs. He treats actresses like sex toys. I imagine he treats his staff somewhere on the same level as furniture."

Roe winces but doesn't disagree.

"It's one thing to be floating around in the background serving a purpose," I add. "It's another to be on your arm, making small talk and being under scrutiny."

"True. And harder to disappear."

"Exactly. At least now I can keep a low profile. Though I do worry about all this." I gesture to all the makeup covering my face. "If I go Under I don't know if this'll show up. We might have to wait to try until my shift is over."

"You think it'll be like a floating white mask?" He makes his skeptical face—the one where the right eyebrow peaks and the left one points in, while the rest of his stupid handsome face stays neutral. He must sit in front of a mirror and practice these things.

"I'm imagining my eyelashes floating around the room like little butterflies when I'm Under."

"That's an image." He laughs. "But how noticeable could it be?"

"I don't know. Maybe best if I do have to go Under for it to be in the dark or low lighting."

"Good call."

With a little distance between us I see that he's dressed to kill too.

"It's a whole themed weekend, then?" I ask.

His three-piece suit is cut in the classic fashion of that decade that I adore. Loose-legged trousers and a low break. A gray suit jacket covers a silk vest complete with tie and pressed white shirt. His fedora sits askew on his head. He could be side by side with Cary Grant in *The Philadelphia Story* and wouldn't be a hair out of place. He rocks the retro look hard. Something about a man in a suit. I'm ogling before I realize what I'm doing and pick up my phone to cover.

"Yeah, I guess he got the measurements and everything for the suits ahead of time," Roe says. "It's extravagant but I dig it." He does a fancy little spin on his heels and tilts his hat. One dimple pops in to say hello before quickly disappearing. I think I ovulate. "Feel free to compliment my hat."

"You actors are bursting with modesty." I busy myself by pretending to check for messages then securing my phone and bag in one of the staff lockers. "So much for a casual gathering."

"An intimate party with Marty Zebulund and a hundred of his closest friends, on a yacht the size of half a football field." At least he sounds as annoyed as I feel. "There's enough money on this boat to finance an entire country."

"He's not really known for doing anything low-key. Kinda like the Texas of Hollywood."

Roe chuckles and I have to stop staring at him. Again. When my eyes flick back, he's grinning a little too hard for my liking.

"What's the plan?" He leans against the door, one leg crossed over the other, and I feel like he should be lobbing an apple up and down. The picture of casual seduction.

"Let's play it low-key until we get a feel for how things are going. I don't want to do anything risky too soon. You schmooze and do your A-lister thing."

"Got it. Are you going to search his rooms or anything?"

"Maybe later." I re-secure a bobby pin into my curls. "If the opportunity presents itself. I doubt he'd have anything incriminating."

"Why don't you plant someone as bait and catch him being a perv on one of those tiny hidden cameras? Why go through all this?" He gestures to the yacht around us.

"And then what?" I hold his gaze in the mirror. "A slap on the wrist and he tweets some BS apology. People in this industry don't care if another pretty girl gets her ass grabbed... or worse." I focus back on fixing my candy-apple-red lipstick. "So long as he keeps producing the hits and making people money, the world will look the other way. After all, boys will be boys. If anything, I'd be asking for it in this getup." I roll my eyes hard to show that I'm not on board with victim blaming. "No. When I take this asshole down, it'll be for something he can't pay his way out of."

"What if he's just a serial sexual predator who preys on innocents?"

"Just." I scoff.

"You know what I mean. What if there's nothing else?"

"He's an evil person. There's more than one skeleton in his closet. I won't stop until he's crawling around rock bottom along with all the other bottom dwellers."

Maybe I said that a little too vehemently because Roe studies me like he's a little scared. Or something. He's focused on me and I don't know what he sees there.

"Okay. You're right," he says finally. "Tell me what you need from me."

"Tonight, you're Hollywood star James Roe." I smile a little to cut some of the tension. "Prove yourself as one of the guys and get as close to Zebulund as you can without seeming obvious. You weren't keen on him last time, so he might get suspicious if suddenly you get too cozy."

"Gotcha. Aloof but charming."

"Good."

"Thanks, Coach."

"You're welcome."

"You know I do this for a living right?"

"Yes. I'm helping." I stall my pacing and wait until he meets my gaze. "I don't want you to forget what's at stake here."

"I'm not." He loses his smooth demeanor and tenses. "Don't forget I have things on the line too."

Okay. This'll be good. We can do this.

"I get the impression tonight is mostly cocktails and getting to know each other while we sail out. Tomorrow is when all the shenanigans begin."

"I agree."

We hold each other's gaze.

"I better go up before anyone sees me down here." He tips his hat and winks. "Good luck."

I roll my eyes but only to keep from swooning like a total loser.

"Break a leg," I correct.

8

Roe

THEY AREN'T KIDDING WHEN THEY SAY MARTY ZEBULUND THROWS one hell of a party. The night starts mellow enough. Many of the Who's Who of Hollywood are here dressed in glamorous gowns and suits, sipping cocktails and making small talk. But it doesn't take long before all the masks of polite society slip down to reveal the baser creatures underneath.

Only two hours out of port and this party yacht is fully in the realm of Sodom and Gomorrah. I can't think about how much something like this costs without my blood pressure rising, so I focus on the task at hand. Finding and infiltrating Zebulund's inner circle. It isn't hard to see who his favorites are; they populate the decks like satellite solar systems, all circling him with their own crowds revolving around them. One of LA's top agents sits on a low sectional couch surrounded by beautiful women a few feet away. There's a publicist I think I recognize in a hot tub, breasts bobbing around him like apples on Halloween.

Two top decks make the exterior. On the lower deck a

massive pool and hot tub overflow with people. Lights are draped across the poles and rails. The top deck is where the fully dressed remain, for now. There's a massive bar with two bartenders. Booze flows. Laughter is raucous. Music is thumping.

Maggie makes her rounds but our eyes never meet. She avoids Zebulund, and since I'm primarily near him, we don't get a chance to talk. I worry about her being spotted for the reporter she is, but she hides in plain sight and nobody notices her. Not when the strippers do such a good job drawing attention. I have to trust that she's good at what she does.

It's about midnight and I'm chatting with an actor I worked with a few movies back about his new baby. I straighten when a hearty slap stings my shoulders.

"James Roe." Zebulund inserts himself between us, and my peer takes the hint and heads off. "I'm glad you could make it, after all, my man." His grip engulfs my hand.

"This is your idea of a small get together?" I half-yell over the music.

Zebulund shrugs, as I avoid the smoke from the thick cigar between his fingers. The on-deck DJ bobs to the beat and more people get up to dance as the bass shakes through my body.

"What can I say? I like to keep my friends happy." He thumbs behind him where the star of this summer's blockbuster is doing a line off the stomach of a woman draped across the bar top. Everybody claps when he comes up for air.

"Thanks for the invite. This isn't my normal scene but I have to admit it's nice to get out."

Zebulund shifts to lean against the bar. His stance is wide, taking up the space of three people. He gazes out like a factory boss watching closely for mistakes. A combination of pride and suspicion, like any minute he'd have to go crack a whip.

"Yeah, you don't get out much, do you?"

Even though he's not facing me, he's watching. This is all

part of the game we play now. He knows that I know who he is. What he has to offer. He knows that I need to get in his good graces and he's going to give me the chance now.

"There's not a lot worth leaving the house for. Once you've been to one of the parties, you've been to them all."

"Then I've proven that my parties aren't the same old?" His cheeks suck in as he puffs the cigar.

This time I gesture with my chin to the stripper twirling around the pole that connects the upper and lower deck. It's clear the reaction he wants, so I lick my lips and tilt my head to check out the split she does upside down and in the air.

"Not even close."

"You're so secretive." He chuckles. "I wasn't sure you were into this." His chin points to two women making out and feeling each other up.

"I'm into it." I swear Maggie owes me for this. Big time.

His laugh is louder and wetter this time. He leans in.

"Any of these women are available," he whispers conspiratorially.

This is a test. I've made it this far in this business because I know what people want to hear. I lean back and make an "I'm impressed" face. A cigarette girl walks by, not Maggie, but all of them are very pretty. This one is a brunette with a dimpled grin.

"Any of them?" I make a show of watching her ass, which wiggles as she walks away.

"Any." He slaps my back again and I bite my tongue so hard I taste blood. His hand lingers on my shoulder. "Some might need a little more convincing than others. You won't have a problem."

I feel sick. Maybe it's the undulating of the ship on an empty stomach, combined with the sickly sweet smell of rich tobacco, but probably the feeling of my self-respect crumbling.

"I better make the rounds. Enjoy yourself." He pushes off

the bar when, like an afterthought, he adds, "The boys and I are playing poker tonight. After things settle down. If you can hang, come to my suite." And like that, he's off in a cloud of smoke and skeeze.

What I really want is to shower in boiling water and then go to bed until Sunday morning when we make port again. That's when Maggie meets my gaze across the deck. She widens her eyes and gestures to a small door under the stairs that leads below deck. I finish my water, on the rocks, and casually make my way over. I go in first. It's an old-school powder room with low lighting and gilded furniture. There's a small tufted couch and a large oval mirror but it seems to serve no other purpose.

She backs in a second later, likely checking to make sure nobody notices. Her ass wiggles and I'm reminded of how I found her earlier—bent over in front of her mirror, sexy garters holding up her stockings, checking out her own figure. Her cleavage was all but in my face. It was torture.

The room is small and she bumps into me with her ruffled ass. I have to shift my stance and clear my throat, hands deep in my pockets.

"Jesus, watch it." I grab her shoulders and spin her around.

"You watch it," she snaps back. She crosses her arms and that makes things worse for me.

"You aren't the one who's had her ass grabbed twenty fucking times already. And that's one of the nicer things that have happened." Even though she's trying to hold herself up, I see now that she has a greenish sheen, and the lines around her mouth are tense. She's already admitted to being uncomfortable with attention and this get-up puts it all out there with a flashing neon sign.

"You're right. It could be worse." I take the heavy oak tray full of empty shot glasses and rolled dollar bills she's been carrying all night. She rocks her head side to side. "Are you okay?"

She looks at me skeptically as she pulls off the strap around her neck that held the tray. When she sees that I'm sincere, she slumps onto the velvet couch.

"I guess I didn't think about how hard this would be. I've really kept myself out of this scene the last few years and it's all too..."

"Much," I finish.

"So much."

I sit down beside her and lean forward with elbows on knees. My leg brushes hers. I swallow.

"I saw you talking to Zebulund. Anything noteworthy?"

"Schmoozing. I was invited to his poker game in his suite later."

"Oh?" She perks.

"Yeah, why?" I didn't expect her to be so excited. Probably won't be going to bed anytime soon.

"His poker games are only with his inner circle. It's a big deal to get invited."

I hadn't done anything to deserve an invite.

"Don't be modest now." She pokes me. "I can come in the room while you guys are playing."

The idea of her naked around Zebulund and his closest compadres twists my gut as if the boat lurched to the side.

"I don't see how that'd work. What if the door's closed and you get trapped?"

She taps her pointed chin. "I'll tap your shoulder when I need a break. You could get up and open the door."

"Maybe. It feels risky."

"Don't get cagey on me now, Roe. This is why we're here. To get information."

"What do you expect to hear from a bunch of guys shooting the shit?"

"I don't know. Seeing who's even invited in there would be good. How he treats them." She studies the scrollwork around the door. "Oh! Maybe I could help you cheat! Like tell you the other hands around the table or something?"

"I can't hear you well, remember. And besides what would that do but piss people off? No, I hate to say this about my own sex, but the last thing we want is to have our ego wounded. They'd kick me out of their little club faster than you can say 'Piccadilly.'"

"That was a random word choice."

"It's the first word I thought of." I pull my hat down lower on my head to hide the blush.

"You're right though." She smirks and flicks the rim of the hat. "Men have very tiny, fragile egos."

"Hey, my ego is hardly tiny."

She laughs and I grip the couch.

"Ugh. How did I get here? I'm so tired." Her eyes drift closed as she rests her head on the wooden paneling. Her neck is long and elegant and her skin is smooth. And even after working all night her sweet smell fills the space. She catches me staring. I study the wall.

"Me too." It's true. I'm tired of all of it. Suddenly, I want nothing more than to go home—Nebraska home—maybe open a small store and work and make a family. I'm struck with such longing for another life I feel woozy.

"Just get me in that room and we'll figure it out," she says, determined again, albeit exhausted.

I agree and notice that for the first time in her plan-making she uses "we" instead of "I." It was only a word choice. Nothing to get excited about.

———

Maggie

EVEN THOUGH I'M DEAD TIRED AS THE PARTY WINDS DOWN, I

insist on joining Roe's poker game. Okay maybe "winds down" is the wrong phrasing, as really it's slowly morphing into an orgy of biblical proportions, and they don't need a cigarette girl for that. I have enough time to wash my face and strip off my clothes before there's a soft knock at my door.

"Now or never," he says through the door.

"Hold your panties." I slip on a robe and answer the door.

He's stripped off a few layers too so that he's only wearing a white button-up shirt, sleeves rolled to the elbows, and dress slacks with suspenders. The hat's gone and his hair has lost some of its slick hold, like he's been rolling around in bed. I swallow. The man is epic.

"Ten minutes. No more. I really don't like this idea." He glances down the hall as his arms cross.

"Yes, sir." I salute him. Ten minutes would never be enough time. We both know that, but sure, let him think he has any control of this situation.

"You strip now or..." He pointedly looks away.

"Uh. Well. I guess I had planned on waiting until we got there."

"I don't think you can risk it. And what am I supposed to do with your robe thingy?" He's right, but it kills me.

"How far is his room?"

"A few doors down. Not far."

"Okay. Fine." I'm stalling because the idea of stripping suddenly makes me super self-conscious. "You just want to see me naked."

It was fun stripping down before, when I was protected from judging eyes. The air is heavy with awkward tension. I lift my head and sniff.

"You got me." He does sarcastic eyebrows. "I love being around beautiful naked women I can't touch."

The fact that he calls me beautiful so casually, like it's a fact known to all, makes my whole face burn. I show him my back and pretend to search the room.

"Hurry," he groans.

"Fine, okay. Get me there quick. And make sure there's a closet or a bathroom I can get in and out of easily."

"I'll make sure. If not, I'll make an excuse and take you back."

"Okay, uh, close your eyes." I take my time loosening the tie on my robe.

"Seriously?"

"Yes. Let's pretend you haven't seen me naked a bunch of times already. I'm at a severe disadvantage here."

He makes a show of covering his eyes with his hands.

"Okay. In a minute, walk out slowly and then close the door."

He grunts an acknowledgment. I strip down and steady my nerves. His shoulder's hard and warm under my hand.

"I'll follow close behind you," I say quickly. "Don't want to bump into anybody." And I don't want him to see all my jiggly bits walking around.

"Fine. Let's go."

"You're awfully testy for someone who gets to keep their clothes on."

He sighs as I go Under. We make our way down the hall, passing several people as we go. None of them see me, obviously, but they wave to Roe.

"This is so fucking weird. I keep expecting them to say something about the naked woman behind me," he whispers through the side of his mouth.

"That's how it should work," I say, even though he can't understand me.

So I poke his butt. I don't know why. Maybe being invisible makes me cheeky. Pun intended. He stumbles.

"Hey, none of that. Not fair. And no talking. Whatever you said I'm sure it was sarcastic."

I goose him again and this time he jumps right as someone passes. The person sends him a backward glance and I laugh to myself. Thankfully, the master suite isn't terribly far. He knocks and I take a deep, steadying breath.

"Come in," Marty Zebulund calls out.

The door opens on a massive living area with rich dark wood paneling and retro furniture. The majority of the space is taken up by a poker table the size of a small pool with fancy cutouts and printed felt. Smoke lingers in the soft light, collecting along the low ceiling, and AC/DC's "Highway to Hell" blasts from unseen speakers. Oh, how apropos.

A few doors open off the main room, probably a bedroom and bathroom, and a kitchen sits to the left side. I let out a sigh of relief and point so Roe can see what I see. The layout leading to the kitchen is wide open and right next to the poker table but has a bar countertop that I can duck behind and come Up for air if I need to. He very subtly dips his chin to show that he understands.

"Roe. You made it," Zebulund calls to him around a cigar. "Grab a drink and join us."

I follow Roe closely, keeping my hands on his waist, so when he stops suddenly I slam into his back, essentially wrapping him in a hug. He's solid muscle so my impact doesn't even register. He reaches back to steady me and then thinks better of it and stretches to cover.

"Thanks." He nods to the table. "Hey."

The others nod back. We head to the kitchen where he opens the fridge. The door opens toward the group so they can't see as he grabs two waters and "accidentally" drops one out of sight behind the counter for me. I mouth a thank you and hide it quietly in the cabinet. I deposit myself behind the counter but stay Under a minute longer as he heads over to join the table, to see who made it to the VIP room.

If he tries to sneak a peek at me, he does so without me noticing. I'm disgusted with myself when I realize that bums me out. There are only four other men, including Zebulund. I recognize another actor and I think an agent. Sure enough, Zebulund begins introductions in his deep, slimy voice.

"You all know James Roe." He points to the first guy—a handsome blond that starred in the last *Super Heroes* movie. "You probably recognize Viktor Karlsson."

I perk at the name, popping my head up over the counter. He was on my list of names too, but also hard to pin down. He's the action star of the moment, built like a Viking, complete with blond beard and ice-blue eyes.

The two actors exchange the international manly chin raise.

"Hey man," Viktor says.

"Long time, no see. We worked together way back in the day on that indie flick," Roe explains, probably for my benefit.

Viktor shakes his head, with what seems like shame. His eyes are bloodshot, and his leg shakes incessantly under the table.

"Don't remind me. I was sixteen and trying to prove my acting chops. I did squinty-eyed crying for half my lines." He has a slight accent that I can't quite pinpoint, noticeable in the blunt way his words cut off.

The room laughs.

"You made a very believable teenager," Roe teases and I relax a little.

Zebulund's at the head of the poker table, rather the seat facing the door, and taking up half the real estate. He gestures to his right and introduces Craig Meisner, a lawyer with thick curly hair and a toothpick twirling around his mouth. I recognize his name as being linked to all the top stars who've found themselves in hot water.

To Craig's right is celebrity agent, Kyle Altman; he's older than my father but rocks pierced ears and a silver goatee. There's a twinkle in his eyes that makes me think of the kid that likes to yank out chairs right before people sit down.

To Kyle's right is Roe, and Viktor rounds out the group. The power in this group is tangible. With each introduction, Roe manages to come off witty and charming with just the right amount of humility. Okay, it wasn't dumb luck and good looks that got him here. He certainly knows how to read people. I'm a little jealous, to be honest. Normally, I tend to say exactly the wrong things.

Being in this room is a big deal. I want to watch longer but the spins and dryness kick in, and so I hide again and come Up. Under the empty bar, I hide while the men deal the first round, say the rules, and set about getting to know each other as only men know how; by giving each other shit and disguising their emotions with posturing. Quietly, I open my water and chug half.

When I feel better, I drop back Under and walk around a little. The music is low and all the other lights are out except the lamp directly above the green felt table, spotlighting their game. The swirling smoke and darkness make for a spooky vibe. Swap the cards and beer for candles and a Ouija board, and you've got yourself a séance.

Zebulund's bedroom is sparse and reveals no secrets. It takes a few minutes to search because I have to stop often to listen. Zebulund's bags and closets turn up nothing of interest. I take another break to get my bearings and finish the water before I make my way back to the table.

I circle the men, studying their hands, feeling a little bored, keeping myself to the shadows. It was silly to hope tonight they'd all decide to spill their deepest secrets. My gaze crashes with Roe's. I stick out my tongue and cross my eyes. He looks back at his hand, as smooth as ever, but maybe I detect a smile?

My modesty fled a few hands ago. So when I pass by him I don't bother covering anything. It's too dark to see me and he's always the gentlemen.

But when I pass Zebulund, I shudder. My body reacts with a familiar tension, waiting to curl up and somehow purge itself. It's childish, I know, but I flip him a double bird with strength I don't feel. As I pass Kyle I stick my head out into the light. Roe glances up to see my floating head. He chokes on his water and falls into a coughing fit. I smile, quite pleased with myself.

"Okay there, Roe?" Kyle asks, smirking at the display.

"Swallowed wrong."

"Relax your throat, bro," Viktor says. He's increasingly drunk as the night progresses.

"You'd be the expert on that," Kyle says evenly.

The table laughs at the quick comeback. Everyone except Viktor, who blushes bright red and glowers. I thought this sort of talk went out with *Mad Men*.

Roe's silent at first but his cheek works like he's biting it. Viktor's nostrils are flared and he glares around at each guy like he's a second from standing up and flipping the table.

"Viktor," Roe says smoothly, "Heard you got the new Pechenko film?"

"Damn right I did." The kid lifts his chin, eyeing each of the others in challenge.

"Nice. I auditioned and couldn't cut it. Congrats, man."

The men all nod and murmur congratulations. Some of the tension lifts. I let out a breath. There's something off about this whole meeting. I'm sure that Roe senses it too. His gaze moves from one guy to the next, seeking out any conflict. It's like all these guys are pumped with extra testosterone and fear, one bad joke from losing their cool.

"That's it, guys." Zebulund stands, eyes squinted from his massive grin. "Everybody's having a great time." He adjusts his junk. "Gotta see a man about a horse." The deck shakes as he clomps out of the cabin.

I don't miss the covert look Roe shoots me. Yeah, he feels weirdness too.

"Come on, man, you know we're just ragging on you because we wuv you," Craig raises his drink in a slurred salute. "Lighten up."

Roe, and maybe Zebulund, are the only remotely sober people at the table. This comment only pushes Viktor further into his dark mood.

"Yeah, heaven forbid anybody not have a good time on Zebulund's dime," Viktor says.

Roe finds my gaze and we share a quick "what the hell does that mean?" look.

"Maybe time to cash out, friend," Kyle says quietly to his hand, adjusting the cards.

"Fuck you." He grumbles something else unintelligible. I sneak behind him to hear his drunken ramblings better. Now we're getting somewhere with this. When he starts to talk again, I lean in. "I know you're sick of..."

Viktor's mumbling into his drink so I can't hear what he says. I shake my head and look up to see if Roe understands him.

But Roe's eyes are wide with controlled panic. The deck dips behind me as the smell of cigar and cologne engulfs me. Zebulund has walked back into the room when I wasn't paying attention and is right behind me. I don't move. If I step even an inch my naked back will be pressed into him. I'm trapped, naked, in front of the man I loathe with my entire being.

9

Roe

My heart races with the effort it takes not to lunge for Maggie. Not only is she absolutely horrified, frozen in place, but we're seconds from being found out. She's positioned between Viktor and Zebulund without either of them touching her, but if she shifts an inch she'll bump one or the other. Zebulund's so close he must be breathing caustic air down her exposed back.

I could flip the table to cause a distraction. Or I could stand up and yell something. But neither of these ideas strike me as genius.

"What's going on?" Zebulund asks.

His arms cross and he examines each one of us. I don't know if he heard Viktor's cryptic little comment or if he senses the palpable tension. Something has to crack. And now.

Suddenly, Maggie sidesteps from between the two and not a heartbeat too soon. Zebulund moves forward to place his hands heavily on Viktor's shoulders. I glance at her for a brief second. She's outside the circle of light but there's enough to reveal her hand covering her mouth, eyes wide. She's shaken, but it's more than that. Something deeper—her gaze is inward and she's withdrawn. I wish I could go to her and comfort her. Instead, I focus on controlling this situation.

I let out a slow breath I didn't even know was stuck in my chest. Viktor winces as his body tenses, curling in on itself, as Zebulund's aggressive rubbing increases. Zebulund kneads the man's shoulders like dough. The actor's eyes water even through his altered state.

"Nothing. We're ragging on Viktor." Kyle's tone is light-hearted. His voice a little too forced.

"But we're all relaxed, having a good time, right?" Zebulund asks.

Immediately the guys chime in with a chorus of, "Yeah, oh yeah, of course."

"Good, good," he says as Viktor's face contorts. "I want everybody to have a good time." His voice is smooth as his thumbs dig deep into flesh.

I have to act. The table we're playing at probably cost more than any car I ever had growing up. It's a beautiful, expensive piece with inset pockets for the cards and chips. Something has to be done. I jerk my hand out and knock over a beer.

"Oh shit. Fuck." I jump back. I leave and quickly come back with a towel to sop up the beer.

"Spills happen, my friend. It's only a table." Zebulund lumbers back to his seat and waves off my worry.

A table worth a fortune, but sure.

"Chill out, Roe," Craig chimes in. "This isn't a first date."

"This is more action than I get on a date, that's for sure." I laugh at myself and throw up my hands.

"You're doing it wrong," Zebulund chimes in and we all laugh. Too hard.

This breaks the tension and though Viktor remains mostly quiet, we find the rhythm again and are back to playing in no time. An hour ticks by at least. I'm more than ready to go. I think up excuses to leave, because I don't get the impression that Maggie is getting anything out of this either. She's been loitering on the edge of the table like a bored poltergeist, going from player to player. I'm straining my eyes trying not to stare at her figure every time she passes me. It's so hard. The not-staring, I mean.

"Well, guys, I'm getting—" I start to say, when a series of things happen.

Maggie drifts past Kyle right as he blows out a puff of smoke. Directly into her face. It happens in slow motion. The cloud floats up her nose. Her eyes shutter closed and her nose twitches. Her face scrunches in an effort to stop the inevitable.

No, no, no...

But no amount of prayer can stop the sneeze that explodes out of her. I can only imagine what it's like for the rest of the table. A few cards fly inexplicably. Kyle jerks violently. Maggie jumps back, hands covering her face—eyes wide and terrified.

"Holy shit." Craig's eyeing the cards.

Viktor glares at the area. "What was it?"

"Something brushed against me and those cards fucking moved. Look, dude." Kyle points to his arms where goose bumps raise the hairs. "I'm freaked out."

Zebulund stays quiet. He studies the cards. There's no way he missed it—he's right across the table.

"The air clicking on," I offer.

"No." Kyle's head shakes with determination. "I'm telling you. I felt something. And earlier I swear I saw a face in the smoke. The shape of it."

It takes all my acting skills to not look at Maggie again. She paces with arms wrapped tight around herself in my periphery.

"This reminds me of this time I was like thirteen," Craig pipes in. "I crashed my little sister's birthday party and they were doing some weird voodoo in the dark, and I swear they called something evil. Like, into the room. I could sense it and then a framed picture fell off the wall and shattered."

"Totally," Kyle says. "The basement of the house I grew up in was haunted." He talks with such enthusiasm the table shakes. "Every time I went there I got chills and sensed something, you know?"

"Careful, you know Marty doesn't like that ghost talk." Viktor's half slumped in his chair, one drink away from passing out right there.

The other men's eyes widen and they glance to Zebulund before pointedly avoiding him. Zebulund tilts his head and smiles with extra teeth.

"All in good fun. But let's continue the game, shall we?" The question is for me.

I dealt the hand, so I ask Kyle, "Your bet?"

"Check," he responds and I keep going around. After a few minutes, I make my way to the bathroom, making sure Maggie follows. Once the door closes, she comes Up to wrap herself in a towel I'm holding.

"I have a really great idea." She grins.

I already know I won't like it.

———

Maggie

ROE SLUMPS OUT OF THE BATHROOM AND BACK TO THE CARD game. He's not happy with me. He's especially not a fan of this plan. Well, he's going to have to deal, because this is all we've got right now. This is something we can work with. I'll turn a stupid mistake into our advantage. We both saw how Zebulund tensed with the ghost stories. We heard Viktor's little comments. We know there's something going on that we aren't privy to. I'm about to find out what that is. And if I freak the living crud out of the scum bucket, then added bonus.

After a couple more minutes in the bathroom and taking some very unladylike gulps from the sink, I go back to Roe and the other guys at the table.

Even though I'm exhausted and this is the longest I'd ever gone Under and Up in one day, we can't stop now. We're close to getting something. The testosterone and fear in that room are culminating to some sort of breaking point.

Roe's still doing a good job of pretending that I'm not there. As they deal another hand of poker, I decide what to do first. Clearly, the weakest link here is Viktor, but if I start with him, he may crack too soon.

Instead, I grab the back of Kyle's chair with both hands and shake it once with all my might. They're big barrel-cut style seats, upholstered with rich brown leather. My shove is enough to cause Kyle to jump. A flush spreads up his cheeks and down his neck. His hand shakes as he reaches for his beer. But to his credit, he doesn't say anything. Roe pointedly acts like he doesn't see it. Only Craig looks Kyle's way. He studies his friend without comment, slowly twirling the toothpick around in his mouth before returning his attention to the game.

Well, that decides who's up next. I saunter over to Craig, the lawyer. He munches obnoxiously on a handful of trail mix, all while the toothpick remains shoved to the side of his mouth. He tilts his head back to dump another palmful into his mouth. I bump his hand, causing it to hit his chin and send food flying. To keep my laughter from being noticed, I step back a few paces. The expression on his face is priceless. He grips the edge of the table like the world is spinning. His chest heaves up and down as he chews. Zebulund notices the food flying, though.

"You okay?" he asks.

The other guys glance up too, and the conversation slows

again. Craig looks to Kyle. Kyle responds with a subtle head shake that Zebulund barely misses.

"Well? What happened?" The chair creaks as he leans forward to glare at the man.

Craig takes a big drink to swallow down the rest of his mouthful. "Nothing. I slipped." He sweeps up the crumbs with his hands and avoids eye contact. But despite his nonchalance, he's pale and keeps glancing over his shoulder.

It's working. All the players are slowly cracking. Zebulund must sense it because his jokes get louder and more offensive. I'm back at Viktor. Poor kid is close to blacking out. He squints one eye as he studies the table, swaying in his seat. I don't know why they don't take him back to his room.

But I'm not here to help. I'm here to see what the deal is with Zebulund and his cronies. I take my finger and run it along the back of Viktor's neck. It's gentle and caressing. He shoots up in his seat and looks around frantically. When he swats the air I have enough time to jump out of the way without being slapped. He's coming off as a crazy person to everyone. Kyle stops mid-drink with the bottle to his lips, staring. His gaze flicks toward Craig, who has dropped the toothpick from his mouth. Viktor notices everyone watching too and stops. He faces Roe.

"Stop." Viktor glares at Roe.

Roe holds up his hands. Everyone sees he's too far away to be messing with Viktor, plus both his hands grip the cards.

"You touched my neck." Viktor shouts at him but he says it almost as a question. Like even as he says it, he realizes it couldn't have been Roe.

"Are we still playing or not?" Roe studies his hand closely.

"Isn't that the question?" Viktor pushes back from the table but stumbles with the effort.

"I'm sure it was the breeze or something." Roe tries to reel them in.

"Yeah, you keep fucking saying that," Viktor grumbles.

"Chill out, Viktor." Kyle's expression is pointed.

It's enough to get Viktor to collapse back into his chair. The two men glare at each other, and for a group of supposed best friends these men are short-fused with one another. I'm about to flick Viktor's ear when Roe meets my eyes and shakes his head subtly. I shrug in question, but he flits his gaze toward Zebulund. That's when I notice he's watching Roe closely. Neither man says anything. Okay, maybe this isn't working. I'm hoping to work up Zebulund, freak him out a little, but as always he's jovial and unflappable.

I stumble to the safety of the kitchen counter and sit on the floor. The night has exhausted me. On top of working all evening and getting accosted, I've spent hours going Under. It hits me hard, and my lips are so chapped that if I smile they'll crack and bleed. The room keeps blurring and zooming in and out. I want to lie down and rest my eyes for a minute. Or a year.

I shake my head and pinch my cheek a little. Definitely won't be able to stay Under if I pass out. This night needs to hurry up and I need a freaking drink of water. But I take a few steadying breaths and then go back to finish what I've started. When in the room I stumble a little, but it's Roe's chair I correct my balance on. He listens intently to a story Zebulund is telling, about some other ridiculous party, and doesn't even flinch as I fall into him. His hand goes to mine. He plays like he's rubbing some tension out of his neck when he squeezes my hand. I'm so taken by the action I can't move. My heart kicks up a notch.

He squeezes one more time and lets go. It causes just enough adrenaline to motivate me. A part of me feels bad for doing this but my gut tells me we are close to getting some reaction from Zebulund. I reach over Viktor, leaning heavily into him, grab his hand of cards, and throw them in the air. Chaos erupts as I rush to the safety of the kitchen.

Roe

WE ALL STAND UP AT ONCE. MAGGIE BARELY MISSES RUNNING into Viktor in her quick retreat.

"I didn't do it!" Viktor yells. "I didn't fucking do that." He sways as he rubs his hands through his hair and face like there're a thousand ants crawling over his skin.

"Calm down," Kyle says, but he's up and pacing, not really talking to anybody.

Craig swears and mumbles about some "fucked-up shit going down in the middle of the goddamn ocean."

To calm them down and give myself some time, I hold up my arms. Maggie stumbles to the floor by the door, I think she's trying to make it to the kitchen but has lost all strength. She's curled in a ball and I worry the blurred edges of her profile will become clear to everyone.

"It's okay, it's okay," I'm saying. I don't know who I'm talking to either.

"Don't tell me it's another breeze," Zebulund says quietly, but I hear it.

He's standing with arms crossed. There's a barely visible sheen of sweat on his brow. A bulbous vein in his forehead throbs fast enough to match my own racing pulse. This is a terrible fucking plan and I know it.

What the hell was Maggie hoping to prove? Zebulund's the only one who isn't in a full-blown state of distress. When Viktor stumbles back and misses his chair, he sprawls to the deck.

"I'm taking Viktor back to his room. It's been a long night. I think I need to go lie down too," I explain.

"Good plan." Zebulund studies me through squinted eyes.

"What time is it even?" Craig runs a hand over his face. He closes one eye to read his phone. "Fuck. I'm still drunk. I'm going to go watch the sun come up." He steps over Viktor without a pause in his step.

Kyle goes to Viktor's side. Viktor's slumped over, head in his hands, mumbling to himself. Kyle helps me stand him up and put him around my shoulders. We grunt with the effort.

"Thanks," I tell Kyle. He leaves the cabin without saying anything else. "Come on, buddy, we're going back to your room."

Zebulund's mostly hidden in the shadows. It's unnerving because I can't tell where he's focused. Thick swirls of smoke disfigure him and I'm so tired I can hardly keep the two of us upright.

"You need any help cleaning up?" I offer, despite my fatigue.

"You've got your hands full." A large stream of smoke appears in the light as I hear a loud exhale. "He's right across the main hall."

He walks into the large bedroom. The door shuts. Maggie's still on the floor.

"You okay?" I mouth.

She nods once, despite all the evidence to the contrary. I half bend down to lend her a hand. She's still Under but her coloring is bad. With an arm around her waist, I pray we don't run into anybody on the short walk to our rooms. How will I get them both out of here without looking insane?

"You'll be in bed soon," I say, ambiguous enough that I could mean it for Viktor too.

Her head rests on my shoulder.

Thank God, I spend hours at the gym each day, because getting these two mostly dead weights twenty yards is a struggle.

"This you, buddy?" I ask Viktor.

He stumbles forward to squint at the door number. "Thinkso," he slurs.

He fumbles with his wallet, half leaning against the doorframe. I take the opportunity to shift Maggie in my arms and stretch my neck muscles. Her face is pale, and I'm shaking from exertion and worry for her. I don't even care about her nudity anymore. The fact that she looks like she's about to slip into a coma drives it from my mind.

How has she held it together this long? Her long neck is exposed as her head lolls back, and the fuzziness at her edges starts to come into focus.

"No, no, no." I shake her a little. She goes back Under with a dry and painful sounding swallow.

Meanwhile, Viktor thinks I'm talking to him and says, "Oh. Wrong card." He was attempting to open the door with a credit card.

"Not a hotel, my man, you have a regular key."

"Oh yeah." His head rests on the door as he searches his pockets.

I sweat bullets trying to make sure he doesn't tip over, all the while I have to gently shake Maggie every few seconds to keep her from becoming visible. Thank God, the halls are all but empty this early in the morning.

"Got it." The door swings open with a slam. He falls face first onto the carpet. "I'm okay."

He gives a thumbs-up from his prone position on the floor. I look to the heavens for strength and guide Maggie in before closing the door. I take a deep steadying breath.

"Almost there, buddy. Few more steps."

The muscles in my back scream in protest as I help him up.

"Young of good ones."

"What?" I ask. He's not making sense.

"You're good. Too good. For us."

"You're good, too. Just faded." I heave him onto his bed and yank off his sneakers.

He's mumbling incoherently again as I go to get him a glass

of water. By the time I come back from the bathroom he appears to be sleeping.

"There's some water and aspirin here on the table, okay, buddy?" I explain.

He says something I can't understand so I lean forward. "What?"

"I wish you could get out." He opens his eyes and stares right into mine. "It's too late though. Hesgotchu too."

"Who's got me? What do you mean it's too late?" I straighten.

But his eyes close and his breath evens out. I run a hand over my face and let out a long sigh. I've aged twenty years tonight. Thankfully, Maggie and I can escape to my cabin now, where I can get her the help she so desperately needs.

"There's a naked woman on the couch," he hiccups out.

My heart thumps. Maggie's passed out on the couch, visible. Her skin is alabaster.

"Sure, there is, buddy."

I pray he doesn't remember any of this tomorrow. His eyes shut and his mouth relaxes open. I go to Maggie.

"Hey," I whisper to her and kneel on the floor beside the couch.

It takes some work but I get her a few sips from an extra water bottle. Her lips are peeling when I ease the hair back from her face. When her eyes flutter open they're bloodshot.

"I can't go Under anymore," she whispers dryly.

"It's okay. You don't have to."

"I'm so tired, James." Her face falls and I think she'd have tears in her eyes if her body could produce any moisture at this point.

Emotion swells in my chest and any anger at the situation dissolves the instant she calls me James.

"I know. Let's go to sleep."

Beautiful, strong, crazy-ass woman. She looks down at her form without moving any muscles.

"Naked," she says.

"You typically are around me."

"Perv." Her smile causes a wince.

I slide my suspenders down and take off my shirt, leaving only an undershirt. She struggles to sit up with my help. I slide her arms into the sleeves one at a time, her head lolling.

"Thanks," she says.

"Come on." I pick her up and carry her cradled in my arms.

At least if we pass anybody on the short walk they'll think we're coming down from partying. Her head is on my chest and I take a deep inhale. She said she doesn't wear anything scented. It's subtle but it's there; a light sweet, clean fragrance.

Finally, in my room I force her to drink another whole bottle of water and eat a few nuts from the kitchenette. She passes out the second I place her in my bed. I kick off my shoes and lay the dress pants on the back of a chair.

Should I be a gentleman and make up the sleeper sofa? That seems like too much work. Maggie's lying there, snuggled deep under the covers, an angelic smile on her lips. It tugs something within me.

What the hell.

The sand in my eyes wins—I fall face first into bed. I'll compromise by sleeping on top of the blankets. With her blond hair tickling my nose I drift off to sleep.

10

Maggie

I WAKE UP SWEATING. BEFORE I HAVE THE COURAGE TO OPEN MY eyes, I register the heavy weight of a man on top of me. A moment of pure panic takes over. What happened? What happened? My eyes pop open despite the protest of my whole being, but it's only Roe.

My racing heart gets the memo and starts to steady. Roe's sleeping soundly. Pretty sweet actually. His eyebrows are parked in neutral and his dark lashes are splayed. We're under a thick white comforter. He's mostly clothed and I'm wearing his shirt. I inhale and it's like a hit of an opiate. This feels like the most intimate thing I've ever done. We're facing each other, his top leg draped over my waist. Our hands lie relaxed, half curled like sleeping children. I should hate this. I should be angry at least.

In fact, I feel content.

As my body fights waking, I think about progress. Not only have I let him see me naked repeatedly, but here I am lying in bed and with him pressed to me and I'm not dissolving into panic.

Roe tugs me closer in sleep. He rolls me so my back is against his chest. We're spooning. I am spooning with man in a bed. And I am not freaking out. I should tell him to get off.

Of me. Tell him to get off of me.

I don't. Probably because I'm exhausted. His warmth is a salve to my discomfort. I should get up to drink a million gallons of water, but my eyes drift closed again with a contented sigh.

When I wake up again, it's to the sounds of Roe cursing. With one eye open I see him pushing up to a sitting position. He's fuzzy with sleep and his hair sticks out in multiple directions. He has a noticeable shadow of a beard. His hands scratch through his hair and he's squinty-eyed with confusion. It's adorable.

"What time is it? Did you hear that?" His mumblings don't really process before coffee and I certainly can't speak. He grabs his phone off the side table. "Damn. It's almost three in the afternoon."

Still... I can't really do more than blink at him.

"I don't remember the last time I slept more than two hours." He shakes his head. It's like he's mostly talking to himself because he seems a little taken aback when he finally notices me.

I still haven't moved. If there were prizes for being the most still I would win them all. Even my analogies are lame right now. He leans closer to me and places a hand on my cheek like a mother checking for fever.

"How are you?" he asks.

I blink once. To me, that translates to, "I've been better, but I'm alive. I could go for a giant cup of coffee and a shot of B12," but that must not have come across because he shakes my shoulder.

"Seriously, Maggie? What's wrong?"

I open my mouth. It's sticky with dehydration. "Coffee," my voice crackles like a dusty old book.

He studies the ceiling for a second. A second later a pillow smacks my head. I'm too tired to take it off. Plus, it blocks some of the obnoxious sunshine.

That's when someone knocks on the door.

"I thought I heard something." The bed shifts as Roe leaves it. "Stay here."

I groan. As if there were any other option. The pillow blocks me from seeing anything but I can hear him walk to the door and click open the deadbolt.

"Morning," a deep voice says.

My stomach sinks.

"Marty Zebulund," Roe says.

I briefly forgot about last night in the confusion of tangled limbs and warm smiles. Despite almost passing out, I remember well enough Zebulund's studied looks of last night. The suspicion. The spectacular failure of my plan. It wasn't a plan really. In hindsight, I'm an idiot. Not that I'd ever admit that to Roe. These powers are wasted on me.

The cool air brushes my exposed thighs, reminding me of my vulnerability. I'm prone on the bed, the upper half of my body covered by the comforter, but the lower half is free to be seen. I'm too afraid to move. I'm like prey. Maybe if I'm still, he won't see me.

"Sorry to disturb you... both." His voice is heavy with implication. So much for that.

"Uh, yeah sorry. I uh, just woke up." The comforter is slid down to cover me.

"I see. That the cigarette girl?"

My heart hammers away and I'm sure the bed must be visibly vibrating from it. Did he spot me last night? Is that why he's here? Did he make some sort of connection? Oh, no. The gig is up.

"Uh, yeah. The brunette." Roe laughs sheepishly.

Relief at his lie is tinged with something bitter. Is it weird that I'm oddly jealous of his other pretend girl? He's only trying to protect my identity but suddenly I'm cataloging all the brunette cigarette girls I worked with last night, wondering which of them is enough to be noticeable to Roe.

"Let's chat," Zebulund says coolly.

Whelp, we're screwed.

"Sure. I'll be out in a second," Roe says.

"I'll wait out here."

As soon as I hear the bedroom door snick closed, I sit up, wide-eyed and panicked. My head throbs from the action but I'm humming with adrenaline again.

"What does he want?" I whisper and even to my own ears, it sounds frantic.

His head shakes back and forth as he pulls on his trousers from last night. The suspenders hang loose at his side.

"I don't know." He slips on a sweatshirt from his suitcase.

"What should I do?" I gnaw on my lip.

"Stay here. Pretend to be sleeping. And drink more water. You're really pale."

I suck in the lip I was chewing to keep from smirking at his concern for me.

He's about to leave when I whisper, "Leave the door open. Just in case."

He frowns at the idea but says, "Stay quiet."

I throw out my hands in the "no duh" gesture.

As soon as he leaves the room, I creep to the door to listen.

"Mind if I make some coffee while we talk?" Roe asks.

I could kiss him.

"Not at all."

Soon the heavenly sound of percolation and the smell of coffee drift my way.

"You're having fun?" Zebulund asks.

"A little too much fun."

"Good. Good." Zebulund laughs his slimy laugh. "Wait until you see the fireworks tonight."

"Get out?"

"I'm known for them."

"Sweet."

I silently gulp down the water and aspirin Roe left me and eat some nuts. Is he really here to discuss entertainment? I have decided to disregard Roe's explicit instructions. We all knew that would happen.

"Listen," Zebulund says with no warning, "About last night."

I don't know about Roe, but my heart moves up and takes residence in my throat.

"What's up?" He clears his throat. Maybe his did too.

"What did you think of everything that happened?"

I can't take it anymore. Roe's delicious smelling shirt drops to the floor as I go Under. It's too soon. My head throbs like I smacked it into a wall. I slowly creep out of the room. Zebulund sits on the small couch facing right at me. But as he doesn't look up, I'm sure he can't see me. Roe sits at a barstool off the kitchenette and his back is to me. I hate being in Zebulund's direct eyeline, regardless of my visibility, or lack thereof. I softly creep across the plush carpet.

"I think it was a great night," Roe says. "The guys are cool, but I'm pretty sure I'm out a few grand."

His eyes flick to me only for a second. I wince. Oops.

"What about toward the end?" Zebulund doesn't give anything away. "With Viktor?"

I widen my eyes at him and shrug. Zebulund's right in front of me now Roe can see me without really trying.

"I think the night... Look, I think Viktor's a stand-up guy. Like I said, we've worked together before. He was trying to unwind and maybe drank a little too much."

Zebulund nods along as Roe talks. He's sprawled out, legs spread and arms propped on the back of the couch. Amazing how one man can take up an entire piece of furniture.

"True. True."

To his credit, Roe's cool as ever as he sips his coffee.

"But what about the other stuff?" Zebulund watches Roe so closely I want to squirm.

"Not sure what you mean?"

My pulse rockets. It's too soon for me to be Under like this and the stress of this situation causes the room to spin.

"Cut the shit, Roe," Zebulund says. His tone is casual but the accusation lodges in the palpable tension like a half-swallowed sunflower seed.

We're definitely fucked. I pace back and forth now. I can't keep still. My neck is itchy. My skin is too tight. Roe shoots me a quick glance. I shake my head.

"No idea," I mouth.

"That. That right there." Zebulund stands up and moves away from where I stand. He points a trembling finger right at me. Well, sort of at me—the general area. "What are you looking at?"

"Nothing. What?" His hands raise, palms up.

Zebulund's pale. Giant circles of sweat stain his underarms. He's fucking terrified. He isn't here to grill Roe at all. He's here for answers. My arms flail to get Roe's attention but he's pointedly not looking at me.

"I'll give you one more chance. I don't like being dicked around."

Roe scratches his five o'clock shadow with both hands. Stalling. I roll my hands like I'm trying to show "go with it." I point to my eyes and make an exaggerated spooky face. His eyes flick back and forth between me and Zebulund.

Zebulund cracks the knuckles of one fist into his other palm. He's about to speak when Roe finally says, "Fine. I can tell you but you'll never believe me."

I wince. The Boy Scout is going to call me out.

11

Roe

THIS PLAN IS BAD. IT'S REALLY BAD. MAGGIE GESTICULATES LIKE A constipated ape and Zebulund's pallor is gray. I have to trust my gut with this. I spent the morning sleeping more than I've slept in months, maybe years. My body reached that point of exhaustion where it shuts down. The moment my head hit the pillow until I woke up wrapped around Maggie I was gone. For just a minute it was like another life. A life where I don't have to work in an industry I hate to keep my family safe from starving. A life where I have a wife and a home and a stable job that lets me sleep.

But then Zebulund shows up, clean and pressed like last night never happened. He's still dressed in the 40s theme, except he's more like a mob boss than a classic actor. The air is heavy with cologne and his gangster fedora casts a shadow over his eyes. Only his eagerness to talk gives away that something more might be going on. The way he's scrutinizing me now tells me that I don't have a lot of time. I swallow and get ready to do the best performance of my career.

"Sometimes, and you have to promise that what I'm about to say doesn't leave this room..."

Maggie stills. She wraps her arms around her body and her face twist with anxious confusion. Zebulund's silence is assent. I don't doubt for a second that he would take whatever I say next and use it to his advantage.

"Okay. I don't tell anybody this. Maybe I'm still a little drunk. But there's no point in hiding this any longer."

"Get on with it." Zebulund pops his knuckles.

"Sometimes I can see the spirits of people who have passed."

I swear to God, in the space that follows I can hear conversations on the top deck. Maggie's jaw sways in the wind and if the situation weren't serious I'd be laughing.

"You think this is a joke," he finally says. He hasn't given anything away but his Adam's apple bobs when he swallows.

"No. It's not to me anyway."

"You see dead people?" he asks.

"Not exactly." I'm winging this now. Be careful and remember every detail of the lie for later. "I can sense spirits. Sometimes see them. But not like in the movies. It's hard to explain."

Zebulund takes a half-step back and sort of falls into the couch. It's the biggest indication of his reaction. "You're telling me that last night there was a ghost in the cabin?"

My most serious eyebrows are in place when I sit across from him. I've practiced in the mirror I know what they're doing.

"I think. I sensed... a, um, spirit."

"You expect me to believe you."

"Not even remotely. I wouldn't believe anybody who said it to me. But I'm living it. And if we're both being honest, I think you, uh felt, her too."

"Her?"

Crap. Too far.

"I think it's a her. I think she's angry. Or trying to share something."

"Really?"

"She seemed to be trying to get attention last night. Like she was throwing a tantrum. It's hard to ignore that." Lord, wasn't that the truth. "But you must have caught me a few times."

Maggie's bent over—her shoulders shake with unheard laughter.

"It seemed like you were looking at something. And then... with the cards. At first..." Zebulund clears his throat. "At first I thought Viktor was playing some sort of juvenile joke. He does that. But then I saw the other two, they aren't actors like you guys. That was genuine fear."

Holy shit, he's buying it.

"I don't want to believe you," he adds. "But I definitely felt something in that room. I kept feeling like someone was standing behind me."

I clench my fist to keep from looking at Maggie. She's right next to him sticking her tongue out at him.

"Right now... I can sense someone here..." She sobers and stands back, the humor sliding off her face.

"That would make sense," I say.

His gaze shoots up. His hand has a tremor as he loosens the tie around his neck. "Why... uh, why do you say that?"

Pause for dramatic effect.

"She's here now." Even I get chills at the way I say it. Daytime and the room is lit up. Maggie shivers dramatically, a cheeky grin on her face.

"Shit."

"She may be haunting you." My gut instinct is driving the show.

"I don't believe this." Zebulund searches the ceiling for answers.

"I understand. I wouldn't buy it either. If things were reversed." Look discouraged, contemplative eyebrows. "I don't think she can hurt you. If that helps."

In my periphery, Maggie mouths something I'm sure is extra sassy, like, "Want to bet?"

"You have to understand that I can't believe this without some sort of proof." Zebulund is up and pacing.

"Maybe see if she hears me. Sometimes, they do. But I don't know."

"You could do that? Really?" His gaze is piercing, glaring in disbelief.

"I don't know. I can try. It's not the ideal setting, but maybe a small test to see."

"Yeah." He tucks his arms under his sweating pits. "Uh, see if you could get her to, I don't know, say something."

"Oh, I can't hear her," I clarify. Also, not a lie. "It's not like that."

He frowns skeptically.

"Maybe I can ask her to do something. She flipped those cards from Viktor's hands."

"True. True. Okay."

Maggie's eyes twinkle like paparazzi filming a drunken starlet. She's way too excited about this.

"Want me to make something up?" I ask.

"No." Zebulund shakes his head instantly. "No offense. But I want to come up with something. In case..."

"In case I'm lying. I get it. Go ahead. But be forewarned; I don't know how easy it is for her to cross over right now."

"What do you mean?"

"I mean, at night in a controlled setting, with more help, I might be able to summon her."

"Like a séance?"

"It sounds like bullshit when you use that word, but yeah, something like that. There were more of us. I think it's an energy thing. I don't know the technicalities. And Viktor was sort of checked out. I think that's why he was the most affected by her." I have no fucking idea what I'm talking about but he seems to eat it up. Maggie gives a sarcastic thumbs-up and rolls her eyes. He chews on his thumb. Thinking.

"Let's try something small for now."

"Okay."

Maggie shakes her head like this is unbelievable but in a good way. She's gnawing on her bottom lip and her eyes are wide in anticipation. She can't wait to fuck with him and this is massively good news—finding out he has a weakness. She's adorable.

"Ask her to..." He looks around the room. "Ask her to turn on the TV." Zebulund crosses his arms, then untucks them, his leg jumping enough to shake the deck.

Maggie practically sprints to the TV. It's an enormous flat screen.

"Spirit, if you are here—" I start as she looks up and down the side of the screen. "Please give us a sign. Please turn on the TV."

Her hands run up and down the bottom panel. And then the side. Panic starts to rise. This should have been a slam dunk. She looks back at me and throws up her arms. She can't find the fucking power button. Her search becomes frantic. The TV subtly shakes from her eager hands. I risk a glance at Zebulund and his nostrils flare.

"Spirit, I know it may be hard to summon the energy for a physical feat of strength." I stall. "After this you can leave in peace."

She shakes her head at my cornball line. She's desperate to find the button that she's pushing anything she sees.

The TV flickers to life. None of us are prepared. The volume is up so loud all three of us jump when the sound blasts through the room. It's a car commercial with a thumping techno beat. I snag the remote and mute it.

"Shit." Zebulund clutches his heart and falls back against the wall. "It's real. I knew. I fucking knew. For days I sensed it. Someone is watching me."

Do not look at Maggie. Do not look at Maggie. Apparently, she's not as sneaky as she thinks. He laughs in that post-scare way, high and halting.

"Hot damn, my man. I knew you'd be good to have around."

Maggie slinks out of the room and slams the door to the bedroom. Zebulund and I yelp in unison and then laugh at our manly displays. He's at my side, one hand rubbing my shoulder.

"That's it. Next weekend your ass is coming to the house to figure this out."

"You want to try a séance?" I ask in disbelief, even though it was basically my idea. "You think the others will go for that?"

"They'll do whatever I tell them." His tone is light enough but there's no modesty in his declaration. He'll get them there. They'll do whatever he asks.

"Okay. I can do that." I run a hand over my face.

I'm sure he thinks I'm relieved to be believed but really I can't believe this worked. We'll get into his house. Maggie and I need a new plan now. Would she be willing to continue this weird arrangement? Would I?

"I'll do my best," I say. "Maybe she's attached to the house or something. I'll do some research but I have to be honest when I say I don't know what I'm doing."

"You show up next weekend and we'll see what happens." He makes his way to the door.

My hands are stacked on my head, elbows splayed. My heart is only now calming down. His head tilts to peek in the bedroom. Maggie lies on the bed in almost the same exact position. Damn, she's good.

"You sure wore her out." His gaze lingers on her legs. I can almost see the trail of slime left behind. "You want to send her around when you're done?"

"I don't share." My voice comes out sharp as a knife and I can't believe how close I am to punching this guy in the face.

"Fair enough." He holds up his hands. "Fair enough." He pulls a cigar out of his pocket and lights it. "Fireworks at ten."

The door handle digs hard into my palm. I give a straight line smile and close the door. Every minute I spend in that man's company, a little bit of my soul dies. Like watching reality TV.

After dead bolting the door, I fall into bed. Maggie sits up with the sheets wrapped around her waist. Her coloring is better but not great.

"I'm sorry," I say and I'm not even sure what I'm apologizing for anymore. Zebulund's comments? Men that abuse power and treat women like objects? The state of the world?

"I'm used to it." She shrugs a creamy smooth shoulder.

That doesn't make me feel better. She's lovely. But she's much more. It makes me sick to think of her being objectified. But am I any better? The sheet shifts slightly and drops down her shoulder, exposing some skin. Here I am examining the area where her neck meets her collar and wondering how it tastes. There's something seriously wrong with me to feel so much attraction toward her while I'm mourning my entire sex. When I look up she's watching me closely.

"Sounds like we have plans next weekend."

"I hope you're free."

"I'll clear my schedule." Her grin is blinding.

———

———

Maggie

WHEN MY SHIFT ENDS I FINALLY TRACK ROE DOWN ON THE topmost deck. I'm exhausted from work and the old dogs are barking, as Mrs. Jenkins would say. Guess I didn't think about the downside of this whole plan, that I would have to actually work. All the while being called kitten and toots, having my ass grabbed and being propositioned. "Want to be famous, sweetie?" I'm still pumped with adrenaline from my outrage as I walk to Roe.

Just my body, not my being. Just my body, not my being.

He's alone and leaning on the rail, staring out at the ocean. His hair is slicked back and gelled and tonight he's in a fancy tuxedo instead of a nice suit. The picture of retro sophistication. He's the visual culmination of all my childhood yearning of black-and-white films. He attracts me in ways I haven't experienced in many years. It's a heady and confusing sensation. Watching him handle the men in the poker game with such ease, knowing exactly how to play each one and make them love him, was fascinating. I could never be aware of all those social nuances.

This is a dangerous road to go down. Instead, I focus on the prize. I envision Zebulund behind bars, the papers slandering him, social media outrage, and all his money gone. That's where my focus needs to be.

"Hey." I lean on the pole next to him and step out of the kitten heel Mary Jane shoes that are part of the costume.

The cool deck soothes my aching feet. I left my tray behind, but I'm still dressed in this ridiculous getup. This side of the yacht isn't as crowded. A few people meander out of earshot, and soft jazz plays over the speakers. The stars twinkle like the backdrop of a set made of diamonds. There's no distinguishing the water surface from the sky.

"Hey." He doesn't look over at me. It's hard to tell his mood yet. I didn't see him much today and when I did he stayed on the outskirts of the festivities. How does he feel about the deceit? What if he's made friends with this man whom I'm willing to do whatever to destroy?

"I could go for a cigarette," I say.

"I didn't know you smoke." His voice is cool and low, like anything more would upset the mood.

"I don't actually. I'm worried it would make my lungs visible when I go Under—"

He throws back his head and laughs. The unexpectedness of it causes my heart to race with pride.

"It feels like the mood for it."

"I think living in LA, my lungs have had about all they can take," he says.

"True that." I twist to lean back and over the edge of the rail to crack my back.

"Could you not do that? You're making me nervous."

Up on my tiptoes most of my body hangs over the edge. The smell of ocean greets me.

"What? This?" The water races beneath me and the blood rushes to my brain. I'm dizzy. It would be easy to slip into the water. I could go Under and nobody would ever know.

"Stop." He tucks his hands under me and drags me back to the safety of the deck. His angry eyebrows are two sharp points. "Such a waste. Of talent," he adds on when he sees me scrutinizing him.

Ah, because I'm nothing if not a means to an end for somebody. "I wouldn't. Not until I bring down Zebulund."

"Careful." He flicks a look around us.

His arms still hold me in place. That attraction at work again. Not even a conscious effort—a gravitational pull. I put distance between us with some difficulty.

"I'm always careful." I blink away stars that dance in my vision. "What're you doing up here, besides sexy brooding?"

"Sexy, huh?" The side of his mouth lifts.

"Puh-lease. You've been People's Sexiest Man Alive twice already, right?"

"You follow my career, I see."

I roll my eyes and study the inky water again. Thankfully, it's dark because, yeah, I'm totally blushing like a teenager. Everybody knows about James Roe's career.

"I'm in the industry. It's my job to know things."

"Hmm." His gaze outlines my face.

"On that note," I take a steadying breath, "if we're going to work together, there's something you should know."

"Okay." He's tense, braced for bad news.

"The reason I started following you is because I found your name linked to Zebulund. My source found out you're being watched."

"What?"

"Somebody's following you." I smooth my skirt. "Well, somebody besides me. I saw an actual person while I was watching you. Funny if you think about it."

He's not laughing.

"But," I press on, "I also found out that you're being investigated."

"How? Who's giving you this information?"

"You know I can't tell you that. It would... I just can't. Not now. Don't ask me."

"What do you mean they're investigating me?" He runs a hand over his face.

"Someone's looking into your affairs. After hearing your talk with Paul, I imagine it's the same person who's taking your money."

"Jesus. This is insane. I'm not doing anything illegal. I'm not the bad guy." He paces.

I grab him by the arms to still him. "I know that." And as the words come out of my mouth, I realize I whole-heartedly believe it. "I want to help you. After all, you got me this far and to the thing next week." I can't bring myself to say séance. "We were pretty good together, er, the working together. Back there. I know I said it would only be a onetime thing. But I think that we should both see this through? I think that your connections will help me, and my friend can help you."

He's calmed down and squinting at me. The teasing creeps into his eyebrows before he speaks.

"Are you asking me to go steady with you, Maggie?"

"Shut up."

"You like me. You want to work with me," he singsongs.

"Never mind."

He keeps humming. Two dimples appear that almost knock me off my feet. I've seen that smile in movies but feeling the full power of it in person is like stepping into the daylight after being in a theater for hours.

"I'm pushing you over." I make a futile attempt to push him toward the railing but he's solid and I'm wispy.

We struggle and wrestle until somehow he has me completely trapped between his body and the rail, I'm facing out toward the water. We stand like Rose and Jack. His entire body presses against mine. I've forgotten what it feels like to be held like this. Consciously. And in good-natured teasing. Not against my will. I stop moving.

He lowers his mouth to my ear. "I don't think." He presses closer.

I feel him everywhere. My pulse kicks into overdrive. If I turn my head a fraction our lips would collide. His heartbeat thumps against my back. I'm desperate to arch my back into him. What would he do? What would I feel? It's too much too soon.

I panic. My heart throws itself against my ribcage, instinct telling me to run. I'm frustratingly stuck between arousal and other. I remind myself that we have a goal. I have talents. We're just a means to each other's ends. A firework shoots up and pops with a silver cascade of sparkles. It's enough to clear my head and get me re-focused. I slip out of his grasp and step away.

"We'll make a plan for next weekend. Something big. I'll need time to search his office."

"We'll figure it out." Roe shoves his hands deep in his pockets.

Above me the fireworks display erupts to the sound of applause as I run down to my room.

12

Roe

TWO DAYS LATER VICTOR INVITES ME TO AN EARLY TEE TIME AT the Los Angeles Country Club. Funny how my appointments were suddenly cleared for the day. This is one of the most exclusive golf clubs in the country, closed even to the likes of me. No point in questioning how he got us eighteen holes last minute. Starts with Z and ends with regret.

It's a typical California day with enough morning chill to make the bright day bearable. My ball makes a satisfying crack as the club collides with it before it zips through the air.

"Nice, that'll be a bogey for sure," Viktor says.

"We'll see."

"The views are incredible here."

We share a sweeping gaze of the fairway. The city is caught in glimpses all around us, peeking through the hills.

"Sure are." He's fishing, I give it to him. "I can't believe you got us in here."

He predictably jumps right in. "That was Marty. He's a member here and pulled some strings."

I give him a "that's respectable" frown. We hop in the golf cart and head down the path following the fairway, our caddies trailing in the cart behind us. A few paps already caught pictures of us, feeding their children for another night. We wave good-naturedly and go on with our game.

The feeling of being watched can really wear on a person. The irony isn't lost on me. Sometimes I forget that there'll never be a time I'm not a circus act to people. And worse than that, if that time comes, I'm in trouble. As we go on, I wait for the other shoe to drop. I'm not naïve enough to think that he wanted to come out here to chat and bond. What he wants remains unclear.

Around hole eight I get my answer. It's been a few holes since we passed any cameras and the caddies work with enough big names to respect our distance.

"I want to apologize for this past weekend." Viktor sports a ridiculous golf costume. The sort of thing you'd expect from someone who'd never actually played, but maybe watched one movie about golf set in the 1920s. He even has a fuzzy ball on his hat. It takes a special kind of man to pull off pastel pink and lime green. And yet here he is.

"Nothing to apologize for." I hit the ball a little too hard, slicing to the left. It rolls into the rough. "Dammit."

I'm much better than this at golf. I'm naturally good at most things but I learned early on that it's not the best way to make friends and influence people. At least not on the first round. I make myself good enough to protect my fragile man ego but still give Viktor an inflated sense of pride. This sounds arrogant, I know. That's why I keep it to myself.

"Ah, bad luck." He tugs at his high collar. "But I was referring to getting drunk."

"It happens," I say casually.

Some extreme need to prove his masculinity, super uncomfortable being teased, and a drinking problem—the man is hiding something. But it isn't my place to reveal his skeletons.

"Well, it's good of you to say that but I was out of line." He laughs. "You know how it gets." With the club tucked in his elbow he mimics pressure building around his head.

"It gets to us all." This is sincere.

"Really? You seem totally unaffected."

"Trust me, it does."

He studies me for a minute and then shakes his head, like remembering to stay on track.

"I think I might have acted like I wasn't grateful. But I am. With my career, with my friends, all that. I was tired and drank too much."

"Okay." But I'm still not sure where this is coming from. "You didn't do anything."

"No? Okay good. Thought maybe I gave a negative impression of Marty and the guys. They're all great. I don't know what I said but I want you to know they've all done so much for me. I wouldn't be where I am without them."

"That's awesome."

"These guys, they could rule the world. Sometimes I think they do. Or at least LA." He laughs, but it's strained.

"Is there anywhere else?"

"You stick with these guys and you're set for life," he says. He shifts to look up at me through blond hair like he's saying something else with his eyes. But I can't read minds. Far as I know. "Your family too," he adds. "Anybody you care about. They'll be taken care of."

My insides go cold. What does he know? What does that imply? I want to shake the answers out of him but that's not how this works. Subtlety is required. We walk again, and he lines up another shot. I wait until he's done with his turn.

"I feel you, man," I say.

"There's not a lot of us up here to see how crowded it is."

He's not focused at me anymore. He's looking toward the final hole, toward the club house's massive expanse. "There isn't a lot of room. When you're here you have to fight to stay relevant."

I swallow. My heart thumps because I know exactly what he's talking about. Sometimes being this high on the celebrity echelon feels like standing on a plateau, and every hot new actor that pushes his way into the crowd sends somebody else over the edge, back into the abyss of obscurity. Or worse, reality TV. Every day in this town I dig my heels into the earth and fight for my spot. Every day I fight for this life, for my family. All good things will come to an end eventually, but I'll stay up here as long as I can to protect those I love.

Maybe I didn't keep emotion off my face this time, because he laughs. It feels a little too strained.

"They're great guys." He holds my gaze. "I wouldn't want to be any other place."

"I get it, man. Me neither." I smile big. Maybe he thinks I'm trying to usurp him as The Actor in the crew, or maybe he thinks I'll spread rumors. Likely, he fights to stay where he is every day, too. "I'm not one to get into anybody else's shit. I like my privacy. I live that way for others too."

"Cool. Cool." He waves down the beer girl who's driving past. "Wanna beer, my man?"

"No thanks." I go with his obvious change of subject.

And just like that we're back in the game.

———

THE CLUBHOUSE IS AN OLD-STYLE SPANISH BUILDING, WITH massive arches and terra cotta roofing. Imagine my surprise when we run into Zebulund, surrounded by a couple of men in suits, when we go in for a post-game refreshment. I'm not sure why they went through the pretense of setting this up. He could have called and asked me if I was free. Though I'm starting to get the impression that it wouldn't matter if I was free or not. I would become free.

He needs to show how easily he can make things happen. I'm supposed to be impressed by his show of money. Money has power, but it doesn't make you special. That's what he doesn't understand about me.

"Zebulund, nice to see you," I say.

I shake his hand over the table. Viktor hovers between the two of us, gnawing on his thumbnail and spitting out little pieces of skin.

"Roe, I'm glad you're here. I wanted to talk."

He has a hunk of raw steak sitting in a pool of blood. It's half finished, and the vegetables surrounding it sit untouched. He tosses his napkin on the plate and pushes it away. A server appears out of nowhere to take it.

After an awkward pause the two other men make excuses to leave, along with Viktor. He gestures to me to take a seat.

"How was golfing?" he asks.

It's the nicest course in the city. I'm sure it cost more than a week's wage at the factory to play one round.

"Fantastic," I answer.

"Good. Good." He sprawls out his arms, taking up three seats.

"Thank you."

Viktor made it clear that we're here because this is Zebulund's club.

"We'll have to play together some time," I go on.

"I don't like to play." Zebulund glances around and leans in. "Are we alone?"

My pulse quickens. I hadn't been expecting the rapid-fire change of subject.

"Just the two of us," I answer honestly.

"I haven't felt anything since the yacht. I'm starting to think I imagined it."

"Sometimes I'll go months without seeing anybody." I shrug but worry he's going to cancel. "There's no saying what causes it."

He leans back, seeming to accept that answer, and I breathe a sigh.

"Viktor apologized then?" He fires again.

That's what this is about?

"Yeah, he did. I told him it was nothing to worry about."

He nods so much it's like a mechanism in his neck is stuck. Maybe a hard thump to the back will unstick him.

"I'm glad. I want you to be part of this group."

There's that weird vibe creeping up my spine again. I feel it anytime I'm with him. It's a sense of foreboding, and more than just the creepy factor. Why do we never talk about what we're actually talking about?

"They're going for the uh, what we talked about?"

"If you think it's necessary."

"It's up to you." Play it cool. Can't have him feel pressured, it must be his choice. "I don't know that anything will come of it. I did read about some examples of people doing it. I was sort of right. Something about the power of belief in numbers. But honestly, I don't know that I should mess with that stuff."

He studies me. I hold his gaze.

"If you don't feel her anymore then there's no point."

He doesn't say anything for a while and I'm sure I've lost him.

"I'll let you know," he says finally.

I think I've made a mistake. Not pushed hard enough. I'm dismissed with a polite smile and take the hint. The two suits return to the table as I walk away.

I need Maggie to do some damage control and I need it now.

13

Maggie

A HIPSTER IS FOLLOWING ME. I THOUGHT I WAS BEING PARANOID at first but now I'm sure of it. It's hard to tell when they're everywhere. A sea of plaid shirts, Buddy Holly glasses, and cuffed pants; but this guy is for sure following me. Roe was going to meet me at the same restaurant near his production lot but the same guy in glasses has been on my tail for the last three places I've gone. I should know. It takes a creep to see a creep.

I duck into a public restroom not far from Echo Park and press a cool hand to my chest to slow my racing heart. The door doesn't lock, but it's the middle of the day and hopefully, he won't be that bold with families playing frisbees within shouting distance. I debate leaving my phone and purse and clothes in the stall and getting out the old-fashioned way but logistically speaking, getting back to my stuff is too risky. Also, who knows how long he'll wait me out?

I peek out the cracked door and sure enough, there he is sipping from a coffee mug and reading a worn copy of what I'm sure is Kerouac or Bukowski. The spy is an evil genius—he'll never be spotted. I only caught him because I'm paranoid.

It's a Pepto-pink bathroom that doesn't look like it's been updated since the 80s. A fluorescent light twitches and graffiti is scratched into the mirror. It's not disgusting but I wouldn't host a soiree here. I go to the last stall in the row and shut the door behind me.

"Abort." I shoot a text to Roe.

I get a "?" in response.

My heart drops when someone comes into the bathroom. I hop onto the seat, balancing on the bowl in a very unattractive squat. Gross, I hate even thinking about the word squat, let alone doing one. It's not a great hiding spot regardless, because there're only so many stalls. I have visions of each door being kicked down one by one as I sit waiting for my doom. I balance to look under the door and see a pair of strappy sandals and let out a breath. Typical dramatic me.

"I'm being followed." I send to Roe.

He bought two burner phones just for our conversations, because he too is that paranoid. How does one go about buying burner phones? I thought that only happened in movies.

Little dots indicate he's typing and then, "Where are you?"

I send a dropped pin but add, "I'll meet you at your place instead, as soon as I can see that he isn't following me anymore." Hopefully, he gets that I mean the theater, but my text remains unread as I put my phone away.

The heels click out of the bathroom and the door shuts again. My hands have a slight tremor as I reach for the lock. They shoot back when the bathroom door opens again. I freeze. It's not the gentle gait of a woman, but the clomping stomp of my follower. Sure enough, when I peek under the door, it's a pair of Chucks. No surprise. He's peeking under each door and I shoot up in just enough time to avoid being spotted.

There is no other door. I have no way out. What does this

guy want? What if he wants to write me into his next great American novel? Whatever the case, my gut says I don't want to find out.

I chew on my lip and study the ceiling. Apparently, two days without stripping in public is two too many. The first door is kicked open. Hot dog! People really do that! Off come my clothes and I tuck my purse and phone into them.

The second door flies open.

I wave a sad goodbye to the bundle before they thump into the trash can. Door number three flies open right as I go Under. The door right next to me. The creep starts whistling. Knocking down each door in a woman's bathroom is a jolly riot. My shirt is still sticking out from the small rectangular trashcan attached to the stall wall. It'll have to stay like that. No time.

My back slams against the wall, taking up as little space as possible, right before the door swings open. It crashes against the flimsy stall, rattling me. My hands shoot to cover my mouth to keep from gasping. The wind from the impact brushes my skin. It's too close a call.

My heart is in my throat, but the guy's face is brilliant. Utter confusion and disbelief. He steps back and searches for a door or window. Sorry, buddy, no luck. He runs around checking all the stalls again, and as he does I shove the shirt into the trashcan. It shuts with a reverberating clunk. My hand snaps back like it bit me just as he runs into view. His face twists with confused rage. He tugs off a knit cap and scarf and runs a hand through his hair.

His face doesn't ring a bell. He's young, possibly, part-Asian. His hair is cut military short and it's clear that the hipster look is an identity to blend in. Evil genius. It's like me being another pretty blonde in the City of Angels. Hiding in plain sight.

"Fuck. Fuck." He repeats my earlier sentiments exactly. "No. She's gone." He's talking into an earpiece. "I don't know. She must've slipped out." I can't hear the other person other than a loud male voice. The man winces. "I know. I was watching too. But she's gone." He brings a fist to his forehead and studies the pink ceiling. "Yeah, no. I know. Fuck, I know."

He kicks a trashcan, spewing debris everywhere. "Yeah, I'm going, I'm going. She couldn't have gone far."

The door closes again. I creep out the stall, still Under, and scope the room. There's a closed sign on the door that wasn't there before and my hipster friend is sprinting away. I leave the sign to get cleaned up in privacy.

Back at the stall, I frown down at my clothes in the trashcan. Feminine wrappers and balled up tissues abound. I take a moment to mourn more lost fashion.

"You sacrificed yourself for a cause. That's more than most of us can say," I say to the romper—never to be worn again. I'm giving up on the clothes but I can at least salvage my bag.

ROE FINDS ME WASHING MY FEET IN THE SINK. NAKED. AS I DO. I went Under as soon as I heard the door but came back Up when I saw it was him. His gaze immediately finds me, snagging on my naked form.

I honestly hadn't expected him to show up. I had planned on going back Under to meet him at the theater and go from there. I'm used to dealing with this solo.

"You came?" I ask.

"I was around," he says coolly.

"Anything to see me naked again." My hair falls loose to hide my smile.

"What happened?"

"Oh, I just decided to take a bath in a public sink like a transient. You know how I do."

"Can you please cover up?" He frowns. Not-amused eyebrows. He shoves a tote bag toward me.

"Hey, nobody looks good in fluorescent lighting." I cross an arm over my chest and dig through the bag with the other hand.

"No, I—"

"Where did you get these?" Inside the bag are a shirt, jeans, and a pair of flip-flops all in my size.

"Rachel."

"Rachel for the win once again. I need to buy that girl a cake." Slipping the T-shirt over my head, I hop off the sink and wiggle into the jeans and flip-flops. "I go commando. Does she want these back?"

"No." He swallows. "She said you could keep them."

"Tell her thanks."

When I do this alone, I'm stuck walking naked through LA trying to find clothes, worrying about what diseases can be absorbed through feet. This is a perk I hadn't considered. Maybe working with a partner isn't the worst thing to ever happen.

"I'm decent," I say because he's trying hard to count the floor tiles.

This sudden modesty for my nudity comes from outta nowhere but whatever.

"Do you live around here? Let's get out of here."

"I'm not showing you where I live."

"Wow. Okay. Because I'm a serial killer?"

"Sorry. But you don't come solo. You bring the paparazzi. Any anonymity I remotely have is gone."

"Fine."

I slip the flip-flops onto my freshly cleaned feet and fill him in on Asian Hipster and the death of my new outfit, which he seems far less interested in.

"I can't believe it," he says.

"I know! I just bought it. And sure, it was on sale, but it was really nice."

He blinks at me.

I blink at him.

"You didn't recognize him?" he asks.

"Newp."

"Would you if you saw him again?"

"I guess." I think for a minute. "Are you going to compile a list of every twenty-something in LA? 'Cause I'm gonna need to solve this before I die."

He sighs. Apparently, it's not the time for caustic humor.

"We have other problems too."

"Oh great." I chug from the water bottle he brought me. Okay, that's pretty thoughtful. "Please, do tell."

"I 'ran into' Zebulund earlier."

I freeze. His use of air quotes throws me off but hearing that name causes me to get serious.

"He's thinking of canceling the séance."

"What?" My stomach knots.

"I got the impression he was testing me out. Like, he wanted to see if I was going to press the invite to his house." Roe leans against the sink.

He's wearing a polo and khaki shorts. As always, when out in public, he has a baseball cap pulled low and dark glasses. Of course, he's even cute in that dorky-ass get up.

"What did you do?" I trust his instinct.

"I didn't push it. But now I'm not sure that he's going to go through with it at all."

"Damn."

Roe pushes off the sink with a sigh. He looks up at me from under the bill of his hat and I feel an unexpected surge of attraction. I clamp it down and focus on the task.

"Maybe he needs a sign that he's still being haunted?" he suggests.

"Well, I guess I know what I'm doing tonight."

He smiles.

"Now, how are we getting out of here?"

He takes off his hat and collects all my hair into a messy heap on my head. He uses the cap to hold it all in place. I'm unable to move because the sensation of his fingertips grazing my neck is almost too much to handle. I'm at war with myself. I physically fight my hands from reaching up to grab him by slipping them into the pockets of my newly acquired jeans.

"Here." He lingers around my neck to tuck an extra strand of hair away. "I'll leave and make sure there're no cameras or stalkers. And after ten minutes, if you get the go-ahead from me, head out."

I can't seem to stop staring into his dark eyes. Brown pupil blending perfectly into the iris. In the direct light do they lighten like a cup of coffee?

"Okay," I manage.

His hand slips and his thumb rests on my bottom lip. His fingertips rest on my dancing heartbeat. He must feel it pounding against them.

"I'll see you tonight."

He turns and leaves and it's only five minutes after he's gone that I realize I have no idea what the plan is for tonight.

14

Roe

I GET OUT OF THERE BEFORE I DO SOMETHING STUPID. As attracted as I am to Maggie, I can't cross that line. Touching her is a slippery slope. It's one thing to think about touching her, but actually doing it could cause me to wobble, and if I'm not careful, I'll fall.

Repeated exposure to her naked body should cause me to become immune to it, instead, it's like studying a piece of fine art. Every time, something new grabs my attention. The way her collarbone slopes in. The way her hair grows in on top of her long neck in two different directions. The way her skin always reacts to my touch.

I push the thoughts aside, focusing on the fact that she was being followed.

We're no closer to figuring out what's happening with the factory, if anything we're further away. If somebody has been watching me for weeks that means I was late to the party. I can't be everywhere. I can't make sure the factory is thriving and keep up with the movies and the guest appearances and press tours. Next month, I leave for Asia to promote my new movie. I have no idea how I'll deal with all of this.

I'm so lost in thought that I don't see the photographer until it's too late. We collide and the camera falls to the ground in a jostle of flailing hands.

"Damn." The photographer curses too late to grab it.

"Sorry. Dammit, sorry." I pick up the camera. "It looks okay—"

As I stand to hand the camera back to the stranger, my vision swims and I stumble.

"Woah, woah. You okay?" The man loaded with equipment steadies my arm.

"I'm okay."

"You sure? You're really pale."

I blink a few times as a flash goes off in my face. Not his. A different camera. Not sure how they found me but I'm plenty far away from the restroom that Maggie will be able to get away safely.

"I'm okay. How's the camera?"

He looks it over. "It's fine. Maybe you should eat."

"I will." I brush him off, not meaning to be gruff but not wanting all these people in my face. "Thank you." I pat him lightly on the shoulder.

He calls out as I walk away, "Picture for my trouble?"

"Make sure you check out *Dartango*." I smile down the anger and stand for the camera, wishing for my hat.

"Thanks, man, we sure will. You're great. Thank you."

A few blocks later I walk into a decent deli and order a grilled chicken breast and steamed veggies. My hunger has surpassed a safe level. All these hours with the personal trainers catch up.

The cashier is young and pretty and says, "On the house," before I can pay. I'm about to reach for a tip when my phone rings. My smiling mother distracts me enough that I step away with my food, forgetting entirely about the cute cashier and the tip. I hover in a quiet corner to take the call.

"Hello?"

"Hey, honey."

"Hey, Ma." I pinch the area between my eyes. It's not good. She has that same tone as the last call.

"How ya doin' baby? How's the press tour? Is that what you're doing now?"

"Ma. You're stalling."

"I was just asking." She lets out a very mom-like sigh.

"I'm fine." I wait a beat. "Are you okay, Mom?"

"Well, there's been bad news. Listen. I don't have a ton of time. Your brother and father didn't want you to know—"

"Why don't they want me to know?"

"They worry about your health. We all do. But it's your company, you should be informed."

"Okay." I sit in a free chair.

"Last night the factory was broken into and vandalized. The machines were broken."

"Which ones?" I clear my throat as the room spins around me.

"All of them, honey," she says, and her voice is raw. She hates telling me these things. "I'm sorry. We think it may have been some teens from the next town over. There was some graffiti and such... some um, alcohol bottles."

"Why would these kids do that when chances are the factory employs their parents?" I shake my head, not understanding.

"There's no logic in evil... or teenagers."

"Okay." I scratch my head. "Have Paul order whatever is needed."

There's a stack of waiting screenplays my agent wants me to read. I had planned on a brief vacation after this last press tour but rebuilding those machines will cost a pretty penny. I could do a few commercials in Japan for some extra cash.

"I'm sorry about this, honey. It's bad luck."

"Right," I say not believing that for a second.

"It'll all work itself out. These things always do. Don't stress. Make sure you're eating."

"I just ordered lunch."

"Okay, good. I'll let you go. Talk soon. Love you, baby."

"Love you too."

My head throbs with this new information. Maggie needs to make the factory the focus. I can't let this still be going on when I leave the country. Zebulund can wait. He won't go anywhere, but people's entire lives are at stake. I'll tell Maggie tonight.

I tuck my phone away and head out of the deli. I give my food to a homeless man on the corner. My appetite is gone anyway.

―――――

Maggie

"Mrs. Jenkins," I call, walking into her mudroom announcing myself. The clickity-clack of Pepper's paws on the wood floors doesn't greet me. "Hello?" I round the corner into the small kitchen at the back of the house. Not to toot my horn but they are the only people who ever seem excited to see me. I miss my usual fanfare.

The guys from next door, Danny and Russell, are leaning with their ears pressed to the door that separates the kitchen from the sitting area. They shush me as soon as I enter the room.

"What are you doing?" In tandem they wave their hands to quiet me without removing their ears.

"Drama," I singsong quietly, setting down groceries. I tiptoe over making an excited face.

"Miss Thang has a visitor," Danny says. Danny always looks like he's running late with slightly rumpled clothes and his hair a mess.

"Ohhh." I shimmy my shoulders in excitement.

"I know that voice. I know I do." Russell's face is scrunched up in focus. Today he's wearing a brown suit and a football tie.

"He sounds young." Danny is scandalized.

"Ah, crap." My smile deflates.

They both look at me like I stepped on Pepper.

"It's James Roe." I wonder if it's too late to go out the back door.

They gasp. I cross my eyes and stick out my tongue. He's been calling me incessantly since he helped me out of the bathroom. I'm salty about being saved, to be honest, not that I even needed it. So having shoes and clothes to wear was nice. Okay, and the water with electrolytes did make me feel better lickety-split. Guess that part was nice too.

But I don't want to talk to him.

I'm also salty because O.G. can't get me in for this freaking séance and I have no idea how we're going to pull it off. I don't want to be nagged anymore. I'm feeling like a hack and seeing Mr. Smooth-As-Glass will only hurt my self-esteem. Also, there's the issue of my growing harder to ignore attraction to him.

Basically, I'm stuck on all routes.

"And that makes you angry because?" Russell asks, a little haughtily, in my opinion.

"Oh, let me take you back to her house. I'm sure she wouldn't mind," Mrs. J. says.

I barge into the room like the sheriff in an old western. "You've got some nerve showing your face 'round here." I point an outraged finger at Roe.

Mrs. Jenkins looks up with a smile, her mink slipping from her shoulder. Roe has a grin that many people would describe as "shit-eating." I find that a little too vulgar but apt.

"Oh, hi, doll! We were just talking about you," Mrs. Jenkins says.

"Were ya?" I ask.

"Hi, Maggie." Roe waves. Still grinning. Even his damn eyebrows are arrogant.

"Here, help me for a minute." Mrs. Jenkins tries to stand and we both rush forward to help her up. We glare at each other behind her back. She pats me and turns to Roe. I use the chance to stick my tongue out at him.

"You want some coffee, Shug?" she asks him.

He looks to me and then back to Mrs. J. His smile is saccharine. "That would be lovely. Can I help?" That's the smile the fan-girls create GIFs of that get reposted a million times.

She waves away his offer before hooking her arm through mine. We shuffle back into the kitchen. We pass Danny and Russell still in the same position, faces frozen in shock.

Mrs. J. picks up Pepper, who followed us in, and sets him on the counter. He spins three times before sitting down, legs splayed like road kill. He blinks at me. Well, with one eye at least. The other stares at the wall. His tongue curls under his mouth looking like a dry-rotted rubber band. Meanwhile, Mrs. J. starts to collect her silver set. I move to the cabinet to get out the coffee grounds.

"Now listen, honey. I know you aren't really aware of what's happening in this town..." She halts mid-task to lean her elbows on the counter, one hand absent-mindedly petting Pepper.

There's a small chance I never mentioned to Mrs. J. what I do for a living. She continues without comment.

"But back in that room is James Roe. He's a Hollywood big

shot. You go in there and wow him." She smacks my bottom. "Shake that skinny white girl booty."

"Oh God."

The guys join us, standing around the island, listening intently.

"Don't talk too much," Danny suggests.

"How rude. I'll have you know I am a delight." I lean back and scowl. Well, I can be. If I try, but I don't because nobody is worth it.

"The first time we met, you spent forty-five minutes discussing the neighborhood association's rules."

"I was trying to politely inform you that you were in direct violation of three of them and you had just moved in."

He sighs and Russell makes a gesture like this only proves his point.

"Whatever. Mrs. J. liked me right away."

Mrs. J. pointedly examines the carafe, rubbing a spot and mumbling about it not coming out.

Russell jumps in. "But..." He shakes his head. "He said your name. Do you know him already?"

"Clearly." Danny's arm flails up in disgust. "She yelled at him."

"This is why she's still single. She's so prickly," Mrs. J. jumps in.

"I am not—"

"I know and it's a shame. She has such great skin. She could date some really rich guys." Russell nods before he even starts talking.

"Wow, I don't even know where to start with that—"

"Aww, I really hoped he came here for me. I thought maybe I won a contest. But I guess he did ask for her pretty quick."

Danny: "Can you imagine a date with *the* James Roe?"

Russell: "Right? I'd pay money to lick him."

Me: "Okay that's—"

Russell: "And those eyebrows."

Danny: "I'd lick those too."

Mrs. J: "I'd lick anything on him."

"Okay." I shake my head and throw out my hands. "Okay, could we maybe stop? He's right out there."

All three sets of eyes flick to me. Three out of three sets look disappointed.

"Have you already pissed him off, Maggie?" Russell asks.

I drop my chin to my chest to show my insult. "I'll have you know we're working together."

"What do you do again?"

"I thought you took care of me for a living?" Mrs. J. looks confused.

"No, Mrs. J., I have a job."

"Wait, why am I paying you then?"

"You aren't."

"Aww, you deserve a raise though." She pats my face.

"Thanks."

"How do I not know what she does?" Russell looks to Danny. "Do you know?"

"I thought she was a maid or something."

"A maid?" Russell is aghast.

Ah, yeah. I know why he thinks that about me. That was a crazy night.

"Yeah, one night she came home in a blue uniform," Danny says.

Bingo.

"Hey, that's true. I saw you come home in scrubs once."

Oh yeah, that too.

"I really thought you were my personal assistant." Mrs. J. is still talking to herself.

Suddenly, all three sets of eyes are on me again. Still disappointed. A new reason.

I scramble to find some lie to tell them. The thought of

revealing who I am makes my palms sweat. I might not be able to stop my flush from giving me away. "I'm an actress."

All three sets of eyes narrow.

"Bologna," Mrs. J. says.

"I could be an actress."

She looks to the men. "She doesn't even know who James Roe is."

"There's no way. You can't lie." Russell shakes his head in agreement. "Look, she's getting all red."

"Oh my gosh yes. Just like that time she stole our newspaper and wouldn't admit it."

Pepper barks as if to throw in his own admonishment. The traitor.

"I was going to give it back," I mumble but nobody listens.

"Maybe we should call her Red instead. Look the red is spreading."

"Stop talking about it!" I press my fingertips to my cheeks.

"So who am I paying?" Mrs. J. shakes her head.

"Give it up." Russell crosses his arms. "What's your deal? Some sort of kinky sex worker?"

"Why would you go there?" I ask.

Danny says, "He watches a lot of HBO."

I take a deep, calming breath. These people can know. It's not exactly a secret, it's just not something I share. Because I don't have people to share it with.

"I'm a reporter," I blurt.

All three seem to digest the information at the same time and sort of nod and frown at the same time.

"Okay, that I could see."

"Yeah, that makes sense."

"I need to call my accountant."

Russell asks, "Have I read anything by you?" He's already got his phone out. "Maggie..." he blinks up at me. "I don't even know your last name. You are very sneaky aren't you?"

"I'm Maggie May." I clear my throat. "Uh, also known as Miss Mayday."

"Shut the front door!"

"And back!" Mrs. J adds.

"You're Miss Mayday!"

"The Miss Mayday?"

I chew my cheek and nod.

"You wrote the piece about the real 'Hollywood Heroes; wives of the most powerful men.'"

"If they ever decided enough was enough..." I half mumble to myself.

Russell says, "Wouldn't be so many degrading jokes, that's for sure."

"Damn straight," Mrs. J. agrees.

"Yeah." My cheeks are on fire. "The men get the credit but these women run the show."

Russell is wide-eyed, head shaking. "And about the guy who was framing people who crossed him by making it look like they were laundering from him."

"Yeah. He's in jail. Well, prison." I lift my chin.

"You're like a superhero." Danny blinks in awe.

"How do you even get this stuff on them?" Russell asks.

Danny makes the mind-blown gesture.

I can't handle the gratitude. It feels dishonest. Or maybe that isn't the word. It's a weird dichotomy of wanting to be proud of my work but shriveling under the blaring light of their notice. But the upside is, I told three people—four if you count Pepper, but I don't know that he even qualifies as a mammal—and the world is still turning. I'm still standing. They believe me. That's the most amazing thing. Not one of them calls me a liar or an attention seeker.

"I uh..."

It's then when we all notice Roe, leaning casually against

the wall. I have no actual idea of how long he's been standing there.

"Tell them what you're working on now. Because it's not helping me like you claim to be."

That's when I realize Roe is angry with me. Very angry.

15

Roe

ALL FOUR HEADS SPIN TOWARD ME. EVEN THAT WEIRD CREATURE on the counter, that may be a cat, spins its head in my direction.

I'm angry. I'm impatient. And most importantly I'm sick of Maggie dicking me around. Everything we've done so far has been for her and her agenda. I'm risking my neck and my career, and for what? Also, there's a box of doughnuts sitting in front of me and the smell is making me nauseous. And that pisses me off too.

She leans over the counter. The coffee sits unmade but this was never about coffee. Maggie's wearing this weird one-piece thing that shows off her legs. They're long and tan and smooth, and I want to run my hands up them until I touch where they meet.

I shake my head.

Focus. Focus. Nobody notices me, they're all too busy talking over each other. Apparently, Maggie is keeping secrets left and right. Well, those days are done. I step around so I'm in her line of sight. She sees me right before I start talking.

"What exactly are you doing?" I repeat.

"I do many things." Maggie flushes but lifts her chin.

She knows as well as I do that she doesn't want her shit exposed. Whatever drives Maggie to destroy Zebulund is more than a desire for revenge. It's deeper and uglier and she isn't about to share it with the room.

"Can you excuse us?" I step toward her and take her arm.

She glares at it and then at me. Her arm snaps away from me. "Excuse us for a minute," she says to the others.

The other three chime in at once: "Yup," "Sure," "I have to go call my accountant anyway."

They clear out of the kitchen and slide the heavy barn door closed behind them. The thing barks. Turns out it's a dog. A second later, the darker-haired fella tiptoes back in and picks it up.

"Sorry." He makes himself as small as possible as he tiptoes back out of the room.

As soon as we're alone we both speak at the same time.

"How dare you show up here?"

"I've had enough of this."

She's rubbing the area I'd been touching. Her nipples are hard.

"Jesus, do you ever wear a bra?" The words come out without thinking.

"Nothing you haven't seen before." She crosses her arms over her chest and lifts her heart-shaped face even higher.

I growl. My nostrils are flaring. I cross my arms and mirror her stance.

"Plus, it's easier in my... career to not worry about under... type things..." She's very red now.

"Yeah, about this career of yours."

She brushes her hair back, leaves her arms hanging loosely, and then thinks better of it and crosses them again. I feel a twinge of guilt at making her feel self-conscious. One thing I've noticed about Maggie from the very beginning is her freeness of being. I hate that I made her think that I'm judging her in any way.

"Listen." I soften my voice. "Things are getting worse and I need your help before it's too late."

"Worse?" her arms fall again.

I explain to her about my mom's call.

"Look you've promised to help me. All we've done so far is get you closer to Zebulund by putting my neck on the line."

"Don't forget I'm getting followed too. And you came here when I specifically asked you not to. I don't need all those cameramen knowing where I live."

"You weren't answering my calls and I'm running out of time."

"They destroyed the machines?"

"All of them."

"I'm sorry. You're right." She reaches out and touches my arm. We both notice. She curls her fingers and drops her hand. "I've been fixating on Zebulund. It can't be a coincidence that the factory got hit at the same time I'm being followed. Something bigger is going on."

"You think they're following you because of my factory somehow?"

"I don't see who else would suddenly care who I am. We must have been seen together."

"Fuck." I scrub my face with my hands.

"I'm as vested as you are. I'll do more digging tonight, okay?"

I nod.

"Any news if this supposed séance is happening? My source can't get me in to his house at all. He only lets his own personal staff host his get-togethers."

"No. I'll see if I can bring a date maybe?"

"I already said that won't work."

"Why exactly?"

"He can't see me." She's speaking through her teeth again.

"Why, though?"

"Because I don't want him seeing my face."

"But why? Did something happen?"

She glares. Then shakes her head, her mouth a hard line.

"What's the plan here, Miss Mayday?" my voice is edged with sarcasm.

"I don't know." She paces the length of the small island. "I don't know. I need to get in that house and I need to search his office. There has to be something."

"Yeah, great. I'm sure he has a letter laying on his desk that says 'I'm guilty of the bulleted list of crimes below.' And where does this leave me? Again, I'm risking my entire reputation and career to get you into his house. But where are we with my factory? People's jobs depend on this." I don't want to share this much but she has to know how massive this is. "An entire town depends on me. If this factory closes, it'd mean a whole town can't afford to eat." My throat catches. I'm showing too much, sharing too much. Her face softens until I add, "It's not some petty vendetta for me."

The color drains from her face.

"I'm sorry—" I say quickly.

"You think that little of me? You think that I'm some angry bra burner that's sick of Hollywood's misogyny?"

"I assumed... it was more personal than that." I run a hand over my neck.

"You're goddamn right it is." She's in my face, her eyes sharp with rage, chest heaving. "You think he's just another asshole that grabbed my ass and I want to get him fired?"

"No, I—" but I can't finish again.

"This isn't about me any more than your wanting to find out about the money is about you. Okay?" Her neck and ears are red. "This is about justice. This is about a man who uses his power to crush and eat everything in his path. This is about a man who can't be bothered to think about anything but his own power. About how people can be used as an end to his means."

"You really think he's pure evil?"

"I think he's the worst sort of evil because he thinks he's helping the world. I see how he is with you and those guys." She holds my stare. "He thinks he's giving you everything. Women and money, they're all objects that give him what he wants. Loyalty. That's what he wants." Her arms flail out in exasperation. She squeezes her eyes closed. Takes a breath. "This isn't about me at all. It's about stopping him."

She's panting by the time she's done talking. I can't argue with that. I don't want to argue with that. She's right, of course. I didn't ever think about her being self-centered. Tunnel-visioned, but never selfish.

Being near her is too much. When I'm away from her I tell myself I've made up the attraction, that I exaggerate it because she's unattainable and damaged and angry. I tell myself when I replay the memories of touching her and smelling her at night that it's never actually like that. And then when I'm around her I realize it's true. It's not like that at all.

It's worse.

More intense. More magnetic. My gaze drifts to all parts of her without my control and I find myself trying to memorize them for later: The way her smile hides. The way she moves her hair over one shoulder and then back to the other, ending it with a twirl around her fingers. She's too much. And I'm constantly battling myself. Knowing and remembering her reaction to my touch. Knowing that she's been used by men. Repeatedly, if I had to guess. I take a cooling breath.

"And how are we going to do that?" I can't help that my gaze drifts to her lips. They glisten from having just been licked.

I wouldn't in a million years make the first move with

Maggie. She's clearly working through some shit. But I can't help how fucking bad my body wants her. How I think of her a million times a day, dressed or naked. It's flashes of the brief smiles she grants me. It's the glimpses of her that I see where she isn't working some angle, where she's entirely in her own body and in the moment with me. When we share a laugh or the same thought. Those are the moments I can't shake out of my head.

Okay, I also think about her thighs a lot too. And her breasts. And her lips. Okay, so I think about her body a fucking lot.

I realize that we've both been glaring at each other's lips, not speaking. "Well?" I prompt.

"What?" She looks up, her pert little nostrils flared. Her lips part slowly as she swallows.

"What are we going to do?"

"You're going to get me into Zebulund's house this weekend." Her eyes move over my face.

I sigh. This whole conversation has been a waste.

"And tonight, I'm going to follow the guy who's following you," she says, her gaze focused behind me.

"Wait, what?"

———

Maggie

KISSING ROE IS BAD. BAD, MAGGIE, BAD. BUT THE WAY HE'S studying my lips, the way his mouth cracks a fraction, it's highly distracting.

Focus on the task at hand. That's what I do. The goal of taking Zebulund down sits in my mind like an elephant on a park bench. But sometimes Roe and his stupid eyebrows that tell me every thought on his mind pop in uninvited. And his stupid lips that just beg to be sucked on. I'm not the girl who thinks about sucking on things. I'm the girl who's set on taking down evil. That's my gift to the world.

"How are you going to do that?" Roe asks me.

And I stare at him for what has to be a solid minute, not comprehending. Sorry, teacher, what was the question? In what was probably a fraction of a second, a thousand different ways of kissing him flash through my mind. Is that what he means? It occurs to me, before I speak, thankfully, that he's talking about my plan.

"Well." I point behind him. "The same guy with a dog has walked past the house three times since we've been talking."

He looks toward the window showing the back driveway and the path leading to my house. He won't be able to see anything. It's on the little black-and-white TV that sits on the counter next to the fridge. It shows the front gate area. He's not even being subtle, the stalker.

"How do you know he isn't paparazzi?" Roe asks me.

"I don't." I shrug. "My gut tells me that a pap wouldn't go through the pretense of pretending to be 'man walking dog.' In my experience, they tend to own their careers."

"What does he look like?"

"I can't tell. Low-quality video. He's wearing a ball cap. Definitely a man, anywhere from eighteen to eighty."

"Oh, good. Solid start," he says dryly.

"The dog is cute, if that helps." I cock a half-grin. "Some sort of retriever."

"To recap: we're looking for an average-sized man with a medium-sized dog." His eyebrows creep lower.

"See, won't take me long to track him at all."

"Wow, you really are a great reporter."

We share a laugh and the tension is broken. Why hasn't he tried to kiss me? I mean, not that I'm sure I could even handle it, but it's throwing me off. There've been so many times this last week where I really thought he wanted to. But he hasn't. It has me questioning all my man-reading vibes. Maybe Zebulund destroyed that too? A cloud covers any good mood I'm feeling.

"You go about your business tonight." I double down, refocused. "Make sure I can come with you this weekend, and I'll track your stalker."

"I have a premiere tonight."

"Oh." I'm a little dumbfounded. He has an actual career as an actor with obligations outside of our shared missions. "Right."

"It's for *Dartango*. Big money. Big names, lots of glamour." He's got coy eyebrows, both slightly raised and flirtatious.

"Mr. Roe, are you asking me out to a movie premiere?" I admit for a minute that my heart races at the idea. But then the image of a hundred flashing cameras. The exposure. The questions. The Googling of "that girl on Roe's arm." My palms itch.

Thankfully, he saves me from a total panic attack by saying, "No. Not you. Get over yourself."

I let out a relieved guffaw.

"Jeez, you really had a moment there."

"Heh." My finger twirls around the ends of my hair.

"I have somebody else in mind." His eyebrows bounce rapidly in excitement.

———

MRS. JENKINS STOPS AT THE TOP OF THE SPIRAL STAIRS AND WE all gasp. She turns her head and extends one sparkling arm, giving us time to truly soak in her appearance. Roe jogs up to meet her. His stellar form is emphasized in a tuxedo cut perfect for his body. He's magnificent but Mrs. J. steals the show. She glows. Her entire being lights up from joy.

I bite my tongue to keep the burning in my eyes at bay. I

never wanted to kiss Roe more than at this moment. Mrs. J. hadn't taken long to choose an outfit. Any other woman would've been hours, but she was done getting ready soon after Roe made his announcement. It's like her entire life of over-dressing each morning culminated in this moment. She had an outfit picked out on the off chance this would be the day she got to wear it out of the house. I have to stop that train of thought because it causes my throat to constrict.

"You look amazing." I clasp my hands to my heart like a starstruck fool. I can't help it.

"Truly. You're a million dollars," Danny adds. Russell nods in agreement and dabs at his eyes with a tissue before fixing the collar of Danny's shirt affectionately.

"I know." Mrs. Jenkins twirls and looks at us all over her mink-covered shoulder. "Do you think the fur is too much?"

"No. No." All four of us encourage. Pepper barks his reply.

She's wearing a modestly cut, satin A-line dress of golden yellow that drips to the floor. Her gloved arms are covered in bling, on anybody else I would assume costume jewelry, on her... I'm not so sure. She wrapped herself in a different mink than the one she was wearing earlier, this one a darker shade to offset her dress. Diamond bobble earnings pull on the tender flesh of her ears and her neck sparkles with matching saffron gems.

Roe's limo is already parked and ready to go outside. His team came here to get him ready because he didn't want to leave and come back. He was made flawless, well more flawless, by hair and makeup. They descend on Mrs. J. as soon as she hits the main floor.

Mr. "I'm just walking my dog" walks by two more times while they get ready. It's every forty-five minutes from what I can tell, but he must have eyes on Roe's car as well. I formulate how I'll track him down as they get ready. The mood is light as they work. Somebody turns on a playlist from the golden days of Hollywood. Crooners and honey voices supported by jazz bands fill the air. Mrs. J. dances with a finger as they work. Danny and Russell waltz flawlessly around the living room, which delights her. She claps and Pepper does a weird hopping thing. That or he's having a seizure.

Roe glances at his very expensive watch, sniffs and goes back to patiently waiting on the outskirts of the room. I tug him by the bowtie into the next room. It's a sitting area with furniture that has never been sat on.

I wrap my arms around him before I can think too much about it. My body is tiny and bird-like as it clings to his solid core. He's stiff, so it takes him a minute before he responds. But when he does he fully commits. He wraps his arms tightly around me, lowers his head and inhales deeply.

"What's this for?" His voice is rumbly in my ear.

I lean back and hold his gaze with mine. My eyes glisten and I can't even be ashamed. "This is... I can't tell you how much..."

"Can't a guy take a pretty woman out on the town?" His cheeky smile betrays his breezy words. He knows how much this means to her. He only just met her and he can give her something I never could. He's got his own super powers; super-star powers.

Suddenly I don't have words. I can't convey what this means to me. I'm brimming with feelings for Mrs. J., for him, even for the Nosey-Neds from next door. I didn't know I was capable of feeling so much at once. It's heady and dangerous. He gazes tenderly and smiles, just a little, as he gently tucks my hair behind my ear. I melt.

The soothing sounds of Ella Fitzgerald's version of "Let's Do It (Let's Fall In Love)" wraps around our embrace, and we start to sway with her voice. I go with it, deciding for once to not dwell on the goals. He spins me out but only to grip my hands. He reels me back in like a yo-yo. We come together and dance around the room. He has moves. Of course, he does. I doubt there's anything he isn't just a little bit good at. My head falls back and I laugh, feeling like I've drunk three glasses of champagne.

He hugs me to his chest and his deep rumbling hums against my body. I close my eyes and listen to the music, feel his body against mine, inhale his clean scent. I breathe it all in. I'm here in the moment and it's so freeing.

The song ends and we stop moving. Our faces are a breath away. I've forgotten why it's a bad idea to kiss him, but the desire is overwhelming.

So I do.

I find his cheek and press my lips to it. A gentle, innocent kiss. I love the warmth and strength that meets my lips. It's chaste. It's over quickly. It's everything I need. My hand is on my lips when there's a quick knock followed by Danny walking in.

"It's showtime."

We step apart as Roe says, "Okay. Be right there."

"Yeppers." Danny's voice is a little too innocently high. I wanna punch him. He turns on a heel and leaves.

"Thank you for your thank you." Roe closes the distance and surprises me with another chaste kiss on my forehead.

I'm touching my lips again. His lids are heavy as he watches my fingertips graze my skin. I still can't speak. I'm sure my face betrays everything anyway.

"I know you don't want to hear this, but please be careful tonight."

I glare because it's what I know. Because it makes sense right now. He rubs his thumb over my bottom lip and makes another grumbly sound. I swallow.

"You too," I finally say. "Mrs. J. has wandering hands."

He widens his eyes comically as he leaves the room.

It takes a few to calm my racing heart. Back in my bungalow, I tuck my hair up in a baseball cap and I put on an over-sized sweatshirt and leggings.

Outside, Danny and Russell give me a look that sounds like "mm-hmm, that's what we thought." Roe and Mrs. J. head to the limo where a few photographers snag some pics. We "accidentally" leaked his locale to the paparazzi and figured it would make for a sweet rep piece.

I work my way into the crowd seeing them off. Just as we suspected, dude is here. Thankfully, the dog is gone now so I don't have to worry about it. I get as close to him as I can. He pretends to be a neighbor sneaking photos.

Roe smiles and waves and signs pictures for a few people and then they're off. Again, I'm momentarily taken aback by his lifestyle. Always having a camera in my face would drive me batty.

I'm right behind the dude. As the limo leaves he turns abruptly and pulls out his phone. I have to dart to the side to avoid being stepped on.

"Yeah. He's off. No, I don't see her."

It's the hipster who stalked me. He isn't just following me, he's following Roe too. My stomach drops out of me. Any buzz instantly evaporates to panic. They know we're connected and I'm not sure what that means.

16

Roe

EMOTIONS PLAY OVER MY FACE AS WE RIDE ALONG IN THE BACK OF the limousine, despite my effort to remain impassive. Mrs. Jenkins, Rhonda, as she prefers for me to call her, presses all the buttons and has two glasses of champagne very quickly. Soon her attention turns to me. I recall Maggie's comments and shift away.

"So. You like my Maggie?" she asks.

"Yes."

My focus remains on the passing apartment buildings. Regardless, her gaze bores into the side of my face.

"Hmmm. Okay. But she's special. Don't think she's the type to boink and be tossed aside."

"I wouldn't—" I clear my throat. "Maggie and I aren't like that."

"Sure. Sure."

"Really, she's not interested in me. Like that." I think of the kiss we shared. Innocent and yet incendiary. I don't even believe my own lies.

"That's a huge load of cock-and-bull. You two almost set my curtains on fire with your heated glances. But okay, do your little song and dance."

My bow tie catches on my Adam's apple until I wiggle some slack into it. Should I explain that I need to take it slow with Maggie? At some point it stopped being a question of "if" with Maggie, now it's only "when?" When will she let me in?

"She's been hurt." Mrs. J. finishes before I formulate a response. Her tone's a little more somber. "She doesn't share much, but I've seen enough to know. Poor little thing has been knocked out all her life. Beautiful people have an easy pass, it's true, but it's not always fun and games. It can't feel good to be sexualized from a young age." Her watery gaze studies the passing crowds outside the window. "Nobody expects anything else from you."

The sun is heavy and fat in the sky and it glares off the city windows. It blinds me if I stare too long.

There's nothing to say.

"Just be gentle with my little bird. She acts like little miss 'nobody can touch me' but those are always the most fragile. The second she is shown love and kindness, she returns it tenfold. She pretends to be a fortress but she so desperately wants someone."

She's drifted in her talking like she didn't mean to say all that. She stops speaking abruptly with a shaky smile. She squeezes my hand. I replay the hug and peck on the cheek. In that moment it felt like everything and now I understand why.

"Mrs. Jenkins—" I press my hands together with my knees.

"On the other hand, that girl needs to be boinked until she can't walk straight."

My wide eyes scan slowly over to her.

"You know what I mean. Wound up tighter than a watch spring. Needs to let loose." She pulls out a compact from her bag and dabs her lips with a finger. "On second thought, forget everything I said. Girl can hold her own. You give her a good orgasm or two and make sure she forgets her name for a while. If it ain't long term, you'll both survive."

I chuckle. My feelings for Maggie are complicated. She hates the world I live in with the "passion of a thousand burning suns," her words not mine, and I can't ever leave it. We're stuck. Not to mention my barely contained attraction to her. Sometimes we're close to ripping each other's clothes off and other times she can't handle direct eye contact. When we cross that line, everything will change.

"Tell me what you'd do if you were me, Mrs. J."

"Rhonda," she corrects. "First, I'd buy an island..."

"No, no." my hand comes up to stop her. "I mean with Maggie. What would you do if you were in my position?"

She studies her hands for a moment. They're covered in silk and jewels but tremble under the direct focus. "I would trust her and be there for her. That's all anybody really wants. To be seen by someone."

What an honor it would be to be fully trusted by Maggie. What it might be like to be the person she goes to for everything, shares everything with. If she'd have me.

"Okay," I say. My leg bounces. I'm anxious for this night to be over. I'm anxious to prove to Maggie the weight of my word.

"But more importantly..." Mrs. J. grabs my hand and squeezes.

This is one of those moments I'll replay when I'm older. A piece of advice I'll turn over in my head in the small hours of the morning when I can't sleep. People who have lived as long as Mrs. J. know a thing or two.

She has my full attention. She holds my gaze and says, "You heard about the G-spot, right?"

———

WE WALK DOWN THE RED CARPET FOR MY PREMIER TO MANY OOHS and ahhs. I tell the world Mrs. J. is a longtime family friend. They eat this up but that's not why I do it. This is for Maggie. She keeps Mrs. J., Danny, and Russell all at arm's length, but she cares about all three of them. Even Pepper, the poor demonic creature.

Maggie would never ask me for anything. She'd never let me worry about her or take care of her. That's why I worry the most. She's reckless. She has no concern for her own well-being. Where is she now? Who was that man she followed?

I trust that she's been doing this for years and she's competent. I'm not her keeper. But I do care. I wish she understood that. That you can be independent and strong and still have somebody to share with. Somebody to support you.

A flash grabs my attention followed by a question. "Is this the mysterious woman you rented out the theater for?"

"Wouldn't you like to know," Mrs. J. snaps. She strikes a pose on my arm and we move on but it's enough to get me focused.

Regardless of Maggie, of what happens, I need to focus. I have a career. I smile and wave and answer the mundane and repetitive questions. It's all a game. I'm just playing it.

We go inside and the movie starts. Mrs. J. falls asleep before the opening credits have even started. I pull out my other phone, the one I use for Maggie, and wait for news.

———

Maggie

I TRACK THE LITTLE BASTARD AS LONG AS I CAN. HE LOST ME A few blocks back. It's crowded and he's quick. Being visible is tricky; following without being seen. Tourists bump into me. My aura is shuffled. I need a better plan.

He turns around, probably sensing me, and I duck into a back alley.

When I peek out again, he's gone.

"Argh." I kick the wall and then regret it. The cinderblock is unforgiving and I'm wearing ballet flats.

Well. I suck. I had one job. One job. And I failed. I glance at my phone. And in less than half an hour even. I do have a text from Roe.

"Mrs. J. is drunk."

"Watch those hands," I respond.

"I would never!" he texts immediately.

"Wasn't referring to you."

The little dots show he's typing. Asian Hipster is slipping away but I wait for Roe to write me back. All the while gnawing my lip and foot bouncing impatiently. Finally, his message appears.

"She asked if I can flex for her. Is she allowed to touch my abs?"

I keel over with silent laughter.

Another text pops up on my main phone. "If you're done goofing off, I have a lead for you," O.G. writes.

What. The. Fuck.

"Go ahead." I send.

"Two blocks south. Go now."

I respond with a thumbs-up and start to jog. It doesn't take long to find it. Though it's tucked away, the entrance in the back alley, it's spotted easily enough. This is some high-security joint. Names on lists and secret code words. I won't be able to walk right in.

"Damn," I swear.

The doorway of a restaurant's back entrance, a little down the way, blocks me from view. The smell of grease and rotting vegetables fills the air.

I text O.G., "Any way of getting me in?"

I don't get a response and it never shows as read. Okay, then I'm on my own.

Two well-dressed men round the corner and I only have seconds to decide. I strip out of my clothes and go Under. I tuck my phone into my clothes and slide them into a dumpster mourning the loss of yet another outfit. From now on, only potato sacks for me.

Ah, naked in a back alley. Totally how I want to spend my Saturday night.

One of the men knocks and the door opens. A tiny little man with beady dark eyes answers. Not the giant man clad in leather like I expected. I'm a little taken aback. The other two men lift chins as I creep closer.

"Briggs and Sutton."

The little man checks his list and stands back to allow them. I creep up behind and tailgate in. Thankfully, they're allowed a large berth. I make it into a darkish hallway without bumping into anyone.

"Straight back," the little guy says in a high-pitched Brooklyn accent.

I follow close behind the two men. When the front one stops I slam into the other one, pushing him into the front. They share a look and I flatten myself against the wall. They shrug and continue on.

The air is humid and smells like herbs and spices. Not like fried chicken. Like an expensive salon. And chlorine. It's some sort of spa. Eww, I hope it's not a Happy Endings sort of place. I don't need to see that.

As they walk, they discuss stocks or something equally boring. They turn to a locker room where my gaze immediately studies the floor.

Naked men. Naked men everywhere.

And not even the hot kind. No. It couldn't be a group of hot firemen or a rugby team. No. It's wrinkled, pasty, beer bellies and stick legs everywhere.

I tuck myself out of the way in a corner. This place isn't for just anybody. One of the hairy man parts I accidentally spot is the mayor of the city. I keep my eyes averted and wait for whatever it is O.G. thinks I need to see.

"Right this way. He told me to send you back." The man who answered the door now escorts Asian Hipster-slash-"man walking a dog" toward a door on the other end of the locker room.

I follow as closely as I can, when a giant, sweaty, pale ass backs into me. Ew. Ew.

"Hey, watch it—" the man starts but stops with a frown when he finds only air behind him.

When this is over, I will shower for days.

I slip a little on the wet floor as I chase after the Hipster and barely make it through. We go down a short hallway to another door. The short man opens it and gestures hipster dude forward. I slide in.

"Please let me know if you need anything," he says before shutting the door.

It takes my eyes a minute to adjust. It's a small steam room. The air is thick with humidity and a soft red light glows overhead. Hipster makes his way toward a shape in the corner. I'm a little concerned for the Hipster. As much as I can care about a man who's stalking me. He's dressed in jeans and a hoodie. He has to be dying in this heat.

Concurrently, I have to note that I feel amazing. Being Under in such a humid environment is life changing. It's like I'm hyper-focused and sharp. Sure, it's stiflingly hot but overall I'm really digging it.

"You're alone?" A deep voice calls from the corner.

My heart stutters with instant recognition. No matter that the face it belongs to is obscured by steam. Zebulund sits wrapped in a towel. He leans back, sweat covering his shadowed features.

My stomach drops to the floor.

"Yeah. I'm alone."

"Tell me what you learned."

17

Roe

After the premiere is over I take a sleepy Mrs. J. home. She thanks me profusely and we make plans to see each other again soon. Maggie isn't at the main house or back in her bungalow. She isn't responding to my calls or my texts. Out of obligation, I head to the after-party at the Four Seasons, thrown by the production company. The guy in front of me may as well be speaking Latin for all I'm paying attention. He's a writer. He's got a wispy goatee and it's painfully distracting. Every time he talks it flops around on a delay, like it's trying to tell me something in code.

"It'd be a great chance to earn your acting chops. A serious role," he says.

My head nods like it's listening but I'm pretty sure he wrote a movie about giant killer house cats. I almost choke on my water when I hear him say "bad pussy."

"That sounds interesting." I pat his arm and start walking away. "Pass it on to my agent. Excuse me, I see somebody I know."

In the bathroom, I call Maggie again. It goes right to voice-mail. I'm going to kill her. As soon as I make sure she's okay. I step out of the bathroom and Rachel's waiting for me.

My heartbeat stutters and skips like a dying engine. For a split second, I thought she was Maggie. For that instant, thoughts of her on my arm at these events teased me. I'd show her off as my brilliant Maggie to every person I met.

Rachel could be her stunt double. But my Maggie has an aura about her that nobody can touch. She glows. And when she's Under it's like she's a beacon.

"Doing okay?" Rachel asks.

"Yup, how are you?"

"Want some?" Rachel forces a plate into my hand. It's an assortment of shrimps and quiches and something gelatinous.

"I just ate a big meal."

She studies me for a second. "Okay. I'm not even hungry." She shrugs. "I'm going to go throw it away then."

"No." I snatch the plate out of her hands. "Don't throw it away." I stack the four small pieces of food like checker pieces and swallow them down.

Rachel watches me over the rim of her champagne glass. "I think the tail was still on that shrimp."

"Extra fiber." Something scrapes along my throat.

"You're sort of an odd duck, you know that?" She drains the rest of her glass.

"Yes."

"Thinking about heading out soon. I'm done for." Rachel sets down a champagne flute and yawns, covering her mouth with the back of her hand. "I've got a documentary and comfy pants with my name on them."

"I'll walk out with you."

I stop and say my goodbyes to a few important people and thank the organizers for a great night. Rachel waits patiently outside the hotel doors.

"Want me to call a car?" I ask.

"Nah. Let's walk. It's a beautiful night."

Rachel stumbles a little as we stroll. I steady her, and she tucks her arm through mine. It's intimate but not weird. She's been working for me for two years and there's never been a worry about line-crossing. We've never talked about it but we aren't each other's types. Whatever tangible zing I feel with Maggie isn't present with Rachel.

"Does it bother your fiancé that you work all these crazy hours?" I ask after we've walked in silence for a few minutes.

"Since when do you ask about my personal life?" She narrows her eyes.

"Ouch." I hold my chest. "Am I that self-absorbed as your boss?"

"No." Her head shakes with a laugh. "You're just private and it seems you expect that of others too. I've always respected that about you."

"I should still ask about others." I shrug because it's true. I've never understood those who tell their entire life stories up front.

"Maybe. But to answer your question, because I don't actually mind talking about my personal life, no, he doesn't. Since he's a hockey player, he's gone a lot for games."

"NHL?" I don't have a ton of time for sports but I know a little about hockey.

She nods and smiles with pride.

"Who's your boyfriend? He plays for the Kings?"

"Yeah, Gordon Fleury."

"No shit!" This time I stop and look at her with a big grin. "He won the Conn Smythe trophy a year or two ago, right? Helped them all the way to the top of the playoffs."

"That's him." She's smiling at the ground. Her long blond hair falls in front of her face.

"Look at you keeping big secrets." I nudge her playfully. "No wonder I'm no big deal. Not when your boyfriend has actual talent. Gordon Fleury. Wow." I think about how many late nights and early mornings she's been here to help me. "Even harder to maintain a relationship."

She takes a minute to respond. "Maybe at first it was. You know, when you're so greedy for each other the rest of the world fades away?"

Her cheeks flush as she speaks. Full of fervent adoration at whatever memories play through her head.

"At the end of the day none of the other stuff matters." She tucks her hair back again. "It's just him and me. The fame and celebrity in both of our careers is part of who we are but not the sum total. If that makes sense."

"You've got it figured out." I smile at her, feeling more than a little envious. She lets her hair fall into her face again.

"It took a bit to manage it, but in the end being together was the most important thing." She's about to say something else when the flash of a light blinds us. To the left is a cameraman.

"Roe, is this your date? What's her name?"

Rachel steps back to give me the limelight I don't want. I smile and wave to the camera and give them what they want.

"This is my lovely assistant and sadly no, her heart belongs to another."

She keeps her head tucked as I put my arm around her and shelter her as we walk away. Just another reminder that my life isn't my own. Rachel may have it figured it out, but being an athlete is different than this level of celebrity. My life will never be close to normal. That's what Maggie has always understood. We're silent another block as I look back to make sure we aren't followed.

"Sorry about that." I thumb back to the cameras.

"I'm around them all the time. Doesn't bother me." She gives me a pitying smile. "You really are good at all that, though."

"Right."

"No, really. I know people like to say 'you fell into fame' but the more we work together the more I see that you do a lot more than that. People think this industry is the dream come true. But it's insane amounts of work. Don't sell yourself short."

I clear my throat. This is uncomfortable. I was plucked from Middle of Nowhere, USA and thrust into success. I do fight to keep it up but I've done nothing to deserve any of this.

"Well, thanks to you."

"True." She smiles. "You keep checking your phone. Am I going to have to draft a statement about a secret lovah?"

She says the last part breathy and I laugh. "No. Just a friend."

"Miss Mayday?"

I nod.

"Hmm," she says and it's very akin to a motherly "hmm."

"What?" I ask.

"She's a reporter." She hesitates. "Just be careful."

"It's not like that."

"Okay good, because I will cut her."

"It's harmless." I laugh even harder.

"Phew. I'm all talk and I actually liked her sassy ways. Also, I don't even know where I'd find a shank on short notice..." She lets out a slow breath. "Just be careful there. I hate to sound jaded, but reporters, they can be ruthless."

"I'm careful."

She comes to a stop in front of her apartment and squeezes my arm. "I'm not good at it. But I would do it."

"What?"

"Cut a bitch." She punches my arm.

"Thanks."

After she's safe inside, I check my phone again. Still no word from Maggie.

That's it. Maggie's GPS shows her at the same location the

last few times I checked. Giving her space is crucial but I need to make sure she's okay.

———

Maggie

I HAVE TO GIVE IT TO THE ASIAN HIPSTER—WHOSE NAME, BY THE way, is Keith, color me disappointed. I expect something cool like Horatio or Vladimir. Anyway, Keith, to his credit, seems to handle the oppressive heat a lot better than I'd have thought. He sweats through, literally but probably also figuratively, as Zebulund fires one question after another at him.

"Where did you see her last?"

"Going into the old lady's house."

"And Roe was there?"

"He showed up later." Keith wipes his brow.

"You let her follow you?"

He nods.

"When did you lose her?" Zebulund is pink and puffy like a turkey after a couple hours in the oven. His fake tan sparkles with sweat.

"I think about a block or two ago."

"And you're sure that you weren't followed here?"

"I'm sure." Sweaty Keith tugs his collar away from his neck and futilely plucks his shirt away from his chest. "But even if she saw me come in here, there's no way of her getting in."

"I'm aware." Zebulund shoots him a textbook withering look.

Keith clears his throat.

"Have you figured out how they're connected?" Zebulund cracks the knuckles on each of his fingers, one at a time, slowly and deliberately. I shudder.

Tonight is all about revelations. First and foremost, turns

out I'm not as sneaky as I think I am when it comes to following people. Maybe I clomp loudly or something. And secondly, they've found out that Roe and I know each other. But I still haven't figured out who they were following first; me or Roe. Maybe it doesn't matter.

"I think she's writing something on him. I'm not sure. They might be dating."

My heart skips at the bad news. They know we are connected.

"Keep someone on both of them at all times."

"That's double the resources." Keith wipes his brow with his sleeve.

"Your point?" Just kidding, that is a textbook withering stare.

"Right. Okay." The poor kid looks like he's seconds away from passing out. His black shirt is soaked through.

"Anything else?" Zebulund asks.

When Keith shakes his head, Zebulund points to the door with one finger. Keith leaves.

The air grows heavy. Zebulund leans his head back against the bench and lets out a deep sigh. I've watched a lot of people by themselves over the last few years. It's not totally unexpected what people do. Lots of random bodily functions, nose picking, bits of unfinished conversations, the occasional song solo. Nothing totally unexpected.

"Am I alone?" he says into the small room. His deep voice rumbles off the walls and sends chills down my neck.

Okay, now that's unexpected.

My stomach clenches. The air's cloudy with steam but his outline is clear enough. I look right at him but he isn't looking at me. He's scanning the room. For something. A sign, I realize. His finger tapping repeatedly on the bench is the only sign that something agitates his cool demeanor.

Here I am with a bowl full of lemons thrown at me from life

itself about to make some sweet, sweet lemonade. The room consists of a tile bench, a box with glowing coils, and a bucket of water with a ladle. Zebulund takes up an entire corner. There are no cards to throw, no TVs to turn on.

He peeks open one eye and searches the room. "That's what I thought."

I roll my eyes. Thought what, exactly? He grumbles something else I can't quite make out. He leans back and closes his eyes again, hands intertwined on his hairy belly.

So, that's it? He wants a sign? I'll give him a freaking sign. I grab the ladle from the tub of water and swing it violently around. Little drops of water fly off the end but go totally unnoticed in this environment. He doesn't even open his eyes.

Something else catches my notice.

The spoon in my hand, just like the rest of me, starts to turn translucent. Like me. What. The. Hell. That same weird bubbly look spreads from where I hold it and up the handle until it's completely gone. I'm clear but distorted when I look down and see myself, and now the spoon and I are one.

Now that I think about it, I've been Under over fifteen minutes, easily, maybe more. I'm not dizzy or disoriented at all. I feel normal. Better than normal, like I sipped from the Fountain of Youth.

The moisture in the room must be crucial here. Does that mean my powers, or whatever less lame word I can use, get stronger when I'm in a wet environment? Maybe the trick is to be really wet!

There's a dirty joke in there.

I can't wait to show Roe. Would he be able to see it? Okay, well this is a new development. Put a pin in that to circle back to later. In the meantime, action.

The invisible spoon submerges in the water. I dump a massive spoonful onto the coals. I hop back to see Zebulund's reaction clearly as a huge angry steam cloud hisses through the room. He scuttles backward up the wall as far as he can go, all the while clutching at his heart.

"Who's there?" His head swings back and forth. "Who did that?"

The spoon bounces off his head, because while I'm a full-grown woman, I'm also a child at heart. An angry, petulant child.

I have no regrets.

He scrambles sideways against the wall toward the door. He moves faster than any man I've ever seen wrapped in only a towel. I beat him to the door. It crashes open when I throw my body against it a second before he reaches it.

A blast of cool air bursts into the room as I run out. He stands there, pale-faced and horrified. A second later the door slams shut. Still in my childish state I hold myself against the door, pushing with all my might. I'm thin but I pack a punch. He tries to thrust open the door and my body is violently shoved but I don't give in so easy. My toes grip the floor without much purchase. I'll be bruised tomorrow. Totally worth it.

In his panic, he bangs his fists, screaming to be let out. A few men in the hot tub outside the room stare at the door. They glance at each other and one starts to get out to help.

That's my cue to book it.

I let go and quickly back away. The next time he pushes, he barrels out as the door flies open. He drips all over and is redder than a sunburned tourist. It's awesome. He collects himself and his pride as much as possible, holding the towel with one hand and pushing back his graying hair with the other.

"I'll talk to management about this," he says to all the slack-jawed men looking at him. He jabs a finger in the direction of the steam room. "That's a health risk."

I laugh and laugh as I make my way to the exit. Out of the humid environment I'm even more keenly aware of the pain it causes me to go Under. Outside my clothes are where I left them so I slide them on. The chilled night air forms goose bumps, especially after such a hot room.

I come back Up and hear, "Funny seeing you here," in an unrecognizable masculine voice.

My feet sprint me away before I can think better of it.

18

Roe

FOR ONCE I HAVE THE UPPER HAND ON MAGGIE. SHE BARRELS OUT of a side door in an alley just as I'm walking past for the tenth time. She's smiling like the actress who got the Oscar. I can only imagine what she's been up to. She doesn't see me and she's most decidedly still Under, as she's totally naked. As always, I try to control my eyes but they're weak and greedy for her. Something's different. Her silhouette is not as sharp. She contorts and blurs much more than normal.

And she's laughing instead of wobbling and pale.

I tuck into a doorway and decide to see what she's up to. She glances around before grabbing a bundle I assume is her clothes and the phone that led me to this alley. Her system for hiding clothes is definitely lacking. If she let me, I could help with that.

I follow her as she rounds the corner to another abandoned alleyway and gets dressed. Her form becomes solid. It's still such a trip to watch. Her spine is bent and curled as she dresses, and her skin emanates a glow that feels ethereal. A glimpse of side boob flashes before she stands to slip the dress over her head.

Time to get a little petty revenge. I sneak up behind her and by the time she has her shoes on I could reach out and grab her.

"Funny seeing you here," I say in a voice not at all like my own, just hoping to watch her jump with fright. Maybe a little scream so I can make fun of her for showing a genuine human reaction.

But I didn't think this through. She's Maggie fucking May. She doesn't even react except that she goes from zero to sixty in a flash.

"Dammit." I chase after her without calling out her name, for fear of getting attention.

She's fast but I have an on-call personal trainer, who must be a demonic masochist in his spare time. I'm gaining on her quickly. She rounds another building where there's still nobody.

"Maggie." I grab her so she doesn't fall in those horrible sandals.

She lands a few good punches as soon as I touch her. My grip tightens as she flails to get out of my grip before she registers my voice.

"Maggie, it's me," I say, trying to get her to look at me.

"Roe."

She blinks. Her eyes focus and she blinks again.

Then she's flailing at me even harder. With more thoughtful punches.

"You sick... How dare..."

"Ouch." Duck. "Maggie." Thump. "Hey, that—"

When she's dangerously close to my junk, I pin her arms against the wall above her head with one hand and the other over her mouth. I press my entire body along the length of her, a thigh between hers to protect from additional kicks. I'm fine letting her get her revenge but I wasn't about to risk the family name over a dumb prank.

"Stop. Chill."

She stops struggling but she's stock still. Her chest rises and falls under her thin dress. She's glaring. But there's something else too—her pupils are dilated, her chin quivers under my palm. She's frozen. Her eyes are wide and unblinking.

She's panicked.

"It's okay. It's me."

She inhales a huge breath under my hand.

"It's Roe," My eyes lock on to hers.

She nods once. Her wide eyes flick to my hand on her mouth and then where the other is still holding her in place. She's ghostly white. A small shudder racks her body.

"Fuck." I release her as fast as I can and step two full paces back. "I'm sorry."

Her arms wrap around her center and she bends forward. She shakes her head and takes a deep breath in and out. I give her all the space she needs. If I could punch myself in the face, I would. My physical power dwarfs hers. It's not fair that I can take her over so easily. She's so strong in my mind. I forget that she's fragile inside. Mrs. Jenkins's warning replays.

I circle around, hands on my head, swearing to myself for my stupidity. Every time I get close to her, I do something fucking stupid and push her away. She'll never learn to trust me at this rate.

When I check on her again, she's against the wall, arms still wrapped around herself, but she's leaning back, chin up, head resting on the brick.

"I'm so sorry I scared you." I step toward her, but not too close. "I thought it would be funny."

"You didn't." She sniffs. "It wasn't."

"I'm sorry," I say again and stare deep into her eyes, pouring all my sincerity into them. We aren't touching. I don't want her to feel trapped in this position. There's plenty of room for her to get away from me.

"Okay."

"I don't know what else to say." Slowly, I lift a hand and brush back a few strands of hair from her lips. "I'm sorry," I repeat.

"I'm okay." She drops her hands to her side. "Stop apologizing."

I wait for her to push past me and huff away. But she doesn't. Her gaze moves to my mouth.

I still. Am I imagining the signs or is she sending them? Her breath isn't calming down. Her eyes are still wide, and her face is flushed. The first move is hers. I already fucked up too much.

But I can show her that I want to kiss her so fucking bad.

I move slowly, giving her plenty of time to leave. Plenty of time to make some witty remark or cutting blow that'll make me laugh. Ruining this is not an option. If she walks away from this moment, I'm done.

I step closer to her. She straightens at my approach. Pushes off the wall. I wait to be rejected. To be shunned. I lean toward her, only halfway. Her eyes flutter closed and her body sways the rest of the way toward me.

When our lips meet, it's a win. My heart runs victory laps. The moment something in her decides to commit to this is tangible. Whatever held her back before is no longer between us. Her body relaxes toward me. I expect the kiss to deepen. I want it to deepen. I want our mouths to open and our tongues to clash. I want her so fucking bad I'm rock solid from only the graze of her lips.

But her mouth slides off mine and she tucks her head into the crook of my neck. Her arms wrap around me and she squeezes so hard she shakes. I'm shaking too.

I wrap her up in my arms. I'm vibrating with the desire to make sure she never feels scared again. My nose nuzzles into her hair as I murmur sounds of comfort. I don't even know what I'm fucking saying.

She shudders out a deep breath and I loosen my grip to pull back and look at her. The soft smile she gives me melts my insides. I feel them actually dissolve.

"Okay. Maybe you scared me a little."

"I'm sorry." I pull her forehead to mine; my fingers tangle in her hair. She isn't trying to get away. She's pulling me closer too. Her fingers grip my shirt like I might drift.

"Forgiven."

We stay like that for a minute. Maybe ten. I'd stay like that for forever. I'd take whatever she could give me until the end of time.

But my phone's chime breaks the mood. We release each other but stay close.

"You can get that."

I shake my head once.

"I promise, I'm okay. Just a weird adrenaline thing."

My thumb brushes over her lips and she shivers.

"Get it." Her head nods toward my phone.

I don't want to but it's Marty Zebulund. The timing. "Hello?"

"Roe." His deep voice is shaken and breathless.

"Hey, man, how are—"

"Tomorrow night. My house."

"Are you okay?"

"We need to get rid—You need to fix what we talked about."

"Sure," I say, thinking as quickly as I can about this odd development. Maggie is leaning against the wall again, watching me through heavy lids. Brilliance strikes. "I need to bring my assistant too. Based on the research I've done."

"Fine. Whatever. Bring your assistant. But nobody else."

"Okay."

"I don't have to tell you that this conversation never happened." It's not a question. It's a threat.

"Got it."

"Good. Tomorrow night. My assistant will contact you for details." The sudden silence of call-ended greets my ears.

Maggie blinks innocently, over the top. "Who was that?"

"What did you do?"

"I have news." She gives me the biggest, cheesiest grin.

19

Maggie

ROE'S HOUSE IS UNEXPECTED. GORGEOUS, ABSOLUTELY. ONLY much smaller than I thought. Smaller even than Mrs. Jenkins's house. It's still worth a cool couple million, but considering what he could surely afford it's modest. Nestled in the Hollywood Hills past a few winding roads, it hides out of sight of all the neighbors. There's a distinctly Japanese feel to it. The roof is low, the dark wood rooms are floor-to-ceiling windows, and the floor plan's wide-open, separated only by thin sliding doors. At least the outer portion of the house. I have yet to see the bedrooms. The pool, which I see walking through to the back entrance, looks like a koi pond that morphs into an infinity pool.

Before entering the house, I stop to admire the view and clear my mind of worries, to just exist. It's late. The adrenaline of the evening has melted away, leaving me exhausted.

I haven't shared with him my new trick. On the drive up here, I caught him up on everything I overheard and Zebulund's reaction in the steam room. But the farther up the hills we drove, the more the heaviness descended between us. There's a distinct shift in Roe's behavior toward me and I can't quite figure out why. His eyebrows aren't sharing for once.

"I never get sick of it," I say, studying the city's twinkling lights below. Despite the ever-present blanket of toxic pollution, the view always takes my breath away.

Literally, too, I guess.

"I know." He sounds lost in thought. He's right next to me, brushing my arm with his. His eyes squint as they search the horizon.

"I've lived in this city my whole life and the sunsets and these hills never get old."

He remains quiet.

"You're from Wyoming right?" I ask.

"Nebraska. We never had views like this, that's for sure."

"What was your house like growing up?"

His shoulders lift to block a breeze that doesn't exist. "We should go in and get some sleep."

Okay, noted. That vault is closed. I'm a little ashamed, or maybe chastened, after our moment earlier. It took a lot for me to admit my fear to him. Even more to touch him willingly and for so long. Was it too much to hope that would be reciprocated in some way? The truth thing.

He doesn't tour me around the rest of the house. I tell myself it's because we're both exhausted and not because of this weird shift between us. Instead, he takes me to a small guest room, clean and tidy, still in the simple Japanese theme, but with sturdy Western walls. The room smells like clean linen with a little hint of lemon. The carpet is plush, so I slip out of my flip-flops immediately to dig my toes into it like warm sand on a beach.

He's studying my toes. I smile sheepishly as his gaze lifts to my face. No accounting for class, I guess.

"There's extra whatever you need in the bathroom." He

points to a door.

It's likely the work of cleaning staff, but it's nice that he's aware of a guest's needs.

"Thanks."

He's distracted and speaks without looking directly at me. Did I go too far in the alley? Could I have pushed him to a point he didn't want to go? Did I completely misread the situation?

"We've got a big day of exorcism tomorrow," I say, desperate to bring the lightness back between us.

With his hands stuffed deep in his pockets he raises and lowers his eyebrows comically, like an actor in an old black-and-white film.

"Good night, Maggie."

"Sleep tight, Roe."

After he's gone I shower. I luxuriate in the hot clean feeling after a day of creepy men and lurking in alleys. The day wasn't so bad, all in all. I replay the kisses. There's a mixture of pride and something else. Guilt maybe? It's been so long, high school probably, since I've allowed myself to enjoy the company of a guy, let alone actively pursued one. My body took over in both of those instances. I'm shocked and amazed with myself. Who knew I was capable of such lust and then acting on it. I mean, everything was PG but I still crave him more.

It's thrilling.

But also scary. So maybe that's why hours later, I lie wide awake in bed thinking. The kisses, the stalkers, the past, the perverts in power. I can't seem to stop the swirling thoughts. Through the walls come the sounds of soft movement. I take a risk.

"Are you awake?" I text him.

Dots appear almost immediately. An idea is formulating. Something to lighten the mood between us, to bring us back to a safe place.

"I can't turn off my brain," his text reads.

"Me neither."

"Gonna make tea. Did I wake you?"

"No." I hit send and start typing before I can chicken out. "Wanna go for a swim instead?"

I close my eyes and throw back my head, covering my face with another extra soft and smelly good pillow, like a total dork. The adrenaline of possible rejection has my feet kicking like I'm throwing a tantrum. I should turn off my phone. I missed this feeling, I realize, and then shame slaps my face, like I don't deserve it.

But I can't help myself. Even though Roe is not a long-term option. He's a great friend and partner in stopping crime. I like having a person to talk to about my... life. And sure, maybe he isn't bad on the eyes.

I can't look at my phone. I can't. And yet...

I lift the pillow and peek at my phone with one eye. My phone sits watching me. Judging me. Still dark with no reply.

"Argh." My moan is stifled by the pillow. I should have specified that there would be no touching.

At the ping of my phone I pop up like a jack-in-the-box. I read the text without breathing.

"Be out by the pool in ten."

I flatten myself out and squeal silently like the hopeless loser I am.

———

Roe

Maggie's shower turned off over an hour ago, followed by the scraping of the bed moving on the wood floor repeatedly. The phone was in my hand to text her when her message popped up. My plan was to let her take the lead after I accosted her in that back alley.

Even though I take my time changing into my swim trunks and grabbing a couple towels, Maggie still isn't by the pool when I arrive outside. I lay the towels on the chairs before stretching my arms over my head and side to side, trying to release the tension. The air is chilly despite the warm day and an eerie mist swirls around the water's surface. The gentle gurgle of the hot tub jets compete with the otherwise quiet night.

When she still doesn't come out, I decide to swim. I pull off my shirt and toss it on one of the chaise lounges. As soon as the water covers me, I push off the wall. After ten tension releasing laps my body finds the smooth rhythm. My focus shifts to breathing, muscles working, and not Maggie's smooth curves. Especially not that little dip right next to her hip bone that's begging to be explored by my tongue.

I come up for air, arms crossed over the edge of the pool. Water drips down my nose forming a little puddle. She still isn't here. I'm about to go back to swimming laps when I spot her clothes and flip-flops. They weren't out here before. My head whips around searching for her.

Maggie doesn't have a swimsuit. I swallow. She hates me. Why else would she have suggested swimming? I close my eyes and take a steadying breath, but that damn little dip appears in my mind's eye.

When I open them again, she's still nowhere to be seen.

"Maggie?" I call out.

She has to be here somewhere. She's messing with me. Then. I feel it. None of the other five senses can find her but she's here.

The water around me shifts, like when someone kicks too close, the hairs on my leg are disturbed.

"Maggie?" I whisper.

All of a sudden she's right in front of me. "Hi." Her face drips and she's grinning ear to ear.

"Shit," I yelp and jump back hitting the edge of the pool. "What the fuck?"

She's laughing so hard the water is jumping all around her. See this is what's not fair. She can mess with me so easily. Belatedly, what I was seeing, or rather not been seeing, hits me.

"How?"

She shrugs. She's grinning so big I can't help but smile.

"I discovered it today. Actually, this is the first time I've tried it in a pool. But I could tell in the steam room today that something was different. I wasn't so drained. Water must be crucial. It makes sense when you think about it. I've always gotten so dehydrated."

I'm nodding as she speaks. She's talking a lot with her hands but we're in the deep end so she's kicking to stay afloat and occasionally has to reach out to hold on to the wall. My eyes remain locked on hers which isn't exactly a chore, because her face is beautiful. Especially right now. She's even more ethereal than before. She's glowing. Her lips are plump, and her smile is genuine.

"What?" I ask. She's asked me a question because she's blinking expectantly at me.

"What do I look like to you?"

"Beautiful," I answer immediately without thinking.

"Oh." Her eyelids flutter. The water overtakes her because she's stopped kicking. I haul her up and she holds on to the wall. Her long lashes clump together. Her cheeks are rosy. "I... I meant when I go Under. Could you see me?"

I look away and then back. Oh fuck. "Yeah." I shake my head when she frowns. "No. I mean, I couldn't see you at all. Until just now."

She falls back into the water with a laugh. "I knew it!" She kicks off the wall and splashes around. "This is so cool."

I'm not happy. I don't like that she can be invisible to me. I don't like it at all. She swims back over and presses the area between my eyebrows with a wet finger, and a drop of water rolls down the bridge of my nose.

"Your eyebrows are frowning. What's wrong?"

I shake off the water drop. "You were already invisible to everybody." Else. "What's so great about this?" My pettiness may be noticeable. My anger grows like an unscratched itch. Why does she have to be so excited about being invisible to me?

My privilege was being able to really see her. I don't think I realized until that moment how much that meant to me. From the moment I first saw her, I've been special to her. We were meant to meet. It's a silly romantic idea.

"Well. I guess because I feel better now. It's like I'm supposed to be in the water. I don't get as sick, and maybe there're other things happening. I don't know, it's hard to explain."

"How often are you going to be able to use this, how often are you in a pool when you need to eavesdrop? I don't see any practical applications."

"You're being sort of a wet blanket. I thought you'd be excited. My superpowers are getting stronger." She drifts to a stop and looks at me.

"Yeah. I guess. It doesn't really change anything, though."

She's followed me to the shallow end. She can stand without kicking now, but she's still on her toes, arms crossed. Her emotions are written all over her face. My bad mood is flaring off me and consuming her.

"I disagree," she says and then is gone.

This. This is exactly what I didn't want. Call me petty but now I have nothing. No reason to feel like there's something to her and me. Now I'm just like everyone else.

"Maggie," I grind out.

A wave splashes me, shooting water up my nose. I sputter and wipe a hand down my face. "Real mature."

20

Maggie

WELL, THIS SUCKS. ROE'S MY PARTNER. SUPPOSED TO BE, AT least. He made me put my faith in him and trust him, and now he's making me feel like I fucked up. No way. He's supposed to be thrilled, curious at worst, but not annoyed. This is why sharing with people is a stupid waste of time.

I go Under and slip to the other side of the pool as soon as it's clear he's being a dick. I may have accidentally kicked water in his face as I swam away.

It's so easy and painless now. I can be in the water all the time and not even worry. I only want him to be happy for me. I want him to suggest experiments to try. Not this bad attitude. He punches the water, splashing himself in the face more. He shakes it off like a wet dog. What could he possibly be mad about? This is awesome! I'm invisible even to him. What's not to love?

Oh.

I'm on a delay but it clicks. Maybe he likes that he can see me when nobody else can. He scans the stones surrounding the pool's edge, probably looking for my wet footprints.

"Maggie, I'm sorry. Are you still in the water?"

My nose barely sticks above the water, my body floating to make as few movements as possible.

"Maggie?" He looks toward the door and punches the water again. "Way to fuck it up again." He's barely audible over the whirring pool filter but it's enough to make me soften a little. I drift toward him. The water softly ripples out around me as I gently propel myself back toward him. He lets out a breath.

"Idiot," he grumbles again and I smile.

"Can you hear me?" I ask but he doesn't react at all. "Roe!" I scream but still no reaction.

Hmmm. His face is centimeters from mine. He makes no movement save his roaming eyes. He can sense I'm close because he's no longer flailing like a buffoon. He's as still as prey waiting to run for it. Or maybe a predator waiting to launch.

"Maggie?" He reaches out a hand, blindly searching for me. It's easily avoided. The water moves a lot, though, and he glares at the area. "Maggie? I'm happy for your powers. I am. I'm tired. It's been a long day."

I come Up right next to his ear and whisper, "And?" before I go back Under immediately.

He startles but not too much. "And you're very good at what you do?" A slow grin lifts the corner of his mouth.

I swim around to the other side, coming Up just long enough to say, "And you're jealous?"

His head whips to the left; he half-heartedly swipes. "And I'm oh, so jealous of your great magical powers."

I swim out of arm's reach and come Up again. "That's what I thought." I kick to stay afloat and my chin is barely above the water. "You can't hear me at all when I yell. I was right next to you. Did you hear anything?"

"When you were Under? No. Wow." He pushes off the wall to come at me but I swim away.

"Are you still mad?" I ask.

"No." The dirty liar.

"Good." It's sort of sweet how he pretends to be happy for me now. Even though his eyebrows still pout. "I learned something else I can do. It's really, really cool. Are you ready?"

"I don't like how you're smiling."

My grin grows Cheshire cat sized. "Don't worry." I go back Under. I pop back Up to add. "Go back against the wall and don't move."

"Great."

I'm Under again as he follows my directions. Time to get a little revenge. I kick right up to him. One of my wet hands runs down his arm. He doesn't react like I think he's going to. He stiffens instead of jumping.

Interesting.

I run a hand down his other arm. His shoulder is out of the water so the trail of water I leave is visible. His Adam's apple climbs up and back down with a thick swallow. The mood shifts from boiling to sizzling.

In a bold experiment, I press my whole body up against him. I have to wrap my arms around his neck to hold on to him, otherwise, I'll slide right off. Our bodies are so slick there's no friction between us. This isn't where I was going to go but now I'm curious.

"Wh-what are you doing? That feels—" His eyes shut and he shudders.

When I wiggle around, my control over the situation slips. He smells too good. He's so masculine and enticing. I'm too attracted to him. I want to run my hands all over him. I swim back a few feet and come Up. "What does that feel like?"

"What did you just do?" His head swivels toward me.

"What did it feel like?"

"It felt like... warmth and soft... but not solid. I knew you were there but I couldn't really feel you." He clears his throat. "It was like how I imagine hugging a cloud might feel, but more than that. More like a ghost. I dunno. That's not it either. It's trippy." He lets out a long breath.

"Interesting," I say. Toying with him is my new favorite pastime.

"You aren't going to tell me what you were doing?"

I shrug.

"Was that the trick you learned?"

I raise an eyebrow at him. I go back Under and he rolls his eyes. I bite my lip in indecision. Act, don't think so much. A tentative hand extends to his bare shoulder. I rub my hand down it. I expect him to move away or grab me. But he's still, he keeps his eyes forward.

I rub my hand down the other side as well. The hard muscles flex under my perusal. There's a little bone at the top of his shoulder my thumbs run over and over again. The water collects in a little pool there before dripping down his arm. I want to lick it up.

And so I do.

I briefly tongue the divot and lust shoots through me. He closes his eyes with a shudder. His arms float out in the water. One grazes my stomach but I don't flinch. He won't touch me. I know that now. He's letting me explore him. He's giving me the upper hand. He understands what I need before I do.

"It's only fair," he whispers as though he's following my train of internal thought. "After all the times I've seen you naked."

He's teasing but right. I give him a wet-willy.

He crooks his ear to his shoulder with a laugh but then relaxes into the same position as before, as I continue my exploration of his body. He's warm and solid and smooth underneath me as I rub all over his upper body, leaving a trail of goose bumps behind. His chest isn't smooth though, and I twirl my hand into his chest hair. They must Photoshop it out of the ads. His nipples are tiny, brown and hard. I get the overwhelming urge to flick my tongue against one. But I don't this time. I'm close enough to bite him though because his breath tickles my ear as he lets it out.

"This feels very... uh, nice. Like a marshmallow massage."

I'm aroused. Very aroused. Shocked at how arousing this is. I never even use the word "arouse" and here I am abusing the hell out of it. I'm glad he can't see me. I'm glad he can't tell how flushed I am. How I keep biting my lip. My back is arching and my breasts ache to rub against his chest.

My hands lower to his abs. I trail my fingertips over nature's speed bumps but they don't slow me down. My fingers toy with his trunk's drawstrings. I lightly scrape my nails along the top.

"Jesus Christ," he gasps.

I grin to myself and dip below his trunks enough to brush where the coarse hair starts.

"Uh, Maggie?" He clears his throat. "What are you doing?"

My grin stretches. I'm reckless and seductive and I love it. I never feel this way. Since puberty, I've seen men's looks hover in the areas that grew too fast, developed stretch marks. Those were looks of something dark and scary. Looks of control. Now, here, with Roe, *I* feel powerful. In control. Like he's barely keeping it together and it doesn't scare me one bit. It turns me on. So much.

His voice cracks as he says, "You should know that, um, my body is reacting to this. I have no control over what's happening. Below."

But I'm very aware of his growing problem. Instead of cold dread, I'm aflame in desire for him. I toy with the tip of my tongue between my teeth.

"Oh boy," he says as I grab his trunks, the loose fabric collects easily in my hands.

We both look under the water just as the material disappears in my hands. There's nowhere to hide.

Roe

ON THE ONE HAND, MY GIANT, GLARING HARD-ON IS VISIBLE FOR all to see. On the other, Maggie just made my clothes disappear off my body.

"Woah," I say with unabashed awe. The material of my shorts slides down my legs but I can't see it happening.

I hold still, afraid to stop whatever magic is happening. These last few minutes have been some of the most intense of my life. Desire courses through my entire body for her. We're moving toward something amazing. Her strength and new-found boldness are driving me wild. Even if I can't see her at all, progress is being made.

She comes Up and holds the shorts above the water, looking like a little kid who caught her first trout. Her face is flushed and her shoulders rise and fall quickly.

"I know, right? I discovered it today. I think my powers or whatever are stronger when I'm fully wet... er, when I'm underwater."

"Amazing." I laugh. "It's amazing. You can make things disappear!"

"See, now this is the reaction I expected." Her arms fly out in a dramatic flop.

"Yeah, yeah." My shorts are out of arm's reach. "And you got me out of my pants."

We glance toward the object in question and seem to remember that we're naked and inches apart. At least fifty percent of us is extraordinarily turned on.

"Umm," she looks up and away. "Right, sorry. I couldn't think of anything else."

I reach for my shorts. One hand ineffectually covers my boner.

"Not so fast. You should get to feel it for a while."

I raise an eyebrow.

She stutters, "I mean, you should see how it feels for a bit to be naked."

"I'm an actor." I lift my chin, like she would. "I've performed sex scenes with thirty people watching. Modesty left years ago." It's not exactly true but I am an actor after all.

"Okay good." The wet slosh of my trunks hitting the stones a few yards away greets our ears. "So then you're okay with that."

"Yup. Feels good." I put my hands behind my head and relax into a sigh. "I'm usually naked out here anyway."

"Well, it's easier to be confident in your skin, I guess, when you have a team of health food chefs and a personal trainer." Her gaze outlines my form. I would pay top dollar to know her thoughts.

She's not wrong. I shrug. My foot slips and I dip under the water, and my erection brushes her thigh.

"Oh shit." I back away and freeze, waiting for her reaction. I expect her to stand and get out of the pool. She shakes her head like it's no big deal. But it is. Based on her reaction today in the alley, it's a big deal to be this close to me.

"Maggie, let's get out and get dressed."

"Okay." She blinks up at me. Did I mention I love how her lashes clump together with water? "If that's what you want."

"What I want is not up for discussion right now."

She looks dejected. I don't want her to think the wrong thing, but my self-control is slipping. I've already scared her way too many times by moving too fast.

My gaze drifts to below the water and back up at her. "It's just... I can't. I don't want to scare you."

"I'm not so easily scared." Her stubborn chin sticks out.

"You're the bravest person I know."

She blinks, her soft mouth opens a fraction. "I'm not brave at all—"

"I want you to be comfortable."

"Dammit. Roe, I'm not a Fabergé egg, if you want to kiss me just fucking kiss me." Her clenched fists come out of the water to slam down, splashing us both. She wipes the drops off her face.

I'm too stunned to move. My dick is urging me forward yelling, "Go, go. GO! This is not a drill!" but my mind is taking a second more to process what she said.

In a whisper she adds, "I mean, if you—"

She won't have to ask again.

She's in my arms. If this is what she wants, what she asked for, then I will fucking oblige. No more chaste pecks on the lips. Her mouth is open. My tongue invades immediately. Seeking and feeling. She meets me and probes back. Her softness fills my arms. Her fingers dig in my shoulders, nails scraping. I moan and she responds in kind. Her stomach is soft against my hardness. Our wet bodies slip against each other. Our arms grasp. We can't get enough traction. We can't touch enough. We can't kiss deep enough.

I can breathe at last. It's not enough to be kissing her. It's knowing that she wants this as much as I do. That I'm worthy of her desire.

But I'm not worthy. We can't go on like this. Too fast. Feeling too much. It's too much. Slow down. I push her back abruptly but not roughly. An arm's length away.

"Fuck. Sorry," I say. "We need to put our clothes on." I'm out of the water before I can kiss her again. My bare ass is on full display.

She's sitting in the same spot, gaze miles away. Her swollen lips are open and her eyes are wide. Her fingertips drift to touch her mouth.

"Now that's what I'm talking about," she says.

I shake my head and laugh. Goddamn, why did I wait so long for that?

"I'm going to take an ice-cold shower."

Her grin grows. "Be right there," she says and I'm a thousand feet tall.

———

MAGGIE DOESN'T JOIN ME IN THE SHOWER. THANK GOD. THERE was no strength left in me to be a gentleman. I shower. Ice cold. For a half hour. Until my lips are as blue as my balls.

I find Maggie curled up and sound asleep in my bed. She showered too, and the smell of my soaps on her skin threatens to regroup the ranks, but exhaustion sets in first. Almost as soon as my arm is around her I fall into a deep, dreamless sleep.

When I open my eyes again Maggie's smiling at me. The room is bright and I know before I check that I've slept more than... well since the last time I was with her.

"Hi," she says and a fresh burst of mint greets me.

"Dirty cheater." I pull the covers up to block my breath.

"I woke up just a little bit ago. I made coffee."

"Is that why you're so perky?"

"I've had a couple cups." She pokes me.

She falls forward easily when I tug her on top of me. My nose nuzzles her neck until she laughs. I want to keep playing but nature calls. With a groan, I roll out of bed toward the bathroom. There's no missing my morning wood but at this point, it's all moot. Nothing she hasn't seen.

When I come back, teeth brushed and lower half under

control, Maggie has helped herself to a shirt and gym shorts. She looks amazing and I have to focus on the task at hand. Which is? Oh, coffee right.

"Coffee?" I ask, squinting at the midday sun.

"Follow me."

At the kitchen bar, once I've had half a cup I say, "What time is it anyway?"

"Late, almost noon."

"Wow. Shit." I shoot a text to my personal trainer, apologizing for missing our session this morning. "I guess I needed sleep."

"Me too."

I appreciate that there's no awkwardness this morning. I wasn't sure how she would be toward me. Retreat was expected. She seems softer than I've ever seen.

"Thanks for letting me stay here. And for last night."

"You're welcome. And my pleasure." My ears burn hot. You'd think I'd never kissed a pretty girl before.

She comes around the bar to where I sit. She walks between my legs and wraps her arms around my shoulders, giving me a hug. Who would have thought of her as the cuddly, touchy type? I'm not complaining. I hug her back and take a deep inhale. She smells amazing.

"I feel really good this morning. I feel good about tonight too." She smiles and I can't help but reflect one back. "I can feel it. I'm gonna get something on Zebulund. I'll bring him down."

A twinge of anxiety tweaks the back of my mind. All the other stuff was set aside since last night. I had only been thinking about us. My love-struck feelings took over meanwhile, she's just as focused as ever. Miss Mayday after all.

"Good. I hope so too."

She hugs me again and my chest constricts without understanding why.

"Roe, why is it so important to you to save this company?" The question seems so out of the blue, the truth spills out.

"This factory employs the whole town I grew up in. Almost everybody. If it goes under, then my whole town will die."

"But that's not on your shoulders. People will move and find new jobs. It's not your job to make sure a whole town flourishes."

I shift in the chair. She's effectively trapped me in my seat though, so I can't move away. I clear my throat.

"I guess it feels like it is. I, um, I'm the biggest success that town has had and I owe them my whole life."

I'm hot under my shirt. Her eyes shift between mine, looking too hard.

"But why? I don't think all people from small towns feel like this."

I scratch my eyebrow. Why is talking about this so hard? Maggie has shared a lot with me. She's let me touch her. I'm touching her now. We're light-years from where we were just a few days ago. Why is the truth so hard to offer?

"When I was younger the factory shut down. It was a different manufacturer then. So many people lost their jobs. My family was hit extra hard because my mom and dad both worked there. They had me, my brother, and sister. John and I were teenagers, eating all the time."

"That's awful." Her face frowns with concern.

"Yeah." I look down. She grabs my hands in hers and links our fingers. "Well, we were poor." I can't share the truth of it. We were destitute. Some weeks the only times I ate were the meals at school. I couldn't tell her I went to bed hungry. How the pain of that haunts me. How, when we did eat, everything was powdered and processed. Cheap.

"Anyway, many of the people around town helped our family. They didn't have much themselves but they always found a way to help us. Even got my parents some work. My dad hurt his back in the factory so he couldn't do much manual labor, but people paid him to do small jobs here and there, and the school had my mom work in the lunch room."

I didn't tell her how my mom would sneak home food that kids threw away and sometimes that was dinner. When I see canned corn or cheap cheese pizza, my stomach burns with acid.

"That's amazing. I can't imagine living in a town like that. Where everybody looks out for each other. I think that's great that you're helping them."

"It's getting worse. The factory isn't making money. I can't keep up like this. Even with the money I'm making it's not enough, and now with the missing money and everything else. It's draining out too fast. A whole town can't live off my checks."

"We'll figure it out, okay?" She rubs her thumb between my eyes, forcing my face to relax a little.

"Okay." For the first time, a little weight eases from my chest.

"I promise. There're few things in life I desire more than justice. What's happening to you isn't fair or right. I'll have all my resources help me. I'll get into places and see what's going on. We're really close to something, I can feel it."

Something big is coming but it doesn't feel good. It feels ominous.

21

Maggie

IT'S NOT AN OVERLY COMPLICATED PLAN, OR EVEN AN OVERLY thought-out plan. Simple plans are best. Get in. Distract Marty Zebulund. Search the house. And, though Roe doesn't know, maybe mess with Zebulund a little. I'm more powerful than ever, closer to the truth and to stopping him. I can taste it.

As far as everyone is concerned, this evening I'm Rachel Bowen, Roe's assistant and spiritual helper. A heavy bag is slung over my shoulder when we reach the door. Next to me, Roe is the picture of cool but he's dreading this. I'll make sure there's nothing to worry about. This is what I do. Marty Zebulund is going down.

Roe and I stand at the door waiting for an answer, as a doorbell chimes an elaborate melody throughout the house. He's rigid with tension. I squeeze his hand once and let go.

A woman answers and the one word that comes to mind is cold. Her sharply accentuated cheekbones, pouty lips, and squinting eyes hint at numerous trips under the knife. Her long brown hair is waved perfectly, her makeup is meticulous. There's no telling her actual age.

"James," she says, reaching both hands out to him.

A forest-green wool dress flatters her slim figure. Expensive jewelry decorates her neck, fingers, ears... really anywhere you can have jewelry she has it. This is no housekeeper.

"I'm Nancy, Marty's wife. Lovely to finally meet you." Her gaze only flicks to me for a fraction of a second.

She's focused wholly on the hunk of man-meat at my side. Roe is the picture of smooth as he bends to kiss her cheeks.

"I've heard so much about you," he says and I fight an eye roll.

Because of a piece I once wrote I know Zebulund is married. I tried to investigate Nancy, but like her husband, information on her was limited. I may not know much about her but I'd love to crack open the brain of someone married to that man. I wait with clasped hands to be introduced.

"You're as beautiful as I've been told," Roe says.

"Oh, I already like you."

"This is my assistant, Rachel." Roe introduces me and I hold out a hand.

"Nice to meet you."

"You too." She looks me up and down before stepping back to let us through. "Thank you for coming to help with all this."

She gives nothing away as to how she feels about the fact that strangers are at her house to have a séance. I nod once with a polite smile. I'm all business.

"Marty should be out in a minute. Just wrapping up a work call." She gestures toward a heavy wood door, behind which a low voice vibrates out to the house. That must be the office. Thankfully, easy to find. We step into the foyer.

"Can I get either of you anything?"

"No, thank you," we both say.

"I can start setting the room up if you like?" I address the question between the two of them.

Straight to business. Look, I'm just here as a helper. Pay no attention to me. I've styled my hair the same way as his assistant, straightened with clipped-in bangs. I'm wearing fake glasses too. Basically, the Clark Kent version of myself.

"Let me show you to the room." Nancy leads the way. Her heels click pleasantly on the marble floors.

The house is as massive and showy as you'd expect. Lots of marble and gold. Honestly, it turns my stomach. Think of all the bare backs this house is built on. I keep my head down. We enter a small room at the back of the house. There's a dartboard on the wall, a small bar, and a poker table.

"The rest of the guys should be here soon. Make yourself at home." She tucks her hair behind her ear. "Do you need me for anything?"

I shake my head and get to unpacking the messenger bag. It's full of random stuff from the holistic shop: candles, sage, crystals, and some other standard mystical paraphernalia.

"James, would you mind giving me a hand with something?" she asks Roe.

It's a struggle not to roll my eyes. She's been eyeing him up like a tasty morsel since we walked in. When he agrees they leave, closing the door behind them. I go about setting up candles strategically. Places where they will illuminate each person but not me as I creep around the table. Naked body plus open flame equals danger. My back is to the door as I light incense; the sound of the door opening alerts me that they're back.

"The house will need to be saged as well," I say matter-of-factly. "Each room."

"And what does that entail?" Zebulund's voice freezes me.

I stand up and clear my throat like Rachel does as I push up my glasses. "Oh, Mr. Zebulund. Sorry. I thought you were Mr. Roe and your wife."

He stalks toward me. His gaze deliberate as it travels up and down my body. "And you are?" He's inches away now and I can't breathe right.

Just my body, not my being.

"Rachel. Uh, Rachel Bowen. Roe's assistant."

Zebulund shakes my hand. "We've met?" He's looking at me. My pulse leaps but I was an actress once too.

"Last week. I set up your meeting with Mr. Roe."

He studies me. I replay the conversation I watched from the closet.

"You complimented my figure," I add helpfully.

"Right. Right. Welcome." The fog clears from his eyes.

He's about to say something else when the door opens again and the other two enter. Nancy is mid-sentence but stops when she sees Zebulund and me. My mouth opens but there's nothing to say.

"Darling, you look lovely this evening." Zebulund walks to his wife, grabbing her hand and kissing her cheek.

Her study of me goes from uninterested to unfettered. She glares as though really seeing me for the first time. Then her features relax into apathy again. Roe and I exchange a glance while the couple chats. I shake my head once when his nostrils flare in question.

"Thank you for welcoming my guests." Zebulund's mouth twitches up in an ironic smile when the doorbell chimes majestically, as if on cue.

"I'll go get the rest," his wife says curtly.

"I hope you don't mind signing a Non-Disclosure Agreement." Zebulund pulls out a stack of papers from under his arms and sets them on the bar with a pen.

"Not at all," I say.

"We all value our privacy," Roe agrees.

"Indeed."

Roe and I step forward and I sign as Rachel. This may be super illegal but whatever, I'm already in the dumpster.

"You were saying something about the house?" Zebulund slides the pen back into his suit pocket, because a suit is obviously what you wear to a Saturday night séance.

"Sage the house, yes."

Here, in this room with him, I'm once again reminded how much space he takes up. How hard it is to breathe. I want to reach to Roe for comfort. That in itself is new and weird.

"What does that mean?" He waves his hand like he's impatient even having to ask.

"It sounds silly. And obviously we don't have to if you insist not. Many people sage their houses with the seasons. Helps clear out any unwanted negative energy. Sage is burned in all the rooms and the negative energy is called to leave."

"Oh, that's what Beth and Gene do." Nancy reenters the room with Craig, Viktor, and Kyle. "I've heard of it. Cleans out the house."

Thank you, Nancy! Though I can't tell if she buys into it or not. And I'm still worried I've made an enemy of her. Never underestimate the power of Hollywood wives.

"You think that'll help?" Zebulund's poker face is impassive as ever.

"I do." I hold his gaze. Lying to him is a pleasure up there with crunching leaves and peeling plastic off electronics.

"You want to walk around my house with a burning weed."

"Yes. It's best if the house is empty and all the windows are open." I push up my glasses. Confidence is crucial when you're lying through your teeth. "The negative energy, spirits, what have you, will be asked to leave."

"You want me to let you walk around my house, windows open, alone?"

"Oh no, sorry. You misunderstand me. It's best if you do it." I glance at Roe, feigning confusion. "He's the one who, uh, who has the negative energy attached?"

Roe nods.

After a brief round of introductions and hellos we move to the table. There're seven of us in all. Marty Zebulund and his wife, Roe and I, Viktor, Kyle, and Craig.

We make our way around the table.

"We're a few chairs short." Viktor points out.

"Ah, no. I'm not going to be part of this," I say. "I'll leave as soon as you're all set up."

"Why?" Viktor pales.

"To be honest, it's not my place. I'm not connected to this spirit. I don't want to get tangled with the energy."

Viktor nods but his brows are furrowed and there's a tightness in the lines around his mouth.

"I wasn't there that night either. My presence may interfere. But don't worry. I've taught Roe all I know because he's got the gift, much stronger than anybody I've ever met."

Roe narrows his eyes and stares at the table.

"We've all signed NDAs," I say to him. This is all part of our shtick. "Nobody can talk about what happens here tonight, right, Mr. Zebulund?"

It takes all my strength to call him by name and act respectful. I feel sick. Roe tentatively peers at the other men, gauging their reactions to this. They're quiet but don't seem silly or teasing. In fact, the whole room is somber. Roe and I may know this is all a hoax, but I realize nobody else is remotely at ease.

"Nothing leaves this circle," Zebulund says.

Roe and I researched what goes into a séance and he's supposed to drag it out as long as possible while I find a way to mess with Zebulund. When he's triggered, hopefully, he'll then sage the house, and when we all leave, that's when I search the office.

That's the plan at least.

"I guess that means I should go too, then? Since I wasn't there that night?" Nancy asks, her voice cool.

My heart stutters. We didn't plan for the wife to be here.

"That's a great question," I say to stall for time.

If she leaves the room with me then she'll keep tabs on me, making sneaking away near impossible. But if she stays they may insist I do too. I can leave and try to sneak back in but none of the windows are open. I'm lost in thought for what feels like hours. Are my concerns written all over my face?

"Why don't you two ladies go get acquainted?" Zebulund suggests. His tone is light and affable for a clear command.

"Of course, darling," Nancy says.

My skin crawls as she cowers to him. I feel sad for this beautiful woman. There's no way she's in a partnership where she feels loved and respected.

"You remember everything?" I ask Roe, still stalling.

"I guess so." His face is smooth but I swear he's thinking the same things.

There's a small shrug in his voice. There's no way to get out of this socially delicate situation. Where's a diversion when you need one? I have no other plan this time. I can't believe this. I'm getting sloppy. Before I started making out with hot actors, I would've never gone into this so loosey-goosey.

"We'll leave you men to it," I say. "Call if you need me."

Sloppy. That's what this is. I came in with too much confidence in my newly developed powers and without a Plan B. Stupid. Stupid. I'm mad at myself as we leave the room; I almost don't hear Nancy.

"Let's go get hammered," she says.

22

Maggie

BOY OH BOY, DID I READ NANCY ALL WRONG. WHAT I SENSED AS cool indifference was actually numbness. Maybe even spaciness. As soon as we walk away, she pulls a small silver case from her cleavage.

"Want one?" She offers me a small pill.

"No, I took some before we left," I lie.

"Xanax? Oxy?"

"No, that other one... with the z."

"Bring any?"

"Not this time."

The furniture in the sitting area is crushed velvet and gilded wood. A massive piece of art hangs on the wall above the burgundy couches, and the floors are covered in rugs that must be worth hundreds of thousands. A small drinks cart is parked in the corner. That's where Nancy heads first. She hands me one without asking.

"Your home is beautiful," I say.

"It's very nice." She looks around as though examining it for the first time; no pride of ownership at all. She sits in a tufted fabric chaise lounge chair across from me, her feet up as she leans back to scrutinize me. She's like a dame in an old film.

"What are you really doing here?"

Thankfully, I expected her seemingly random question. My features remain neutral but my heart is a runaway train. No doubt Zebulund sent her to sniff out information from "the assistant."

"Just to help set up and take down."

"Right." She takes such a long sip as she scrutinizes me and half the drink is gone by the time her glass lowers again. "Are you and Roe an item?"

"No." I laugh a little, keep it light. See we're just girlfriends, chatting about boys. Gag me.

"But he's so gorgeous."

I suck in my lips. She's asking it but I don't think she's even sure she believes it.

"I'm engaged to someone. A hockey player."

"That's nice. That's gotta be fun." She finishes her first drink and goes to make another. "Hockey players are delicious."

"I agree." It's risky but I add, "Marty has his charm." The vomit creeps up the back of my throat.

A delicate eyebrow arches. "Doesn't he though. A real Hollywood Hero..."

That phrasing. Why is it making my heart slam against my chest?

"That's a shame about Roe though." Her eyes drift to the side, like she's thinking about him. "He's very nice to look at."

"Yep." Must maintain composure. Must get out of this interrogation intact. Must get back to the men.

"I've heard Roe is a real hard-ass too." She shrugs and her eyes take longer to open. Not even two cocktails in and she's slurring and half asleep in the chair. The shift in tone is obvious. Maybe her work is done.

"He has his moments." This is taking too long. Roe is waiting.

She finishes her second drink. I haven't even sipped mine, but I bring it to my mouth when she looks at me.

"I need a drink," she says through half-lidded eyes, "but he sent all the damn staff away for this."

"Oh?"

"Trustsnoone," she slurs.

"I'll make you one. Gin and tonic?"

She flips her hand up in a gesture that conveys "whatever floats your yacht" and I jump at the chance to make her unconscious.

"Rachel, how'd you get into all this?" she asks while I'm fixing her next drink.

"My aunt was really big into it." It's almost worrisome how good I am at lying. "She's a big believer and taught me a lot. I'm mostly too busy but I like to help. When Roe mentioned it, I thought, why not?"

"I've heard Roe is tightlipped. How'd you find out about this talent of his?"

"By mistake. I walked in on him talking to someone once. He tried to play it off, but I sensed the spirit."

"You've got a gift too?"

"Not as much as him." Oh man, I wish I could record this conversation to show Roe later.

"What's his deal? Is that why he's so private?" She's watching me closely through narrowed eyes. I suspect this may have been part of what Zebulund wanted from her and she knows it. Thankfully, so do I. She's still on the clock for her husband.

"Partially, I suspect. You know he wants to be taken seriously. If this gets out, he knows nobody will believe him."

"True. I don't even believe this." She blinks at me. "No offense."

"None taken." I hold up my hands. "Not for everyone."

"You said partially." She's pretty shrewd for a drugged-up drunk.

"Well. Everyone has their demons." I play coy.

If they think they can get answers out of me so easily, they've got another thing coming. She pats the chaise lounge next to her, dropping her feet as I deliver her drink.

"Sit here."

I obey.

"It's just us girls. You can tell me. I'm not going to tell anybody." She takes a long sip of her drink and licks her lips.

Long pause. What can I say?

"He's got a giant cock," I deadpan.

I mean, it's not that far off the truth. Even if it wasn't the juicy gossip she was hoping for. She coughs on her drink and leans forward.

"What?"

"You can't tell anybody." I hide my face in my hands. "I can't believe I told you." When I peek at her through my fingers she's still blinking. "Yeah," I say, dead serious. "It's actually a problem. For like wardrobe and his girlfriends. He gets horny too fast and he can pass out. You think oh sure, giant cock, great. In theory. But in practice..." I punch my fist against my palm. "Not so much."

"No way." She's leaning forward so much she almost falls. "You've seen it?"

"One time," I lean conspiratorially closer, "during an outfit change at a photo shoot."

"And?" Her eyes are wide; they watch my mouth as I speak.

I glance around for effect and lean closer. "Are you familiar with butternut squash?"

"Shut up."

"It's not as glamorous as it sounds." I shrug. "He's very self-conscious about it."

"Damn."

"But this is between us girls. If he... I mean... I'd get fired in a heartbeat."

She waves away my concerns and lies back in the seat. Her legs shift, rubbing against each other.

"Here." I pour her another drink.

"It's not fair." She takes it and throws it back in two gulps. "Those good looks and being hung like a horse."

"I know. It's a curse for him but I think he makes up for it in other ways."

"Oh?" Her cheeks are flushed.

"Yeah. I've heard the girls he brings around the sets. To his trailers. They're loud and grateful."

"Oh lord." A flush creeps up her neck and she fans her face.

"I think because he knows he can't, you know, fuck them." Her gaze never leaves my mouth as I enunciate clearly. "He uses other skills to get them off."

"Wow." She fans herself ferociously. "That's got to be hard for him."

"Oh, I'm sure it's very hard." I'm shameless. She can't sit still. "Are you okay? Do you need another drink?"

"Just hot." Her eyes focus far away. She seems to notice me and sits up a little. "I'm a little tired. I think I'll call it a night." She stumbles as she gets up.

"Let me help you to your room."

"No. No, I'm okay." She straightens, trying and failing to compose herself. "I just need some sleep."

She climbs the stairs messily and I sit still with my drink, casually watching her leave. My limbs are tingling with adrenaline. On the inside I'm panicking. Hurry, hurry. It's already been a half hour at least. I need to get to the guys and quick.

———

Roe

MAGGIE HAS A PLAN. SHE ALWAYS HAS A BACKUP PLAN. I REMIND myself of this as Zebulund and the others sit staring at me, waiting for ghosts to show up like fashionably late party guests. I got nothing. I wipe my sweaty palms on my jeans and keep myself confident and casual.

"Let's start simple," I say. "Keep in mind, I've never actively sought a spirit out. Typically, they just show up."

Everyone gathers around the table. It's like the poker game with less smoke and booze. The atmosphere is heavy. Whether or not the other guys buy what's happening, they certainly aren't excited about it. I can't say that I blame them.

"My assistant already got all the candles and stuff ready. I guess, maybe we should start with this." I gesture to the board in front of us.

I've never seen a Ouija board in person, only in the movies. Numbers and letters in a freaky font. Options for Yes and No and a Good Bye at the bottom. This one has drawings of the night sky and sun and moon around the edges.

"You gotta be kidding me," Viktor says. He's lounging back, trying to look cool but fidgeting with a Zippo lighter. He smelled of booze when he walked in and has since downed a whole drink.

Zebulund shoots him a warning look. Zebulund's smile is terrifying. Like a shark grinning at you.

"I'm just saying." Viktor pops each knuckle on both hands as he talks. "What if this is a terrible idea? She wasn't exactly being nice to us last time. What if we piss her off?"

"That's not our intention here. We just want answers and then Marty can ask her to leave," I make up on the fly.

Because Maggie is pissed. I've never met anybody so set on a purpose. She's like the main character in a superhero movie.

"We don't know what we're messing with here," Viktor says.

"I felt something last weekend. Something that was angry; and this is a really fucked-up idea in my opinion. Not that anybody asked."

Kyle and Craig are suspiciously quiet. Maybe they aren't sure what they saw last weekend, or maybe they're waiting to form an opinion based on how the night goes. Whatever the case may be, the air is heavy. Craig twirls the toothpick around his mouth slowly and watches the exchange, as we all do.

Maggie's still nowhere to not be seen and I have no clue how long I'll have to wing it.

"Okay, well, to Viktor's point, why don't I try calling out to her before we use the board?"

This seems to please Viktor, and Zebulund agrees.

"Like I said, I've never done this before—"

"Just do your best," Zebulund cuts in.

"I read it's best to keep relaxed. It probably wouldn't hurt if we're all a little more open to things."

Zebulund gives the okay. The other three sit stony. I swear to God, the tension is so thick I could swim in here.

Okay, here we go. I close my eyes and start speaking.

"If there's a spirit nearby that wishes to communicate with Marty Zebulund, we ask that you make yourself known."

I repeat it two more times. No Maggie. But I am freaking myself out a little.

When I open my eyes Zebulund is watching me closely.

"I'm sorry, I don't see her," I say, scanning the room.

This doesn't seem like news to him either. He taps his fingers in a slow pattern along the tabletop and remains quiet. This idea feels stupider by the second. I hate that I'm here and Maggie is stuck bonding with his wife. His wife. That poor woman. Or maybe she prefers this life. Money is a powerful aphrodisiac. A familiar mix of rage and disgust works up from my gut.

I clear my throat and keep myself calm on the outside as

much possible. Okay, acting. Acting like this isn't a stupid waste of time. Acting like Zebulund isn't seconds away from calling this whole night quits. I surreptitiously glance at the door every chance I get. I try a different tactic and suggest we all hold hands.

"No, come on. No," Viktor snaps, immediately tucking his hands almost completely in his armpits.

Zebulund holds out both hands and the rest have no choice but to follow. Viktor's hand is clammy and cold. Kyle reluctantly follows suit. I have no plan and feel very fucking stupid.

I repeat the invitation a few more times, mixing it up. Each time I mentally scream for Maggie to hurry up. Each time I open my eyes to nothing. Each time disappointment worries me.

"I'm sorry. It doesn't seem to be working," I say as we all drop our hands.

Zebulund leans back and lights a cigar from a little contraption hidden in the table. I didn't even know it was there until he tapped and twirled the wood surface in a specific pattern.

"That's cool." I point to where he pulls out a cigar cutter.

"Thanks."

"Oh yeah, Marty loves that stuff," Viktor slurs. "He's got them all over the place. Secret doors and shit."

Zebulund puffs out a massive plume with a bunch of rapid puffs. He points the smoke right into Viktor's face, which causes the blond to double over in a coughing fit. The door to our room is still closed. It hits me belatedly, that'll cause an issue for Maggie.

I shoot up out of my chair. Craig jumps.

"We aren't sitting in the same order." I gesture to the other men, not Zebulund. "You stay there, Marty. There, now we're in the same order."

"Was the door open or closed?" I make a show of looking around.

"Does it matter? She's a fucking ghost," Craig says. "She can just go through it."

Fuck.

"Fair point," I say.

It's dark enough, let's hope I can draw attention away if needed. Zebulund is facing toward the door. The power seat. I blow out a few candles around the outer edge of the table and decide to figure it out as I go. I'm on my own for this.

"I've got nothing else. Let's try the board." I sit back down.

The men all shift in their chairs and mumble different version of okay.

"Place two fingers of your right hand on the planchette."

"What the fuck is a planchette?" Craig asks.

"It's the heart-shaped piece of wood," Kyle says.

I raise an eyebrow at him.

"I assumed from context." He points to the board

Before this morning I didn't know what it was called, but Maggie and I did a cram session on all things dark arts.

"Do you want to ask the questions?" I ask Zebulund.

"Better you do it. You're the one who sees dead people." His tone is flat and his patience is worn very thin.

"Okay." I clear my throat and put my pointer and middle finger on the planchette. It moves easier than I thought it would. The others each add their fingers and it wiggles with each addition. It's obvious why these are so creepy. It's as if they have a life of their own. "If anybody is here and would like to be heard, now's your chance."

The game piece hovers in the middle of the board, jostling slightly. Honestly, at this point in the game, I'd probably have a heart attack if it started moving. All jokes aside, this shit is getting heavy.

Nothing happens, though.

"Please speak," I ask again. "We're here to listen. Don't be afraid."

The piece jerks under my hand. I gasp. It was a very manly gasp, of course. The others are wide-eyed as it jumps from the letter "D" to the letter "I" and then to "E."

It stops.

"What the actual fuck?" Kyle says.

The toothpick falls out of Craig's mouth.

Zebulund has a sheen of sweat on his forehead.

Then Viktor, the bastard, starts laughing. Like a fourteen-year-old that just farted.

"The look... on all your faces." He slaps the table and the board jumps. "You're such little girls."

None of us laugh. Not even a little. We gawk from one another back to Zebulund. I don't know Zebulund very well but from the way his hands clench the side of the table, I'm genuinely afraid for Viktor.

"Listen, it's not too late—"

But Kyle's eyes are wide and horrified. The muscles in his neck are straining from holding himself so rigid. I follow his gaze to the Ouija board, where the small piece of wood moves around the alphabet. By itself.

"What the f—"

23

Maggie

I'M LATE, I'M LATE FOR A VERY IMPORTANT DATE! I JOG DOWN THE hall toward the room where the séance is happening without me. I didn't mean to be gone so long. Thankfully, in the grand scheme of things, Nancy got drunk crazy fast. Let's hope Roe has been able to keep the situation contained. And doesn't murder me for being so late.

I race to the bathroom off the main room and strip out of my clothes. I'm about to run next door when I'm struck with an idea.

See, there's something else I haven't told Roe yet. Last night when he left for his shower I came out of the water and went Under. I was holding a towel and that went invisible too. It only lasted about five minutes, but it made me realize something amazing: when I'm fully saturated I can make things invisible. Which means he won't be able to see me either.

Insert evil laugh here.

I turn on the tub and lie down. The water fills around me. I go Under and feel my body absorbing the moisture. I'm a sponge. Even if I can't do anything more than freak out Roe, this will be worth the wait. Once the tub is full, I completely submerge myself. I go invisible even to my own eyes. No hazy outline, nothing. I watch myself disappear.

I lie there for a minute longer and when I look around me, the tub is half full. Apparently, I'm an optimist. I know I've left Roe way too long, so I hurry out. The extra droplets soak into my skin. They evaporate into nothing.

"Incredible," I whisper.

I make sure my hair isn't dripping too much, though I do feel it running down my back a little. I imagine it's being absorbed too. With a glance over my shoulder, I tiptoe out of the bathroom to make sure I'm not leaving a trail, but it's clear my body has absorbed any extra moisture. How long does this mean I can stay Under? Just when things are looking up, another obstacle. The door to the room is closed.

Shit.

At that moment a cackle of obnoxious laughter meets my ears. I use that as my opportunity to open the door and slip in. The breath I've been holding whooshes out when I see the room is barely lit and nobody registers my arrival. They're too busy glaring at the laughing Viktor. The men are all crowded around the table, jaws hanging open. Except Roe, who has angry eyebrows, and Zebulund looks like he's about to whip out a .45 to cap Viktor.

I creep past Roe but he doesn't see me. I wave a hand right in front of him. His gaze flicks to each person around him but never on me. Ha! This is too amazing.

There's a gap between Viktor, who's still leaning back laughing, and the lawyer guy, Craig, who's leaning to the other side, covering his mouth. I slip between them and grab the planchette.

The piece dances around but nobody notices because they're all so focused elsewhere. Roe starts to speak, always the peacekeeper. I blow softly on Craig's face. He pulls back and his eyes drift down. I can pinpoint the second he sees my actions because his entire body stiffens and the color leaves his face.

"What the fuck?" Roe stares at the board.

A second later all the men fixate on the board with similar masks of horror and confusion. I scramble the piece around a little and bring it to the bottom. Maybe they'll understand that I'm trying to say something.

"Don't touch it," Roe says. "She's here."

"Like I'd fucking touch that," Craig whispers.

"Jesus." Kyle runs a hand over his goatee.

Viktor looks like he's seconds from throwing up. None of them move toward me.

The planchette slides to the first letter. "Y." I have to sort of flick the piece jerkily, to avoid it disappearing with me. I can't control that yet.

"Y," Roe says. Then, "O," "U," "R" and "E."

I still for a moment.

"You're," Viktor croaks unnecessarily. He's far from laughter now.

I glance up at Zebulund. He's stock still as sweat drips down the back of his buzzed hair into the soaked collar of his dress shirt.

"N," Roe continues to translate as I move the piece. "E, X, T."

I freeze again.

"You're next," Kyle says.

"Who?" Viktor asks.

Roe's focused on me now. I give him a questioning look. Am I visible to him now?

"I can see her." He points to where I'm standing.

So, that's a yes.

All heads whip toward me but none of them see me, so their gazes go back to the table. So what was that? Maybe five minutes of being totally invisible, even to Roe. I rest my hand fully on the game piece but it doesn't go Under with me. Any of the clear feeling the tub gave me is already starting to wear off.

Now, here we're to the part I've been looking forward to ever since we hatched this insane plan. I take the piece and ever so slowly turn it so the pointed end faces Zebulund. I drag it jerkily off the board and toward him. Every centimeter it moves, his shoulders tense a little closer to his ears. The sound it makes in the silence is deafening.

By the time the piece comes to a stop in front of him, he's visibly shaking. And just because I'm still so pissed off...

The board flies right at his stupid face.

———

Roe

IT'S MINUTES BEFORE ANY OF US SPEAK.

"She's gone," I finally say.

Again this doesn't seem to surprise Zebulund. He's been staring at the pieces where they fell. Maggie ran out of the room. I'm still not sure how she was able to be invisible to me for as long as she was. But I can't think about that right now. I need to figure this out. Make sure he does what he needs us to do.

"I think it's imperative that you sage the house right now. We'll all leave." Maybe that'll do it.

Zebulund's gaze finds me. It's the most emotion I've seen, other than good-natured teasing.

"You need to do it while she's close by," I press. "I'll tell you exactly what to do. Then I'll come back when you're done."

Zebulund looks at the others.

"They should leave too. You need to clear the house as much as possible."

Kyle and Craig gape at Zebulund for instruction but Viktor is already shrugging into his jacket.

"I can't wait to get the fuck out of here." At the door he turns and looks at Zebulund. "I don't want any part of this. I'm done."

Zebulund blinks once. "I'm sorry to hear that."

Viktor's courage seems to falter for a moment, but then his gaze drifts to the planchette on the floor. It resolves him. He lifts his chin and leaves the room.

"I didn't know it would be like that," I try to explain, but Zebulund holds up a hand.

"Gentlemen." His friendly smile is back as he addresses Craig and Kyle. "I'll see you Monday."

They look at each other and then leave, having been dismissed. Dread clings to my neck. I have no idea what Zebulund is thinking but it doesn't feel good to be alone with him. Once the room is empty, he faces me squarely.

"Tell me what I need to do to solve this problem."

———

Maggie

ONCE AGAIN, TIME IS NOT ON MY SIDE. ROE CONVINCES ZEBULUND to take his time and sage every room. Which means literally burning sage in each room and telling the evil spirits to leave. Thankfully, that means I should have several minutes at least of quality searching time in his office. I'm standing in the doorway, still Under, as I listen to Roe explain the details.

"I'll go drive around with Rachel to kill time. She's waiting for me in the car. Text me when you're done, and I'll head back."

Zebulund doesn't respond. As Roe leaves he subtly motions me to follow. When we're almost to the front door, he stops to tie his shoe.

"Go as fast as possible," he whispers. "Look for a secret compartment in his desk. He supposedly has them all over."

Our gazes clash and hold. We're both thinking the same things, sharing the same fears. But we're so damn close. I nod. I so fucking got this.

He's gone out the front door.

Zebulund appears in the hallway, the lit sage in his hand. He lets out a low sigh then makes his way up the marble staircase to the second floor. He walks as though he has no worries in the world, whistling as he waves the burning plant.

Even if Zebulund rushes, this house is still huge. The water is wearing off, so rehydration is crucial before I start. I go back to the downstairs guest bathroom I used and sit in the half-full tub, dipping my arms and upper body in as much as I can. I dribble on the tap to avoid making noise and drink until I feel revived.

His office door isn't locked. There's a large leather couch and a heavy bookshelf to the left. A wall of movies and a large flat screen TV take up another wall. His desk is simple and uncluttered. If there's a hidden compartment I can't see it after a few minutes of looking. I mean I guess that's the point, but I also don't see any unaccounted-for space either.

This is not going to be as easy as I hoped.

I try and fail several times to get into his computer. Every second that ticks by I grow more frustrated. What was I thinking? That his computer would just be sitting here like Pandora's box? This was such a stupid plan.

I'm so frustrated in my search that I don't even know Zebulund has entered the room until he speaks.

"You aren't welcome here."

I shoot up. Zebulund's standing in the doorway. His eyes move around the room. That's the second time tonight I allowed him to surprise me. I'm getting too distracted.

"I want you out of here. Leave me alone."

I rest my palm against my racing heart as he continues to talk and sage the room. He's talking to the ghost, not me. Relief floods me so fast I collapse back and have to steady myself. Instead of fainting I hurry to a far corner out of the way. He wanders around as the heavy spicy scent fills the air. It burns my nostrils. I take small breaths in through my teeth to combat the headiness.

He makes his way to his desk and opens a compartment that there is no way I would have ever found. A lid pops open after several complicated movements and then there's another step just to retrieve something. Even having seen him do it I'm not sure that I can duplicate it. Oh, his phone. Damn, that would have been nice to get.

His thumbs move around the screen with little clicks. The familiar whoosh of a message-sent follows. He sighs and slides the phone in his pocket and then puts the compartment back into the desk.

His attention is snagged by his computer monitor. My face scrunches up with frustration. Sloppy. I'm being sloppy—it's still lit up. He looks around. I hold perfectly still. He sets the sage on the side of his desk, the burning side hanging off the edge, and then goes to the computer and types before I can get over there. He's too fast anyway; I doubt I would've been able to catch his password.

As I watch over his shoulder, he clicks into files and enters more passwords to get into folders. Each one of the guys in the inner circle has his own folder, as well as a few other names I recognize. I can't catch much; screen grabs of bank accounts, complicated-looking spreadsheets, pictures; but he pauses on nothing long enough to get anything useful. It's like he's just checking to make sure everything's still there.

Damn this amateur plan. A few names, that's all I get.

He leans back and checks his email, sage apparently forgotten. The effects of being Under are catching up. I'll need to leave soon. After knowing how good it is to be Under while wet, everything else feels like sitting under a hair dryer.

After a few minutes he scans the room and gets up. He picks up the sage from the edge of the desk and starts swinging it around. I'm not sure what he's doing but it doesn't seem good. I press myself as flat as possible against a wall and follow him, keeping myself out of his vicinity, but manage to get myself stuck between his desk and the corner of the bookshelf.

He walks toward me, his hand out in front of him. My heart races. I bump into the curtains and they billow out at my mistake. His attention immediately shoots toward me. I have no choice but to stay where I am. He sets the sage back down on the desk, allowing him to have both hands out grasping at the air in front of him.

He hasn't come at me like this since the time I don't think about. It's different than messing with him with Roe and the others nearby. I need to move. Standing there with a heart that won't settle is doing me nothing. He may not be able to see me, but he'll sure as hell touch me in just a few more inches.

I'm rigid in place—reverted back to my younger self. The girl that's intimidated in his presence. Even in my most angry moments, he always fills up too much space physically and emotionally. He takes and takes and I'm nothing but another source for him.

My heart's racing. A combination of fear pulsating under my skin, and rage at my own inability to move, makes the room spin. Only two more steps and I'm caught. There's no going back. I let loose a sob but he can't hear it. He doesn't even flinch. How can he not hear the way my heart slams against my chest?

I close my eyes at my weakness. I can't look at him. I can't fight him. He's got me and he doesn't even know.

Just my body, not my being. Just my body, not my being.

My whole body shakes. He steps forward and his hands miss me as they spread out but catch me on the way back in. A combination of things happen at once.

The sensation of his hand on my naked body snaps me into action. My eyes shoot open. I place two hands on his chest and shove with all my might.

Right before he screams, his eyes widen to comic proportions. It's not a manly yell, it's the gasp of a frightened child. He stumbles back as there's a knock at the door. When he falls back against the desk the burning sage is knocked into a wastebasket filled with paper and used tissues.

The banging grows louder. A small wisp of smoke rises from the trash can. He's green and sweating with his hand grasping his chest.

"C-Come in... Hurry!"

Roe bursts into the room.

"What's going on?" His gaze bounces from the terrified man to the trash, which is now totally lit up and smoking like crazy, and me shuddering and naked in the corner. I shake my head. I know I must look horrified. Roe's fear is blatant in his features.

Zebulund falls into the couch. He doesn't answer Roe's question. He runs his hands through his hair and stares at the window where I had just been standing.

I'm still Under but I won't be able to hold on much longer. The adrenaline and fear are doing something to me. The room is smoky and burning my eyes. I'm thirstier and dizzier than I've ever felt. I feel like I can't hold on to the power.

Roe stares helplessly at me. I point to the rapidly growing

fire. It's sucking moisture from the room. I'm weakening at an even faster rate than usual. I can't hold on.

He runs out of the room and reappears a moment later with a fire extinguisher, just as I collapse to the floor. His eyebrows are all screwed up and his nostrils flare. He's fighting himself to come help me. Zebulund mumbles with his head in his hands. Roe glances between the three emergencies, likely deciding which needs him first: me, fire, or Zebulund.

Every second the moisture sucks from my skin. I'm steaming away like damp wood thrown in a fire pit. Smartly, he chooses the fire, which grows larger with every second.

Roe pulls the pin from the extinguisher and points the hose toward the flames. The sound around me is muffled but a high-pitched wail reaches my ears through the clouds. I'm on the floor watching things from a new angle. Roe is frozen. His gaze scans the ceiling before coming back at me. To my intense surprise and dismay, he drops the extinguisher and hurries to Zebulund.

Okay, maybe he isn't that smart. He can't know the fire is drying me out, but he should at least understand that FIRE BAD. I don't understand his logic but I'm losing the ability to care. He's racing to help Zebulund. I know he can't leave with me. There's no way of getting me out of this room. We're screwed.

I come Up, lying totally exposed on the floor of my abuser's office. This day has not gone at all as I'd hoped. I'm too far gone to be anything but numb and I watch the scene around me as another person might. A detached movie reviewer. I feel nothing and have no fear. It's freeing.

"What do you need?" I think Roe asks. His voice is muffled and far away.

Zebulund is angry. Only a slice of him is visible through the gap under the desk. He's gesticulating toward the fire but he doesn't seem to notice me on the floor behind the desk.

Every time I blink it takes my eyes longer to open. So tired. And thirsty. I'm so far past thirsty that I need a new word for it.

I'm hallucinating. In my desperation, I imagine it's raining inside the office. Cool drops of water soak into my skin like I'm the world's driest sponge. I open my mouth and let the fake drops seep onto my sandpaper tongue and dribble over cracked lips.

I close my eyes and succumb to the fantasy.

24

Roe

MAGGIE REALLY REALLY NEEDS TO WAKE UP. I CAN ONLY KEEP Zebulund distracted for so long. The second the overhead sprinklers go off he starts yelling.

"Why the hell didn't you put out the fire?" he screams at me.

"I thought you were having a heart attack."

"Get those fucking things turned off!"

It takes several attempts, but at last he heaves himself off the couch. The pouring water and leather seats make for a slippery struggle. He launches himself to his desk, using his body to protect his computer. I point the fire extinguisher at the trash. The flames have already been doused but the explosion of chemicals and steam might buy some time. Once the smoke stops the sprinklers do too. Thankfully, Maggie's gone. Not even I can see her. The door's open so hopefully she made her way out. Zebulund swears and futilely grabs a few things on his desk and shakes them off.

"Where are towels?" I ask.

"Next door, there's a closet."

He's not swearing as much when I return. Still very angry. After we've cleaned up, he checks to make sure his computer's still working.

"Shit." He slams a fist on the desk. "It won't turn on."

"It doesn't mean it's ruined."

He's nodding but I can see his thoughts are far away.

"She hasn't left," he whispers.

I collect the soaked towels. His office is in shambles. Papers are soaked and curling. The air reeks of melting plastic.

"Did you see her? When you first came in?" he asks me.

"I did."

"The sage shit didn't work. The séance didn't work. My office is ruined. I'm at my wit's end." All his joviality is gone.

"I know. I don't understand..."

"I know you never promised anything." He waves for me to stop talking. "I hoped."

"You could always call a priest... or maybe someone in the city. It's LA, there's bound to be someone who can figure this out better than me."

Unfortunately, I know it won't stop. Not anytime soon. Not until Maggie gets what she needs. We're further from the truth than ever and in danger of losing everything. I'm cold and wet and tired and hungry and I just want out of here.

"And what would the media do if they found out about that? People rely on me. Hundreds of people have jobs because of me. If they think I'm losing it... I have to be at the top of my game at all times." He scratches the space between his eyebrows and picks the sage out of the trash. It's sopping and makes a wet thump when he drops it back in the basket. "If it weren't for the things you've said and we've all seen, I'd think that maybe I'm cracking."

My breath whooshes out. I don't pity him, exactly, but I understand the fear of feeling like you're losing touch with reality. The feeling of a couple hundred people depending on you completely for their livelihood. Admittedly, it's a lot of pressure. But pressure we both chose. Nobody is making us do these jobs.

But I do it without using people as a stepping stool.

"I need people in my life that'll tell me if I'm going insane." He's surprisingly honest and raw. I hate that I've had the same thought a hundred times since I started in this town. "I need a reality check from time to time." He slumps into his office chair. His gaze roves around the room surveying the destruction. "All this money and power, it's hard to know what's real and what's not. And then even if it's not real, does it matter if everybody in your life thinks it is?"

I don't answer. It's obvious that these questions are rhetorical. I feel like I should say something, but I've got no answers.

"I'll call people to clean this up." He lets out a long sigh. "Thanks for trying to help at least. Go home. Get some rest."

His whole demeanor is different. He looks exhausted. He looks old.

"Are you sure there isn't something else that I can do?" And for the first time, I might actually mean it when I ask.

"Nah. I'll be fine. You're a good egg, Roe. I wish there were more people like you than like Viktor." It was a surprising reference to the man. I don't say as much. "I thought he was like you, but I see now that he has some real problems." He shakes whatever he's been thinking from his head and looks at me. "But not you. I can tell you know what side of the line is right."

Sitting slumped in that chair, he looks fragile and tired. He's not the powerhouse that he normally is and I don't feel pity, I cannot allow myself to feel pity, but for the first time, I'm wondering exactly where this path is headed. I think Maggie and I started with clear intentions, but things are getting muddled and complicated. Our simple plan is involving more people and emotions than I'm prepared for. The repercussions may reach people who don't deserve it.

I need to find Maggie, to talk to her. Maybe we should back off a little while until I figure out something. The noose around my neck gets tighter every day since I met Zebulund, but for the first time, I understand that's also the day I met Maggie.

————

MAGGIE'S SLUMPED IN THE PASSENGER SEAT OF MY CAR AGAINST the window. Her hair's damp and she's shivering in a sundress. I get my jacket from the back seat and wrap it around her shoulders. She pulls it closer but doesn't say anything.

I'm not sure where we stand with each other. There are a thousand things I want to say but I know well enough that this isn't the time.

We don't speak for a while. I drive out of the long driveway, the tires thumping over the expensive tiles that make up the path. The gate slowly opens for us. It's after ten as I maneuver the winding hill roads. The headlights reveal what's coming as we reach it; the rest is emptiness. Only when we're safely on the 101 do I speak.

"I think we need to lay off Zebulund for a while."

I can't see Maggie well, but her gaze on me is tangible.

"Oh yeah? Why's that?" Her voice is steady and bland. I don't trust it.

I have to be careful how I approach this. Lest I wake the beast. The steering wheel squeaks under my grip.

"He's unraveling. He won't give up any information if he feels like things are spinning out of control. He's only going to take measures to hold on tighter." We round a bend and I slow way down to focus.

"He's shaken, Maggie. He looks broken. Look, I don't like the guy, but I'm not sure that I'm comfortable destroying a man."

As soon as I say it I'm aware of how unconscionably selfish

it sounds. To my surprise, Maggie doesn't lash out or go off. Instead, she's quiet.

"You're right," she says at last. "You've done more than enough to help me."

I glance at her and she's looking at me. We pass under a street lamp and I can see her features are serious, no hint of sarcasm. There's another long pause.

"I've asked too much of you," she says. "This... this isn't your battle." Her voice cracks and something crumples in my chest.

"It doesn't have to be your battle either. You can let go. Trust that scum will get his. It's not our job to dole out punishment for people."

She nods, her lip is pulled in and she's chewing on it. I don't understand what's changed. We're both changed after this night and I don't fully get why.

"I'm not going to ask you for anything else." She doesn't say it in that catty passive-aggressive way. She genuinely means it.

I pull into my driveway and put the car in park. Without thinking, I took her to my house, but she may not want to stay here. Probably not. I leave the car running. The garage flood-lights illuminate us as we study each other. Her acceptance is too easy.

"But you aren't going to stop, are you?"

"No." She doesn't drop her gaze from mine.

My blood is boiling again. My hands tremble. I want to shake her if only to get some sort of reaction.

"Maggie." I let out a sad breath. "What's that expression? Anger is holding onto hot coals and expecting someone else to get burned. You have to let go of it."

"You don't know..." Something flames behind her eyes. "You can't ask me..."

"I know he did something awful—"

"Please, just stop. I know I've made a mistake in mixing you up in my plans. I'll help you with your stuff still, like I've promised, but you're done helping me. I won't ask you to do anything that goes against your personal code of ethics anymore. I understand. I really do."

I can see it. I can see the wall forming around her. Every word like a block of ice covering her, taking her back from me.

"Zebulund may have you fooled, but I won't stop."

I let out a sigh and drop my head back. She thinks I've been duped. The conversation is over but neither of us want to leave the car yet. It's like we understand that the second we do our connection is severed. I'm not ready, despite my frustration. I want to clutch her to me. I want to keep her safe. Safe from herself. I want to heal her.

"Did I ever tell you about my first real job?" she asks.

I'm shocked by the rapid subject change but shake my head, thankful for a few more minutes with her. She clears her throat. She's facing forward, no longer looking at me.

"I was interning in college for the theater department. It was a coveted position. The director was this big deal Hollywood guy that wanted to really work on the craft that he missed. His words." She picks at her thumbnail. "He was the cool artsy teacher that all the girls crushed on. Cultured, handsome without being oppressive." She glances at me and I get the impression I was just insulted. "I was different from the other girls. I know everybody says that, but I was genuinely fascinated by theater and acting and the way people could be whoever they wanted. It was magic to me. He took me under his wing. He was my boss and mentor and we hit it off from the beginning. I got his weird humor and he got mine and it made me feel mature to make this sophisticated man laugh at all my silly jokes.

"One day after work, we went out drinking. The play had just done its last show, finals were over. I was light as air. I wasn't even old enough to legally drink but he took me to all these bars where they didn't care. They knew who he was and

I was somebody because I was with him. His wife was going to meet up later and so I never thought anything of it. I was just so thrilled because all these people talked to me like I was in the industry. We talked shop and it was just so cool." She notices she's destroying her nail bed and fists her thumbs, dropping her hands to her lap. "I did shot after shot of tequila."

My fists clench; I hate where this story is going. My stomach's in knots and I don't want her to go on.

She pries my hands off the steering wheel and squeezes my fingers. "This isn't bad. This is just something I've been thinking about. Like maybe where things shifted for me."

"Sorry." I uncurl my hand and the blood flows back into my fingertips. I'm making it about me.

"Eventually, we're back at his place. I was obviously way drunk but so was he. Like really drunk. And I thought 'this is so cool' people will never believe I was with him partying like this. That I got to see him like this. We had deep conversations. I can't tell you how important this was to me. Like, it meant that I was special.

"We were leaning against the counter talking, and he asked me to kiss him. Just like that. Like it wasn't a huge deal. Like he wasn't my mentor and friend. Like he wasn't married and I wasn't his student. I told him no. And sort of laughed it off. He was drunk, I told myself. He wasn't thinking. But he kept on. He kept saying, 'Come on. Just a little kiss on the lips. Aren't you curious?' And even then I thought, 'Well, jeez he wants to kiss me, that must mean I'm special.' But it didn't feel good. I knew it wouldn't stop with a kiss. I was confused.

"A little part of me thought, maybe I should do it to keep him happy with me. I didn't want him to think I didn't appreciate all he did for me. Maybe it was some sort of test. But I kept telling him 'No' and eventually his wife came home and I left. That was it. Didn't force himself on me. Things were different after that. He never said anything but soon he found a new protégé. I was replaced. He stopped talking to me."

She glances quickly at me but can't hold my burning gaze.

"The worst part was the regret. I kept thinking, maybe I should have let him kiss me. Maybe I did owe it to him. He only wanted to kiss me. Nothing more. I couldn't even talk to anybody about it because it felt so small compared to other stories. I was ashamed that it affected me so much when maybe some women would have loved it. But I was changed."

Maggie's quiet. My skin is hot with rage. Muscles twitch outside my control. I want to murder this guy. It wouldn't be hard to find out who he is and bash his kneecaps in. I sit, hardly moving, hands clenched between my knees for fear I'll reach out and break something.

"It's hard to understand your value when you think you're one thing but people treat you as something entirely different," she goes on. "Something like an object. I've always heard the comments. My whole life. I was eleven the first time I got cat-called. I remember it distinctly. I was playing hopscotch with my friend and a car drove by. I looked down at my tank top and shorts and realized my body had changed." She laughs without humor.

"Some random family member at a reunion picnic who saw me eating a Popsicle told me I was going to be popular one day. I was fourteen. My teachers told me to cover up or I'd cause trouble. I'd always known that my body was my responsibility and anything that happened because of it was my fault. But even after all that I still thought I had something else to offer. After what happened with my mentor, I knew better. I should've known. I should've known that if I put myself out there, drank and laughed and wore clothes without worrying, then I'd be teasing men. I thought he was different. That he didn't see me that way. And to be clearly thought of as a sexual object changed my value to myself for the first time. I thought that even the people who say they expect more of me are just..."

"Just what?" I study her face.

"It's hard to know what's real and what's not." She shrugs. Her words are raw and mirror my own thoughts. Zebulund's words. But this time it's a revelation. "I guess by the time I met Marty Zebulund, I was already jaded."

Whatever she shares next might shred me to pieces.

25

Maggie

I TRAIL OFF. THIS IS SOMETHING I NEVER TALK ABOUT. IT'S NOT
even something I think about. Roe has to understand, really
understand, that this is so much more than revenge. That this is
about every incident in my whole life, in every girl's life. Every
girl who feels unsafe. Every person who feels unsafe. This
whole culture.

"By the time the thing happened with Zebulund... I was
already jaded. I sort of went into it understanding how the
world works. Zebulund spotted me in a casting call. I made a
joke in the audition and he laughed and I knew I was on his
radar. He wanted to talk to me. I knew he was a huge deal. He's
one of the first names you hear in this city."

Roe nods his agreement and I keep talking. I've already
shared my whole life story at this point, I might as well go big.

"I was called up to his hotel room. He was in a robe when
he answered the door. One voice told me that I needed to leave
and go back downstairs. The other voice warned me not to
blow this opportunity. Other girls would kill to be here. I

thought I was worldly and womanly. I thought I knew so much. I would play him. Give enough without crowding any of my own ethical lines. I quickly learned I had no control over the situation. Not ever. I was an idiot to put myself in that position. I get that now. But I thought maybe I was different. Maybe he thought I was really talented. That I wouldn't be like all other girls. But I was just like them. Even after that incident with my mentor, I held out this hope. Isn't that crazy?" I wipe away a tear with a bitter laugh. Apparently, I'm crying.

"You don't have to—" Roe's eyes shut for a long moment before he opens them again. "If this is too hard."

"I have to tell someone. I can't live like this anymore. I feel like it's just sitting in my body like a cancer and eating me from the inside out."

He takes a deep breath. "I know it sounds trite. But you're so brave right now."

I smile falteringly and go on. He thinks I'm brave now. But he needs to know the truth about me. I'm a coward. And worse.

"By the time he got to making his advances, I wasn't even surprised. Mostly I was numb. I thought of the career I would have. Told myself that I owed him this. That this was my duty. I closed my eyes as he rubbed my shoulders and said I was beautiful."

I stop talking. My stomach churns bile up my tight throat. All those nights afterward when I could still feel his hands rubbing my shoulders, his fingertips on my breast. My shame at selling out. My shame and regret for not knowing if I should stay or go. Even then, even when we had crossed all my own personal lines, I didn't know how to leave. I swallow and gather the courage in me, fisting my hands into my sides to quell the pain.

"He went to take my shirt off and I knew I couldn't go any further. I couldn't do it. I couldn't start my career this way. Even if that's what I was told to do. Even if that's how the system worked. I wanted to leave at that moment. But he was already... into it. His robe was open. I had my eyes squeezed shut but he... he wanted me to touch him."

Roe sits with the back of his hand over his mouth. His eyes shine and his eyebrows contort in disgust. This is when he changes his opinion of me. This is when he sees me as a whore. A drama queen. Or worse, a liar. But I have to get it out. He has to know the truth about me. I push my fists harder into my sides, hating that I'm sniffling.

"I told him 'no,' that I didn't want to touch him. I told him I had to go. He said we'd just started, that I was a good girl, that he really liked me. He just wanted to help me. That I wasn't like all these other girls. That I had talent and humor and a willingness to work for it that would get me far in this business." I wipe a tear from my cheek. "It was everything I had been dying to hear. I fell for every line. Even still, when I'm super low, I hold on to those kernels, praying he meant it. Even when he rubbed himself against me. Even later I would doubt how it all happened, thinking maybe I was being dramatic. But no. In that moment, I was terrified and wanted to leave. I told him no, but he said I was already committed. He sort of pulled himself out and rubbed himself against my thigh. I couldn't... I didn't stop him. I didn't know what to do. I didn't move. I let him. I know I shouldn't have. He ended up coming on me. Telling me that I was a good little girl and he knew that I liked it."

All the horror of that moment sits on my chest. I feel him still. I hear the grunts as he humped me. I smell his sweat and cum. And see myself sitting there taking it. My arms are wrapped so tight around my middle that I feel like getting sick to release the pressure.

"He told me to go take a shower. I locked myself in the bathroom, and after I threw up and shook and cried. He knocked on the door but walked in anyway. He had a key. The lock was pointless. I should've known he'd be coming back for more. To really seal the deal.

"He looked around for me. Called me. He was in total shock. That's when I realized I was invisible. I went Under for the first time. I didn't even know I'd done it. I thought maybe part of me died. I actually sort of hoped for it in that moment. I know, melodramatic, but I did. I was standing right next to him but he didn't see me. I just ran for it. Naked. I grabbed my coat and purse and ran for it. I don't know what he thought happened." I let loose a shuddering breath.

"I never went to the police. He hadn't raped me after all. People would think I was making something out of nothing. It wasn't nearly so bad as what some women go through. What century was I from that a little dry hump destroyed me? I could never come forward about something like that. After that, I was thoroughly disenchanted with this town. I wouldn't leave the bungalow. I was depressed. It was only when someone on TV made a joke about him and his hotel room that I started think-ing. I decided that the cycle had to stop, and it would be me to stop it. I would take him down because I was done anyway. There was no me anymore. I was erased. I became Miss Mayday that day and never looked back."

A deep breath allows me to steady myself and keep my gaze from Roe. I'm afraid to see what he thinks of me now. How he will see who I am.

"I know that it was idiotic of me to go into that room. I just... You hear the stories. But you think you'll be different."

"You have to stop talking." His voice is carefully controlled.

I suck in my lips. My heart is breaking in my chest. I study my hands as a fat tear drops into them.

"Fuck—fuck! I want to murder them." Roe rages.

I look up in shock at the outburst. I've never seen him like this. His eyes are wild and glossy.

"I want to rip their hearts out, Maggie. And you..."

"I know." I squeeze my eyes shut.

"No!" He gets out of the car and slams the door so hard it scares a sob out of me.

He's leaving me. He's done with me. I'm a coward. A child with a pathetic story. Now he knows the truth. He growls something unintelligible outside the car and kicks up a clump of rocks as he walks around in front of the headlights. The door whips open. He drops to a crouch beside me and reaches for my hands, but doesn't touch me.

"Can I have your hands?"

I turn so that my knees are out of the door a little and my upper body faces him. I lay my hands in his. His skin is on fire. He shakes me gently to get me to look at him.

"Maggie, fuck no. You don't know. You're saying you do but you don't. These so-called men, these fucking cowards, were in positions of power over you. They used it and manipulated—" He's red and his eyebrows are contorted with sadness. "They made you feel like you were wrong."

"But it wasn't that bad—"

"Fuck that!" Roe roars.

"I should have left. I should have never gone—" I'm crying and can't go on.

"Maggie this is not your fault." He shakes his head. "This is in no way your fault."

My throat is closed.

"These men abused you. They abused their position of power. And if it made you feel awful you are allowed to feel awful. People can't tell you how bad your abuse was. They didn't live it."

"I wasn't raped. It could have been much worse."

"Fuck." He runs his hands down his face. "I can't believe we live in a world where 'at least I wasn't raped' is a defense. You were sexually assaulted. This is not your fault in any way. Your mentor should have treated you with respect. Zebulund—I can't even think about him and not feel sick. I'm going to go to jail for murdering him."

I squeeze our linked hands and lower my head onto them. I'll apologize for all the snot later.

"What? Talk to me. What's wrong?" His voice is strangled.

"You believe me?" I ask.

"Of course, I fucking believe you." His gaze roams my face but still burns with anger.

"And you don't think I'm a whore? You don't think I put myself in the situation and it's my fault? That I liked the attention? Dressed for the attention. Teased them?"

His face falls, becomes instantly blank. He stares deep into my eyes.

"No, Maggie May. I think you're a million amazing things. I don't think what happened to you, what these men did, defines you at all. They are master manipulators. You are not the sum total of their pathetic actions. They do not get to define you. Do you hear me?"

I nod; my chin quivers pathetically. I'm shocked. I had no idea how badly I needed to hear this.

"What all these men have said and done to you," he squeezes my shoulders, "your whole life, is not your fault. You didn't deserve it."

With that, I fall out of the car and crumble into Roe's arms. We kneel, dirt digging into my knees. I've never felt as light as I do in that moment.

I don't deserve what happened to me.

It isn't my fault.

He believes me.

I have value.

26

Roe

SHE GOES WILLINGLY INTO MY EMBRACE AND EVEN WRAPS HER arms around my neck. She's quieted down some. No more great heaving sobs, only occasional sniffles. I carry her into the house and lay her on the bed. She immediately curls in on herself, hands in fists, looking up at me with glassy eyes.

"I'm making you a bath. Okay?"

Her eyes are red and heavy with exhaustion, but she consents. I bring her a wad of tissue before going to fill the tub. I can't catch my breath. I've never felt this level of rage before. My emotional control is gone. Thankfully, I'm an actor. I don't want to scare Maggie. And I don't want to make her confession about me. Whatever it takes to make her comfortable with me, I'll do.

Over and over I replay every interaction I've had with Zebulund. Every stupid joke, every comment to pacify him when I should have been beating the life out of him. My hands are shaking so hard I have to tuck them under my arms. All the comments I've made to Maggie, telling her to let go of her revenge. My stomach clenches with guilt.

"I'm an idiot," I say to the room.

"No, you're not." Maggie leans against the doorframe. "It wasn't my intention to make things worse for you. I only wanted to help you understand why I'm the way I am."

She steps forward. She's disheveled but beautiful as ever. As soon as I think it, I feel ashamed. I'm having a hard time reconciling the immense feelings I have for her with my guilt. How can I even think about my wants right now? Her needs first. From here out.

But what does she need?

"I'm fine," I finally say, realizing people usually respond when spoken to. "I only wish—" I stop and shake my head. This isn't about me. "I understand now."

"Really?" She lets out a slow breath.

She steps closer.

"Because if I can stop him, if I can stop just one girl from going through—"

I shake my head to stop her. "I understand."

The small bathroom swirls with steam. Color returns to her cheeks immediately as her shoulders relax. Her gaze moves over my features, snag on my lips, and I feel it as much as if she leaned forward and licked them. I clear my throat.

"Okay, well, I'll let you get to it. I'll stay nearby. If you need anything, just—"

I can't speak anymore. No blood to brain. Her pulling up the hem of her dress. No matter how many times I see her naked it's never enough. It's worse because I just want to touch all that much more. I try to speak but my tongue is too big for my mouth. It needs moisture, it needs...

I clear my throat again and back away but bump into the granite sink. I focus on the cool surface under my hands and grip so hard that the rough edges dig into my palms. My breath comes out through puffed cheeks. There's the ceiling. Would you look at that? That's a nice light fixture. There are Maggie's hard nipples poking the fabric. There's Maggie's exposed stomach.

Shit.

Back to the ceiling. Count the inset light fixtures. One. Two. Two gorgeous, perky breasts. No. Lights.

"Roe?"

Three. Four.

"Roe?"

I stay focused looking up. "Mmm-hmm?"

"Can I have your help?"

Oh boy, I cannot do this. "I should go."

"I need you to stay."

Hearing her say "I need you" saws away at the last remaining thread holding me together. The counter digs deeper into my palms.

"I need to go," I say.

"Is this better?"

I look down and she's gone. Like totally gone. I let out a breath.

"Yes. Better." Her dress is on the floor.

The bath is a large marble infinity tub that overflows before filtering and recycling the water. It's more efficient than any other on the market. Super green. Right now I've never been so jealous of a fucking tub.

The water laps over the side and though I can't see her, she's right there. I don't see even a hint of her. The water doesn't even seem to get displaced except a little at first.

She is the water.

"Incredible." I'm momentarily distracted by her powers.

She comes Up and says, "Thank you."

Her skin glows and she's grinning. A fat drop of water balances on her lip.

"Maggie," I say her name like a curse and look away again.

"I'm sorry." I can tell from her light tone that she's anything but sorry. "I can't talk to you while I'm Under."

That's right, she had said she needed something. I can do that. I can do whatever she needs.

"What do you need?" Does my voice always sound that high?

"I fell earlier. In the office. When I collapsed. I hit my shoulder on the desk."

That was just what I needed to hear. It was a ragey version of a cold shower.

"Are you okay? Need an ice pack?" I step into action.

She shakes her head and looks truly pitiful as she winces. I take a step toward her.

"I don't suppose you can rub my shoulders?"

"I really, really don't think that's a good idea." I grip the back of my neck.

"I understand. I'll do it myself." She lifts her right arm to her left shoulder to rub. The action causes her back to arch and pushes her breasts toward the ceiling.

What have I done to deserve this?

She winces and I'm on my knees behind her before I realize it. I press my thumb in circles into the soft skin between her shoulder blades. The tips of my fingers rest just above her collarbones.

"Ohh, that's amazing," she moans.

I start listing the Academy Awards winners for Best Actor starting with the most current year and going backward in my head. I'm on Daniel Day-Lewis, for *My Left Foot* and not *There will be Blood*, when she moans again.

"A little lower."

My thumb circles down the tense muscles lining her spine.

"Ah, yeah, there. Did you just say Dustin Hoffman?"

I cough and take my hands out of the tub, wiping them on my jeans. "If that's better, then I'll get going."

"Can you go a little lower?"

I'd been at her lower back. Any lower would be her...

"Maggie," I gasp out her name. It feels like all I do is gasp her name lately, or curse. "You're killing me."

She peeks over one shoulder, surprisingly agile for being hurt.

"I'm killing you?"

"Yes. And if I rub your... you any lower, I'll die."

"Wow." She purses her lips and furrows her brow. "If just rubbing my ass kills you, then I worry for your health with all the things I want you to touch."

My mouth freezes. Words want to come out but they are all backed up. My brain seems to have stalled out and my cock is straining against my pants, screaming, "What are you waiting for? Go forth and touch!" I close my eyes. I can't look at her as I make the stupidest choice of my life. But truly, I want what's best for her. Touching her is exquisite but she may need time and space.

"Trust me when I say, there is truly nothing I want to do more than explore these ideas of yours." My gaze falls under the surface of the water to her breasts, pink nipples just barely peeking out of the water. "I'd really, really love to."

Her nipples break the surface of the water and harden. With every subtle movement the water shifts around them. The skin of her neck is flushed and one of her hands is on her thigh under the surface, moving up and down.

My mouth is open. I'm sure something is about to come out. I force myself to look at her face and finish the thought. The stupid, stupid thought.

"My feelings for you are... big. There's no rush. I don't want to scare you."

She turns entirely in the tub but lifts her legs in the process so she's hugging them by the time she faces me. I can tell she's biting back a laugh.

"You don't scare me."

"You're right. You've never been scared of me."

"That's not exactly true." She swallows and looks around the room.

I think again to the first time she watched me. How I was cruel to Rachel to protect her and wonder if that's what she refers to.

"You were scared of me?"

She looks up at me through wet lashes. Her skin glows ethereal and it's surreal to see.

"I was scared of how I felt for you." For the first time, her coy seduction slips. Her eyes flit down and up again. "I haven't been attracted to anybody, not for years. I didn't even think I was capable, but the first time I saw you in the flesh, the first time, I really looked at you..." She focuses on the edge of the tub before meeting my gaze again. "I haven't been able to stop thinking about you in ways that are entirely new to me."

"Oh." My mouth hangs open and my Adam's apple bobs. I can't remember anybody ever telling me something so honest and truthful. It floors me.

"I keep telling you it's okay. That I want to. That I want us to be closer. But you keep fighting it. I know you think I'm fragile. And in a lot of ways I definitely am. But after talking to you tonight and coming forth with all that dead weight I've been carrying around, I understand that I'm ready to move on. I'm ready to claim my sexuality for myself. It's okay if you don't feel the same way. But don't say it's because you're trying to protect me. I don't need protection." Her gaze dips and she licks her lips. "I need satisfaction."

———

Maggie

IF ROE LEAVES THIS ROOM, I MAY DIE. MY HONESTY LEAVES ME raw and exposed like a patient in the middle of heart surgery. Here I am with my chest ripped open and my heart totally exposed. He places a hand on my cheek. *Don't you dare. Don't you dare leave this room.*

"You're an amazing human," he tells me. "I'm so lucky to know you. I've never thought for one moment you were weak." Then he stands up and leaves the room.

Frick.

I stare dumbfounded at the door. Okay then, at least I'm rejected in the nicest way possible. Doesn't help the horrible sensation in my ribcage, like someone's repeatedly stabbing me. I can't catch my breath.

I go Under as I actually go under. I can't even handle seeing myself right now. My back slides down the smooth surface of the tub as the warm water engulfs me entirely. The water settles around me in record time. I don't sink toward the bottom of the oversized tub. Instead, I sort of hover.

Like this, floating in water almost the same temperature as me, I feel something close to Nirvana. Or maybe that's too spiritual for what I am at this moment. I feel neutral. Maybe that's a better word. Nothing weighs me down. I don't even feel like I need to breathe. I can stay suspended here in this equal state of neither rising nor sinking forever and feel nothing and do nothing.

Let the rest of the world sort out its own problems. I'm being selfish. I deserve the tiniest pity party after that. For a long time, I float with just my face out of the water.

Roe doesn't return and I think about calling for a ride. I bet Danny and Russell would love to come pick me up from *the* James Roe's house.

I take my time toweling off and applying good smelling

lotion. Ah, the perks of massive amounts of disposable income. This lotion alone is probably squeezed from the cheeks of cherubs.

Everything I told Roe is true. I'm not having some sort of emotional hangover or rebound-type situation. I'm not mixing up my confusion of lust for him with my abuse. I'm not seeking redemption through the touch of another man while not healing and covering the pain.

For years I've been hiding. Roe's the first man to make me feel like I'm worth more than the sum of my looks. He makes me feel things that I didn't even know I was capable of feeling. I'm ready to claim myself. I'm tired of not knowing myself on that level. On a sexual level. I'm twenty-five years old and I don't have any clue what I'm like in bed. Or what *I* like in bed. I don't know how to have an orgasm with a man. I've never even tried. Some would say that I'm technically still a virgin.

Okay, fine. All would say that.

A few sloppy fondles in high school that meant nothing, and then the incident with my mentor not long after that. I don't go out and meet guys. I'm not naïve. Just lacking in experience points. But I don't want just anybody. I only want Roe. My cheeks burn and I press cool fingertips to them.

He's the only one I've found myself fantasizing about. The only one who fills my thoughts when my mind is left to wander. I think about doing things with him that I didn't even know I wanted to do. But I'm not scared. I'm not being bullied. He has no power or influence over me that could be used for nefarious purposes. I mean, except maybe his insane good looks, but he doesn't even wield them as a weapon.

I'm attracted to him. And more than that, I have feelings for him. Some would say strong feelings for him.

Okay, fine. All would say that.

I'm pretty morose by the time I leave the bathroom. I drag

my feet through overly plush carpet and hurry past Roe's room for fear of further pity. But something snags my attention. Roe.

He's sitting on the edge of the bed. His elbows are on his knees, hands clasped, head down. It's almost like he's praying. His entire room is lit up with dozens of candles. When I pause near the entrance, he shoots off the bed like he's been waiting for me.

"What's with the fire hazard?" My voice comes out soft, despite the teasing.

"I know, it's silly." He runs a hand through his wet hair. He's shirtless in jeans. Freshly showered. The fine soap he uses fills the air. His toes wiggle in the carpet.

I'm still only wrapped in a towel. And I'm very aware of that fact. I clench it tighter, worried it might try to jump off my body and make a fool of me. I take a step back, but he raises a hand.

"I just thought..."

He steps toward me. His movements are confident and lithe. It's hard not to study his form like fine art. He looks up at me through come-hither eyebrows.

"...It might be nice for when you show me all the places you think about being touched."

27

Roe

"Yes. Like that." Maggie smiles at me with heavy-lidded eyes. "Perfect."

I bite my lip and study her every movement. She groans in delight.

"Mmm, nice."

"The trick is to wait until the bubbles break through from the other side."

Maggie's making me pancakes. This must be what contented happiness feels like. Pancakes on a lazy Sunday morning, pretending the rest of the world doesn't exist. My eyes roam her body hungrily. She pauses in her explanation to look at me.

"Are you listening? This is important. Everybody should know how to make pancakes."

My chin rests in my palm as she flits comfortably around my kitchen. I replay some of the highlights from the night before: how sweet her nipple tasted in my mouth, how warm and wet she was as I slid a finger into her, how her scent wrapped around me. It's forever and officially my favorite.

"You're so not listening." She leans over the kitchen island and gives me a soft kiss. "You're lucky you're cute."

I'm half a breath away from sighing like a Disney princess— smitten. And yes, I'm comfortable enough with my masculinity to say smitten.

She pulls back but I stop her. Once again I kiss her, only this time I delve in to explore her mouth. Our kissing quickly goes from Disney to HBO. It is my life's duty to kiss her as often as possible.

"Not cute enough to burn food for," she mumbles against my mouth before going back to the stove. "How many do you want?"

"Whatever." My voice is rusty from misuse. You'd think our evening of exploring each other would have led to some relief, but nah. I'm spent but not sated. Last night was all about discovering what Maggie likes. And I liked that very much. Now, I'm free to imagine all the things I wouldn't allow myself before. All the different things we can try together.

I can't think about a time when I'm not around her. It unsettles me. Things have moved fast since I met her, especially my feelings. But I'm not ready to analyze that.

She sets a fat stack of carbohydrates in front of me. Butter melts on top of perfectly golden-brown pancakes, dripping syrup down the side. It's like a commercial. My stomach growls loudly. The fork shakes in my hand as it moves through the sugary calories. I hate wasting food. I cannot waste food but I can't eat this. I haven't earned it. All the bliss of a moment ago evaporates.

Little progress has been made with the factory. If I start celebrating it's as good as saying I've stopped caring. No. There is still too much work to be done. I push the plate away.

Maggie grabs my fork from my hand and uses it to take a

bite as she wiggles her ass into my crotch. I'm momentarily distracted again as I wrap my arm around her waist and nuzzle into her delicious-smelling neck.

"What's wrong? Are they not cooked all the way through?" She takes a big bite and her tongue comes out to lick some syrup from her chin. "They're perfect," she says around a mouthful.

I talk against her shoulder blade, rubbing my face against her like a cat. If I could just capture this right here and not think about anything else...

"I'm just not feeling good," I say. "Finish them for me?"

Maggie puts the fork down and turns in my arm to level a stare at me. I have the overwhelming urge to hide behind the counter.

"Are we going to talk about this?" she asks.

Her easy flirtatious mood has gone. Now she leans back against the counter with crossed arms, away from me, but I only loosen my grasp a little.

"About my stomachache?"

"About your eating disorder."

"You're crazy. I have a stomachache," I say and drop my arms. She can go now but she doesn't.

"We've spent a lot of time together these last few days. Ask me how many times I've seen you eat?"

"This is ridiculous." I lift her but she locks herself into place.

"Zero times. I've heard your stomach growl countless times. I've seen you pass offer after offer, making excuses. But not once have I seen you eat. Honestly, except for the fact that you aren't dead and clearly must eat something, I'd've spoken sooner." She gestures to my shirtless form.

"It's for a movie." I'm by no means anorexic. I'm lacking fat because I train hard.

"No, it's not."

"I eat enough. My trainer provides a strict meal plan."

"Listen." She chews her lip, seeming to analyze this excuse. "I've been in this town my whole life. I went to a high school for the performing arts. I can spot an eating disorder from a mile away."

"You're being a little dramatic."

"You're being purposely thick-headed."

I lever her off my lap and stomp toward my room. No longer feeling lovey and touchy and certainly not wanting to be shirtless. She's ridiculous. This is some sort of tactic to push me away because we got too close. Fine. She can be like that. Maggie follows and shoves my door open, waving a spatula.

"We're not done having this conversation."

"We are though." I pull a T-shirt over my head.

"You have an unhealthy relationship with food." She jabs the spatula into my gut.

"I don't." My rage is growing. She has no right to pretend to know me. She has no right to talk to me about this.

"Fine." She scrutinizes me.

She heads back toward the kitchen and I think I've won, so I let out a breath. This conversation makes me absurdly uncomfortable.

"I'm going to toss all these then," Maggie calls from the other room.

I hurry to the kitchen in a second. She holds the plate poised over the trash can.

"Stop. Why? You eat it." I won't have her throwing it away. Four perfect pancakes made with real butter and real maple syrup. It could feed a few children easily. She shakes her head and the food slips a little toward the trash. I quickly snag it from her.

"Fine. I'll eat it." I shrug casually, contradicting myself. After this, I'll run a lot. And skip my lunch protein shake.

"What were you just thinking?" she asks.

"Nothing," I snap.

"Were you thinking about throwing up?" She shakes her head, talking as much to herself. "No, you won't waste food. Were you calculating all the pushups you need to do?"

"You're insane."

She takes the plate from me and hovers it over the trash. I whip it out of her hands again and cradle it in my arms. She raises her eyebrows.

"I'm acting insane? You're holding that plate like you birthed it. I'm not crazy and you know it. You need to talk to someone."

"I don't."

"Then why don't you just eat and not think about it."

"Because I have to watch my figure," I say with venomous sarcasm.

"Listen, I get this industry is harsh. The standards are hard but you're going a step past rational. You're being highly irrational when it comes to food."

"No."

"Then eat. And don't exercise at all today."

This isn't her business. I have no reason to share this with her but maybe she'll get off my fucking case.

"You act like... it's nothing weird," I say. "The hunger pains, they just remind me."

"Remind you of what?"

"Of being hungry. And poor. It reminds me of why I do this."

My cheeks burn as my statement hangs in the air like flies over rotting fruit. I surprise myself. My past is my business and nobody else's. She turns off the burner and removes the pan from the heat.

"Do what, exactly?" she asks, less accusingly, but infuriatingly patient. "Act?"

"Yes, act. But mostly the other stuff. The press tours, the

pictures, the interviews, the invasion of privacy, the mind games, and networking. I hate it all. I fucking hate it. But the hunger pains take me right back. They keep me strong."

She frowns.

"Puberty was the worst. I was desperate for food all the time. It was all I thought of. More than sex." I hope to ease the tension but her frown remains. Telling her all this seems ridiculous in comparison to what she went through. Do I really want to explain all the nights curled in bed crying from pain? Share about the headaches and dizzy spells? The desperate times I ate from the dumpster behind the doughnut shop by my house? It's humiliating.

"I'm sorry you went through that. Truly." She comes around to me and kisses me softly on each cheek. "No child should ever know hunger."

I look away. It's embarrassing to talk about this. I don't want her pity or the shame.

"But do you see how this isn't healthy?"

My fists ball and I turn my face away, even when she climbs into my lap. Trapping me.

"Your thoughts about food. They're not rational. You'll never get to that point again, Roe. You'll never lose everything and be destitute. Or rather, it's highly unlikely. Even if your career tanks you must have millions saved, invested? Your house alone would set you up for a few years, living modestly. Especially if you invested wisely. I call bull." Her tone is still patient, but her accusation surprises me.

"Excuse me?"

"Yeah. Bull. You're miserable and you're torturing yourself but I can't quite understand why."

I want to shove her off me and end this conversation. How could she take such a nice morning and ruin it? Why would she want to undo all the progress we made last night by driving a wall between us?

"There's nothing to understand," I say.

"You need to talk to someone about this."

"I'm not telling people my shit. The last thing I want is people telling me what I need." I scratch at my stubble.

"Is that why you're angry? You don't want people knowing your business?"

I throw my arms out as I yell, "I'm not angry." Okay, maybe I'm angry now.

"You are. You starve yourself. You don't sleep. You're miserable and unhappy. I just don't understand why."

"What could I possibly be unhappy about? You said it yourself. I have it all. I'm the poster boy for Hollywood success. What's not to love?"

"LA is soul-sucking." She scoffs. "There's plenty not to love."

"You're jaded. Understandably so," I add quickly as to not totally undo all the progress of last night. "Not everybody hates it here. You can't just throw this away."

"What?" she asks.

"This." I gesture to my house. "This lifestyle. I can afford anything. People will do anything. Give me anything."

"So?"

"So!" I hate that I'm yelling. Gotta calm myself down so I slap on an affable tone. "I owe it to the world to pass it on. To be grateful."

"You don't, though. You aren't responsible for everybody else." She's so convinced of her own rightness.

"You don't understand; I owe them everything. That town. They kept me and my family alive. My parents did whatever they could to keep us afloat."

"You've more than returned the favor." She shakes her head like the math still isn't adding up. "What's this really about?"

I stand up and she falls off my lap and lands in a heap. I'm speechless. She won't let this go. I growl as I rub my hands through my hair.

She stands with a glare and leans against the counter, taking in my freak-out. I hate how calm she is. How crazy she's making me feel. Such a different crazy than last night. She sighs.

"I don't think you feel like you deserve it."

Well, duh. "I don't."

"Why?" She crosses her arms.

"Why are you pushing this so hard?"

"Why are you avoiding the questions?"

"I do what I do and it's nobody's damn business." I scoff and sound ridiculous. This interrogation sucks.

"I disagree."

"With what?" I growl.

"I think it's exactly my business."

This stalls me; I stand gaping.

"I care about you and I've gotten to know you. We've been intimate." She says this with only a hint of shyness. Very matter-of-factly. "And so I deserve to understand why someone I care about is hurting. Because that's what you do when you care about someone. That's what you did for me." Her logic is sound but her voice cracks, giving away her emotion.

I soften. She really has shared so much with me. I clench my jaw.

"People don't get this level of success for nothing."

"What do you mean?" She lifts her chin.

"You've heard it all. I won the looks lottery. Don't you know? I shouldn't be here. I don't deserve it. I lucked out. It's going to go away as quickly as it came unless I pay some sort of penance."

She grabs my hands. "You're brilliant. You play the game like you were born for it. Not many people can. But you're also genuine somehow. Plus, you have this thing. People talk about *It* all the time. People are desperate for *It*. But you really have *It*. That Thing. I get to see it firsthand every day.

Even before your fame, I bet you were always the center of attention."

I stare at the floor. She's right, but it's never felt earned. She can't understand that. There's no such thing as getting everything. There's always a cost. She lifts my chin with a finger and her gaze penetrates me.

"Also, you're a brilliant actor. You give me chills. It's unreal. You should know that I don't say that lightly. Like I've said, I've been in this town a long time. It's not dumb luck that you're here. Not by a long shot." Her tangent does weird things to my chest so I break the tension.

"I thought you've never seen my movies."

She shrugs and the old Maggie coolness is back, but she's playing at it because the corner of her mouth lifts.

"I lied." She kisses my nose. "I didn't want it going to your head."

Her ease of intimacy compared to when we first met is surprising. For someone so cold and angry she's very good at it. It's like it's all been lurking under the surface. And she just needed to find someone deserving of it. Which means she thinks I'm worthy of it and that has me feeling like the best fucking guy in the world. More than all the accolades she listed. Her eyes pull down in a sad little frown and her tone grows serious.

"You deserve more than most and then some. But you're not happy. This city is eating you alive. That's what it does. This industry. It'll pump you full of whatever you think you need temporarily so it can get what it needs but it'll leave you drained long term. It's not luck. You made it here, you've sustained it here, because you're brilliant."

Despite her intent, I feel worse again. Because now it feels like maybe it is my destiny to be here in this career and even she believes it. Like I don't actually have a choice in the matter.

Maybe I've waited too long to respond because she says,

"But just because you're good at something doesn't mean it's your passion. It doesn't mean you have to do it."

"What. And just walk away?" I ask. "From all this. From everything?"

"Yeah." She shrugs.

"It's not that easy."

"But it really is. Take your money and run before there's nothing of you left." She wraps her arms around my neck. Her eyes cloud a little with sadness. her thumb caresses my lips then presses the area between my eyebrows, soothing them. "I give you permission to leave." Her voice is tight.

"But you said I have a talent for it."

"So? I have a talent for packing U-Hauls very efficiently but I'm not a mover for a living."

"That's an odd example and not exactly relevant." The side of my mouth lifts. Because, Maggie. "You aren't awarded lots of money for your packing ability."

"The point is still valid. You don't want to admit it to yourself because you're holding on so desperately to this false truth you're living."

"Jesus, Maggie. Way to cut to the quick."

She holds my stare. And there's something she's not saying, something on her mind.

"You're allowed to be grateful and still walk away," she finally says. "Nobody expects you to be miserable. You get to choose your life, Roe, that's how this all works."

———

Maggie

ROE DOESN'T THANK ME FOR MY BRILLIANCE. HE DOESN'T SAY anything. But he does smile at me in a way that makes my heart conga around in my chest. He grabs my face and kisses with something that feels deep with meaning. When we pull away from each other, we're both panting. What I told him is true. He should leave. He isn't happy here, but I'm surprised at how bad that idea hurts me. I don't like how much I've grown accustomed to having him around me.

He snatches the flight-inducing pancakes and takes a big bite. We share the now cold breakfast in silence, occasionally smiling at each other or pausing to lick syrup off the other's mouth.

I'm happy. It feels weird, to have fallen for Roe in a way that I can't even begin to understand. I'm not throwing out the L word but I'm not *not* throwing it out there either.

There's a nagging at the back of my mind, though. Some weird self-revelation I had when I spoke to Roe. About living a life for the wrong reasons. My mind keeps wandering back to that. Pointing out the statement and waving its arms at my hypocrisy. I nudge it away.

Things have changed between Roe and me, but my mission hasn't. I haven't changed. I need to bring Zebulund down. More than ever, actually. A plan formulates in my mind while I clean up plates. Roe is showering when my phones buzzes.

"If you're done with the gooey eyes, check the news." It's from O.G.

I raise an eyebrow at his salty tone.

"What did your phone do to you?" Roe asks, walking into the room with only a towel wrapped around his waist and a smaller one in his hands.

"It's giving me lip..."

Now see, this is why we can't get things done. He towels out his hair and different muscles fire off like pistons in complicated machinery. He's a freaking body soap commercial. My mind wants to go back to last night. It wants to replay every delicious moment. I'm seconds from giving in when my phones buzzes again.

"Entertainment Exclusive, now!" my phone yells.

"What's wrong?" He's at my side, reading over my shoulder. "Who's O.G.?"

"The Original Gangsta, obviously. Turn on the TV."

He does as I ask. The screen fills with an image of Viktor. It's a mug shot and he's got a black eye and busted lip. He's glaring. Roe clicks up the volume. A Botoxed reporter drones away.

"...sources at the renowned gay bar say that Viktor Karlsson was in the process of being kicked out for starting a fight with a bartender who cut him off when he pulled out a gun and shot it into the ceiling."

I gasp and glance to find Roe stony and listening closely.

"Viktor Karlsson was held at the LA County courthouse on several charges but released on bond early this morning." The camera switches to a male anchor with gelled-back dark hair and a hawkish nose.

"When contacted for a statement, this news agency found the actor had been dropped from his current representation for his violent outburst and as far as we can tell has not been picked up by anyone else."

The camera switches back to the female anchor.

"If you recall, this isn't the first run-in with the law Karlsson has had. A few years back a similar incident occurred that ended up getting him fired from his current movie."

"It's not looking good for Viktor," says the male anchor. "This morning, Marty Zebulund announced his regret to have dropped him from his production company."

The screen flashes a stock photo of Zebulund and as always my stomach roils at the sight of him. A statement appears as the anchor reads it.

"We regret having to cut ties with Viktor Karlsson but Slingers Production Company has a long-standing reputation for excellence and his violent behavior cannot be rewarded nor ignored any longer."

I snort. Roe's frowning so deeply his eyebrows could block him from a rainstorm.

"Social media is blowing up with outrage," the female anchor goes on. "@LAGal2354 said, 'Violence like this shouldn't be rewarded. Good for @Slingers for giving him the boot.' Well, it's sad no matter what you think."

"That it is," the male agrees as the camera focuses back to him. "Switching to happier news. James Roe has been rumored as the lead in the next Guy Horatio film. The movie hasn't even been filmed yet but there's Oscar buzz."

"It couldn't happen to a more deserving actor." The female finishes but Roe shuts the TV off and runs a hand over his face.

"Fuck," Roe says.

"Fuck," I agree.

"It's like Zebulund was writing me a message."

I nod because that's exactly what I get out of all that too.

"I didn't tell you, but yesterday, after you left, Zebulund said something. At the time, I was having a moment of regrettable pity toward him."

I growl without meaning to. He faces me and holds my shoulders.

"Trust me, it won't happen again. But he made a comment. Something about me being a good egg, seeing the right side of things. The same sort of shit he always says. But this time, I think he was warning me. This is not a coincidence. These stories back-to-back."

His neck is red. He's carefully controlling his rage. I am not.

"I hate him so much!" I yell as I stomp my foot. Like a child.

Roe doesn't even hesitate. "Me too."

28

Maggie

ROE TAKES ME HOME AFTER BREAKFAST. I'VE BEEN NEGLECTING MY duties as unpaid housekeeper and need to regroup. We're too caught up in each other. We both seem to want some space after our heavy revelations to one another. Or rather we need to. Yet, neither of us seems to want to leave each other's sides as we say goodbye.

It's absurd. You'd think I'm going off to war, the way our hands clasp desperately to each other in the driveway behind Mrs. Jenkins's house. We can't stop kissing each other and then smiling like idiots. Ugh. I love it.

But really, we need to get things done. We agree to regroup tomorrow night for dinner. He has to film all day and I need to make a plan. As close as I feel to Roe, I made a choice. I'm not involving him in this anymore. I can't tell him that because he'll try to change my mind. He wants to do what's right but this is all my fault. He's gotten in way too deep because of me. I promised to help him and all I've done is manage to make his life infinitely more complicated.

Roe thinks the Zebulund threat was for him but I think it's more than that. He's getting too close to the flames. Zebulund is showing that he has the power to destroy anybody in a single breath. I bet he didn't even lose a wink of sleep last night.

He framed Viktor. He's somehow responsible for the entire shift of the public against the actor. It's that easy to sway the masses. A few tweets, a few news stories, and a career is ruined. I won't have that happen to Roe. Not now, not after I know what he's been fighting for.

When I check on Mrs. Jenkins, she's napping, so I take out her trash, clean up the kitchen, and do a little bit of housekeeping. All the while my gears spin, making a plan. I need access to Zebulund's files. I need to get real dirt on him. I need an exposé, but it's further away than ever. All I have is a few names.

After I take care of the house and a few emails, I start my search on the names I found on Zebulund's computer. They don't get me far. One is a lawyer from the Valley. There's no connection to Zebulund or Roe as far as I can see. The other is a director I recognize. He's done a few films for Slingers but that's nothing crazy. I can't help but see the news in my searching. The media blows up with examples of how awful Viktor is and always has been. I feel for the guy. He did his best. He's obviously working through some issues. Poor guy. His whole life is ruined. Personal and professional.

But suddenly the universe is on my side when I get an email entitled, "Is this Miss Mayday?" from Viktor himself.

———

VIKTOR WANTS TO TALK TO MISS MAYDAY. HE WANTS TO TELL HIS side of the story. Who am I to say no? He gives me his address and I head over to Beverly Hills. It means revealing that Miss Mayday is Roe's assistant, Rachel, but it means he will give me the biggest break in this story yet. It's a calculated but necessary risk. I'm so close now. The tide has turned and Zebulund is going down.

I've just pulled up to the gate of Viktor's mansion when he stumbles out from the side door leading to the garage. His blond hair easily gives him away. He can hardly walk.

"Viktor!" I yell through the heavy iron gate.

His whole body turns toward me comically.

"Ahoy!" he yells.

"I'm here to talk."

It takes him a bit to make his way toward the gate.

His face is a muddle of confusion as he tries to place me. "You're Roe's assistant? Did he send you?" A breeze carries the strong scent of alcohol before he reaches me.

"Nothing like that. I want to talk to you about what happened."

"Don't you know? I'm gay and I have a violent side. I carry guns. I'm un-h-h-hirable."

"I don't know that actually." My eyebrows raise. "Why don't you tell me the truth?" I hold his gaze. "You did email me that you want to tell your side of the story."

And there it is... I've now used Rachel to pretend I'm somebody else. Again. I really need to send her chocolates.

Wheels turn behind his watery stare. "Ms. Mayday?"

I nod.

"Does Roe know?" He squints as he types a code into the keypad hidden in a brick column to my left.

"A girl's got to have some secrets," I say though I'm not sure why I lie. Reporter instinct mostly. Also, Roe should have plausible deniability. I've risked him enough. "He doesn't know I'm here or who I am."

I slip through the gate and follow him through that same side door around the house and go through a laundry room roughly the size of my bungalow to a sitting room. He slumps into a large white linen chair. From a flask, he takes a long sip and looks at a painting on the wall. I follow his gaze and study the art too. It's modern, messy, splattered-looking, but I don't know enough about art to know anything more than that.

"I'm gonna have to sell that." His gaze settles on me but he seems a little startled. "Oh, right the assistant." He looks at me expectantly.

"You know, it's not over. It's just a bad day." My comfort comes out weak.

He snorts.

"Any publicity is good publicity," I lie.

I don't know why I feel compelled to make him feel better. Maybe I do feel bad, maybe he got caught up with Zebulund like Roe did, not necessarily willingly but knowing that resistance is futile.

"Well, that's just not true is it?" He looks at me through a lock of white-blond hair that's fallen forward. Even though he's drunk and obviously in the middle of an existential crisis, he's tangibly attractive. When his gaze locks on me I don't have the ability to look away. His eyes are the color of the Grecian ocean contrasted against white buildings and a clear sky.

They're bloodshot though. And his blond beard is a mess.

"All I'm saying is you don't need to start auctioning your house just because you were outed."

His head falls back and his Adam's apple is highly pronounced. It bobs when he groans.

"You have no idea."

"Seriously, it's not the issue it once was. Most people don't even think about sexuality anymore, and those that do have their own issues to work through."

I relax back into the couch. The room is decorated in a trendy sort of outdoorsy, Norwegian theme, with exposed wood and lavish furs.

"You really think that, don't you? You're cute. Tell me one

openly gay male who plays the action roles I do... did." He slings back another drink from the flask. It must be empty because he leans back for too long and then examines the thing like it might magically make more.

I don't speak because there's some truth to what he's saying.

"But even if it were true." He burps. "It wouldn't matter. He's ruined my reputation and that means more than anything. Nobody will hire me. Hell, I'll bet nobody is allowed to work with me. I've been blacklisted," he slurs. "He probably has a phone tree set up to bring his enemies down. Calls one person and a few hours later all of Hollywood knows I'm a leper. They won't go near me."

There's a buzz and he struggles to get his phone out of his tight slacks.

"Look another tweet," he says. "'@TheRealviktor is gay? Are you serious? Is nothing sacred? #Transformation movies have now been ruined for me. Gross.' See." He shows me the phone. Another notification pops up as he does. "Oh, an email. Surprise. I lost my sponsorship with Tag Heuer." The phone slams against the wall with an expensive cracking sound.

"You really think Zebulund did all this?" I keep my voice steady as the adrenaline kicks up.

"Come on, you're a smart cookie." He rolls his eyes and his head goes back too.

I do know. I just want him to tell me how I can bring the man down. I want to get information out of him while he's angry.

"Just like I know you aren't Roe's assistant," he adds.

I freeze. My knees go numb but I make no outward indication of freaking out.

"I saw the way he looks at you. That man's crazy for you. Shame you're lying to him too."

"Listen," I say, ignoring that for now. "I believe you, but what can you do? Zebulund's untouchable right?"

"Everybody has an Achilles' heel. He found mine."

"So let me help. Let Miss Mayday bring him down." It has to be something a little more substantial than a fear of the after-life. I hope.

Viktor hesitates. He holds my gaze but his mouth remains a tight line.

"I want to help." I'm delicately pushing the balance here. I hope I don't go too far—seem too eager.

Eventually, it's like he decides. He leans forward and lowers his voice. "He's got dirt on everybody. That's how he operates. He spies on them. He's got dirt on your man, and the fact of the matter is it's too late for him already." His eyes drift over and go dark. "If Roe crosses him, if he even questions him, that'll be the end."

"Where does he keep his dirt?"

I'm too blatant, too bold with my question. It slips out before I can stop, but I'm aggressive and impatient when I'm on a lead. He gives me a skeptical and surprisingly sober look.

"You really want to help me?"

Him and every other person under Zebulund's thumb. I nod solemnly, holding his gaze.

"Fine. I'll pretend to give you a big speech about how you didn't hear this from me. But honestly, whaddo I care? I want the world to know. I want someone to do something."

"I'm your girl." I'm pouring all my determination into my voice.

"All right, you asked for it." He purses his lips. "Zebulund has a small house in the mountains about an hour's drive north, outside of the city traffic." The color fades from his face. "He took me there once. Made me give him a BJ and then took a picture of it. Told me he wanted to be a team but just wanted to make sure I stayed on his side. I really thought, even then, that he cared on some level about me. I'm an idiot."

The admission stuns me into silence. I'm furious for him. I want to scream. Another of Zebulund's victims.

"He won't keep getting away with this." It's a promise. The venom in my voice causes him to look up at me.

"Anyway." He glances away again. "There's a computer there and a remote hard drive. Not attached to the Internet. He keeps backups of everything there."

He's so pitiful. So broken and sad. And this is all Zebulund's fault.

"What he did to you was not your fault. You were the victim. He had power over you and he took advantage. You're not a bad person and you didn't deserve it." I repeat what Roe said to me, hoping to give him comfort.

His eyes are glossy and close to tears. He sniffs and his jaw flexes.

"Thanks. But you have no idea what you're talking about."

———

I STARE AT MY PHONE IN DISBELIEF. IT'S RINGING. IT'S RINGING, and it's O.G.

I wanted it to be Roe returning my nine hundred calls. There's so much to tell him, about Viktor, about the cabin. As much as I don't want to get him involved any more he deserves to know the truth. That Zebulund has people following us, but more worrisome is that he's likely trying to find a way to black-mail Roe. Please don't let it be too late.

I feel a hint of dread. But I think of Roe. His touches. The way he looks at me and the things he's shared with me. There are no secrets between us anymore.

My thumb hovers over ignore. O.G. and I have never talked on the phone; our only communication has been texts.

Ignore. I can't think about O.G. right now. The phone immediately starts to ring again. I slide to accept the call.

"Hello?" I say hesitantly.

"How nice of you to finally answer." The voice is unrecognizable. I mean truly. It's robotic. It's both masculine and feminine. It's being filtered through distortion and layered.

This is so weird. It could be awkward but it's O.G. We've been something like friends for years.

"Well, I'm driving and it's hands-free in city limits, you know that."

"But you're outside the city."

"Creep," I say, only slightly kidding. Because it really is weird that O.G. always freaking knows where I am. Ew, what if he can see me peeing? I shake my head.

"It's what I do," he responds, not missing a beat. "So you're probably wondering why I called."

"Sure am."

"Too much to text. But you need to know. It's about the accounts you asked me to watch."

"Okay, is this a conversation I should pull over for?"

"Yes."

Well, that's ominous. I do just that at the next gravelly turn off. It's more than halfway to Zebulund's mysterious cabin. The sun is setting and in my eyes, another reason to pull over. I debate waiting until tomorrow night, when I'm supposed to meet with Roe, but I'll be in and out quickly. I'm about to announce that I'm stopped but O.G. knows that.

"I did some more digging on your fella."

I smile despite the serious tone. My fella. Hehe.

"Since you can't see me, I should tell you that I'm rolling my eyes," O.G. goes on.

"You were digging," I prompt.

"Yeah. At first, even I had trouble. This guy has nothing. No skeletons. No parking tickets. He's squeaky clean. Honestly, I don't trust it."

I don't say anything because I know Roe. I feel like I always have. I do trust him.

"Nothing for days, but then this morning," the robotic voice says, "all the money has been moved."

"Moved?"

"Dispersed into several other accounts. Shady and fake accounts. They're all fronts to get the IRS off their backs. It looks like money laundering."

"But why?"

"That I'm not sure about. The factory is hardly making any income. Laundering that amount of money seems excessive. The amounts are not minuscule but typically these accounts are in the millions."

"It doesn't make sense."

"I'm just the messenger."

"Who's laundering it?"

"The first company is owned by a Michael Rutherford," O.G. says.

"I know that name." I gently pick at the steering wheel. "How do I know that name?"

"I thought the same thing, so I kept looking. The next company is owned by a Matt McLoughlin."

"It's ringing a bell."

"What if I say Detective Matt McLoughlin?"

"Okay, cut to the chase." It's on the tip of my tongue. Or brain rather. "Why do I know these names?"

"Last name, there are a few others but I won't bore you with those."

I roll my eyes at his dramatics. If he weren't so bloody helpful I'd kill him. Well, if I ever meet him. The sun is just about to set. The last sliver slips behind tall firs and pines as the wheels of my mind turn. When he speaks again my heart sinks.

"Dominick Dartango."

"No." It comes out as a whisper. That's Roe's latest role.

That's the character he wrapped up press for last week. The others too, I remember now, they're all his characters. I shake my head.

"It's true," O.G. continues. "They all have social security numbers too. Look real enough if you're in some IRS office somewhere. Money is laundered. Rich get richer. Poor get poorer. Another day in America."

"Whose social? Not Roe's?" My insides are ice. I trust Roe. It's not him. It can't be. I sit stunned. My head shakes because it refuses to accept. Or maybe that's my heart.

"Not his. Still trying to figure out whose."

I let out a breath. "It doesn't make any sense. Why would Roe be behind this? He wants to help his town. He doesn't want the money."

"Are you sure about that? How well do you really know him?"

I think for a minute, really sit back and think about who he is and what I know of him. Of how much I learned about him these last few days. He isn't making himself so miserable just to steal money.

"No," I say firmly. And then I say it again because I'm so damn sure. "There's no way he did this. I'll talk to him. I'll ask him what's going on. But he didn't do this."

There's a long pause. I look to see if the call disconnected. I'm surprised to even have reception this far up the mountain as it is. The numbers tick away on the call to show O.G. is still there. There's another cough.

"Okay. I agree with you."

My hackles are still raised though. "Listen, I know we only recently met but—" I'm set to fight for Roe but then it registers what O.G. said. "Oh. You do?"

"Yeah. This doesn't make sense, and it doesn't fit what I've discovered about him in my own research."

"Oh," I say again. "Good. And also," I go on after a pause, "if you're going to commit federal offenses on such a grand level, why would you use the names of characters you've been? It feels a little on the nose."

"Bingo. And I found this information a little too easily. It's hard to explain but to me it feels like I was supposed to find it."

"He's being set up."

"That's what it seems like."

"It has to be Zebulund. There's nobody else who'd want to do this and not want the money." I squeeze the steering wheel and shake it but feel like going outside the car to scream into the abyss of the mountain valley.

"I agree again." Another cough. "On that note, where're you headed?"

"You don't already know?"

"You're being rash. Go home. Talk to Roe."

"Thanks, Mom, but I'm going to get this son of a bitch. I can't wait until tomorrow. "

"Look, I have to go." The coughing fit goes on longer this time. "But turn around. Don't do anything stupid. I like your pretty face."

"Flirt." I hang up the phone.

Immediately, I dial Roe but hear nothing but silence. My phone says No Service. It feels like an omen. I ignore it and throw my phone into the center console. But then pick it back up again. Always have another plan. I compose a text that sits in the outbox, waiting to send.

"I found out some things. We've got to chat." Hopefully, it'll push through when I get service and let him know where I am. I text the address just in case and send it his way. It also gets caught sending.

I pull back onto the road and drive for about thirty more minutes. The light is weird this time of night, that post-sunset glow makes the passing headlights blaring, so I'm more cautious than I might normally be. I almost miss the turn off for the gravel road leading to his house. The driveway is long and narrow and my tires crunch loudly even with the windows rolled up.

The cabin is modest but obviously still a few million easily, nothing compared to the ostentation of his main house. There are no lights on and no cars around. I ease on the driveway's cement pad. A motion sensor sets the light on and my heart stops for a minute. I take a minute to collect my thoughts. All I need to do is go in. Get the computer. Get out. Three steps. Easy.

I stare up at the dark house.

"What the hell?" I say out loud.

This is a stupid plan. This is a very stupid plan. If I were watching myself on a film right now, I'd be screaming at the heroine that she deserves to die for going up here alone. I check my phone and shocker, no service. Well, I refuse to be another damsel in distress. I grab my Mace and knife from the glove box. I don't own a gun. That might've been a bad choice.

"Just leave," I tell myself.

Come back tomorrow with Roe in the light of day. Don't be a bimbo. Don't let them paint you with that brush. As much as I don't want to drive all the way back home, I'm not going to die before I can bring Zebulund down.

I put the car in reverse and make my back down the driveway. The reverse lights don't provide enough light, so I roll to a stop and put the car in drive. I'll drive up to the house to turn around instead. But before I shift gears my passenger door opens. Zebulund slides into the seat next to me. The car tilts with the new weight.

"Hi, Maggie. Can we talk?"

29

Maggie

ZEBULUND SLAPS THE MACE OUT OF MY HAND AND IT FLIES INTO the back seat. The knife is gone too before I think to use it. A second later he yanks the keys out of the ignition. I'm defenseless in the middle of nowhere.

I'm an idiot.

"Before you scream or do anything else pointless, understand that I'm not going to hurt you." He's smiling jovially. "You always assume the worst of me, Maggie May."

"Give me my keys." My voice is level despite the hammering of my terrified heart.

"Let's go inside and talk."

Hell no. Screaming is pointless but maybe I can go berserker on him and get away. As it stands now, I won't get far without GPS and a plan. But I could make it to the road and wave down help. I was stupid coming here but no more stupid or rash choices.

The belated realization sinks in that he refers to me by my

real name. Of course, he does. He's got me here. He knew I was coming. He obviously knows who I am.

"If I wanted to cause you pain I would have done it by now."

He says it so smoothly it doesn't even feel like the threat that it is. He can hurt me. Easily. His smile is still sincere. He leans back casually, his arm leaning against the door. I have no clue about this man. I've been feeling like I've had the upper hand these past months as I got closer to the truth. But his demeanor, even the fact that he's here, says that I've grossly underestimated him. I need my keys. I need to leave but I've lost the upper hand. I never had the upper hand.

I'm an idiot.

"Let's talk here."

He lets out a dramatic sigh. "No, that's really not going to work for what I have planned."

My insides liquefy. My kneecaps tingle. He's going to kill me.

"Calm down. You should see your face. I'm not going to murder you, Miss Mayday. I want to talk."

"Give me my knife and Mace back."

He gives me a look that says "nice try."

"I'm not leaving this car without some security. Sorry if I don't take you for your word."

"Funny thing about that. How you think I'm the untrustworthy one. When I've only ever been honest about who I am and what I want. I have yet to see the same from you."

I scowl. I won't let him talk me out of my convictions. I know how he operates.

"Regardless." He draws a black handgun out of his pocket. "I hope you know what a position I'm putting myself in here."

In a display of weakness that makes me hate myself, I shut my eyes tight. Despite his promise to leave me unharmed I have to face the facts. He has a gun.

"Take it. I don't think you're stupid enough to shoot me. Just in case, I have security cameras." He leans forward next to me and waves at a camera by the motion-sensor light.

I want to cry and scream. He's pressed against me. My whole body shivers. My insides heave. I take the gun. I do it hesitantly because this has to be a trap. Or a trick. But it's a real gun. And loaded. I know how to shoot a gun because I went to get my conceal carry license shortly after my run-in with Zebulund the first time but never ended up buying one.

But I know how to use it if I need to.

"Come in." He heaves himself out of the car. Right now, with his back turned, I could shoot him. "We'll talk. I think we need to clear the air."

There's no option that I can think of other than to follow him. He isn't remotely concerned I'll shoot him where he stands. I grip the gun like it's my last hope and follow him into the house.

The small cabin has a high-ceilinged front living area with a huge fire pit in the center. It's a modern circular design and a sleek exhaust fan I can't even hear. I stay close to the door with the gun at the ready. Somewhere to the left of me, in the kitchen, I guess, he putters around breathing heavily. He walks past me and holds out a plate of assorted cheeses and meats.

"You'll excuse me if I don't partake," I say dryly.

"Suit yourself." He smiles with a shake of his head.

With a gusty sigh, he settles into a large worn recliner that is clearly "his chair." I'm far less at risk when he's this relaxed so I lower the gun but don't move. He lets out a contented sigh and lifts the footrest, legs crossed. With his plate balanced on his lap, he takes a bite of a greasy piece of sausage. There's an audible pop as his teeth pierce the casing. A piece of cheese follows it immediately.

"You're so quick to assume the worst of me," he says with his mouth full.

Nausea is my new normal. I blink pointedly at him.

"I know, from your point of view I'm the bad guy. You were new to the industry, you didn't understand how things work. Perhaps, I expected too much too soon of you."

I freeze. I can't hear him talk about that day. It was both better and worse when I thought he didn't recognize me at his house for the séance. Had he known all along?

"I don't know what you're talking about."

"Did you think I wouldn't remember you? Say what you will about me, but I never forget a lover."

He says *lover* like it was mutual. Like it wasn't sexual abuse. My vision fuzzes at the edge from my rage. I can't believe I'm standing here alone with him again and he's telling me we were lovers. I can't believe my mind is forced to replay events from his viewpoint. I must scoff because he looks up at me.

"Don't act like you didn't want it. Maggie, I cared about you. We shared a connection. Or so I thought. You came up to the room that day. To me, and most people, that means you wanted to take things to the next level."

I swallow. They're just words. They don't mean anything. He's playing me. I know this. And yet...

"You're beautiful and clearly smart. I misunderstood the situation. You came to me and said those things. I thought you wanted it."

I squeeze my eyes shut again. I want to scream. I want him to stop talking. That night I didn't say anything—I hadn't wanted it. But he's making me question everything. Why is he saying this? I never said things. Had I?

"I know it's easy to make me the enemy but I promise you I never wanted to hurt you. I want to clear the air. I thought we shared something special."

My stomach feels carved out—sharp pains cramp me. Maybe I misunderstood. Maybe I repainted history to appease the guilt I felt about the whole situation. Maybe I'm not the victim I think I am.

My brain is a turbulent sea of rights and wrongs and blacks and whites until my thoughts gray out. I wish I could see things outside of my own thoughts. I wish I could see things rationally. I want to curl up in a ball and cover my head. I don't like this. I don't want to be this person.

No.

"No." I said no. I said I wanted to stop. I never asked for any of this. I think of what Roe said. It's not my fault. I don't deserve this. I told Zebulund no. I wanted to leave. He's doing this to me. He's putting doubt in my head. He's making think that it was my fault.

He's watching me closely. Maybe he truly believes what he says. Maybe he really tells himself his victims want these things. His victims aren't victims to him. They're his lovers.

A slick, sour dread twists my gut.

There's a gun in my hands. Heavy with power. Cold and serious. It would be so easy. It's not the justice I hoped for but I can't think of any reason not to kill him. I raise the gun and point it at him. I will kill him.

———

ZEBULUND'S HEAD TILTS TO THE SIDE. HE GRINS AND THEN refocuses on his food, not at all intimidated by the deadly weapon pointed at his chest.

"Before we go on," he chucks a piece of cheese in his mouth, "you should know that there're three cameras pointed at you right now." He slurps excess spit from the sides of his lips. "I like to make sure I have proper documentation."

It clicks. That's why he makes the comments about me wanting it. He's got plausible deniability. I want to cry and scream and shoot all of these bullets into his body. But he's not going down that easy. I think of his other victims. Of Viktor and how he was taken here. Forced to perform fellatio and the pictures of it. And then something else clicks.

"You should know that there are no backup computers here with files, so go ahead and dash that silly idea."

I close my eyes against the betrayal. And my stupidity. It was Viktor who led me here. I walked right into this. My mind was too distracted to make the connection.

"Don't be too mad at the poor kid," he says, reading my thoughts. "He's all mixed up. Poor, sweet boy has learned his lesson and wants back in my good graces. He gets now that my threats aren't empty. He sees what I can do." Zebulund smiles a sad smile that conveys a warm love and pity. It's so genuine I get chills.

I lower the gun with tears burning in my eyes. I clench my jaw to steady against it. He holds the plate with one hand and adjusts his junk with the other.

"People constantly underestimate me. Do you think that I got to this position out of dumb luck and empty threats?"

He's a sociopath. He can pretend emotions but feels nothing. Everybody around him serves a purpose and when they no longer do, he cuts them out. It's clear that he genuinely believes he's helping people. That he serves a role.

"You thought you could pass as his assistant." He flops a hand out. "Uh, hello. I met her. And you. You're two different people. I have to admit, it did make me laugh."

"What. Do. You. Want." It takes all my effort to speak.

"I want you to understand how the system works, okay? I work hard to provide a lot of people with their dreams. You bleeding hearts paint me as a bad guy but you know what most people say about me? What people who really know me say? That I'm a good guy. That I look out for the people I care about. Do you know what I provide people? Their dreams. I never get time off. I'm always working, planning, trying to make sure everything is perfect. It's exhausting. But it's a fair exchange. I get them what they want. I get what I want." He swirls his finger around in leftover grease before licking his plate clean. "I only want to take what's due to me."

"What do you want with me?" I clarify.

"You need to understand how things work." He places the now empty plate on the table beside him, lowers the footrest and leans forward with his elbows on his knees. "I'm not the bad guy here. I'm in charge of retaining balance. I gave you a chance to make all your dreams come true and yet you try to come after me? All your little news stories, they're a pain in my ass. All you liberal media types are all the same. You think you're the first to want to catch me?"

"Fuck you."

"All you special snowflakes." He laughs. "Think you can change the world but there's a system here. I provide for many, I'm due what's owed to me. That simple."

I repeat my previous sentiment.

"Maggie, I'm tired." He sighs again and rubs his eyes. "I'll cut to the chase here: I want you."

I stumble back. A new type of terror ices me.

"Not like that, doll, come on now. We've had our fun, and you ruined it. I want you to work for me. I want to own your loyalty."

"Right."

He stands. I tighten my grip on the gun.

"I'm serious. I've been tracking you for some time."

This startles me and it must be obvious because he grins.

"I can't have a loose end. You left that hotel in such a rush. You disappeared. Poof." He snaps his fingers. "It really got to me, I'm going to be honest. I'm still not sure how you did it. Probably the same way you're getting all this information."

I hate how visible I am. I wish I could go Under. I can't stand him seeing me. But there's no point. Nowhere to run. If I leave now, I'll have accomplished nothing. At least he's talking.

"I couldn't find you. Nobody knew you. Tell me how you did it?"

I don't say anything.

"Didn't think so. Anyway, I had to stop looking for you because one by one people all around me, very close to my inner circle but not quite in it, started getting arrested. It was the darnedest thing."

He stops and tilts his head back, mouth open, exasperated.

"There's this new reporter on the scene. She has information there's no way she could have unless she was in rooms there was no way she was in. You must know this really threw me for a loop. I'll admit you got me there." He waves a finger at me like I was a naughty kid and he's Santa.

"At first, when I found out who you were—" He stops to chuckle. "Oh, this is really great, it was my wife who showed me your work. She's a fan of yours ever since you wrote that silly little article about the wives of Hollywood. Poor twit has no idea what she did. When the pieces fell into place, I thought I'd just threaten you. Get dirt on you, do whatever to make you stop." He takes a few steps toward me.

"The noose around my neck was getting tighter." He pauses like he hasn't rehearsed this monologue. "Okay, not really. The noose wasn't even close to my neck." He stops right in front of me and holds my stare. "You should know you'll never be able to bring me down. You'll never be able to stop me. I'm in so many pockets, you can't even imagine. That's how it works in the real world. I'm protected because I keep everyone else safe." He starts pacing again and waving his hand around. "So less like a noose, more like a gnat. Annoying me and needing to be crushed.

"But after that séance. After you walked right back into my life, I knew it was a sign. My wife was over the moon that you were undercover at our house. I was worried she'd blow it all. Honestly, I was just going to blackmail Roe for loyalty, but then he brought you into my life. Does he know that you're a reporter?"

"No. Please. Don't tell him. He has no idea."

"Looks like you've gotten close." He looks me up and down and shakes his head with something like disappointment. "I thought reporters knew better. You really can't help yourself around men, can you? Spreading for whoever shows you a bit of attention. Poor Maggie."

His words slice me. My neck inflames. I curse myself for the outburst. I may have done more damage than good. Now's the time to go back to not speaking and not giving anything away.

"I'm not sure how you've convinced him he can 'see ghosts' but you're talented. I truly believe we're made to work together."

"You're insane."

"Listen, this'll all go a lot faster if you just agree. I've given you your little gun so you can pretend to have a semblance of power but you don't. I own you."

"You'll never own me."

"You act like it wouldn't be beneficial to you. Money out the ass. Cars. Whatever you want."

"I want you to rot in hell."

"Jesus, can you just wake up and see the world as it is?" He slams his hand into the wall next to my head.

I'm shaking so hard I might be sick.

"You're too smart to pretend it's black and white. Right and wrong. I'm getting older. I'm tired. My help these days sucks. It'll be easier if you just come work for me and share whatever bit of technology you have."

"I can't be bought."

"Everybody has a price."

Why didn't I bring a recorder or something to take to the police? Not that it matters. I'm out of my league. All I have left are my scruples.

"You can never buy me. You'll never own me. My only goal in life has been to bring you down and I will not stop until you're rotting in jail. Everybody'll know what a pile of garbage you are."

The moment I say it I know I've revealed too much about myself. He's smart. He's evil. And he's conniving, sure, but he reads people damn well and knows how to play them.

"Why are you being so difficult about this? Do you know what an opportunity you have? How many people want to be in your shoes?"

It echoes what he said to me four years ago. He's close to me now.

"Other people would beg to be offered this."

"Give me my keys." I grip the gun tighter.

"Fine." He drops his head. "We'll do it your way."

He saunters to a side table and grabs a tablet. He hands it to me and gestures that I read it. I flinch. Without lowering the gun I scan it. But I can't absorb what I read.

"What's this?"

"I'm not as sneaky as you but I do have connections. I can find things out too. This is James Roe's background and his financial records. And all the ways he's been stealing money from the poor people of his town to fund his lifestyle."

"Liar."

"Facts are facts. The police aren't going to care. His family and neighbors aren't going to care."

I keep scrolling and see my name, Miss Mayday, at the bottom of the text file.

"Look, here's the deal." He checks his watch. "Either you help me or I go to the press with the news of Roe's money laundering. I'll send this file to your editor and have it published before you can start your car."

The world spins around me. There has to be a way out of

here. There has to be justice. I've been working too long and too hard for it to be over like this.

"No. No. I can't."

"Fine." His breath is sour and disgusting when he lets out a long exhalation in my face. "Then let me just mail this."

"You're a monster."

"You aren't listening." He slams the tablet down. "I'm trying to explain. I run this industry. People need me. I provide so much. You don't even know how much I provide for people. You're the selfish one here." He smooths his hands down his front and takes a steadying breath. "We'll make a good team. Now, agree to this or I'm ruining Roe's life. He'll never forgive you for this."

My head shakes.

"You chose to go up to that room that night, Maggie. You wanted the accolades and roles I promised you. I would have given them to you. I'm not an asshole. I only wanted what was due to me. One moment of pleasure and the world could have been yours. But you had to throw a hissy fit."

I'm ice cold. I'm sweating. Roe has given up everything to help those he loves. He's given so much to me. He's made me feel worth something. There's no way I can do this to him. I can't let my one-sided selfishness destroy him.

Just my body, not my being.

But those words don't work anymore. Not after my night with Roe, when I see how much my body is connected to my being. I can't move. I'm overwhelmed. This is not how this is supposed to go. He's evil. I'm Miss Mayday, I'm supposed to bring him down. It's all I've been working for. It's everything that matters.

No. That's not true. Roe matters. His work. His family and hometown. They matter. I know the decision has already been made.

"F-Fine. I'll work for you. Leave Roe alone. Keep his career intact and flourishing. Leave the factory and that town alone. I'll work for you." I swallow down the bile. There's no other choice. "I'll do whatever you want."

"Whatever?"

"I won't... I'm never going to touch you."

"You think that, don't you." His lip curls and he steps closer.

He's delusional. This isn't happening.

"Maggie, you're beautiful and young and I'll have whatever I want from you. As long as you're a good girl I won't hurt Roe. But you'll do whatever I ask. Don't ever forget that." As he speaks, his hand moves to my neck. He slides his fingers around it, completely engulfing me. His thumb traces my chin and slides into my mouth.

He applies enough force that I gag. My whole body shakes beyond my control. Four years. For nothing. No, not for nothing. I'm back here in this same place. I can't stop. Why am I not doing anything? Why do I always freeze when I should fight? What's wrong with me?

"Good girl." He pulls his thumb out and moves it around my lips, wetting them. "I like Roe. I don't want to get him involved in all this. I'm glad you're seeing the light."

For Roe. Roe has suffered too much. It isn't fair. His whole town won't suffer for my own mistakes. I focus on Roe to stop the terror that threatens to consume me.

I grasp at straws. I have to say something. I need to feel like I can do something.

"You need to stop harassing women."

He slaps me across the face before I even see it coming. "Don't ever tell me what to do."

I'm so shocked I gasp and feel like I can't catch my breath.

"It's not harassment. They want it. Most women beg for it. They know their place."

I cradle my burning cheek. I'm stunned speechless.

"I'm already helping Roe. And I'm running out of patience. Take it, or leave and ruin more lives."

"You promise Roe will be safe."

"I really am a good guy. People tell me all the time. But you've pushed my buttons." He walks a small circle around me. "I need to know that you mean it. I need to know you're serious about this because you're giving me a lot of lip."

"I'm serious," I say with hatred burning in my eyes.

"Not good enough. Beg me, Miss Mayday."

My face throbs. I may be in shock. I can only make one choice at a time.

"P-Please. Please let me work for you."

"Get on your knees." His mouth is curled with sadistic pleasure. I think he gets off on this more than any sexual act.

I refuse to cry. I refuse. But as I drop to my knees warmth streaks my cheek. I'm in front of him. Like so many others. I look up at him, holding his gaze, acting like I've never acted before. I'll do what needs to be done. I'll protect Roe.

"I want to work with you. Please."

His hand goes to the back of my head. My stomach churns. I can't... if he thinks... not after last night with Roe. I can't.

His free hand takes the forgotten gun from me and puts my keys in its place. The gun was only a futile symbol. He was right; I never had any power here. I was played before I walked in that door.

The hand still resting on my hair moves to my cheek to cup it. He pats it and it stings the already sore spot.

"Good, little girl. I knew you'd see the light."

30

Maggie

SHIVERS WRACK MY BODY AS I TRAVEL BACK DOWN THE MOUNTAIN. It's weird because I'm totally numb. In a different part of my brain, I note that I'm in shock. Driving is probably a bad idea.

Several miles later I pull over to throw up on a patch of wildflowers.

"Just my body, not my being." I've been repeating the words over and over.

What happened back there has the power to make me feel worse than that hotel room all those years ago. I can't allow it to. And yet.

I can no longer disassociate from my body. It does mean something. My body *is* my being. I did this for Roe. I'm healing because of him. He's done so much for me. He's taken care of me from the beginning. Even when I didn't want to accept his help. From the first time he put his coat around me to the conversation this morning. He's shown time and time again what trust is. What a healthy relationship feels like.

This sacrifice will be worth it. I have to believe that. My

mind cannot drift back to that cabin. It cannot think about the promises I made. I especially can't think of the way Zebulund touched me. Just to prove he had the power. Just to see how far I would go.

I swallow down a gag. I can't pull over again. I don't have time.

This is the same road that'll take me to Roe's house. As soon as I get reception, I call him. He doesn't answer. It goes straight to voicemail. I leave him another urgent message.

"Call me as soon as you can." I don't want to say too much in the message. Just in case. "Please. Call me. Before you do anything else."

He has a late shoot so I race to his house. I'll wait for him there. There's no way in hell I'd ever work with that man. Not a man. Garbage dressed in a suit. I'd grovel and lie all day if it meant Roe was safe, but I would never fucking work for him. I begged him. I shake the image from my head. He forced me to look up at him. Made me subservient to him. I promised myself I would fight to bring him down and there I was begging to work for him. How? How did I get to this point?

My phone buzzes but it's O.G. I don't want to hear how right he was. I don't want to do anything until I can clear the air with Roe.

Everything will be okay because justice will prevail. I'll make things right. I'm not keeping secrets. I'm trusting him. I made a stupid choice to go up there without him, but I'll make it right. I'll make everything okay.

I don't know when I start crying, but when I get to Roe's house tears stream down my face and my chin won't stop quivering. I suck in a shaking breath and knock on the door.

"It's open," Roe calls.

A relieved sob coughs out of me at the sound of his voice. It'll be okay now. We'll work this out together. I did what I had to do to protect him because that's what you do when you...

I stop in my tracks... When you love someone.

I love James Roe. It's painfully obvious now. Why else would I beg like that? Why else would I let that monster think he's won? We'll figure this out together. He will tell me everything will be okay.

He's at the kitchen island. Head down and not moving. There's still flour on the counter from this morning. Pancakes and kisses give me hope. For the first time in hours I don't feel covered in slime.

But then I really look at Roe and the smile falls off my face. He's hunched over a tablet, reading something. His hand is fisted in his hair and the other is gripping the back of his neck.

He looks up at me and I know in that second something is wrong. Something is very wrong. His eyes are bloodshot and his eyebrows are twisted with fury I've never encountered on him.

"You knew about this?" He slides the tablet to me.

It's my column. The familiar heading and cartoon avatar. The date reads today. But I haven't turned in a story in weeks.

"This doesn't make sense. He promised me—"

My hand covers my mouth as I read, "Hollywood Hero Steals from the Poor." It's an exposé on James Roe and the company he's embezzling from. All the details that O.G. shared with me are highlighted in bold text.

My world implodes.

31

Roe

It's all gone. Everything. Just as I knew it would happen. Nothing is safe or secure. My career is over. Maggie's face is drained of color except for a red welt on her cheek.

Maggie.

I lunge for her right as her knees give out. Her whole body shakes in my arms.

"Roe." She grips my shoulders for her dear life. "I didn't write that. You have to know that I would never write that."

It hurts too much to look at her. This morning feels like a lifetime ago. It *was* a lifetime ago. I was a different person then. It will forever be known as the Before. Before my career ended. Before my town was destroyed. Before my family disowned me.

"He lied. He promised me he wouldn't publish it."

My chest cracks in half. I don't want to believe. All this time she was collecting facts to use against me? This couldn't be true. Not after what we shared. Not after last night. It doesn't add up.

"You wrote it?" My voice is surprisingly cold and even-tempered. The opposite of hers. She's frazzled as a live wire. She's pleading with those large eyes.

I deposit her on a stool and step back. She falls to her knees in front of me anyway. Her arms are wrapped tight around her middle.

"No. Please, no, I didn't write it, Roe. I came here to tell you everything."

Seeing her like this—shaking and groveling, it turns my stomach. Gently, I wrap her in my arms and pick her up. She seems to come apart with relief.

"What's happening?" I ask.

She starts to spill out an explanation. It's hard to follow and she's stuttering. Something about Viktor and Zebulund and planted stories.

"Stop. Take a breath. And slow down." I've never seen her like this. She's a mess. I stop her again when she says she was driving up the mountain.

"You went to his cabin alone?" My rage isn't well hidden.

"I know it was stupid. But I was driving and my source called and told me all this stuff about you. About money being stolen. But I knew it wasn't true. I knew it was blackmail." She takes a deep breath and stares desperately at me. "I knew you would never do that. I trusted that it wasn't true. I was furious that someone would set you up like that. I wasn't thinking clearly. I didn't want you to be any more involved in all this than I already got you. I wanted to go get that computer and stop them before they could hurt you. I realized it was a stupid plan when I got there so I turned around to leave... but it was too late. I was set up."

Despite my fury I hug her close to me. Somehow I can't let her go, even though I'm angry and scared and don't know what's up or down.

"I promised to work with him. And he said he'd leave you alone."

The numbness closes back in. The world is pressing down. I haven't eaten since breakfast. My stomach rumbles. We both hear it but she doesn't say a word. Maybe Maggie is right about my relationship with food, because this went down after I ate those fucking pancakes. It's not real but the thought keeps coming back.

"That article posted hours ago. Before you even left Zebulund's cabin," I manage to say through a closed throat.

"But he didn't know. He asked if you knew who I was. I told him no."

"It was a test," I say. "He must've known you'd come straight to me." I'm numb. Rationally I know it's not Maggie's fault. And yet...

"I would never do that to you, Roe." She reads my mind.

"I know."

"I'll print a retraction."

"It doesn't matter. The information is out there." How long until the police come for me? How long until everything else falls down?

Her face is raw with pain. If I wasn't lost in my own rage, I'd comfort her.

"It's already out there, Maggie. Even if your name is taken off, it's still fact to anybody who looks into it. I was an example. Like Viktor."

"I'll make it right. I'll do whatever I need to do."

She really believes it too. After all this. That familiar conviction is clear under the green pallor and quivering chin. I know the truth, though. It all had to come crashing down someday. Nothing good last forever.

"You have no idea what I—" Her phones buzzes. We both stare at the screen when she pulls it out. "I don't know this number."

"Answer it," I say icily.

She slides her thumb across and puts it on speaker. "Hello?"

"Nothing personal about the article." Zebulund's familiar voice oozes derision. "But I did warn you. You can't cross me. This was your warning. Lie to me again and this'll seem like a picnic."

The line goes silent.

Maggie finally breaks, seeming to understand that she really is his pawn now.

"I can't work for that monster. I don't know what to do. What are we going to do?"

We.

Is there a "we"? Or has this always been about her? I want to comfort her. I want to ease her pain.

But.

But what about all the starving nights? My family. The town that rallied for me. What are they doing with this news? I need to think. I need space. I need to fix this.

"Roe?" Her voice cracks and I feel it in my soul.

"I need to go home." It's all I can say. I want to make her feel better but I'm reeling. My life is over. I know it's not fair to be mad at her. But I can't think about "we" right now.

"Please don't hate me. Please look at me." She comes forward again and grabs my face. "Please."

My will is crumbling. I want to find solace in her but I can't. I need to fix this.

"I'm not mad. I'm ruined."

"We can fix it." She pulls my shirt. "I-I'll fix it."

"What can be done?" I'm shut down. I know that I sound far away. "I need to go home," I repeat.

I start calculating sums, thinking about what I can sell to make things right. Most of my money already goes back home but I will find a way.

"I'll come with you. Explain everything to them. They'll know it wasn't you." She's desperate.

But she's done enough. Her heart was in the right place, but she was so set this whole time she never really thought about me. It was always about her. In the back of my mind I always knew it. She couldn't possibly care about me as much as I cared about her, but I wanted to believe.

It's clear the moment she surrenders to the truth. She straightens, wipes the tears from her face. We were never going to work. Our desires were too different. Our worlds too different. Gently, I nudge her back.

"I need to go alone."

32

Maggie

WHAT IS THIS? THIS NUMBNESS. SOMEHOW I'M BACK AT THE bungalow though I don't remember driving. Reality is distant. The world keeps going but I'm not. Nothing feels real or important.

My life is ruined.

Roe blames me. He's too nice to admit it because I shared with him my darkest shame. And I blame me too. I brought all this upon him.

Zebulund weaved him in and systematically dismantled his life because I dragged him kicking and screaming into his twisted world. My vendetta trumped all. My sights were set on one thing. It's because I wanted to stop Zebulund from hurting anyone else—and that's still true—but I also hadn't realized how much rage and shame I'd been holding onto until I unloaded on Roe. I wanted Zebulund to feel that burning fear and disgust, the way I did. I hate that time after time he gets what he wants, uses who he wants to and goes on living a life of luxury.

He needs to feel pain on a level that all his victims have. And I'll do whatever it takes, no matter who I take down in the process.

Maybe I'm not so different from Zebulund.

All for nothing. Evil wins. And it always will because that's the truth. Everybody knows the real Golden Rule: he who has the gold makes the rules. To think I was naïve enough to hope to fight that.

I curl up in a ball on my bed and sob until I pass out. When I wake the next morning I'm left with the sharp pains of regret and loss.

I check my phone hoping maybe I dreamed it all. But the Internet is on fire with rage. Some at Roe but mostly at me. Calling me a liar. A whore. I took advantage of our relationship. At some point, pictures were released of Roe and me. In one we're embracing. In another kissing. Seeing it burns fresh pain through my insides. I miss him so much already. How am I supposed to go on now that I tasted happiness? It's a cruel sort of injustice. At least before I could pretend that my revenge was enough to keep me warm at night.

What will I do now?

It's time to make this right. Whatever there was between Roe and me, I've destroyed, but I can still help him. The bamboo fan spins slowly over my head as I discard plan after plan. Zebulund must have other weaknesses—I could start working for him and try to get him that way.

But I'm exhausted. Tired of scheming and working angles, trying to get information, trying to worm information out of people. I'm tired of living this life I never wanted. Some days it helps to know I've put criminals away or hurt them. But my main goal will never be reached.

Zebulund's proven that he's always a step ahead of me. No matter how I think I have him, I always lose. He always has something on me. For a dark moment, I contemplate my options of doing something drastic. He can't use my body if my body is gone... But I can't go down that path. I can't throw away this talent or whatever it is because I've made mistakes.

What would it be like to work for him? I suspect there'll be some sort of test. How many awful things will I do to prove myself worthy to him?

I shudder out a sigh.

There's a knock on my door. I jolt up. Maybe Roe came back. Maybe he has a plan. A small part of me hates how quickly I've come to depend on him. How much I've built my little life around him. I run to the door and whip it open.

"Oh my God, your face!" Danny says with a shocked expression, with Russell mirroring it behind him.

My heart crashes to the floor with disappointment. I press my cheek and find the skin highly sensitive. I forgot about it to be honest. Everything else in my body hurts so bad that the slap pales in comparison. My insides are crushed.

"It's nothing."

There's a crumpled tissue in his hand and Russell has a supportive arm around Danny's shoulders. A new dread finds a crack to seep in.

"What's happened?"

"Mrs. J. isn't doing so good." Russell steps forward. "We thought you may want to come see her."

I slip into a pair of flip-flops and follow them across the lawn. Over the last few days, she's been napping every time I've gone to check on her. If I hadn't been so caught up in my own world I would've noticed the pattern.

The three of us are silent as we hurry toward her room. I try not to run but my legs are lunging toward her. How can I always be so self-centered? One of the few people in my life who cares about me. I wasn't here for her. I was at Roe's house. I was wrapped in his arms, doing other things, when I should have been at her side. Easing her pain.

A nurse is next to the bed as I slip into her room. How long has she been here? She smiles at us.

"I'll go take a break," she says and steps out of the room.

The lights are low. The canopy bed is so large it makes Mrs. J. look like a porcelain doll among the pillows. Such a powerful presence in every room reduced to this. It kills me.

"Mrs. J.?" My voice cracks and I don't think I can cry any more tears yet there they fall. I gently take her hand.

The guys ease to her other side. I'm grateful for their presence. It keeps me from falling to pieces completely. Every time I think I've hit my lowest low, something new reminds me that it can get worse. Much worse.

But this isn't about me now.

She turns her head at the sound of my voice and smiles before her eyes open completely. Her eyes blink and sleepily take in my face. I have my bruised side in the shadows and covered by hair.

She shakily says, "You got laid."

"Not quite."

The boys try to stifle laughs.

"Well, you had an orgasm at least, I can tell. No point in lying."

My blush burns my cheek, reminding me of all that happened since that moment of bliss.

"I know Roe didn't cause that." Her shaking hand points to my face.

"He would never hurt me," I agree.

The boys exchange glances and Mrs. J. chuckles.

"Oh, girl you got it bad. Why so glum?" Her hand is dry but smooth and so frail.

"No. No, Mrs. J. I'm here for you. How are you feeling?"

"I'm fine. Just stiff. And old. I don't want to talk about it. Why do you look like someone is dying? It ain't me. The good Lord can't have me yet." There's a steel resolve in her voice that makes me feel better. "Tell me about your man."

The boys are way too interested. I shoot them a glare. They don't even have the shame to be abashed.

"There's not much to tell. We had a good night but now he's on a plane to get away from me."

"Men. They're idiots."

"No. This time I think it was me." I slide a chair next to her. My gaze strays to the guys. "Might as well get comfy too. I was too focused on my career. He got in the crossfire."

"We saw the article." Russell crosses his arms. "We don't believe it."

"It's not true. He would never do that," I say doubting they'll believe me.

"Did you write that then?" Russell asks.

"I didn't."

"We didn't believe that either," Danny says.

"You didn't?" I ask them.

"Hell, no," Mrs. J. adds. "Also, it didn't sound like you. Not your voice."

"Makes no sense. Why would he use the names of his characters? It points right to him," Russell says.

"Exactly. But there's nothing to be done. I called my editor, and she's printing a retraction and taking my name off. But the story is getting way too much publicity. It's been copied and reposted a million times no doubt."

They're all silent.

"I'm still confused," Danny says.

How much do I tell? These secrets and lies and manipulations are tiresome. I just want somebody to tell my woes to. After a moment's hesitation, the whole story from the very beginning comes tumbling out. Well, except the invisibility stuff. I don't want them to think I'm crazy.

I start with the hotel room and end with the cabin. It

doesn't matter if I tell them about Zebulund. It's not like they can do anything. I can't do anything. Nobody can. When the story is over, silence greets me. The three of them take their time digesting.

"It's my fault. I went up to that room—"

"I'm going to stop you right there." Mrs. Jenkins holds up her hand. "You forget how long I've been in this town. Nothing about what you said sounds like anything less than the truth. I've had my fair share of hotel rooms... and closets... and offices." Tears hover on the brinks of her already watery eyes. "It doesn't matter if you went to his room or he came to your trailer. He wanted you and he would've had you. Men like that don't care."

I take a deep breath in and let it out, shocked that another person believes me and doesn't blame me.

"It happened to me once too." Danny sniffs and Russell grabs his hand. "When I first got into broadcasting. A morning show host. Super popular. He told me he'd set up my career. At the time I told myself it was mutual." He looks to Russell. "Now I understand that it was abuse. I had no choice."

"I'm sorry." I don't know what else to say. It doesn't make me feel better that we all have stories. It makes it worse. Are there no good people? Is everyone a predator when given an ounce of power?

I let out a sigh and stare at Mrs. J. Even now she has makeup applied and her hair coiffed. She's classic Hollywood.

"Why are some men so evil?" I ask with a shaking voice.

"Here's the truth, sweetie," she squeezes my hand now, "there are always bad people. Just like there will always be good people. We've all been hurt by someone. Prejudiced against. You can't help what happens to you. Know that it is part of you but doesn't define you. And you need to talk to someone. A professional. You don't have to just get over it. It doesn't make you weak."

The guys nod in agreement.

"I just hate that I can't stop him. I can't work for him. I'll die. It'll be the antithesis of everything I've fought for."

"Maybe it's time to stop fighting. Maybe it's time to move on and start living your life."

"Maybe."

"This can't be it," Russell says. "Something has to be done. It's not fair."

"I'm starting to think that's just life," I say, aware of my morose tone.

"It's not your job to make the world right, sweetie. You just survive," Mrs. J. says.

Her encouragement offers a bit of release but also sadness. There should be justice. There should be rightness. But I'm so tired. I could leave this town and change my identity and could live on the run from Zebulund.

I also want a life with Roe. How am I supposed to go on? How could I ever?

Mrs. J. interrupts my thoughts. "Now, someone bring me my wacky tabacky so I can get out of this damn bed."

————

I leave Mrs. J. with a bowl of Cheetos and a sleepy smile on her face as I head back to my room. Walking away from this town would be amazing. To try to forget and, well, maybe not forgive, but definitely forget. But what about everything that brought me to this point? I'm caught up in them. There's no way to make it right. If Roe were here, we could work through this.

But he left. He doesn't think the same. All his talk of being a team was empty. I genuinely thought that maybe it meant something to him. That in our most intimate moments of connection the things we said to each other, all those hopes and dreams, could actually bring us a future.

After our night together, I confessed to him dreams of teaching acting, of developing self-confidence in my female students. Of acting, not in film but on the stage, maybe. Something I would have never thought even to myself. I never allow myself to dream of acting because it's associated with so much darkness, but my theater days in high school and college were some of my happiest memories. There's something about the camaraderie and thrill of theater that I have yet to find anywhere else.

Roe told me he dreams of picking roles based on interest, not just to boost his career. He might hate the Hollywood machine, but he likes acting. Mostly, he just wished to go back home and live a modest life. I found that most surprising. He, like me, was never enchanted by the wealth but understood its power. But it doesn't matter now. I have to push away thoughts of him. How he looked happy sleeping on the pillow next to me. I squeeze my eyes shut at the pride I felt feeding him those pancakes, seeing him eat. It all feels too raw and too much. I can't stop the swirling thoughts.

My phone rings as soon as I walk into my bungalow. My heart beats faster even though I've tried to stop getting my hopes up that it might be Roe. I stand there with my phone in my hand, not really seeing it.

My heart pouts and goes back to its cave of sadness when O.G.'s name appears. I've been avoiding him. This whole calling me thing is harder to avoid. It goes to voicemail. A second later a text pops up.

"Answer the phone. Stop staring at it," his text reads.

I flip off the phone. A second later it buzzes again.

"Classy. Answer when I call this time."

It rings. Resistance is futile.

"Hello?" I'm not even pretending to sound happy.

"I know when I'm being avoided." The modulated voice greets my ear.

"Says the robot," I say as I sit at my kitchen counter.

"Why are you mad at me?"

"I'm not."

There's a pause before he says, "I don't live in town. I can't meet easily. But if you want to I could try to find a way."

There's a hopefulness in the voice that twists me with guilt. I realize we're friends. Weird friends that rarely talk to and never see each other, but friends. O.G. has been on my side from the beginning. I shouldn't take out my feelings on him. Besides, I'm angry at the world but not him.

"I'm sorry. I wasn't avoiding you. Well, I was but only because I feel stupid for going to the cabin when you warned me not to."

"I'm sorry. I wish I could've been there to help or do something. But there was nothing—"

"It's not your fault. You've only been trying to help from the beginning."

There's a heavy silence between us.

"Are you okay?" he asks.

"Besides being under the thumb of an evil sociopath and losing the only guy I've ever loved? Yeah, I'm alive."

I expect a pitying phrase of comfort. A condolence on the end of my career. I'm not expecting an annoyed scoff followed by, "Oh, please."

"Huh?"

"You're acting like this is the end of the world."

"It's not?"

"This isn't the end of anything. Come on. I chose you for a reason. You can do better than this."

"Chose me? What? Better than what?" A few different things about that statement jump out at me.

"You aren't trying." Even through the distortion, annoyance is clear.

Now it's my turn to scoff. "I assume you saw somehow the whole exchange with Zebulund?"

"I did. I apologize for not helping in that case, but that's not what I'm referring to."

"Please enlighten me. Since I'm your chosen one." I roll my eyes. It's nice to feel annoyed. It's a mild salve to the pain of loss and defeat.

"First of all, let's get something straight. You aren't the chosen one." There is an emphasis on "one" that I want to clarify but I don't have time because O.G. presses on. "But yes, you were selected. Not only because of your talents, but because I thought you had gumption. Something more than others in your position. I thought you were a catalyst for change."

"I was naïve." I'm hurt. "I thought I could change the world too. But I'm a coward. I groveled. There's nothing left to do. Aside from running."

"Running isn't a viable option. He's too powerful."

I blink at the factual tone. That option is scratched now and I go back to feeling deep pity and fear for myself.

"But you have an option," the voice says. "An option you could've done from the beginning."

"I don't see any way out. Please enlighten me, because I'm losing my mind." I drop the sarcastic bite in my voice and plead with O.G. "I've gone my whole life thinking there was some sort of justice for the evil out there. As juvenile as that is. It's becoming increasingly clear that there is no justice or fairness."

After a brief silence he says, "There is justice when people choose to fight for it."

"I thought that's what I've been doing."

"No. You've been hiding."

I grumble. I can't help it.

"You do more than most, true, but you're still not being totally truthful."

I shake my head, not understanding. But then I get it.

"You can't mean coming forward? About my... about what happened."

"That's exactly what I mean."

"After all these years? People wouldn't have believed me before. But now? And after that story? There's no way."

"So, the only reason to come forth is to be believed? That's the only way it means something?"

I open my mouth but have no answer.

"There are always going to be bad people." There's a coughing fit and I want to tell O.G. to see a doctor. "There's always going to be evil. That's not why you step forward. I'm not saying that you should. I'm not telling you what to do but somebody has to do something. Somebody has to be the person who steps up."

"Nobody would believe me. I'd lose everything."

"What's left to lose?" I wince. "Isn't there a quote about rock bottom being the best foundation?"

I pick at some cracking varnish on the counter and think about his words. "What if I do and nothing comes from it? What if I put myself out there and it does absolutely nothing? He walks away and nobody cares."

"I think you have to be prepared for that possibility."

I drop my forehead to the counter. It's cold and painful. I don't care.

"But what if just one person finds solace in it? What if it helps one person come out against their attacker?"

My chin begins to quiver. But he doesn't stop.

"What if it causes one man to tell another man that that toxic talk isn't okay? What if it challenges the system in place?"

I sigh. "This is why I told myself I was going after him. To cause change. To help other people."

"Exactly. No matter what happens with him, someone has to be the one to stand up. Someone has to risk it all. It's about power. Someone has to take it back. I believe in you, Maggie. I believe that you are that person. I always have. You have to believe it too."

I bite my lip and take a steadying breath. If I speak now my tight throat will give my tears away.

"Look, I have to go. But I did choose you for a reason. Make me proud."

"I'm scared." My voice cracks.

"You wanted to change things. You have the power to do that. I trust you'll find a way out of this. That you'll see the truth and stop lying to yourself."

The call ends abruptly. I don't have a chance to say anything.

The phone may as well be a paperweight for all it's giving me. I can't come forward. What would it do but make even more people hate me? I have to find another way to bring Zebulund down. My story won't matter.

My eyes squeeze shut. My heart is pounding because it's getting the memo before the rest of me. It knows I'm about to make a choice. A very scary and stupid choice.

O.G. is right. I'm lying to myself. All these years set on revenge, but the truth is I've been living a lie. I use my powers and my stories as protection. I'm still so afraid that my words don't matter. That if I come forth about my abuse I'll be called a liar and a whore. All my life I've felt that my body was vulgar. That it was wrong and dirty and shameful. That all this really was my fault somehow. I thought I could cover myself. But I can't anymore. I can't go back to lurking in rooms of criminals and living that lie.

People will call me names. All the people cursing me for the article about Roe proves that. But it doesn't matter. I'm done hiding the truth. From myself. For the countless others.

My strength isn't revenge. My strength is courage. With or without Roe, I know what I need to do. I know it isn't my fault. I accept what happened to me. It doesn't define me.

I need to free myself. Telling Roe about my abuse helped me reclaim my body. Now it's time to reclaim my life.

33

Roe

IT TAKES EXACTLY ONE NONSTOP FLIGHT FROM LOS ANGELES TO Omaha to realize what an idiot I am. By the time the plane bumps onto the tarmac, I'm fully enraged with myself. My anger earlier was misdirected. Maggie wanted to work as a team and make things better but I left.

"Idiot," I mutter to myself. My neighbor shoots me a dirty look.

They do a double take of recognition so I look away and lower my hat. I'm on the only available flight home. Which means a cramped middle seat on a puddle jumper built before I was born with no Wi-Fi. It doesn't matter. My parents and the town are likely thinking the worst of me.

I'm desperate to call Maggie. She's probably... I don't even want to know. Anger may be best-case scenario at this point. Anger is better than hurt or apathy.

I left her to work with that scum who's the real reason my life is in ruins.

I'll fix it and help her out. As soon as I can, I'll go back to help her. And pray I'm not too late.

As soon as the door opens, I'm up and out of my seat. I shove into the aisle but so does everyone else. It takes a thousand years for my phone to switch from airplane mode. As soon as bars appear I try to call Maggie, to explain the reason I left so quickly, and that we'll figure it out together. My blood turns to ice when I see a message from Zebulund come through before I can do anything else.

"Call me."

I can only stare at my phone for a minute. People around me shuffle and shove. When someone bulldozes me forward my feet finally get the memo. I have no choice. If I can help Maggie, I have to talk to him. I trudge with the flow and dial the man who's ruined my entire life.

"It's nothing personal. I hope you know." That's how he answers my call.

I have no idea what's happening around me. Traffic pushes me out into a crowded gate waiting area. Zebulund's heavy breathing and cool demeanor are all I hear.

"You're kidding me."

"Nature of the business. I had to teach her a lesson. Both of you."

I have nothing to say.

"I get it. I was tracking you, getting information on you, and you wanted a reporter to help look into it. You went to the best. I understand."

It sinks in. My hands shake so badly I can hardly hold the phone. Zebulund was tracking me, ruining me, long before Maggie ever entered the picture. I thought she got me caught up with him. That it was her meddling that made him do this. I've made such a mistake. I need to talk to her. Every minute and mile away from her feels like an unbreachable chasm.

What if I've undone everything I've worked so hard at with her? What if that ice wall is back up between us?

"You need to leave Maggie alone." My voice is shaking with barely controlled rage.

"She's too talented. I need what she has."

"No. You don't. She'll never work with you."

"She will. She already agreed. Didn't you hear? I used you to show her that she doesn't have a choice in the matter at all. And I am sorry about that. You and I can be beneficial to each other. This doesn't have to be the end of our friendship."

"Friendship." I stare at my surroundings, unseeing. I shamble out of the crowd to the terminal's big windows. Outside, past the tarmac, acres of cornfields wave gently.

"I'm perfectly fine letting you rot. It's too late for Viktor. The tide's turned on him and he's served his purpose. But you, I can still save your reputation. I can get people to do anything. Things they swore they would never do. Just look at the video I sent you to see my point."

"What video?"

My head spins. I say the first thing that comes to mind while my brain processes all that he's telling me. I hate him but a small part of me worries. What if I need him after this? What if he's the only way I can help save my town and everyone I love? Even Maggie. What if I need him on my side to help her? Fuck. I hate this man, and the control he has.

"In your email," he responds. I can feel him wrapping up the call.

"I can't think about that right now." My voice is dry and wrought with sarcasm. "I'm too busy racing home to try and save a whole town from bankruptcy."

"Who cares about that town. You still have your money."

Maggie was right. Again. His conniving and manipulation go so much deeper.

I make a choice. Maybe it's the families racing around me.

Maybe it's seeing the lands of my childhood. Or maybe it's because Maggie has truly changed me to my core.

"I wouldn't work with you if it were my last option in the world."

To think, one time I found his laughter genuine. Now it's obvious mockery.

"That's what your girlfriend said before she got on her knees and begged for it. Everybody has a price, my friend. I know hers and I'm learning more about yours. Finally. You were a hard nut to crack."

"Fuck you," I murmur into the phone.

Families are walking past. It keeps me from screaming profanities like I want to. A growing numbness spreading through my body. Maggie on her knees... it couldn't be.

"I only wanted to teach her a lesson. Remind her of my power. I think you need reminding too, my friend. I run this town. And now I see where your weakness lies. Maggie cared for you. You care for that town."

His threats do nothing compared to the truth of his statement. That's how Maggie sees it too.

"I'll hear from you soon." The call ends abruptly.

"Girlfriend on her knees." The words repeat in my head. With shaking hands, I open a video attachment. There's no sound at first. It's a high angle of what must be his cabin. It jumps around. First, she's by the door with a gun and then he's in front of her. It's been edited for his purposes. Just like everything around him. Then the sound clicks on.

"I want you to beg for it. I want you to beg me for Roe's sake."

He's tormenting her. I want to puke. When she starts to say something his hand smacks the side of her face. Her head flies back. My sight goes red.

The welt on her face. I remember now. I've been so self-absorbed. I didn't think. The video jumps again and she's on her knees. I can't watch. I can't look away. She's begging him now. She's saying that she wants to work for him. It stops.

I close the video. My body thrums with anger. I can hardly see. My heart slams against my chest.

Maggie. I made such a mistake.

I could take this video to the press, but what would happen to Maggie? It doesn't look good in the video. He makes it seem like she wanted it. I'm such an idiot. I call her and there is no answer. I'm not surprised.

My phone rings again and I jump. I need it to be Maggie. It's not.

"Rachel?"

"Hey, have you landed?"

"Yeah. Just now." My voice is tight.

"What's going on?"

"Too much." I shake my head. "I need to get back to LA right now."

"Okay. Didn't you say you just landed?"

"Yeah, but I made a mistake. I need to see Maggie. I can't reach her."

"Okay hold on." The soft familiar sound of typing comes through. "Well, the next flight isn't until tonight. Otherwise, you fly all over the country to get home at basically the same time."

"Shit."

"I have a suggestion."

"Yeah?" I pace the terminal.

"Your mom has been calling nonstop. You need to talk to her. Since you're already there, go explain things in person. That's why you flew down there, after all. Take the time to think of what you need to say to Maggie too. I'm not sure what happened there, but I did see the article. You're all over the news."

"She didn't write that."

"Glad to hear that. I like her. I didn't want to hurt her."

"She cares about me."

"You're easy to care about." Her voice is soft, and I'm taken aback. People rely on me but I'm not used to people caring for me. I hear her typing some more. "For now, go do what you went there to do. Smooth things over. I'll make sure Maggie is okay and you can meet up when you get home tonight."

"You're right." I run a hand through my hair. "As always."

"I know."

"Promise I can make everything right."

"I can't promise that. I can tell you that things'll work out. They always do. Maybe not as you expect but sometimes better."

I want the factory to be okay. I want the town to have its lifeline. I want Maggie to be okay too.

I just want Maggie.

MY RENTAL CRUISES DOWN A TRANSFORMED MAIN STREET ON autopilot. It's weird how easily it all comes back. Being home is weird. Despite the dread at seeing everyone, a small part of me feels like I can take a true deep breath.

It's in better shape than in my memory. The image in my mind is filled with empty buildings with boarded-up windows, broken glass in the streets, the smell of depression in the air. But this town looks like a Hallmark Christmas movie town. There are flower beds in the median, the street signs are replaced with wrought-iron poles, and old-fashioned light fixtures on every corner. Every building is occupied; the strip mall flourishes. There's a lot of traffic. The town is thriving. My jaw hangs open as I observe all this.

When I pass the factory, there's a constriction in my chest. Thoughts of Maggie are pushed aside to focus. There are only about five cars in the parking lot. It's the weekend but there should be more people here than this. I head past to the nicer neighborhood, where my folks live. They wouldn't let me move them into anything too ostentatious.

"We'll never be able to fill it," my mother said. I bought them a modest home east of the factory as they requested.

I probably should've called before coming down here but they need to see me in person. They need to see my face while I explain everything. Makes it harder for them to shut me out. Before I can turn into mom's driveway, several cars pull out in succession and leave back toward the town proper.

I recognize a few neighbors and friends. My mother's is the last car to leave. She doesn't notice me in my midsize sedan as she passes. She has no reason to suspect I'm even here. I turn around and follow the caravan. Where is everyone headed? Every mile twists dread deeper into my gut. What if they're going to the factory to decide layoffs? What if they're planning to gang up on my parents? What if everyone blames them?

They lead to our small civic center's parking lot. It's packed, and by the time I find a spot across the park on the other side of the road most everyone is already inside. I slip into my hoodie and tug my hat lower on my head. Before they get their pitchforks and do anything drastic, I need to talk to Mom. How much have they been keeping from me? How bad has it gotten?

Once inside the storm doors, a hundred plus people all talk at once. The community center isn't equipped to handle this many people and they overflow into the hallway. Every possible chair is in use.

I slip into the crowd unnoticed. Only bits of conversation make it to my ears. Not surprisingly, there's an air of outrage and disbelief. As feared, I'm the hot topic.

"After all these years, still never been back."

"Lived here his whole life. To think he would steal."

My shoulders lift to my ears to block out the accusations. I have to find my family and explain. I search the room, careful to keep my face as hidden as possible. To my horror, my mother and father make their way to the podium.

My heart sinks. My mother is older. Somehow she became a grandmother while I was too busy to come back home. Too busy was the excuse I made.

My father looks older too. He shouldn't be working still. My stomach churns with guilt. Behind them is my brother, with his wife and the niece and nephew I have yet to meet. They all look haggard and tired. It's poor luck they have me as their brother.

"Attention." My mother taps the microphone and it buzzes but the murmurs around the room die down. "Hi, all. Thanks for coming today. It means a lot."

Dozens of angry people shake their heads at her.

"I brought some cookies. They're in the back. And thanks to Darla for the lemonade."

A very pregnant woman waves from behind the podium. It's Paul's wife. I haven't seen her in years. She's got a toddler straining on her hand while her belly proclaims her pregnancy. Paul gently lowers her into a chair. There's a small round of applause. I scan the audience again and feel confusion. There are angry faces, but it doesn't feel like they're directed at my mother. I start to inch my way through the crowd up the side aisle.

"Now before we get to business, let's address the elephant in the room." I freeze, being said elephant.

The grumbles grow louder. But the snippets only confuse me more.

"I know." My mother waves her arms and calms the room. "Obviously, we know the story is a lie."

Say what now?

"That woman is a liar and should be ashamed to call herself a reporter!" A man, I think it may be Ned from the gas station, stands and yells. "We should bring her out here and tell her what this town really thinks of her."

I look around in disbelief.

"I don't know about that." My mom uses her patient voice. "But I've been trying to get ahold of Jimmy all morning. Now if you know my boy, you know that he's probably taken this all on his shoulders. Probably on a flight down here as we speak."

There are soft, pitying murmurs. My dad places a supportive hand on my mother's shoulder.

"We as a family decided it would be best to keep him out of the loop." She glances sheepishly to my father who may not know about her phone call to me. "But we see now that was a terrible idea. Things look way worse than if we were up front with him from the beginning.

"We need to try and figure out what's going on before he gets here. Now, don't forget. He thinks his help to this town is still a secret. He doesn't know y'all figured it out years ago."

"We'll do whatever it takes, Kathy," another man shouts out.

"Your boy saved this town and we stand by you and your family no matter what," a woman adds.

My hands clasp behind my head. I'm going to cry. Like the proud feminist I am, I'm about to lose it. They know what I've been doing. They support my family still. After all this time.

As I bring my hands down, I pull my hat off. I make my way to the podium as the whispers get louder. My mom's still speaking about organizing committees when she notices the disquiet and turns to me.

Her eyes widen and her hands go to her mouth. We're embracing a second later. My dad and brother and sister join in too. The auditorium breaks out in cheers.

Yup, I'm crying. Full on. No shame.

After a minute I wipe my face. The relief I feel. It's unreal. I can't even speak. My brother shakes my shoulders and calls me names. My father's face is twisted in happy pain.

"Well, darn," my mother says with a sniff. "I don't suppose you missed all that."

"I heard it all, Ma."

I go to the podium. It's time to clear the air. I can't handle people thinking that Maggie is to blame for all this.

I grip my ball cap and go to the microphone.

"Hey, everyone."

They clap and I shake my head with modesty. Something about seeing your former baseball coach clapping for you is almost too much to take.

"You can't imagine what your support means to me." My throat tightens and I grip the podium.

"Just returning the favor," someone speaks up.

"Growing up here, when things were so hard. You all did so much." I point to Mrs. Hale. "Giving us produce from your garden."

She waves my comment away.

"Giving us jobs." The former principal of my school squints when I gesture to him. "All of it. You all made me who I am. You gave our family a chance. All I ever wanted to do was give you something in return. I'm so sorry that this happened. I'm so sorry I couldn't stop the money from being lost. And I'm sorry to say I likely won't be able to support you much longer."

My brother steps up to me and nudges me. He grins. "The money isn't gone."

The crowd studies us as I stare in disbelief at him and the rest of my family smiling happily. "What do you mean?"

"As soon as we discovered it was starting to disappear, we transferred it out to safe accounts. We used your movie role names for the account names. I guess we didn't think it would look shady. But it's not laundered money. It's just our money getting interest."

I'm clutching at my heart through my shirt. I only notice

because my mom grasps my hand. "Don't wrinkle your nice shirt."

"I don't understand," I say.

There's no foul play? That's why the police haven't arrested me. Because it's all legit. I blink. So Zebulund wasn't setting me up. He legitimately thinks I'm laundering money. No wonder he's so keen to have me.

"Why wouldn't you just tell me?" I ask.

"You were killing yourself for us. We didn't want to make it worse."

"But when you called? You said money was going missing."

Paul steps forward. "It was. But just little pings on the account, almost like tests to see if we were watching."

"Maybe scammers?" Dad says.

Or Zebulund wondering about my connection to the business.

My mother steps forward tentatively. "I didn't know they were already taking care of things when I called about the vandalism. Turns out it really was just punk kids."

"This is crazy. So there's no issue?"

"Not anymore. Whoever was poking around at first stopped when the money disappeared."

Zebulund must have thought I got scared and sent my money somewhere safe. Their actions to protect me only made me look worse.

Another question forms. "Why are you all here then?"

"We're angry about the article. We want to clear your name. We were just deciding the best way to go about it." She glances at my dad, sheepish. "There's something else."

"Okay." I swallow.

"We want to close the factory."

"Is it doing that bad? What about the jobs?" I run a hand over my face.

"That's the thing. Your dad wants to retire. We want to travel while the grandkids are in school. Your siblings want to invest their money into new businesses. To be honest, the town doesn't need the factory. We're sort of tired of it."

"But all the jobs? What will people do? When it closed last time it almost destroyed us."

"Industry changes. We aren't a factory town anymore. But we're thriving. The factory's been downsizing for some time. I was trying to do it slowly so you wouldn't worry or feel guilty. But it sort of backfired."

"Why all the secrets?"

"You stopped coming home. You stopped talking to us. You were obviously killing yourself working for us. We just didn't want to make you feel like it was all for nothing. We thought we were doing the best thing for you at the time. We were going to tell you when it was closed so you could slow down."

It's weird having this conversation in front of the whole town but there aren't secrets anyway.

"I'm fine. I really am. Work is work. But I don't understand. The factory is closing?"

"Yes," she says.

My brother studies the floor.

"And people are okay with it?" I look to the room. A hundred plus heads nod in agreement.

"But what will we do with the building?"

"That's what we were meeting to discuss. And then that article went out."

I'm taking this all in as I go back to the podium.

"I want you all to know that Maggie didn't write that story. The Maggie May I know would never write that story. She is an honest, brave, strong person. She was trying to find out what was happening to the money."

There are glares of disbelief but they keep listening.

"I don't want you all thinking poorly of her. I was being blackmailed by a very bad man. And apparently, for much longer than I even knew. But nothing that happened had anything to do with Maggie." I think of the strong-willed woman and can't help but smile. "She's wonderful and would do anything to help me." And did.

I glance at my mother. She's got knowing eyebrows. So that's where I get them from.

"I only came home to make sure the factory was safe and you knew that I would never hurt this town. But now I see that was all for nothing."

"Not true," my brother says. "Now we get to see you."

———

Roe

BACK AT HOME, MY MOM'S HOME, I SHARE WHAT HAS HAPPENED. Everything with Maggie. From the beginning. Well, mostly. I can't share about her talents and instead hint that she's just a strong journalist. Also, I don't share how intimate we were. The relief that the town is fine, not only fine but flourishing without me, allows me to focus wholeheartedly on how massively I screwed up. My love for her is written all over my face. I can't help it. Talking about Maggie makes me that way.

"She sacrificed everything for me. For nothing. He abused her. Again."

"Poor girl." My mother shakes her gray curls. "It's a cruel world."

"I need to make it right for her. But what could I possibly do at this point to undo what he did to her?"

She taps her chin for a minute. "It sounds to me like all she ever needed was you and your support."

"I'm such an idiot."

She grabs my hand and squeezes. "You'll make it right."

"I'm grilling up ribs for dinner. Been marinating overnight."

My dad rubs his stomach in anticipation. "Are you going to eat with us?"

I feel my mother watching me closely. I'm about to give my normal brush off but think about how I haven't eaten since pancakes. Pancakes make me think of Maggie and just like that, guilt is making me want to not eat. I see now that maybe it isn't how I should be viewing food. As a reward and punishment system.

"Sounds great," I say.

"Help me shuck some corn," Mom says.

My phone vibrates and I reach for it so fast I almost drop it.

"Is it Maggie?" my mother asks, ever hopeful for me.

"I don't know the number." I slide to accept it. "Hello?"

"Hello, Mr. Roe. This is Maggie's friend. Please turn on the TV to Entertainment News."

"Dad, turn the TV on," I ask him with my hand over the phone because he's closest to the remote. Then I ask the phone, "Who is this?"

"A friend." The voice sounds weird and garbled. "You have some serious making up to do."

The line goes dead and I growl at it. "I know that. If you stayed on the line, you could have told me how."

A text pops up and I blink at the same number. The text states, "You'll figure it out."

I stare at the phone in disbelief and with more than a little concern but am quickly sidetracked by the sight of Maggie on the screen. The caption on her image says "Maggie May, Journalist." She's sitting in a studio. Someone runs off screen after adjusting her mic as though they rushed into all this.

Her voice is strong but her hands holding the paper shake. I should be there holding her. I can't tear my eyes away.

"Hi, I'm Maggie May. You might know me as Miss Mayday. I'm here today to set the record straight about a few things."

I sit in front of the TV, turning it up way louder than it

needs to be. People collect behind me, but I'm only vaguely aware of them.

"First and foremost, let me say that I never wrote that story about James Roe. Mr. Roe is a man of impeccable character, and the lies propagated about him aren't true. I didn't write that story, but it was my fault that he was involved in this mess. He has nothing to do with anything I'm about to say." She holds the camera in an intense stare. It's the determined woman I know so well. It's like she's looking at me, willing me to understand. "I'll find a way to prove he has nothing to do with the allegations against him."

Someone gasps behind me but I can't move my eyes. Another person says, "That'll be easy. We'll fix that."

"I've already contacted a lawyer," my dad says.

I don't turn though. I can barely blink. Even now she's protecting me. Trying to help at her own risk.

She looks down at her paper and clears her throat.

"Let me read this press release I wrote. It's already been sent to the Associated Press and all major news outlets." She takes a deep breath and reads. "When I was twenty-one, just out of college, I went on an audition that was rumored to make my career. I met a man that needed no introduction. His reputation and name proceeded him. That man was Marty Zebulund.

"I know what I say next will be turned against me. I know I can't stop people thinking the worst of me. I know all I can do is tell my truth. But here it is: Marty Zebulund assaulted me. He touched me and sexually abused me even after I clearly told him 'no.'

"I have no way to prove this. It happened four years ago. I've shared the details in a police report. I waited so long because I thought my voice didn't matter. I thought that nobody would believe me or if they did, it would be swept under the rug. I'm hoping not for justice, because Marty Zebulund has made it clear that he holds the power in this town, instead, all I hope is that I can give courage to men and women who are being abused to come forward and say enough is enough."

My face is almost touching the TV, I'm so close. That brave, beautiful woman. Her biggest fears. Coming forth, revealing her hand. She's done too much.

"Marty Zebulund wants me to come and work with him. I'm sure my life will be ruined after this. More than that, he hurt the man I love."

Behind me my mother gasps a little "Oh."

"This is my official notice of rejection, Marty Zebulund. I will never work for you. I will never stop finding ways to reveal your true character. I will uncover how you blackmail everyone around you. I know you have officials in your pocket. I don't have any way of proving that. Not yet. But I'll never stop. And if they find my body in the ocean one day, the world will know it's thanks to you."

"She's crazy," I whisper.

"Your reign over my life is over," she finishes.

The screen goes dark, but I keep staring at it.

"I can't wait to meet this woman," my mother says.

———

IT TAKES EXACTLY ONE NONSTOP FLIGHT FROM OMAHA TO LOS Angeles to realize what I need to do.

As soon as the wheels touch down I power on my phone and call Marty Zebulund.

"About time," he answers.

I close my eyes and swallow back the emotions threatening me. I'm an actor though, so I act. If Zebulund thinks I'm the type of guy who'll launder money, then that's the guy I'll be.

"You were right about everything."

34

Maggie

I SPEND MOST OF THE MORNING IN THE BATH. PARTIALLY OUT OF necessity, partially because it just makes me feel better. I alternate between visibility and going Under. After my confession, my phone won't stop ringing, just as I assumed. I turn it off. The police filed the report but, clearly, didn't have plans to go further than that. I suspect the paperwork will get "lost."

Like all the others.

I do feel lighter though. Obviously, physically floating in the water but emotionally too. I'm glad I came forward. I have nothing to hide from the world anymore. I can start the process of moving on. Danny and Russell used their local news connections to get me on the air and apparently I was great for the ratings. So, in my small way, I've already helped at least two people.

Danny told me he was proud of me. Russell even hugged me. I smile and sink back Under. Peace is within my grasp, except the ever-present nagging of my broken heart. When Mrs. J. opens the door and lets herself in I'm startled out of my

Zen moment. I come back Up before she sees me... or doesn't see me? She's spritely today so I can only begrudge her a little when she makes her way to the closed toilet to plop herself down. I scoop some bubbles around to cover myself.

"Please, girly, modesty is long dead and gone." She flicks a bubble clump at my face. "But I'm not. Get dressed. I need to run an errand."

"I can't leave the house."

"And I can't live without my medication."

Well, boo.

Not twenty minutes later she's directing me somewhere. We passed the closest pharmacy five miles ago.

"Give it up. Where are we going?"

"Just drive. I don't pay you to ask questions."

I flick my eyes to her. "You don't pay me at all."

"I see why. You're too nosy."

I may be wallowing in a cloud of self-pity but I'm not blind. My heart picks up the pace as we get higher into the Hollywood Hills.

"If this is some ploy to get me to..."

"No questions." She holds up a hand to cut me short. "This isn't about you."

Soon, it's clear where we're going and she doesn't need to navigate anymore. We turn onto the road to Roe's house but when we reach his driveway, it's lined with cars. This is odd. Roe doesn't have guests. He doesn't talk to people.

"Is that a news van?" I'm genuinely curious what this is about.

Mrs. J. glares.

"That was a rhetorical question," I say defensively.

The driveway is cleared enough to drop her off at the front door, which pleases me.

"What are we doing here?" I shift into park. "And don't you dare snap at me. We're here. I can ask questions."

"Who says *we* are doing anything? I'm here to support a friend." She struggles to unbuckle her seatbelt.

"Fine." I lean over to help her. "I'll be back in a bit to come get you."

"I need help getting up the stairs."

I just saw her walk down her own steps without a struggle. It's probably better to just go with it at this point. Plus, I'm curious. Something's up. Only the smallest fraction of myself wants to see Roe. Like a sliver of a pie chart. I'll look at him and all the embarrassment and pain will rush back in.

I need to go back under my sheets where I'm safe.

Roe's property is gated but the entrance to the backyard is open and Mrs. J. heads that way, toward the sounds of a small crowd. Once around the corner, I see something astonishing. There are two large cameras pointing toward a podium. That explains all the attractive people in the audience. Twenty-plus chairs are set up facing it. It's like a wedding reception in a beautiful resort but there's no sense of love in the air, only a looming dread.

Roe is nowhere to be seen. Not that I care. Maybe only the tiniest pie-slice of caring.

I settle Mrs. J. into a chair and make an excuse to leave.

"Just stay." She grabs my hands. "Please, I'm asking you." It's the most serious I've seen the woman. It ages her and tugs at my heart.

"I'm only going to see about a drink. It looks like a party. Let's party."

"I want a highball. See if you can make that happen. Did I ever tell you about the time I got Sinatra to make me a highball?"

"Tell me when I get back." I pat her hand.

I'll get her what she wants, but I first I want to find out what the hell's going on. I won't be bamboozled.

Do people still say bamboozle?

The yard isn't very big. I carefully skirt the chairs to avoid falling into the pool. The pool. Ugh. So many happy memories in that stupid pool. But it does give me an idea. I slink behind the outdoor shower, slip off my clothes, and go Under. When I peek my head out there's nobody looking my way. I'm a little hesitant, wondering if anybody else can see me like Roe, but not a single head turns my way even after I wave my arms frantically. I quickly make my way to the pool and slip into the water.

Soon I feel full, that's the best way to describe it, or maybe charged. Like a good meal and a nap. Not even Roe could see me. I climb out. The sliding back door is open so I'm able to slip in without causing any suspicion. Upon entering the living room my heart sinks to my feet.

Roe stands, his head lowered slightly to listen to Zebulund. Marty freaking Zebulund. Good to see that he and Roe have patched things up. I step closer. There're only a few minutes left before Roe will be able to see me. But right now he doesn't. Not even when I stand right in his eyeline. He's frowning at what he's being told.

Zebulund's wife is here, too. Oh lovely. She's dressed in a silk two-piece suit, that no mere mortal can pull off. Her face is somber, but her blinks are slow, and she wobbles.

"If this is some sort of setup—" Zebulund whispers.

"I care too much about my career to risk it," Roe interrupts.

Zebulund studies him closely. "Fine."

"We stick to the script. I say I regret my actions and am donating to your charity. You say that you believe the allegations are a lie. We both win."

I ball my fists. No way. No freaking way. These two are in cahoots now.

Zebulund scratches his chin causing an audible rasp against his five o'clock shadow. I see up close that his eyes are bruised. His skin sags around his eyes and his pallor is ashen.

Have I caused him a little stress? At this point that would be the best-case scenario.

"I'm going to mention my lawsuit for libel against her, too. She started this fight. She gets what's coming at her," he declares.

"Sounds good. Helps discredit what she did to me too," Roe says. "You sure you want Nancy to talk?"

"Yes. People love the wives standing by their men."

They both inspect the woman as she smiles sweetly and sways.

"You better make sure she can stand at all," Roe says. It's like a stranger talking.

He's so angry. My heart drops to my feet. Even hearing him, I still can't fully accept it. It doesn't match up with the Roe I know. It doesn't make sense.

He heads out to the yard and I feel myself growing thirsty and tired and somehow even more sad. I'm about to follow him back out to get my clothes when Zebulund speaks to his wife.

From a few feet away it could look like he's caressing her but as I step closer I see that his hand is gripped hard on the back of her neck. Her face is forced toward him.

"How are you, baby?" His tone is almost sympathetic. Almost. He pulls out a silver case and rattles it. It's like Pavlov's bell, causing her eyes to shine for just a moment. "You need another one? Glass of wine?"

Her eyes dim again but she shakes her head once, slowly.

"You know I love you, right? I go through all this for you? For our life. I want you to have everything. I love you."

"I know. I love you, too." She raises a hand to his cheek.

"That's a good girl." He leans in to kiss her ear and her eyes shut. Fresh hatred and sickness spiral through me.

I regret ever judging her. She's as much his victim as the rest of us. If not worse. She's chained to him by money and paperwork.

I can't watch any longer so I make my way outside. I don't want to be here. I don't want to try to understand why Roe would align himself with pure evil.

Back behind the shower I get dressed, come back Up, and make my way back to Mrs. J. She held my chair with her fur muff.

"Wow, thanks for the drink," she says dryly.

I blink at her. It takes me a minute to remember. "Oh. Sorry. I got sidetracked."

"Are you okay, toots?"

"I don't think so. Can I please take you home?"

"Just a little longer." She puts her arm around my slumped shoulders.

Why won't Mrs. J. let me go? I'm not needed here. I'd rather be a million miles away if Roe's going to say hard things about me, even if I deserve it.

Roe trudges up the podium's stairs like a politician caught cheating. He scans the crowd but for once he doesn't see me. I'm just another blonde in the crowd. Has he ever seen me?

Yes. He always has.

I hate that my stupid fragile heart still holds out hope. I shut my eyes against the images that bombard me. When I open them he walks to the microphone with that familiar mask in place, the one he uses when he addresses anybody.

Anybody but me.

Right before he speaks, his eyes lock on mine. No stutter. No hesitation. It's like he's known where I am this whole time. My heart skips. No surprise, but his face changes. It goes from solemn to determined.

Of course, he sees me.

He's always seen me.

———

Roe

MAGGIE SMILES AT ME. IT NEARLY MELTS MY DETERMINATION. What have I ever done to deserve that beautiful, kind smile? I almost forget why all these people are in my yard. I want to run up to her and wrap my arms around her. I want to inhale her and tell her how much I love her.

But she's here because of my machinations and I can't hold her until I undo some of the pain I've caused her.

Zebulund and Nancy walk outside and stand behind me. I hate that she sneaked inside and heard that conversation. More lies and deception. Not that I actually saw her. I can feel when she's near me and right before I left, the merest shimmer started to appear. I know it was her. It's why I left so quickly—I couldn't handle seeing her until I know she's forgiven me.

I clear my throat. "We're ready to get started."

The crowd silences. I wait for the lights on the cameras to blink to life. My gaze alternates between them and the crowd, but it drifts to Maggie without my meaning to. I'm always seeking her out.

"I grew up poor," I begin when the producer gives the sign. "Far below the National Poverty Level. Poor beyond what any child should have to go through."

So far, I'm on script. Garner sympathy with a tragic backstory.

"It caused me to believe that at any moment all that I've earned would be taken from me. Even with all my success these past few years, I was convinced that I didn't deserve any of it. I was just waiting for someone to come along to take everything from me. To point out to the world that I'm a sham. Poor, uneducated, undeserving of everything that has happened to me. Because it's impossible to reconcile this life with the life I knew."

Maggie frowns at me. Maybe because she knows I never

open up about who I am and my deepest insecurities, or maybe because she doesn't understand why we're all here.

"The day I met Maggie May, I thought I met the person who would ruin me." I take a breath. "I was right."

Still on script, I see the moment Maggie swallows what I've said. Her skin shimmers like she's struggling not to go Under. Mrs. Jenkins holds her in place, God love her. Mrs. J. shakes her head and Maggie stays sitting, her expression thunderous.

"Maggie has ruined me. Ruined me for the image of myself I had in my head. Ruined me for living a lie. Ruined me for hiding out." I smile at her as her frown melts into confusion. "Ruined me for any other woman in the world."

Her hands cover her mouth. I'm officially off script. In my periphery Zebulund shakes his head. I'm sure he planned for my betrayal. I pray he didn't have time to hurt anybody else I care about.

While I can I carry on. "Maggie has shown me not only what true strength and beauty are, but what character really means. I've never met anybody so motivated by justice. I was barely surviving when I met her. It didn't take long for her to save my soul."

I clear my throat, because yup, I'm getting weepy.

"Maggie." Half the crowd turns to look at the person I'm addressing. "I love you. Thank you for making me understand that I'm strong enough to walk away from all this."

Her eyes shine.

"Thanks for not only showing me what strength is but showing the world what true courage is."

Zebulund keeps his face stoic and whispers in my ear, "I'm done with your little lovefest, Roe."

"Just wrapping up." I give Zebulund the same winning smile he's given to me and so many others, time after time, right before he fucks them over. I hold up a finger and turn back to the audience.

"But I digress. Let's get to the true reason we're all here."

Maggie's eyes widen when I say, "Anybody who has been abused by Marty Zebulund, please stand."

Without hesitation the entire audience stands.

Behind me, he curses me loudly. "You have no idea what you're playing at."

I look again for Maggie. Understanding dawns on her face. It's not a press conference. It's an ambush.

"Everyone here today has been abused by Zebulund. And we're all here to stop that from happening again. Who'd like to go first?"

A woman in the front row steps forward—she already has a microphone in her hands.

"I was eighteen and Marty told me to go to his trailer. It's been years since he made me touch him, but I've never forgotten." She turns around to Maggie, who stands with her hands over her mouth. "Thank you for giving me courage. I went to the police this morning."

Another woman comes forth and shares a similar story. Each one of them thanks Maggie. Each one of them filed a police report. Zebulund can make an accusation here or there go away, but it's a lot harder to sweep several dozen under the rug.

As each woman speaks, the camera records them.

"This is ridiculous," Zebulund whispers into my ear, still calm. "You think this little show is going to do anything? You have no idea how deep my influence goes. You've ruined your life and anybody you've ever cared about."

"I know what it feels like to lose everything. I'm not worried." I glance at Maggie, who's in the center of a crowd of women, and a few men, who talk to her about their pain. She's lost in a sea of tears and hugs and confessions.

Zebulund's threats go on, but my eyes never leave her. Viktor steps forward and her shock is visible.

"I'm so sorry," he says. "I was scared shitless. You're so brave. You didn't deserve that." He glances toward us. His brows furrow. "I'm done living in fear. I'm done."

She hugs him after he shares his story. Zebulund takes the microphone.

"These accusations are absolutely not true." To his credit, he keeps his cool. No dramatic confessions and sweeping speeches about how they all deserve it. "I'll be filing lawsuits for slander and emotional distress against each and every one of you."

He could probably get away with it too. He could probably contest each one of these reports and somehow get away with it all.

"This is ridiculous." Zebulund sweeps past me but pauses to say one last thing. "You're ruined. You have no fucking clue what you've done."

He's still smiling and he says it so low that only I can hear him. I look past him and to Nancy.

"Let's go." He tugs on her wrist

But Nancy doesn't move. At least not toward him. Instead, she breaks out of his grasp with a firm tug and stands in front of the podium. It's the most clear-headed I've seen her in our brief acquaintance. Her voice is so soft when she first speaks that she's almost unheard over the crowd.

"What are you doing? Come here." For the first time, Zebulund loses his cool. His eyes flick wildly to her and then the cameras.

She clears her throat and the crowd stops talking.

"My name is Nancy Zebulund. I met Marty when I was sixteen. That was the first time I told him 'no.'" Her voice shakes but gains momentum. "It's been thirty years since then. A cycle of me saying 'no' and him pushing me further."

Zebulund is statue-still as he watches his life unravel.

"Two years ago I discovered a reporter who gave me hope.

Her stories made me think this town could change. She had the strength and courage I did not. Maggie May thank you for being a light in the darkness."

I didn't think Maggie could look any more surprised. The two women hold each other's stares as though it's just the two of them.

"My cowardice ends now. I will go to the police for the rapes." Nancy pauses and nods once with determination. "And for everything else. I've had the power to stop him for years, but I was... I didn't." She lifts her chin before facing him. "You're done hurting people."

Two LAPD officers step out of my house and handcuff Zebulund.

"You'll regret this," he says to the world. One of the officers reads him his rights. "What am I being arrested for?"

"Numerous counts of rape," the first man says.

"Obstruction of justice," the other continues. "Blackmail. Money laundering. Planting false evidence. Embezzlement."

"It's a long list. But don't worry, we'll go over them all."

The three men head toward the door but Zebulund is a big guy and drags his feet.

"This is a lynching. There's no justice here. I demand you call my lawyer."

I make a concerned face and lean toward him.

"You know, when I told Kyle and Craig about how you blackmailed me and the dirt you had on them, they decided to sever ties. You're going to need a new lawyer. I forgot to mention that earlier."

"You can't arrest me. You have no proof."

"Actually, that's not true. Your lovely wife sent all the evidence to us early this morning." The first officer smiles warmly at Nancy, who blushes. "We just needed some paperwork."

"I have men who'll protect me," Zebulund insists.

"Not with this publicity," I say. "Nobody will touch you with a ten-foot pole."

He glares with so much heat my eyebrows are at risk of singeing. As he's being taken away, he trips on nothing and falls face first into the gravel. When he stands up again, his face is bloodied.

"That's abuse. I'll sue."

The cops exchange an eye roll before continuing to lead him to the car. He folds forward with a wheeze as if he's taken a blow to the gut.

"Look you can beat yourself up," The taller cop says. "In fact, I encourage it. But only because there are cameras everywhere recording what you're doing."

"I'm not doing it. Can't you see that—" He's cut short as his head whips to the side and his cheek reddens instantly. His eyes are wide and wild. He looks all around and finds me. "You! This isn't possible... How are you?"

"It's a ghost," I say, dead serious.

His color drains and his eyes remain wide as he's lowered into the police car. I scan all around the area for Maggie. But she must have gone for another dip because she's invisible even to me. I make my way through the crowd and talk to a few reporters but I can't find her anywhere. Or Mrs. Jenkins.

Maggie's gone. I wanted it to be enough. I wanted to tell her, only her, how much I love her. How's she changed me. I wanted to wrap my arms around her and never let go.

By the time the chairs are all put away the only people left are Rachel and me. She comes up to me and smiles.

"I think we can agree that went better than expected."

I hug her and she blinks her surprise. She deserves a raise. Big time.

"Thank you for helping get them all here on such short notice."

"Us PAs stick together. We also talk. A lot." She blushes.

"I couldn't have done it without you."

"Least I could do after you saved me from being another person in this crowd." She shrugs.

I wave it off, that was lifetimes ago. Pre-Maggie. Everything is pre-Maggie or post-Maggie. I look around with despair weighing on me.

"She's gone, I think. I saw her walking her older friend to the car."

"I can't blame her." I slump. "I fucked up royally."

"She might need some time. Don't be too hard on yourself." She pats me on the shoulder and says goodbye.

After I walk her to her car, I grab a beer and a bag of chips and head back outside to wallow. In the lounge chair under a deep black sky with twinkling silver stars I lie back and let myself think of nothing. I'm halfway through my beer when I think I hear a soft splash.

"Maggie?"

I'm greeted with silence. The water is still. I groan and sit back.

When I open my eyes again, there's a beautiful naked woman in my lap.

———

Maggie

IT'S NOT EVERY DAY I FIND MYSELF NAKED AND STRADDLING ONE of Hollywood's biggest stars.

But I'd like it to be.

I have a whole speech prepared. About love. About courage, and finding it in myself through him, and yadda yadda.

It's all gone now because he's kissing me with abandon before I can even say hello. He's kissing me so wonderfully I forget my speech. I can't even remember my name.

"Oh, Maggie, Maggie, Maggie," he says.

Oh yeah, that's right. I smile against his mouth. His mouth trails off my lips to nuzzle my ear and neck. He inhales me deeply even though I'm dripping wet.

From the pool.

Pervert.

I'd been soaking in it waiting until the time was right to strike. I sent Mrs. J. home in my car. She's totally capable of driving—she only chooses not to when it's convenient for her. After many minutes of wonderful kisses, I pull back, still very, very naked and aware of it.

"Hi," I say.

He closes his eyes like I've said so much more. "Hi."

"I'm very, very naked." I lean back.

The adoration in his eyes melts to something far more dangerous. "You really, really are."

"You have me at a disadvantage."

"Not possible for Miss Mayday. You always have a plan B."

I let out a sigh. "Sadly, Miss Mayday has retired and it's just boring old Maggie now."

He chuckles and squeezes my thigh like it's all he can do not to do more. "You're anything but boring."

He holds my gaze as he reaches for a towel and wraps it around my shoulders.

"Thanks."

He kisses a drop of water off my nose.

"Today was amazing... I never would have..." I cup his face with both hands. "Thank you."

His eyes cloud over. "I needed to do something to help. Zebulund sent me some footage from the cabin. What you did for me. And then my reaction. I'm so sorry."

"I don't want to think about it. It all brought us to this point."

He brushes his hands down my neck and shoulders. I

shudder with pleasure. He clutches me to his chest. I relax onto him, between his legs on the long chaise lounge. His heartbeat soothes me.

I feel like we have so much to say to each other, but instead, we both lie there in silence. After a while, I finally say the thing that's weighing on me the most.

"You think he'll actually go to prison?"

"Hard to say. Once the initial scandal wears off and something else distracts the media he may be able to bribe some people."

I stay quiet because it's honest but it sucks.

"But I think the people here today were just a fraction of who he's hurt."

"I agree."

He squeezes me tighter.

"Are you okay? With how everything turned out?" he asks.

"I am. I'm still a little afraid that he'll go free on some technicality. But all this was more than I ever hoped for. I'm so happy. I still can't believe you did this. How did you get him to agree to do this?"

"I groveled."

I groan. All too familiar.

"I told him that I wanted to work with him. That I knew there was no way to bring him down. I said we needed to have a press conference where we both agreed you were a liar."

I can't help but wince.

"I'm sorry. Even lying and knowing the end game, I hated doing it."

"It's okay. Trust me, I get it."

"Let's not think about him right now."

"Great idea."

We sit in silence for a while more. Another question pops up.

"How did you get Nancy to go against him? When I met her

she was trying to get information from me about you." I giggle when I remember the lie I told her. Which turned out to be not much of a lie at all.

"I had no idea. I had nothing to do with it." He pokes my shoulder. "Why are you laughing?"

"No reason. I'm glad she's going to be free of him. I can't imagine what sort of life she's had."

He mumbles an agreement and runs a hand up and down my back. Again, we fall into comfortable silence.

After a few minutes, I say, "Oh, hey, Roe?"

"Hmm?"

"I love you, too."

Under my ear his heartbeat picks up the pace. I nuzzle into his chest.

"That's really good to know."

"For a while now. Just in case you were wondering. I can't help it." I shrug.

"I think I've loved you since I saw your nipples... Ouch!" He rubs his ribs where I've pinched him. "Every time I see you I love you more, Maggie May."

I sigh. His voice is serious now. Deep and rumbly. I never want to leave this spot. "You're the greatest thing that's ever fallen into my life. More than the money and the fame and everything associated with that."

I look up and he's staring down at me.

"And you've made me feel seen."

EPILOGUE

Maggie

"REMIND ME AGAIN WHY WE COULDN'T JUST PAY SOMEONE TO DO this?"

Roe and I take a break to lean against a stack of boxes and drink water. Roe wipes the sweat from his brow with his forearm and grins at me.

"And deprive you an opportunity to show off your sweet truck packing skills?"

"I regret ever sharing that talent with you."

It's a perfect spring day in LA. I'm only a little sad about leaving the city and the moderate year-round temperatures. Just a little.

"Why pay someone to do something we are perfectly capable of doing ourselves. Plus, we have all this help..." He gestures to the yard.

Out the open door, the guys and Mrs. J. sip drinks with umbrellas and sprawl in lounge chairs on the lawn. Pepper is on the lawn, paws up and tongue flopping out of his mouth. I'm pretty sure that's normal.

"I'm exhausted," Mrs. J. says.

"Moving is hard work," Russell agrees and pats Danny's knee.

"You guys are fired!" I call out.

"Good. I couldn't lift another finger." Mrs. J. uses a paper fan to cool herself off from their strenuous activity of gossiping about the rest of the neighbors. I'd worry about her with me leaving but she has the guys and has decided to hire a full-time nurse. After a patience-testing tutorial, she's even keen to video chat me from time to time. Though I still don't understand how to get the camera to switch around, she assures me I'll get used to it.

Rachel and her fiancé Gordon come back from the truck with their own bottles of water, arms around each other's waists.

"I think that's about all of it," Rachel says with a sort of half smile. "I can't believe moving day is already here."

The four of us had hung out as often as our complicated schedules allowed these past six months. I never thought I would have so many people in my life that cared about me and that I cared about in return. My therapist often reminds me there is no limit on love. Instead of feeling panicked, I feel full. Who knew?

"It's sort of sad," I say, and Roe tugs me close to his side. "But mostly happy."

"Plus, we will be back for your wedding," he adds. "That's only three months from now."

"It'll fly," Rachel agrees. "What are you going to do now?" She addresses the question to both of us since she knows Roe's next film isn't scheduled until September.

"We're both looking forward to a break," I say. "Maybe I'll see if the local paper is in need of a reporter." I look up at Roe. "How bad is the crime in Pennsyltucky?"

He raises an eyebrow, one deep dimple showing. "You

should really know where we're going to live. The locals have high expectations for the girl I'm bringing home."

"I kid. I kid. You know me. I researched all about it. I probably know more than you. For example, did you know that your very own hometown is the largest distributor of canned chickpeas?"

"I did not know that."

"You're welcome."

"Because it is not true."

"It could be true."

"My life would be so boring without you, Maggie May."

"Obviously." We hold each other's gaze so long seasons may pass.

Gordon clears his throat. "That reminds me, I need to see the guys. I'll be right back."

"I'll come with. I want to know the final score of the Dodgers game," Rachel says and tugs Gordon after her as she walks away.

"I was thinking about that," Roe says.

"About the Dodgers?"

"No. I was thinking about your life in Nebraska. I can't have you getting bored."

"Pfft. I never get bored." Since Zebulund's arrest and subsequent conviction I've slept more and picked up more hobbies than I can count. Some more successful than others. "I could garden. I've thought about trying that." But even as I say the words, I imagine a field of weepy brown flowers and hard clumps of earth. "Or something."

He gives me skeptical eyebrow.

"I could totally garden."

"Sure," he says seriously. "I have no doubt you could do anything, Maggie May."

"Thank you, James."

"But you might be busier than you think very soon." His

right and left eyebrow take turns jumping.

"Oh? Am I pregnant and you didn't tell me?"

"Not quite." He pokes my ribs. "Last night when I was video chatting with my mom, she told me what the town decided to do with the factory."

"Tell me." I grab his hands and pull them behind my back so he's wrapped tight around me and I'm looking up into his eyes.

"It's gonna be a theater."

"No way! That's perfect." My mind spins with possibilities. Local plays. Events that incorporate the whole town. Bake sales to raise funds. Maybe Mrs. J. wants to donate to the costume department.

"I thought so too. You did mention missing acting. Do you think maybe..."

I bite my lip. I haven't let myself think about acting for years but now the thought excites something deep down inside. A little fizzle of adrenaline. I think of the lights and stage and costumes. I squeeze Roe so tight he wheezes. It's nice to feel a little more than ribcage these days.

"I think that sounds really great," I say.

We pull apart and I glance around the small bungalow one last time, seeing if there is anything I forgot. I hang up my metaphorical Miss Mayday hat and grab my keys. I'm ready to move on. So ready.

"You know what I just realized?" Roe's question interrupts my thoughts.

"That you're the luckiest man on earth?"

"No." He narrows his eyes. "I already knew that."

"Smart man." I boop his nose. "What?"

"We never figured out why I can see you and nobody else can."

I tilt my head. As far as we know, nobody other than Roe has ever been able to see me. Though my activities of invisibility are mostly in the testing phase these days and usually pertain to bedroom experiments.

"It's because you're the only person to see the real me. To see past all this superficial stuff," I say seriously.

"I like that." He kisses me.

"Or maybe you're broken in the head," I tease.

"One of life's great mysteries, I suppose."

I lock the door to my old home and get ready to go. Roe stops me with a gentle touch to the elbow.

"From the moment I met you, I felt something deep in me. A primal instinct to seek you out and protect you." His gaze locks mine. "Like we were meant for each other. We were meant to find each other."

I think of O.G. I need to send that man a fruit basket.

"I felt it too. I was too scared to admit it. I was so angry about it at first because I was scared." My voice is a whisper. "It was cosmic."

Roe goes on, "I always thought I had to maintain the burden of living alone in this world. I wore every negative aspect of this industry like a battle scar. But it's not a burden, it's a privilege, and I get to share it with you now. You've blown me away from the beginning. Your passion and dedication to change is so unseen in the rest of the world. You exist to make the world better. I'm proud to know you. I'm so honored to be in your life. Your love means more than all the accolades and awards I've ever received. I want to be the best person possible to be worthy of your love every day for the rest of our lives."

His impromptu declaration has my heart racing. "You already are that person. I'll never find another that sees me the way you do." A slow grin pulls up my cheeks. "Are you asking me to go steady?"

"Yes." His face is fully serious as he reaches toward his pocket. My heart is slamming around for totally new reasons now. "Let's go steady forever."

ACKNOWLEDGMENTS

It's impossible to write this without feeling so much gratitude for all of the people in my life all the while worrying that I'm not going to adequately convey how much you all mean to me.

JR - I don't even know where to start. No single person has pushed me and encouraged me all the while believing without a shadow of a doubt that I could reach all of my dreams. I can't promise you an Aston Martin, but I promise you are the reason I believe in the transformative power of Love.

My Daughter - For showing me that I'm capable of much more than I ever thought possible and making me want to be the best version of myself.

Mom - For once telling a NYT best-selling author that I had "something special" with a gleam in your eyes and emotion tightening your throat. Thank you for having faith in me, but trust me, everything great about me comes from you. And for Jack, for giving her the Happily Ever After she deserved.

Tracy - For the middle of the night texts and the FOREVER talking about plot holes and characters as though they are as real to you as they are to me.

Ben - Good gravy, you have to be sick of this book for all the times you've read it. But knowing you, you're gonna say how much you love it. Your tough love made me a better writer.

Lauren - For unflinching insistence that everything I write is great even when it's really actually garbage. You are the ultimate cheerleader and sister.

Cassie - Thank you for the laughter and deep conversations, and for bringing a little bit of culture to this gal's life.

Judith - For making me laugh when it was really hard to even smile.

My BETAs - You were SO helpful. You were chosen for a reason.

LERA - The first time I went to a meeting, I knew I met my people. Such a powerful group of badass women (and some dudes) that helped me grow into Piper.

Thank you to all of my friends and family who have cheered on this crazy pipe dream over the years. I am so lucky and thankful for each and every one of you.

ABOUT THE AUTHOR

Piper Sheldon writes Contemporary Romance and Paranormal Romance. Her books are a little funny, a lotta romantic, and with just a little twist of something more. She lives with her husband, toddler, and two needy dogs at home in the desert Southwest.

Sign up for her newsletter at pipersheldon.com/newsletter so you don't miss a thing!

f facebook.com/PiperSheldonAuthor

🐦 twitter.com/piper_sheldon

📷 instagram.com/pipersheldonauthor

SNEAK PEEK

Read on for a sneak peek of Book 2 in The Unseen Series, "The Untouched," coming out July 2020.

THE UNTOUCHED

Julia

"No, Susan, I wasn't done speaking."

It feels great to finally say the words out loud. Well, not really great. It would have felt better if I said them in the moment—across from Susan in the staff meeting—but just venting my frustrations now helps... a little.

"And I wasn't done, Dan. This is my quarterly presentation so I would appreciate if you kept your comments and concerns to the end. Or never," I add spitefully since it's my imaginary retelling anyway.

The wind whips off Lake Michigan through the back alleys of downtown Chicago stealing my words with it. Despite the city being quiet at almost 2 am the clicking of my sensible pumps along the ground is hardly audible. I tug my knit hoodie higher to protect my ears from the biting wind. The dumpster grease smell makes my eyes water.

My steps slow as the anger wears out. These shoes aren't really meant for stomping around the city for hours. These eight-hour heels have worked enough overtime. I slow to a stop, the spring wind still cutting through my layers.

"So there." But there's no heat behind my words. My anger dissipated into regret. Why couldn't I have stood up for myself in the moment? Why couldn't I be the person that speaks their mind, that doesn't give a flying fig about upsetting anybody else's delicate sensibilities?

If I don't speak up nothing will ever change.

"Hey," a voice calls out. It's muffled over the wind but clear enough. "I'm your ride."

My head snaps in the direction of a car where the driver is calling out to me. I can hardly see him. He's leaning over the passenger side towards the window closest to me. He's youngish? Maybe thirties? He's driving a small silver sedan with a rideshare sticker in the front window.

I shake my head no. My voice that was so strong only a second ago has gone missing again.

"You sure? Come here. You shouldn't be out this late."

I don't move. I'm several feet back. He couldn't grab me without getting out of the car.

I shake my head no again, this time with more gusto.

"No? Really. It isn't safe. Let me give you a ride." There's something about his tone, a little too pushy.

I can't make him out but clearly but I can feel his desperation. He really wants me to get in that car.

I step back and head the other direction. I cut through the alley to get to the next block in a few short strides. There's a chance he's got the wrong person.

I sneak a final glance over my shoulder. He shakes his head and drives off. I let out a huge sigh of relief. At what point in a woman's life does she stop feeling so damn scared when she's walking alone? Not just dark alleys in the middle of the city, but to the water cooler at work past a group of men. At what point do the men stop going out of their way to leer?

The alley ends on Oak Avenue. Three blocks from home. The light from The Pho House casts a green tint to the scene. The smell of dumpster grease has become overpowering. I wait a beat to decide where to go next.

The silver sedan rolls to a stop in front of me. I see my startled reflection in the window as it lowers. The rideshare man leans towards me again, tilting his head in a way that has to be rehearsed.

So not looking for somebody else. My knees tingle as the adrenaline kicks in.

"There you are." He smiles. Full on teeth. His hair is shaved and he's got a thing strip of facial hair along his jaw line like the least popular member of a boyband. The desperation in his eyes rings all my woman's intuition warning bells. His gaze never stops scanning his surroundings. His hand grips the steering wheel, the one not waving me closer, so hard his knuckles are white. "I'm worried about you."

He's not to be trusted. Not at all.

I glance to the left and to the right. Nobody is around. No shops are open. Nobody to hear the screams. I step back into the alley, keeping my attention on him.

One. Two. Three. Four. Five. Steps. I'm hidden in shadow now.

The further distance from the car the better. I'm half way back to the other block when the driver's focus flicks behind me.

Rough arms haul me from behind in a massive bear hug, lifting my tiny frame off the ground without even a grunt of effort. This new man is huge and smells like onions. I scream but the gloved hand clamps over my mouth.

"Get her in the damn car!" The driver's yelling is lost in the roaring wind.

I fight with everything I have. *And though she be but little, she is fierce.* Elbow to the gut. Stomp on the insole. Head slams back to nose. Crack. Curse. Oomph!

Rapid fire, like a dance routine I've rehearsed a thousand times.

My attacker grasps his nose and falls forward to catch me with one arm as the other reflexively tries to staunch the bleeding. I'm too fast. I duck down, spin away, head deeper into the alley.

The other is out of the car now. The big one and the seducer. That's what they do. One coaxes the women out. The other grabs them and shoves them into the car.

My face, as I'm told, is often interpreted as innocent. My naturally large round brown eyes have a way of giving me doe-eyed naivety. My petite dancer's frame hides my age. So many times I'm mistaken for a child despite my almost thirty years on this planet. It's the reason the Susans and Dans of the world talk over me in meetings. It's the reason nobody listens. I'm constantly underestimated.

It's exactly what gives me the advantage.

Made in the USA
San Bernardino, CA
25 July 2019